SIN

A DARK & DIRTY SINNERS' MC: THREE

SERENA AKEROYD

Copyright © 2021 by Serena Akeroyd

All rights reserved.

No part of this book may be reproduced in any form or by any electronic or mechanical means, including information storage and retrieval systems, without written permission from the author, except for the use of brief quotations in a book review.

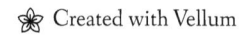

❋ Created with Vellum

SIN

DEDICATION

TO MY DIVAS and my Posse.
    May Sin be sinful enough for you.
    Much love,
    Serena
    xoxo

UNIVERSE READING ORDER

FILTHY
NYX
LINK
FILTHY RICH
SIN
STEEL
FILTHY DARK
CRUZ
MAVERICK
FILTHY SEX
HAWK
FILTHY HOT
STORM
THE DON
THE LADY
FILTHY SECRET
REX
RACHEL
FILTHY KING
THE REVELATION
THE ORACLE
FILTHY FECK

PLAYLIST

If you'd like to hear a curated soundtrack, with songs that are featured in the book, as well as songs that inspired it, then here's the link:

https://open.spotify.com/playlist/6MupuNrCuWWETEg8U1Dj9V

FYI

DARLINGS!

So, a couple of things.

If you love this series, the crossover with the Five Points' Collection will give you a lady boner! Drool alert. For a comprehensive reading order, just turn the page! <3

You come across the name Padraig in this book, but the way to pronounce it, according to a legit Irish lady (thank you, Mandy!! [Update 2022: RIP, sweetheart. <3]) is Podrea.

Content warning: this book contains scenes of graphic violence and a miscarriage.

Much love to you, my darlings. I hope this book melts your heart... and your panties. ;)

Serena

xoxo

ONE

TIFFANY

IT WAS the smirk that did it.

I hated smirkers.

I really fucking hated them.

My best friend's brother was a smirker, and he seemed to think he could pull it off, but Luke couldn't. In fact, Luke Lancaster couldn't pull off a holiday sweater, never mind a smirk, but that was just my opinion. As far as I could tell, the prick had more female attention than even this guy.

And his smirk?

It suited him.

At the Satan's Sinners' clubhouse in West Orange, New Jersey, I'd admit to feeling like a fish out of water. Some of the girls from the country club had pretty much dared me to come, and because I was a moron, I'd let them work their wiles on me.

I wasn't even mad at them, more at myself. Peer pressure—who'd have thought I was still vulnerable to it after school?

See, this was why I liked Lily. In fact, hell, no. *Why I loved her.*

She was like the sister I should have had. She got me, and I got her. But she was on a tight leash—her dad was as big of a prick as her brother—and that was why I'd decided to spend my Friday night in this dump, because she was stuck hosting some stupid meal for her dick dad.

Well, okay, dump was a strong word. The place was quite nice actually. Surprisingly so. And the view? Sweet Lord in heaven, yeah, the view was more than worth it, even if I didn't know what I was sitting in—something disgustingly sticky—tucked on a sofa beside a biker who looked like he was preparing to get sucked off by a woman wearing very few items of clothing.

That would be awkward.

Entertaining, maybe, but mostly awkward.

I mean, I'd watch. I'd be nuts not to, wouldn't I? I had to watch. This entire thing felt as much like a social experiment as part of the psychotherapy major I'd tossed down the drain. There were so many women with daddy issues here, and so many men with god complexes that, six months ago, it would have been my idea of a wet dream.

Now?

I wasn't sure whether to be amused or disgusted. I'd already seen some chick popping pool balls out of her ass.

Yup, you read that right.

I hadn't even known you could get two balls up there, but she'd proven me wrong. Proven a couple of bikers wrong too—they'd taken bets on how many the poor bitch could shove up the brown eye.

They'd evidently never learned anything about anatomy.

That she could get a couple up there was a miracle—if you loosened your definition of what a miracle was—but eight? Did they think her rectum was Mary Poppins' carpet bag?

Still, that had been a humorous interlude, if disgusting, and I'd made a mental note to A, never play pool here.

B, use Lysol on my entire body when I got home.

C, destroy this entire outfit, because there was way too much DNA on it.

Entertaining though it was, the reason my friends had come here was to get laid by biker dick.

More daddy issues.

Apparently, being treated like a piece of ass was on their to-do list. Well, it wasn't on mine.

I had no such issues. Dad might not be a saint, but he was cool. Cool enough to support me as I tried to figure out what the fuck I was doing with my life after I'd 'messed' things up at school, at any rate. And I didn't need to get back at him by being gangbanged by a bunch of bikers who wouldn't understand the word 'respect' if Aretha Franklin screamed it at them.

Of course, all those thought processes happened before I saw him.

He had his hand down some woman's pants, and his smirk set fire to my body in a way that made my eyelashes aroused.

My fingernails tingled too.

Everything about him screamed sex and sin. But even worse than that? He screamed a promise fulfilled.

He would give you sex and sin, but you'd love every fucking minute of it.

I was no virgin, and I'd played around in college, but fuck, he made me question if I was technically a virgin.

Because, dayum, he should be illegal in at least thirty states.

Shamefully, I thought all that while he was finger fucking some wannabe porn starlet who made a banshee look quiet.

As I nursed the same bottle of beer I'd been drinking all night—no way was I going to be under the influence with these guys in my vicinity—I watched him work.

And work it was.

Even if he did it so fly that he should have been selling something. Hell, vending ice to the Inuits would be easy for this guy. Shit to a horse farmer even easier.

His laughter was just as mesmerizing as the smirk, and the way his dark eyes twinkled was clear, even from over here. He was a man who lived and loved life, and he charmed me without even having to say a word, with a laugh that lit up a face that'd make an angel sigh. He was all rugged charm, a wide brow, strong nose, stubborn jaw, but his coloring? Heaven. Dark hair, close to black, creamy skin that was beyond lickable. Perfect dark brown stubble on his chin that framed lips, which were apricot in color—they were even more lickable than the rest of him. Shit, that was really saying something.

Inwardly drooling, I watched him, though it was shameless, ogling the tats on his forearms that roped over thick muscles revealed by his wifebeater, the strong shoulders that the leather cut he wore didn't hide, and the long lean legs that were covered in denim he filled out better than the Coke advert guy—yeah, I *just* wanted to make lurrrrvve to 'him'—and carried on observing when someone pointed out to him that I was checking him out.

I didn't stop, didn't let my gaze flicker away when he started to move toward me now that he'd finished finger fucking the chicklet, and that smirk was back in business.

But he braked to a halt when I smirked back.

That response?

Dynamite to him.

I saw it. I saw my cockiness hit him square in the face, like I'd smacked him with my fist. I saw his visceral reaction to my lack of coyness, to my lack of flirtation.

I gave him back what he'd given me, and suddenly, he was just as ensnared.

I'd seen all the women around here cooing over the men like they were the second coming of Jesus. Not only my friends, but the clubwhores too. I knew what they were. Not only from *Sons of Anarchy*, but because talk about the clubhouse ran rampant in the small area where we lived.

My family and Lily's were new in town, but it seemed like the Sinners were at the top of the list of the gossip chain, and to be honest, I was as curious as someone who gawked during the aftermath of an accident. The clubwhores lived in and, get this, did the laundry, made the food, and fucked all the brothers for board and lodging.

Blew my mind too.

Regardless of my personal opinion, these women had actual positions in this place, and they were all over the bikers like chlamydia.

Seriously, none of the chicks here looked like they were even capable of playing hard to get. Well, maybe one. There was a tall motherfucker with a scowl meaner than Odin's, who stood glowering at a pretty pixie with a murderous scowl, whose only enjoyment at this 'party' seemed to come from glaring at everyone and no one.

Seemed to me like she was claimed by the Enforcer—he had a patch on his cut which was kind of neat because at least we knew who was who—who was staring at her like he owned her. Since she was the only one not dropping to her knees to suck any dude's dick in the building, I figured they were lovers in the middle of an argument.

I got to my feet, even though I was going to miss out on the blowjob beside me, and knowing I had the man's attention, I began to walk out of the bar.

Considering the hype, this place wasn't that cool. It was pretty disappointing. But then, I lived in a pool house and had my own cinema room. I was rich and could afford the best. Spoiled? Yep. I admitted it. But why the town was so obsessed with what happened within these walls, I didn't understand.

As far as I could see, the job of a biker was to fuck, drink, and shoot the shit.

Oh, and ride bikes.

Simple.

As I strolled outside, he grabbed my arm the second I was in the yard.

"Where you going, darlin'?"

I almost rolled my eyes at the endearment, even if his accent did things that confirmed he should be illegal in more than just the thirty states I'd thought earlier. Because he turned me on so fast, I kept my voice cool as I told him, "Somewhere you're not welcome."

A husky chuckle escaped him, and I hated that it made my bones turn molten. "That doesn't sound very friendly. Look at what we'd both be missing out on—"

"Nothing to miss out on," I countered. "I'm not going to fuck you. Not when your fingers still have some other woman's pussy on them." I shot him a look over my shoulder. "They might get off on it, but I don't."

Though he'd liked the challenge back in the bar, it figured it'd piss him off when it came down to playtime. "If you're too good for this place, then why are you here?" he demanded, like I'd spread my legs for him and was suddenly saying no.

"Never said I was too good for this place." My smile was sweet. "Just said I was too good for you."

Those stormy eyes of his narrowed as he pulled back his arm. "What's your name so I know to never let you back in here?"

"Why would you do that? Don't you want to fuck me?" I knew I'd confused him, so I spelled it out. "You're not good enough to fuck me now, darlin', but that doesn't mean you can't work up to it." I twisted around to pat his cheek. "Looking forward to your efforts."

His nostrils flared in outrage, making me smirk harder at him, but when his gaze dropped to my lips?

I knew I had him.

And I sweetened the deal.

I licked my lips, letting my tongue run along the bottom one.

Leaning into him, I pressed my hand to the leather cut he wore, and murmured, "You can have any woman in there. They'd be on their knees in an instant. But me? I won't do that. You can't have me." I smiled. "Yet."

Winking, I carried on strolling until my butt was in my Jag and I was driving out of the clubhouse's courtyard.

And the guy, the biker who had 'Sin' embroidered on his cut?

He stood there watching me as I rolled out and onto the open road.

TWO

SIN

FIVE DAYS LATER

SHE WAS DRIVING ME CRAZY.

Like, officially crazy.

And the weirdest thing of all? I actually liked it.

I liked that she didn't grab my dick and offer to suck it the second she saw me. I liked that I hadn't even managed to sniff at her pussy, never mind see her tits. And I liked that I never knew what the fuck was going to come out of her mouth.

She was a challenge, and somehow, she'd tapped into my stupid competitive streak.

I'd seen her that night, sitting beside a bleary-eyed Storm as he got sucked off by one of the club bunnies, looking like a princess among the paupers.

It wasn't that she'd looked down on us—if she had, that'd have pissed me off, and I wouldn't be interested in the bitch.

No, she hadn't been amused or obnoxious. If anything, she'd been watchful. Like she was taking it in. A baby at a circus. All wide-eyed and intrigued.

I hadn't even known her name. The only thing I *had* known was her license plate number. I got one of the deputies in the police department who was on our payroll to run her plates and get me some information on her.

Of course, I couldn't be interested in one of the cute girls from the country club who was just rich, could I?

No, she had to be a Farquar, didn't she? Fuck's sake. The prick had pretty much transformed West Orange, making the already upper-class town even more swank with gated communities that offered a thousand luxuries to the ultrarich who were tired of space-poor Manhattan.

One thing West Orange had in abundance was space, well, it did until Tiffany's father had fucked that up and brought a bunch of yuppy yahoos into my backyard.

Still, I wasn't about to blame that on her.

The fact her daddy was behind the ruination of my town wasn't a sin that could be laid at her door.

I crossed my feet at the ankle as I stared up at the sky, my hands tucked behind my head, thinking back to the meetings we'd had since that first time. A drink at the club's bar, a burger in the diner. Each time, she'd sit at another table, and I'd have to talk to her like we were fucking strangers.

Then, last night, when I'd finally gotten her to agree to come out here, we'd been at the park. The fucking park. Her on a swing like she was a kid, and me feeling like a weirdo being in a goddamn jungle gym when I was over the age of eight.

When a rumble sounded in the distance, I smirked with satisfaction.

She was here.

She drove a Jaguar, and fuck, I could hear the vibrations through the ground as the sportscar roared its way up the slight incline to my driveway.

I was one of the few brothers who had two homes. I lived at the clubhouse for the most part, but when shit got a little crazy there and I didn't want to be a part of it anymore, I came here.

Sanctuary.

From my past, my present, and my future.

All of which were somehow uncertain.

The past was fixed for most people, but for me, it wasn't.

Everything could change in a heartbeat, no matter how deeply I set my roots.

Still, those were thoughts for another day. As the wheels soared over the gravel of my driveway, spitting the stones every which way, I didn't bother looking up.

The door opened. I heard the slight sound of music—Sum 41? Really? —before it shut off, and the door slammed closed.

I knew from the direction of her steps that she wasn't heading toward the house like most folk would. She was heading toward me. Like she knew I'd be just as difficult as she was.

And that was the truth.

Any other bitch, I'd have been waiting for her on the porch, and soon after, I'd have taken her through to my bedroom.

Because it was Tiffany?

Because she was difficult?

I thought I'd be difficult too and make her hunt me down.

As she moved around the driveway, the sound of gravel crunching petered off, and then her footsteps were silent once she was on the lawn.

"Well, isn't this romantic?" she mocked as she approached me, and though her cockiness might have grated, I appreciated a woman who knew her worth.

Maybe that was because of my past though.

I didn't want a virgin, but I liked the chase, and there was precious little of that around here. What with the clubwhores and the daughters of rich fucks in town who wanted a walk on the wild side, we were surrounded by pussy.

Even the ugly fucks like Jenssen got laid on the regular.

Sons of Anarchy might have given us all a bad rep with business, but where the cunts were concerned, we were drowning in their cream.

"I aim to please," I rumbled, letting my eyes drift shut.

I'd had a swift glance at her from the corner of my eye, and my dick was already taking charge of my body.

Fuck, she was hot. That chick from *The Matrix* hot. All cheekbones and sass-itude.

Her hair was different than the first time I'd seen her two weeks ago. A little shorter, a lot bouncier. It had bright blue color at the ends now, and it made her eyes pop so they looked almost turquoise instead of blue or green.

She wore a halter top that had her tits spilling out, but then the most conservative shorts—knee-length and tailored—and a pair of ballet flats that shouldn't have been sexy, but somehow were.

Those tits, holy hell, I wanted to bury my face in them.

Fucking suffocate as those tits sucked the air from my lungs like she sucked the cum from my balls.

Heaven.

When she maneuvered to my side without a word, settling beside me on the plaid blanket I'd set down, her perfume swept over me.

Cool, crisp, and clean.

Like apples in the fall, with just a faint hint of blossom to give it a feminine tang, then a rich warmth that made me think of musk.

She was the most feminine woman I'd ever seen, so confident in herself, in her sensuality, that it made me want her more than any other bitch I'd wanted in a long time.

When she was lying flat beside me, she asked, "This your idea of a date?"

"Not fucking you over the pool table at the clubhouse, am I?"

A snort escaped her. "That's what you do on a regular date?"

Her lack of pique surprised me. All bitches were jealous, just look at Giulia. She'd come into Nyx's life and was headbutting and nose shattering any clubwhore who dared to get in her way, and only fuck knew what would happen when he eventually claimed her.

Cammie had been wrecked as well, not that she'd had the brains to stay away from a fucker like Nyx. Just because he was possessive and didn't share his pussy didn't mean he was staying with the bitches he claimed for a short while.

Giulia was different though.

I got the vibe that, once he pulled his head out of his ass, he was going to patch her in.

Sweet fuck, that was going to be a blast to watch. Nyx wasn't the kind of man to be led around by his dick, and Giulia was a stubborn piece of sass that wasn't about to let him get away with shit.

My lips curved at the thought of the showdowns we had coming our way.

We hadn't had a real party in too long. What Tiffany had come to was more of a Friday night thing. No visiting chapters had come to stay, and when that happened? Shit turned real, fast.

The second a slut came onto Nyx after he'd made Giulia his, I just knew she was going to break bones, and it'd be better than ringside seats at a championship boxing match.

"Why here?"

I blinked, just remembering she was there. And I didn't mean that in a bad way. It wasn't that she was forgettable, it was that she was calming.

She wasn't an attention seeker.

I liked that.

It actually made me more aware of her, even if I could zone out some. It meant my body knew she wasn't a danger to me, and in my world, that fucking mattered.

I rubbed my chin. "I live here."

"You do? I thought you guys lived in the clubhouse."

"We do, but I have my own space too."

"Why?"

"Some brothers like the community. Some don't. I like a bit of both."

"When do you come here?"

"When the noise gets to be too much for me."

"It is loud there, isn't it?"

I only nodded, but that was an understatement. "Most of the time, I can deal with it, but then, some days, I just can't." I wasn't like Mav, dealing with PTSD and survivor's guilt, but somedays? I just needed a fucking break from the noise.

"How come?"

Rolling my head to the side, I graced her with my attention. She surprised me because she wasn't giving me googly eyes. Her head was turned to the dying rays of the sun, and she was basking like a house cat in its warmth.

My lips bowed slightly, and I gave her an honest answer, because everything about her demanded it.

She wasn't like any other bitch I'd come across.

I just fucking knew it.

She wouldn't take my bullshit. Wouldn't accept it. Would make me be me.

And maybe I should walk away from that, head in a completely different direction, because being honest wasn't my forte...

Seeing a chance to deflect, I muttered instead, "You don't suit your name."

She snorted at that, unoffended. "You think I don't know that? Mom had a fetish for dolls. She had this one she called Tiffany, and lucky me, I apparently had her eyes."

I laughed. "Had? Past tense? I hope Mom's not as much of a nut job as she sounds."

A shrug had her wriggling her shoulder. "Depends who you talk to."

"Meaning?"

"Meaning, she says she isn't, but I disagree. We have a room with thousands of dolls in it."

I mock-shuddered. "Sounds creepy."

"Doesn't just sound it. It *is* creepy. Creepy as fuck."

My lips twitched again. "You prefer, I dunno, Tiff?"

She rolled her head like I had, turning it so we were looking at one another. When she stared at me, her blue-green eyes were lazy and relaxed. Just looking at her was like listening to a meditation tape for an hour.

"You can call me Tiff," she murmured. "Or you can call me by my middle name."

"Do your friends call you Tiff?" At her slow nod, I inquired, "Okay. I'll bite. What's your middle name?"

"Lexie."

"Lex. I like it."

"I'm glad you do," she teased, "but that isn't what I said."

"You're not a Lexie either. You're a Lex."

"That's a boy's name."

My gaze drifted down to her tits. "Think I'll have to settle with Tiff, seeing as you're no boy, sugar."

"Figured that out a long time ago."

She reached down and placed her hand on my belly, and heat arced between us like someone had doused us with a flamethrower.

She released a hissed breath, one I'd have matched, but my control was too strong, before I drawled, "You know where this is heading, don't you?"

"I know. But I want you to know that I'm not like any woman you've ever met."

I was aware of that already. It was why she was at my home.

Why I hadn't boned her yet, why I had brought her here—where incredibly few women had been before.

She had class.

It exuded from her pores.

And that made me respect her.

It made me want her more.

"That isn't news to me, Tiffany," I said, turning my gaze away from hers.

I laid there in the dying sun, and stared at nothing—mostly, a copse of trees with some birds that were making a goddamn racket—while she rested at my side.

It wasn't how I imagined this date going, but to be fair, dating wasn't my scene, period. It hadn't been since I'd been patched into the Sinners' MC.

Dating and cuts didn't go together. What we'd done this far, I wasn't sure even constituted as dates.

I mean, a couple who dated shared a table, didn't they? Did more than yell at each other across a fucking bar?

When she curled onto her side, her legs entangling with mine as she pressed her face to my arm and rested her hand farther down on my stomach, I knew that I'd have tossed off any other bitch, told her to get in her fucking car and get the fuck away from me.

But with Tiff, that didn't happen.

If anything, my initial tension drained away when she hummed, "It's pretty out here."

"Thanks." It was. Not exactly my pride and joy, but I spent a lot to make it look this naturally unnatural.

"You garden?" she teased.

"No," I said with a snort. "I pay someone to look after the place."

"Why?"

"Because it's mine."

If that sounded possessive, then so be it.

My house and my bike were the two possessions I owned that I gave a fuck about. They were the only items that couldn't be easily replaced.

"Did you give the landscapers free rein?"

I smiled at the idea of Garry Johnson calling himself a 'landscaper.' Garry was salt of the Earth. His company was called Green-Fingered Garry, for fuck's sake. Not that I said any of that, even if it rammed home the difference between her and me in a big way.

"Why?"

"Because I can't imagine you planting a patch of peonies," she muttered with a laugh.

"Peonies?"

"Thought as much." She wafted a hand over in the direction of the house. "Those flowers are called peonies."

I shrugged, I hadn't known that. "Thought they were wildflowers."

She giggled. "Sounds about right. I'm almost relieved. You're breaking all my glass ceilings here, Sin. If I thought you were into flowers too? I'd start wondering what the hell you guys were doing at that clubhouse of yours."

"Nothing that delicate little ears like yours should be hearing."

"Not so delicate. You grow up fast in this world."

"Which world?" I scoffed. "You're rich, Tiff. Rich as fuck. What do you have to worry about?"

"Staying rich," she replied dryly. "Not me, per se. But Daddy? He has to worry about that kind of thing. It's no easy life."

My brow puckered. "Then don't spend as much. He wouldn't have to work as hard—"

"I actually don't," she said flatly. "Mom does though. Every item I'm wearing? She bought. My place? To Dad's specs."

"Why?"

"They want me to stay close to home."

"Why?"

"We're tight-knit. They hated when I left for college." She shrugged. "I just wish Dad didn't have to work so hard."

"So, you're not a spoiled rich kid then?" I mocked.

"Well, it depends on your definition of spoiled. I mean, I am, but I don't even have an Insta account to show off all my shit. That means there are plenty of kids brattier than me."

I laughed. "No Insta? Shame, I'd probably get a kick out of watching you do duck faces."

"Why look on IG when you can see them in the flesh?" She leaned up onto her elbow and pulled a pout, then she smiled at the same time, diminishing the ridiculousness of the exaggerated pose, but it didn't take away from how fucking kissable her lips were.

How pouty.

Fuck.

She had a mouth made for sucking dick.

I bit the inside of my cheek at the thought, but I couldn't stop myself from reaching over and tracing that delectable curve with the tip of my finger. Her lips parted ever so slightly, and when I outlined her Cupid's bow, she swallowed. It was too dark out to see her eyes, but I could see her movements, could feel them. She pushed harder against me, pressing closer like she didn't want any space between us, and I got that.

I did.

I didn't want space between us either.

"You come here to be fucked?" I rasped.

She tensed, but I didn't regret asking the question. "Excuse me?"

"Trying to figure out what your purpose is," I said, and when she made to pull back, I half sat up, grabbed the back of her neck, and forced her to roll on top of me. The second she lay on me, I loosened my hold some and she instantly stopped struggling, but I stayed in her face.

And she stayed in mine.

"That was a dick move," she snapped.

But she didn't roll off me.

"First lesson. I *am* a dick."

"No shit, Sherlock," she snarled, yet she didn't back away.

"Second lesson, I'm not one of those pussies you've dated before."

"No, you're just a dick," she growled under her breath. "First lesson, I'm not a slut. Second lesson, I won't let you get away with treating me like shit. Especially when I don't deserve it."

"Meaning there are times you will deserve it?"

"I'm no angel."

"No, you'd be fucking boring if you were."

"I'm many things, but boring isn't one of them."

Slowly, I rolled back down so I was lying on the ground with her blanketing me, and again, she didn't fucking move.

"Why are you here? You want a hard fuck? Is that it?"

"Didn't get it, did I?"

"Not yet. The evening's still young," I replied with a laugh.

She huffed, but shuffled on my body, pressing her hips into mine before she resettled. I got the feeling she wasn't trying to turn me on, but get comfortable.

I wasn't averse to the idea, even if her hip bones dug into me like knives.

I didn't usually like skinny bitches, but there was something about this little heathen I appreciated.

Like she'd said, she wasn't boring, and fuck me, I was so fucking tired of boring snatch.

"I'm here because I liked the look of you."

Her prim tone had me scoffing, "You're here because you think I'm pretty?"

"Oh, sugar, you know you're more than pretty," she purred. "Taming you would be impossible."

She didn't say it like that was a bad thing.

"Glad we got that out there," I said, but I moved my hands to her ass and squeezed her butt cheeks.

She didn't rear back and slap me, and I liked the fact that I wasn't sure what she was going to do.

Unpredictable? Yep. She was that in spades.

I rubbed her ass, then murmured, "I don't date."

"You'd have fooled me."

"This isn't a date. This was me testing the waters."

"I can see that, even as I can see that you don't consider our other meetings to be dates. Have you tested these waters? What now? You going to haul me into your house and fuck me on the kitchen counter?"

Well, she didn't sound averse to that idea.

I laughed because she was funny, even if she didn't really mean to be. "I won't fuck you."

"No? Why?"

Was that a pout in her voice?

"Because you want more than a hard fuck. I ain't the kinda guy you piss around with, Tiff. I think we both know that. I'm the kinda guy you country clubbers screw then giggle about once you're safely back home as you wince every time you cross your legs for the next few days, because you can still feel my dick inside you—but you don't want that."

"No," she whispered, her voice smaller than I'd anticipated. "I don't."

"You don't know what you want, do you, sweetness?" I rasped, liking that. Liking that she wasn't here to fuck, even if she did want sex.

I didn't play games. Ever. Even if my brothers thought I did.

"I just know I want you."

"Whatever I'll give you?"

"No. Whatever I want to take," she drawled.

Her fire had me rolling up again, and as I speared my hands through her hair, holding her to me, I brought our mouths together. Nipping her bottom lip, I muttered, "Don't think you can play me, Tiff."

"Same goes." She nipped me back, giving as good as she got.

In the blink of an eye, I switched positions, rolling us over so she was beneath me. Her legs parted, her hips rocked up, and all of a sudden, I was resentful of my fucking jeans, because her heat?

Paradise.

Talk about a molten hot pussy.

I rested my arms on either side of her head and leaned over her. Dipping down, I pecked her lips, here and there, nipping and teasing, lashing my tongue along the curve of her Cupid's bow, tasting her and enjoying her little pants and moans.

When her hands came to my butt, digging into me, I grinned, even as I carried on, tempting us both.

Then her tongue snapped out, catching mine, and I dove right in.

Fuck, kissing was an underrated aspect of sex in my opinion. Most men went straight for the goods.

Me?

I loved kissing.

Tongue fucking.

All of it.

It was hot, but no one let me play. Until her.

She tried to tempt me into taking it deeper, but I remained on track, sliding my tongue against hers, eating her as she began to eat me, starting to understand what I was doing.

When deep grunts escaped me, and her tiny mewls echoed around us, I pulled back, aware that both our mouths would be red in the morning.

She groaned when my weight shifted, my dick pushing into her softness, and I reached for the hem of her halter top.

Dragging it up, I revealed a pair of tits that were porn star worthy. That they were real was even more eye-popping.

That they were covered with a lacy bra thing told me she hadn't been screwing with me.

In the past, bitches had arrived at the door to my room at the clubhouse wearing coats and nothing else. Shirt dresses with no panties or bras on. Sending me the clear message they wanted to be used.

And fuck, if I wasn't enough of a gentleman to give them what they wanted.

Tiff?

She didn't know what she wanted.

The only thing she knew was that it involved me.

She wanted me.

And I wanted her.

So I dipped my head and rolled my tongue around her bra-clad nipple, sucking on it through the thin lace. It wasn't the most supportive of her tits, and they shifted to the side some, but fuck, they were juicy.

I squished them together, thought about burrowing my dick between them, and almost had my eyes rolling into the back of my head at just the idea.

Nipping the hard peak, I tongued her some more until she was squirming beneath me.

Then I let my mouth drop lower, shuffling back on my knees so I could kiss her belly.

I glided my nose down her center, along her covered cunt, and scented her arousal.

Fuck, she smelled delicious. Like honey and heaven and hell rolled into one juicy morsel.

My mouth watering, I pulled back so I was kneeling between her legs.

"Take off your clothes," I rasped.

"Take off yours," she countered, making me grin.

"You want to see the goods first?"

Resenting that the sun had begun to set, casting long shadows over the already shaded part of the yard where we were lying, I wished I could see her face at that, but she just sniffed. "Can't see anything in the dark."

"No, I like it like that."

I sensed her confusion. "I thought you'd be into visuals."

"Sometimes I am. Sometimes I'm not. Tonight, I'm not. Strip," I commanded, giving the order and expecting to be obeyed.

Though she huffed, I heard and felt her move around, but I surprised her by helping her with the task at hand because any distance between us, I soon discovered, was too much. She shivered at the touch of my fingers swiping over her legs, then groaned when I moved them over her belly and tugged her tits out of the thin cups of her bra. When I reached the waistband of her shorts, I nipped along the line, then tugged at it with my teeth. She moaned, then dragged them down herself, and I grinned and began nipping at her panties too, until she released a groan of irritation and did the job for me. Well, as much as she could, considering I was between her thighs.

Within seconds, fabric whispered against fabric, and when she tossed the bundle at my chest, I grabbed her clothes, sorted between them, and found her panties.

The thong was tiny, and it scented of her even more. I reached down for my fly, pulled out my cock, and wrapped the scrap around it. Then, I reached for her hand in the gloomy twilight, and dragged it over to my dick.

A sound escaped her, thick and guttural, delicious enough that that simple noise had me twitching.

"Fuck," she rasped, her hand shaping me as she jacked me off. Her words were just as thick, and I knew she was savoring me.

Knew it, and fucking loved it.

With a gulp, I tipped my head back as she carried on exploring me, and when the heat of her tongue flickered at the tip? I nearly died and went to heaven.

Dragging off my cut, I quickly tore off my shirt, and worked around her hands and mouth to unfasten the button of my jeans.

She helped drag them down to my knees, and when her nails scored down my thighs, rolling around to do the same to the backs? I nearly fucking came. Her tongue flattened around the tip of my dick, and when she began to hum around the glans, I gripped her hair and tugged her back.

Spit connected us, a thick wave of it, so heavy I felt its weight against my dick, and blindly, I reached down, touching her lip before I swiped my hand through the saliva that bound us. Collecting it on my fingers before I bowed over her and joined our mouths, I stuck my wet hand between her thighs, coating her in both of us, and I found her clit, rolling it between my fingers, rubbing it hard and fast until she shuddered against me.

The little orgasm had me grinning against her mouth, but it didn't stop me from fucking her there with my tongue. She panted against me, melting into my hold, never once struggling against the tight grip I had on her hair.

The more I took, the more she gave, and fuck, it was like poetry.

She didn't whine or squeal, she accepted what I wanted her to have.

And that fucked with my head.

I speared a finger inside her, testing her readiness. She was tight but molten hot, and ready for me to fuck.

That didn't mean I was ready though.

I let my finger retreat from her heat, then reached up and thumbed her nipple. Her tits were heavy, and the weight in my palm made my cock weep.

I held her there, explored her curves, then slowly, I moved her back and released my grip on her hair.

Grabbing her ankles, I levered her legs up high, bringing her knees to her chest. She didn't stop me. Not once. When I bowed over her, swiping my tongue along her folds, giving her clit a quick flick, reveling in her taste for just a second, she arched her hips up, wanting more.

Needing me.

I thrust into her and flickered the tensile muscle around, getting more of her addictive flavor in me, then I reared up, dragged her wet panties off me, and settled my cock between her parted pussy lips.

Pressing her ankles higher, so that her thighs stayed between us, I let my weight rest against her. She was mostly restrained, but her arms instantly came around me, her nails digging into my shoulders before she reached down and around, touching me where she could reach.

"Want you inside me, Sin," she whimpered, and the words messed me up inside, because damn, there was nowhere else I wanted to be either.

I sawed my hips back and forth, coating my cock in her cunt juices, then when I was slick, I reached between us and slipped the tip inside her.

The heat of her had me freezing. Tiff too.

We both released a breath that was more of a whistle, and when she rasped, "Are you clean? Please tell me you're clean." I wasn't sure whether to be amused or offended.

"Wouldn't have touched you if I wasn't," I whispered, because there was no time for messing around with this shit.

"I'm clean. Haven't been with anyone in months." Her hips arched up slightly. "I'll get the morning after pill tomorrow. Fuck, please, just put it in."

I groaned under my breath, knowing this was stupid, but somehow needing it all the fucking more because of just how hot she was. Just how perfect her cunt felt around me.

How many brothers had been trapped this way?

I could ride with her to the pharmacy, make sure she swallowed the fucking pill.

Indecision warred with need, and dumb fuck that I was, I let need win.

When I slid into her?

The first pussy I'd ever slid into without a condom?

It was like a fucking revelation.

Nothing beat going in bareback.

Nothing.

Her cunt was tight, hotter than lava, and sucking me down into the heart of her.

Perfection.

Absolute perfection.

When my entire dick was cosseted in her pussy, I settled my weight on top of her, just savoring the experience.

It was how sex should be.

Real and raw.

Fucking flawless.

But when I didn't move, that had her fidgeting all the more. She squirmed beneath me, her nails digging into my back and hips, at my waist. I let her, loving the feel of her writhing around. Then she moaned, "Fuck, Sin. Please!"

Who was I to argue?

I gave her what she asked for, even if she didn't know what that was exactly. I did.

She wanted me.

And fuck, I knew I wanted her.

That night at the clubhouse, that party? She'd been the only bitch who'd caught my attention all evening.

Sitting there, prim and prissy, while the debauchery went on around her, touching her but not contaminating her?

I wanted that.

I wanted her.

And because what I wanted, I usually defiled, I did what I normally did.

I took.

I fucked her hard, fast, and wet. I gave her what she asked for and took for myself.

She screamed with every drag of my cock out of her, and as I thrust in to the hilt, I bounced off her. I fucked her fast, and her cunt clamped down around me, trying to hold me inside, trying to keep me hostage.

I'd never wanted to be captured more than I had at that moment.

I didn't stop until we both roared our release to the world, and even then, I didn't stop pumping my hips, needing to feel every twitch of her cunt around me as I drowned in the sheer wonder of fucking without a condom.

When I finally came down, I pulled back, not enough to pull out, but I grabbed her legs and dragged them around my hips. Then, I settled my weight on her some more, using that to keep my dick inside her as I slumped atop her body.

When her arms came around me again?

I didn't know what the fuck this was, but I knew I didn't want to move.

Not ever.

Not even in a million years.

THREE

TIFFANY

THREE WEEKS LATER

WITH THE BIG SHADES ON, the scarf, and topped by the helmet, I didn't look like me.

And I was glad for that as I strode into the pharmacy, marching the walk of shame as I muttered, "Morning after pill, please."

When the old bitch behind the counter glowered at me, but fulfilled my request after insisting I remove the helmet, I longed for the days of anonymity that came with living in the city.

New York was wonderful in times like these. Pharmacy clerks didn't give a fuck if you bought a million condoms as well as a million carrots to stuff inside them, so long as your credit card was working, you didn't give them any shit, oh, and you didn't stick a gun in their face while you did it.

Here?

I felt like every purchase you made was being judged by a clerk.

It pissed me off, but not enough to drive fifty minutes into the city to grab the morning after pill when I could get it here.

Sue me, I was lazy.

And I knew Sin had work to do, so riding on his bike wasn't something I did often, and this was my excuse to ride bitch as he so charmingly phrased it.

The second the old cow gave me the bag once my payment was verified, I retrieved it from the paper, gave her a false smile, and said, "Let's save the earth, no?" before shoving the bag back in her face.

As I walked out of the store, I unpacked the pill, tossed the trash in a can by the door, and, making sure Sin was watching, I popped it in my mouth.

The first time this had happened a week ago, he'd bought the pill himself, and had practically watched me gulp the thing down. Hell, he'd been more intent than when I sucked him off. You'd think I was deep throating the pill for all the focus he gave me.

But I got it.

I did.

He didn't trust me then.

Now?

Different matter entirely.

After that first pill, I'd sworn never to do it again. I'd felt like death warmed over, but here I was, another mistake notched up, and I felt bad. So fucking bad. This wasn't why the pill existed, and I needed to make better choices.

Of course, it wasn't just on me.

When I settled on the back of his bike, my legs clinging to the sides of his, my body molding against his, I sighed, loving the freedom that came with riding bitch.

I sometimes wasn't all that easy with showing public displays of affection, even if we were at home. It wasn't something that came naturally to me, to be honest. Why sit holding someone's hand when you were watching a movie when you could sprawl across the sofa in comfort? My brain wasn't wired to be clingy. But riding bitch? I either clung, or I'd be tossed off the bike and be left on the highway—I liked those odds.

The second my arms were around his waist, my head on his shoulder, he kicked the ignition. The throb that lit me up from the inside out made me want to fling my head back and holler.

But that'd draw attention to us.

I didn't need that right now.

So I contained it with difficulty, then twisted my head down when, as we drove down Main Street, I saw Lily walking into the new diner.

I wasn't sure if Sin noticed, but I hoped he didn't. We'd been keeping things on the downlow since that first night, but we were spending more and more time together at his place.

Because I didn't work, I usually waited for him at his home, to which he'd given me a frickin' key.

Crazy that I had the key to his house, right?

It kinda messed with my head. That meant something, didn't it?

I knew Sin wasn't the kind of guy who trusted easily, but he trusted me with his home.

Even while that made me feel all squirmy inside, it also made me nervous. And happy. A little, befuddling cocktail that I'd swallowed down with a load of cum the night before.

Just thinking about what we'd done last night made every part of me twitchy.

Damn.

What he could do with his dick should be illegal.

I'd even hazard a guess and say that it was.

Entirely.

In some prudish states, that is.

Just remembering him sliding into my butt was enough to make my eyes cross. It was why we were here. He'd torn two condoms getting into my ass, and with the third, the last in the pack, we had a winner. But that had screwed us over for when he'd fucked me after. Boy, was it worth it.

I'd never had anal sex before, but fuck, I wanted to break all the boundaries with Sin. Break all my inbuilt rules, and he made it so goddamn fun.

It was like... God, it was stupid, I knew, but because I couldn't give him all of me, I wanted to give him access to every part of my body.

Just not my heart.

Because in that way lay danger.

I mean, I was already in danger, so I didn't need him tugging at my heartstrings too.

Something about him got to me.

What started off as a hookup turned into friendly booty calls, turned into us spending his free time at his house, chilling out, sometimes in the yard, sometimes watching TV. Him grilling outside, me watching and shooting the shit with him after I'd made a simple potato salad—he wasn't to know my housekeeper had made it, and I wasn't about to tell him. He bought a double wide hammock that we enjoyed together—don't have sex in hammocks, kids. *Don't. Do. It.* Then he gave me his key so I could wait there for him after he pulled a long shift at work.

I knew something was happening. His shifts had changed, and he never told me exactly what he did anyway. I mean, I didn't really want to know, considering he was a biker, and I'd Googled the Sinners. I knew they were one-percenters, which meant they did all the bad stuff. But Sin wasn't bad. Even though his name kind of implied it.

Lately, he'd been gone for longer periods of time, and when he got back, his eyes were gritty—I'd even watched him put eyedrops in.

That, to me, was so crazy intimate that I still couldn't get over it.

Watching a man in the hall light, opposite the vanity in the bathroom, tipping his head back to put in drops? It felt pretty much like I was watching *my* man, not just *a* man.

I squeezed him around the waist, and his hand came to my thigh. He loosely gripped it with a casual possessiveness that both thrilled me and unnerved me as we drove down the back roads toward his property.

We were at the top end of the town line when we were at his place, and I loved how much open space he had.

My yard was bigger, my house better, but somehow, I preferred his.

With its wild yard that he had a guy called 'Green-Fingered Gary' fix— I'd met him one day—which was so beautifully done it was like wandering into the woods, I'd fallen for it, him, and the house itself. Though simple, plain, even, it was clean and just beautiful with some vintage touches that came from an old property.

It was from the forties, at least, and the floors were from that era. The kitchen he'd had restored so the cabinets, which were detailed, had been returned to their former glory. He'd put in a marble counter, replacing what he'd told me had been scarred Formica, but that and new appliances made the room inviting, which was fitting as the living room opened up into the kitchen.

His bedroom was empty except for a bed, a rug, and two nightstands with simple lamps on them, and I loved that too. I liked how little fuss there was anywhere. It was the opposite of my place, where antiques rubbed shoulders with works of art to expose just how rich we were to anyone who came to visit.

It made me realize how much of a showplace Mom had made the house rather than a home, and while I was grateful for what we had, I appreciated the simple things at Sin's more.

When we slowed down on the drive up, he tapped something on his hog, and as we rolled down the hill toward the house, the gates to the driveway slowly opened.

Only when they were closed again, at my back, did I truly relax.

This house?

With this man?

It felt like the only place I could be myself.

It was making me question who I was.

Rich kid. Spoiled. College dropout.

I was living at home permanently because I had no idea what I wanted to do with my life after making a mess of a delicate situation in college. I currently spent my days with Sin, waiting on Lily to go and have another pedicure, or...fuck, that was pretty much it. Talk about wasting myself.

When he parked, I jumped off the bike and dragged the helmet off my head, eager to escape such thoughts. Tugging off the scarf, I let my hair flow behind me, all while he sorted out the bike and got to his feet.

I didn't bother to wait for him, just headed for the house.

Unlocking the door, I trailed into the kitchen where I started some coffee.

I needed it.

It had been a helluva morning thus far.

When I opened the fridge to grab the bag of stuff I brought with me, I felt him enter the kitchen and wasn't surprised when he tugged me into him from behind.

His arms came around my waist, his head dropped to my shoulder, and somehow, that move right there hit me square in the ovaries.

I wanted to melt, I wanted to tense up, but he gave me no choice.

"Need to stop making a habit of this, Lex," he rumbled, making me laugh at his use of my middle name.

He was a clever shit.

He knew I wasn't comfortable with being held like this, so he disarmed me, as per usual, by calling me that when he knew I didn't particularly like it. That was when I rolled out the big guns and called him Padraig—his real name. Yup, he'd told me it.

"Lex-ee, Sin. It's an extra syllable, Padraig."

His lips twisted. "I don't know what that fancy word means."

I narrowed my eyes at nothing, then twisted my head to glare at him. "Don't do that."

"Don't do what?" he inquired, brow arched.

"Act like you're dumb. You're not."

"Just wondered if you'd figured that out yet or not."

Instantly, my shoulders hunched up. "Sorry."

I knew what he meant.

He shrugged. "It's okay."

No. It wasn't.

Quite clearly, it wasn't.

He'd felt my reaction when I'd spotted Lily.

Shit.

I cleared my throat. "I don't want to tell her."

"Why not?"

"Because she might tell my dad."

"So?"

He was so beautiful, and I totally didn't think he knew it. Sure, he was cocky, but around me? With time? That faded away.

But his pitch-dark hair was glossy in the early morning light, and because we hadn't done anything other than roll out of bed to get on his hog, it was soft rather than crispy with gel. His face was worn from lack of sleep—not just because of our escapades, but because of whatever the club had him doing—and his eyes were...crap, stormy.

He was getting ready to fight.

I didn't want that.

So I spun in his arms, didn't let him move away by slinging mine around his neck, and admitted, "When someone's nice to you, do you find it hard to say no?"

"Tiff—"

"I don't mean me and you. I'm not manipulating you. I'm trying to make you understand." I sucked in a breath. "When someone is a bastard to you, you can be rebellious. It's easy to say no. It's easy to think 'fuck you.' But when someone's nice? When they reason with you, when they turn your world on its head to make you think you're wrong, and they use everything you've done as a weapon against you, all while saying it's in your best interests, and all while doing it because they love you? It's harder to say, 'fuck you,' isn't it?"

He scowled at me, but it softened as he read how earnest I was being.

This was no bullshit.

This was my life.

"I guess."

"That's my dad," I whispered. "I love him. I do. But he's definitely old school. He gives me more freedom than most daughters who still live at home, who still buy shit on his card, and who dropped out of college, get from their father, but that's because I live like my mother. He understands that. He molded her a certain way, and as long as I live in her image, that's fine." There'd been a time when he'd wanted to bring me into the business but, of late, that had changed, and that just made me feel even more worthless. *Useless.* Like my mom. A pretty butterfly whose only role in this world was to look pretty and to make men smile.

"But you're not boning a dude from the country club. You're boning a biker," Sin said softly.

"Exactly. If he thought you were on the up and up, if we'd make an advantageous match, he'd have no problem with this. But I know him. He'll... He'll kill me with kindness until I find it hard to say no. He'll learn stuff about you that I don't know, and he'll use that as ammunition to break us apart.

"I know there are things about your life that no sane father would approve of. I'm not an idiot. I know you have a past, and I'm sure your present isn't squeaky clean, but I don't need him pushing his nose into it. Can you get that?"

He didn't answer that, instead, asked, "You think Lily would tell him?" He knew how I felt about her. Knew I considered her to be a sister from another mister.

"I don't know. You're a Sinner," I said drolly, reaching up and running my fingers through his hair. When his eyes fell to half-mast, I almost smiled at his visceral response to my touch. "She might think telling him is in my best interest. I don't know that I wouldn't do the same if I thought she was dating a Sinner too."

His eyes popped open at that. "We're dating?"

I froze, then when there was only amusement in his eyes, muttered, "Jerk."

He grinned at me, his entire face lighting up as he squeezed my waist. "We're dating, angel," he rumbled, dipping his chin and letting his scratchy stubble scrape down my nose like the jerk he was. When I pinched his butt in payback, he snorted out a laugh, then hauled me high so I could wrap my legs around his hips.

He pushed me back into the fridge, and I didn't even mind that a magnet was digging into my hip. I was just more focused on the look in his eyes, on that intense stare that made me melt and tense at the same time.

"What is it?" I whispered.

"I get your reticence, I do. I even understand why you don't want your friends and family to know, but this, what we have, it's not going nowhere. You get me?"

I bit my bottom lip but nodded.

He was right.

"Okay," he muttered, blowing out a breath. "So long as we both know that."

"Yeah. We do."

His eyes darkened. "Good. With that in mind, I want to fuck you with no condoms. I'm clean. You're clean. And I don't need us rolling out of bed at the asscrack of dawn to grab the morning after pill because we had too much fun the night before."

My lips hitched up in a grin, and I squeezed my arms around his neck.

"Aww, poor baby," I retorted, then squealed when he darted forward and nipped my chin.

"You know precisely what I'm saying." The intensity in his words and on his face? God, it hit me hard. In places that I couldn't afford to respond to him like this. Places like my goddamn heart. "I want you raw. Never experienced anything like it. Don't think I ever will again—"

Before he could say another word, another terrifying word, I whispered quickly, "I'll get the shot." I mean, hell, I'd been intending on having this conversation with him anyway. It was to my benefit that he brought it up first.

He dipped his chin. "Good." Then, "When?"

Snorting, I muttered, "I'll get an appointment with the doctor today. So whenever they can fit me in."

"Even better." He let me down at that, evidently no longer worrying I was going to run off and faint, or go screaming for the woods at this conversation.

But I got it.

We weren't that great at talking.

Doing? Being? Yeah. We rocked at that. Especially when we were together.

Now that I was on my feet again, I grabbed the coconut milk from the fridge, and the regular stuff for him, then began making us coffee.

I was well aware that I moved around his kitchen like it was mine.

Even more aware that he hadn't said anything when I rearranged his cupboards so I could fit some of my things in there.

As I doctored our cups, he slung himself onto a counter stool and asked, "What are your plans for the day?"

"Talking with the doctor is one of them," I answered dryly, and since my back was to him, I shot him a sassy grin over my shoulder when he just grunted. "Tonight, I won't be here until late."

"Me either. After eleven, at least."

I nodded.

Work.

It went without saying.

It also went without saying that I couldn't ask what he was doing. Which technically sucked, but I wasn't sure I really wanted to frickin' know.

He didn't ask either, but I could see he wanted to. It amused me that he could be fair though. This big, badass biker who liked to grill and sit in a hammock, and who maybe killed people for a living or delivered drugs—

dear God, I could just hear the conversation with my father if he ever discovered what was going on here—being *fair*.

Because I couldn't ask him what he was doing, his logic was why should he be able to ask me? Feminists didn't all come with burned bras, it seemed. They wore cuts too.

Because he didn't, because he let it go, even though he was curious, I explained, "Meal with Lily and her dad and brother tonight."

Tension hit him. "Yeah?"

I frowned, but hummed too. "It was Lily's birthday yesterday. They have a family meal thing on the day itself, but then I get invited the day after to a more 'relaxed' meal. You okay?"

"I don't like that Luke Lancaster fucker. He came into the bar and—"

"And what?" My eyes lit up. "Oh man, please tell me you were the one to break his nose? He's been bitching about that ever since it happened."

"No, but I wish I was."

I grinned. "But a biker did it?" I hooted. "Love it. Bet he didn't tell his dad that."

As I snickered when I handed him his coffee, he gripped his hand around my wrist and stated, "Don't trust that Luke fucker, Tiffany."

I wasn't sure if that was a command or him telling me that he didn't trust him. Frowning, I stared at his tight grip on my wrist, and muttered, "Don't worry, I don't even like Luke." I'd had a crush on the pretty boy back when I was younger, but there was something weird about him that gave me the creeps now.

He relaxed some. "Good. Keep your guard up tonight."

My brow puckered, because I wasn't sure why he thought that was necessary. I ate at Lily's place a few times a week, maybe once a month with both her brother and father in attendance.

"Okay," I agreed slowly, knowing something was happening here that he couldn't explain.

I just wished I'd heeded his warning.

Maybe if I had, things would have turned out differently.

FOUR

LUKE LANCASTER
LATER THAT NIGHT

WHEN LILY FLINCHED at Father's hold on her shoulder, my lips snagged into a nasty smirk, before I had to stop when it made me move my nose. Even that fraction of an inch pulled on the break, and the tape I had on the bridge, snagged on my skin, dampening my mood, even as it fed my desire for revenge.

Tonight was my night for vengeance, and the plan was already underway.

Lily gently tilted away from Father, just a tad, not enough for him to notice. But me? I noticed everything. Of course, I knew what Father was doing to her, what he'd been doing for years, but with a man like our father, there was no stopping him.

I knew because I was reared in his image.

Lily was weak. Exactly like Mother. The opposite of Father and me.

We were men of old. Vikings who raped and pillaged, took what we wanted, owned whatever we dared claim.

Did it sicken me that he was fucking her?

Yes.

Not much sickened me, but that did.

Even if it didn't surprise me.

A man like Donavan Lancaster wasn't one to be denied anything he desired, but even though I knew, there wasn't much I could do.

Not yet.

I was biding my time.

There'd come a day when he'd topple from his pedestal, and I'd be ready and waiting to take advantage of his weakness and to claim everything that was his and make it my own.

It was a day that wasn't far in the distance. The second I'd shown him my sanctuary, I'd known he'd fall into temptation too.

And he had.

His end was approaching.

My lips curved in earnest when he moved to the head of the table and Lily relaxed. My gaze switched between her and her best friend. Tiffany was an annoyance, but in this instance, she was going to help me.

Without even knowing it.

I watched her as she guzzled the drinks I'd insisted Conchita use to accompany this meal, and I handled the bar myself, slipping small amounts of the drug I'd ground up into her drink over the course of the evening. She was starting to look shaky on her feet.

Lily's tension at our father's impromptu speech about how he missed our mother, and how he wished she was here to see us both—farcical considering he was the reason she wasn't here in the first place—actually came to my aid.

She was tense, on edge, and ever since he touched her? In another world.

I knew how that worked.

A safe place.

Like anywhere on this rotten planet was truly safe.

Her wandering off to Narnia helped me because she didn't recognize the state Tiffany was in.

There'd been a time when I liked Tiffany. I liked her goo-goo eyes over me, but something changed, and ever since, she'd turned into an irritation. When her crush had died, I'd tried manipulating her into wanting me, but she'd rebuffed me one too many times, and only Father telling me to back off had made me stop. I wasn't the kind of man who took no for an answer—which was why tonight was going down the way it was—but for business? I got it.

Tiffany's father was a cash cow for some important people, our family included, so who was I to turn down free money?

When the interminable meal was over, I wandered off without a farewell. Heading outside to where I parked my car in a dark corner of the front yard, I waited for Tiffany to stagger toward her car, leaving Lily and Father back in the house.

She almost tripped and fell on her face, but she caught herself just in time. Her purse landed on the ground, and I almost laughed, watching her try to collect the crap she stored in there.

By the time she was back on her feet, she was shaking, and she almost slouched over the wheel.

Without the drug, she'd probably just be riding the limit, but now? She was a danger to everyone on the road.

Which was what I was banking on.

Loving that my new car was fully electric, which meant it purred to life rather than roaring like Tiffany's did, I began tailing her.

It was painful and pitiful watching her crawl down the driveway in her beast of a car, but when she sped up as she approached the highway that would make the journey to her house take five minutes, she stalled the engine. A few seconds later, she was back in motion, but she was going too fast. When she slipped down the shoulder, the tires spinning, I was almost disappointed when she wasn't involved in a worse crash. Still, beggars couldn't be choosers, I thought, as I pulled up behind her and slid out onto the asphalt.

She was moaning when I reached her, but luckily for her, she wasn't harmed. Puke covered her front, though, and she reeked of it. I was used to worse stenches, however, so I didn't curl up my nose, just was careful not to touch any of the filet mignon Conchita had served us as I reached for the phone she had put in the dock on her dash.

Holding it up to her face for it to unlock, I rummaged around her messages until I found the biker I was looking for.

Sin.

The unofficial guard dog the biker had set on his bitch.

A bitch whose blood I was going to taste tonight.

I thought about how tracking him had been so easy. Surprising, but easy. Tiffany was more fastidious than anyone let on. I was fucking gorgeous, but she'd never fuck me. Never even cast a look my way since she was a teen. What the fuck she saw in that scum, I didn't know, but it was to my good fortune that she was deciding to rough it.

I'd been following the bikers for about a week, tracking the ones the Sinners' Enforcer had set on his cunt of a woman, and the pretty boy fuck called Sin was the one who was usually on the snatch's tail.

That was how I'd put this plan together.

Following him had led me to discover that he was boning Tiffany.

Fucking slut.

She was snippy with me, but would spread her legs for that biker trash?

The thought had rage flushing through me, and though I wanted to take it out on her, I decided not to waste my energy on this bitch.

Giulia Fontaine was the woman who deserved my wrath, and with that fucking biker of hers out of town, tonight was my night to party.

The second I'd found Sin's number, I typed out a message.

Tiffany: *Got into a crash. Can you help me?*

Sin: *Fuck, are you all right?*

That he responded almost immediately had my brow rising.

Did the filth have feelings for his uptown girl?

My lips snagged into a grin at the thought, and as I hummed the Billy Joel song under my breath, I replied.

Tiffany: *No. I don't feel so good. Can you come and help me?*

Sin: *Shit. I'm on the clock.*

A pause when I didn't reply.

Sin: *Christ. Okay, I'll be there as soon as I can. Send me your live location.*

I sent it, carefully wiped the phone down, then I dumped it in the dock where I'd found it.

Squeezing her tit on the way out of the car, hard enough for it to hurt, for her to moan in her drug-induced state, I chuckled at the noise and, with a jaunty step, retreated to my car.

Blasting the radio as I pulled out onto the road, I headed toward the town where the Sinners' new bar was located.

The second Sin had left, the second that bitch was alone, she was mine. Giulia was about to learn how it felt to wish she was dead.

The dead felt nothing.

The dead were free.

Life was the prison, and I was about to become that cunt's jailor.

FIVE

TIFFANY

I SQUINTED at my phone as it started to ring. The light blared into the darkness, making my eyes ache until I grabbed it and pressed it to my ear after a quick glance at the time told me it was two in the morning.

Shit, I'd slept the whole day *and* night through.

I'd woken up at Sin's in a daze, we'd talked about what happened, and then he'd dropped me off here. That was pretty much all I remembered as I connected the call, wishing I was at his place and not my parents' home.

"Are you okay?" was Sin's greeting.

"No." Sin's voice made me wish he was here. Christ, what I wouldn't give to be waking up in his arms like I had yesterday. Misery filled me, misery and want and need as I whispered, "I still feel sick, and my head is killing me." I blew out a breath, then, knowing I'd caused him some trouble last night by having to leave work early, I asked, "Everything all right?"

"Not exactly." His breath gusted down the line. "I need to tell you something. It's big."

My eyes widened, which made my head pound. "What? Are you okay?"

"Everything comes at a cost, Tiff. My staying silent about what we discussed this morning means I have to listen to my Prez. It won't be for long."

"What won't be for long?" I rasped, sitting up, then hiding a moan as the ache in my head transmogrified into a monster.

He grunted. "I should have explained this morning, but fuck, we had other things to talk about. I should have been on the road last night, I just couldn't let you wake up alone this morning. I had to see you before I left."

"Couldn't let me wake up alone? Explained what this morning? Sin, what the hell are you talking about?" I whispered, my eyes watering as tears started to burn along the line of my lashes.

"My going away."

My heart nearly stopped. "Where are you going?"

"Our sister chapter in Ohio. I'm on the road already, halfway there."

My mouth dropped open. "Are you kidding me?" I whispered rawly. "You didn't think to come and say goodbye?"

"This isn't goodbye. I told you, Tiff, and I'll keep on telling you..."

I reached up and rubbed my eyes, blurting out, "I'm so confused."

"Don't be. I'm being punished. It's okay. Everything will work out."

Maybe I was being stupid, or maybe the drugs I'd been given were addling my brain, because I just wanted to cry some more.

"I don't want you to go." It was all I was capable of saying, but it wasn't enough. Didn't encompass at all how his words were messing with my already aching head.

"And that's why I didn't come and say bye to you, angel." He cleared his throat. "I'll call when I get there."

I frowned at the ceiling, which was impossible to see in the darkness. I'd turned everything off, switched off everything but the AC, anything and everything to make the place as quiet as possible.

Hell, if I could have turned off the fridge, I would have.

But even though it was silent, I still felt hypersensitive, and I listened to his breathing, listened to every nuance in his tone as I rasped, "Are you breaking up with me?" Was this just bullshit he was spouting? Had something else happened last night that I didn't remember?

"No," he stated sternly. "Listen to me, this is not over. It will never be over."

Never was a long time.

And I knew what the club was like. In Ohio, a day's drive from here? God only knew what would go down.

Maybe I *was* losing him. Only, I didn't think I could bear it if I did.

Calmly, he stated, "Tiff, it will all work out." I didn't miss the sternness to his tone, but that didn't mean much when he was on the fucking road to Ohio and this was the first I was hearing about it.

"How can it?" I asked miserably, wriggling my shoulders as an ache in them made itself known to me. "What's happening here?" I rasped. "Really, I mean."

"I didn't want to—" He grunted. "Fuck. Luke Lancaster used my absence at the bar to sneak in. He attacked Giulia Fontaine, our Enforcer's woman." He cleared his throat. "He's dead, Tiff. She killed him."

"Oh my God! Lily! I have to call her—"

"Yeah. Well, you can do that later. This has implications that I can't talk about over the phone, Tiff. Just remember, you're mine, and I'll speak to you later."

He didn't wait for me to reply, didn't wait for me to say a damn word, just cut the call and left me blinking at my screen, squinting as the pain of the light felt like it was piercing my eyes with the strength of a laser.

Even as his words sank into me, horror did too, and when I couldn't focus on my screen, I hit Siri and demanded, "Call Lily."

I knew there was no love lost between the siblings, but he'd died and...

Shit, was I supposed to be sad about it? After how he'd treated me?

I cut the call, focusing on the blob of the red button long enough to hit it. It didn't take a genius to figure out what had happened. I distinctly remembered Luke touching me last night, before Sin had arrived and helped get me home. I knew he'd been the one to drug me, and now I knew this about Giulia? I was unsure what to say, how to empathize-slash-sympathize with Lily, when the fucker had drugged me for the nefarious reason of attacking an innocent woman. So no, I wasn't sure what to do or how to help. Wasn't sure if I even could.

Lily and I were close, closer than close, but where her family was concerned, she was pretty tight-lipped.

I thought about calling Sin again, thought about asking him for more details, but even that felt beyond me.

I sank back against the pillow, my skull throbbing like it had been hit with a hammer, even as it settled into the down-stuffed layer.

Everything had just changed, my world had shifted on its axis, and I'd slept through it.

I reached up and rubbed my temples, but even as I started to cry again, I could feel my eyelids start to lower as sleep beckoned me into its embrace.

Tomorrow, I'd figure out what to do. Tomorrow, I'd learn if Sin really meant it, and I'd work out how to help Lily.

Tomorrow was another day, and hopefully, it was a better one.

I'd never know just how shittier my tomorrows were going to be.

SIX

TIFFANY

TWO MONTHS LATER

"DUST TO DUST, ASHES TO ASHES..."

As I stared into the hole where my father lay, I tossed some dirt onto the shiny casket and blinked back tears.

This was all avoidable.

That was all I kept on thinking. It was like a litany in my head, an endless song that was on repeat and I couldn't switch off.

I wanted to.

How I wanted to.

But I couldn't.

It was impossible.

The record was already in motion, and I'd lost everything.

Everything.

The only thing I hadn't lost?

My sanity, and honestly, that was a hard-won thing.

A hand moved to my lower back, and I quickly turned around, recognizing the scent, and buried myself in my best friend's arms. Lily hugged me tight, exactly how I needed to be held, as she whispered in my ear, "Sweetheart, come on. You need a breather."

I needed more than that.

Gnawing on my bottom lip, I let her draw me away. Behind her, there was her new boyfriend, Link.

He was, to put it kindly, a bruiser. Blond, very blond, very stacked, and the definition of ripped. I'd seen him before at the clubhouse on the few occasions I'd been there, and what I'd seen didn't make me predisposed to like him, but now that he'd claimed Lily?

There was definitely a change in him.

He looked around the cemetery like it was full of enemies, and that was the exact opposite of the truth.

Not even my mom was here. I was by myself with Lily, Link, and a few bikers who were on the road, just up the path, watching the show like it was entertaining. Not even my father's business partners were here. It was like Dad had been erased or something. By everyone who was supposed to care for him except for me.

I wasn't even sure how this had happened, and so swiftly too. It had all started the night when Luke had been murdered by one of the Sinners' Old Ladies.

She was here as well.

Sitting on the back of her man's bike, looking like a queen atop her chariot. It didn't matter that she was riding bitch and doing so behind a man that made Lucifer himself look friendly. She appeared regal, even as she looked watchful. They all were.

I wasn't sure what they expected to happen, but I got it.

Ever since that night, things had changed, and my world had turned upside down.

Lily's dad had warrants out for his arrest now, and as a result, his business assets were frozen. Turned out my daddy had been relying on Donavan Lancaster like he was his own personal piggy bank. With those funds cut off, his real estate empire came toppling down around him.

And the fallout devastated all of us.

But devastation was something you could come back from.

What you couldn't?

A bullet to the head.

"I can't believe he killed himself," I rasped to no one in particular. Hell, maybe I was muttering it to the world.

Maybe the universe could answer, because I sure as shit couldn't.

"I know, love," Lily whispered mournfully, and her grief was genuine.

She loved my dad. Everyone did. He was awesome. Mom was too, but she was a bit of a pain in the ass sometimes, and now more than ever. She wasn't taking the family's fall from grace into bankruptcy lightly, and she was starting to irritate me.

The only reason we were staying afloat was because of Lily.

We were staying in her home, living on her dime, all because the IRS had taken every piece of property my father or his company owned, freezing every single one of his assets.

She'd even offered to float us enough money to cover the company's debt, and while I'd taken her up on that offer, and had used it to funnel funds toward the employees who were suddenly being laid off, there wasn't enough to cover the amount of monies outstanding.

Especially when a mountain of those debts belonged to Lily's family anyway.

It was a clusterfuck.

But it was something we could have survived. We could have ridden it out.

However, there was no riding out anything when you were six feet under.

I paused, unable to take another step away from my daddy.

Pain flooded me, and a keening cry escaped my lips as I clung to Lily, letting her embrace me, burying my face in her hair as I sobbed out my grief.

My world was nothing.

Everything was built on a lie.

We weren't rich. We were indebted to the max.

My parents' marriage wasn't strong—if it was, Daddy wouldn't have killed himself when Mom threatened him with divorce because he was poor.

Everything was...

Gone.

All of it.

All ruined.

Dust to dust, ashes to ashes.

That was my life.

Only, my heart still beat and my body wasn't withering into nothing—I had to remember that.

I could survive this.

I was stronger than my father.

The thought had me sucking in a sharp breath, one that was loaded with guilt for thinking that about Daddy, but it didn't help me fight the cascade into panic.

She must have realized how close I was to freaking out on her, because Lily squeezed me again. "Come on," she murmured, "we need to get you home."

Home?

What was that anymore? Where was it?

I bit my lip but nodded, and the silk of her hair rubbed against my face. A hand grabbed my shoulder, big and strong, and a husky voice stated, "It's okay, Tiffany. Everything will be fine. With time."

Those were the key words.

With time.

I peered up at the big, mean biker who had the power to make grown men piss themselves, and who was softening his tone for me.

Little old me.

"Thanks, Link," I rasped.

He shrugged. "Sucks, doll. Sucks."

It really did.

Somehow, with a couple of words, he was capable of condensing my feelings. I didn't resent that, if anything, it made me feel like I wasn't alone.

"Yeah." I reached up, knuckled my eyes, and dragged the tears away. "It does."

Lily snagged a hold of my hand. "We need to get some food in you."

Her look was pointed, and I turned away, not even wanting to think about why she was saying that.

She swore I was pregnant.

I was refusing to believe it.

Look, when a woman's world collapsed around her, she missed her period, and sometimes, when things were really stressful, she barfed.

Simple.

Stress related.

I pinched the bridge of my nose, trying not to think about Sin.

I'd have to tell him soon.

I'd have to, if what Lily said was true.

This morning, before we'd left for the funeral, she'd appeared at my bedroom door with a baggy in her hand. Then, she'd almost refused to leave until I used the damn test.

The only way I'd gotten out of it?

I puked, and after I puked, Mom had wandered in like Greta Garbo, her hair in a fucking turban of all things, demanding to know why I was sick.

I'd lied, of course. I'd told her that I was just feeling under the weather and had taken that moment to make a dig at her refusal to attend the service today. But I was only putting off the inevitable.

I knew the second I got home, Lily would make me piss on a stick, and I had a nasty feeling I knew what the result would be.

As we wandered over to Lily's car—my Jag had been one of the things lost to the debt collectors—Link veered toward his bike the second he'd dropped us off.

He kissed her with a tenderness that made my heart ache, made me long for Sin, and she smiled at him with so much love that it hurt to behold.

A shaky breath drifted from my lips as I climbed into the car, and when she got behind the wheel, switched on the AC, and turned to me, I knew why.

The bikers kicked off before they spread around her like she was being shielded on all sides by metal.

As a protective detail, it was better than what she'd originally had when her dad was around. All her guards were gone now, replaced on the regular by Prospects from the MC, and it was weird to always have her tailed by dudes on bikes, even if I was glad for her sake.

When they were situated, she cranked the ignition, and we set off.

"It's going to be okay, Tiff."

"I can't let you float us forever," I whispered, turning my face to the side as I peered out onto the gravestones.

It was hard to see, thanks to one biker's 'tail' getting in the way, but I focused on the gravestones, thinking about how Lily's dime was going to be covering my daddy's funeral too.

"I don't deserve you," I whispered, my eyes flooding with tears. "Friends don't do this for friends. This is too much."

"Hey, enough of that!" she chided, and her hand slapped down on my pant-clad thigh. "We're more than friends, we're like sisters. You know that."

"I do, but still. This is going above and beyond, even for sisters."

"Hardly. How much money do you think I need? And, sweetheart, I don't say this to hurt you, but your mom can't be poor. You and I both know she can't survive without having money. It's impossible. If she does, we'll lose her too."

"She's being so awful," I whispered, because I knew Lily was right. If Mom had to be poor, she'd slit her wrists, and then I'd be left with the doctor's bills in the aftermath too.

The only consolation was that Daddy's debts weren't mine. They were Momma's, sure, but she was going bankrupt too. You couldn't get blood out of a stone, and somehow, Mom's heart had turned to that in the past few weeks.

"She's like a mother to me too," Lily reasoned, and while she was right about that as well, while my folks had been kinder to her than hers had ever been, it just wasn't right.

"You're too good to us."

She whistled past that, saying, "Your mom can stay with Link and me as long as she needs, Tiff. You don't need to worry about her. She can have that half of the house." She shivered. "I hate that side anyway."

Her father's side.

It wasn't hard to figure out why.

He'd always given off bad vibes, so had Luke, and that was one of the many reasons why I'd never let his come-ons turn into something else.

See, back when I was eighteen, I thought it was the height of romance for Lily and me to be best friends and for me to be with her brother. Luke was handsome, he was charming when he wanted to be, and he was the heir to an empire. What wasn't to love?

Well, on the outside, he was all those things, but I'd stopped looking at the outside a long time ago.

The inside was all that counted.

And I'd seen early on in those silly, girlish desires for Lily and me to be tied in a familial way that Luke was not good people.

He was rotten to the core, but no one saw that because he was a damn fine actor.

When I didn't say anything, Lily heaved a sigh and changed the subject. "Are you going to tell me who the father is?"

"I might not be pregnant," I muttered, my tone gruff. I sank into my seat, hunching my shoulders as I tried to avoid this topic too.

Nothing, absolutely nada, was high on my conversational agenda right now.

It all involved a future I had zero control over, and at the moment, that just made me feel like I was going nuts.

"You're pregnant. You're never sick, Tiff. Ever."

"My daddy just died, Lily," I grumbled, peering at the highway now that we'd driven out of the graveyard.

West Orange wasn't my favorite place in the world, but Daddy had brought us here for his new development.

A development that was now in the can.

Just like Mom's and my future.

It wasn't a concrete jungle, but it was nearly there. As part of his agreement with the county when he started building the subdivision here that brought a lot of Manhattan's richest people to New Jersey, the area had been spruced up with flowers and plants and shit, but it wasn't enough. You couldn't polish a turd, at least that was my opinion.

"Tiff?"

"What?" I queried absentmindedly.

"The father didn't...he didn't hurt you, did he?"

Sin had, but not in that way. "No. He'd never do that."

My words were truthful, and I felt her tension lessen some. It was like the air in the car had warmed up ten degrees with her relief.

That she loved me was a given. That I loved her was clear, but it was, in the aftermath of this nightmare, wonderful to be reminded of that love.

To know that, come what may, she'd have my back.

"Who is he?" she whispered.

"You don't want to know."

"Wouldn't ask if I didn't."

My throat grew choked as I whispered, "Link knows him."

"He's a biker?"

Her squeak almost had my lips twitching. Only, nothing was funny about this situation.

Nothing.

"Yeah. He is."

"Who the hell is he?"

I hated how we were both talking about my being pregnant without me even admitting to it.

Was I ready to become a mom if I truly did have a bun in the oven?

I couldn't imagine it. I wasn't the most maternal of people anyway, and I was young. Christ, I was barely twenty-three.

Placing a shaky hand on my stomach, I wondered if there was a kid in there, if that kid could feel me, could sense my emotions, my stress, and my concern for the future.

I wouldn't have been ready for a baby if I'd still been loaded.

But to be facing this without a penny to my name? Without the man I'd come to care for in a ridiculously short span of time at my side?

Fuck, was it any wonder I was terrified?

"I need to get a job," I muttered.

"Huh?" Lily swerved the wheel so hard that the bikes had to swerve with her. Her shoulders hunched just like mine had when, in different stages, the bikers turned around to glower at her. Link drove up beside her and tapped on the window. She waved him off and carefully mouthed, "Sorry."

His stare was hard until he fell back a pace, returning to the moving circle around us.

It was hard to imagine Lily with a biker. She was all class. We both were. And yet, somehow, we'd both fallen for bikers.

Rough and ready men that moms warned their daughters about.

Men who said daughters ignored their moms over, and who they tried to toy with until they got burned.

When they did, they were burned badly.

Just like me.

Only, Sin hadn't meant to hurt me.

He couldn't help that he'd been transferred. If anything, it was my fault. And Luke Lancaster's. May he rot in hell.

"You can't get a job."

"Why can't I?" I mumbled. "That's what people do, isn't it? Work when they have no means of supporting themselves?"

"You're different. You don't need to work. You have me."

I released a shaky breath. "You have to stop saying that, Lily. Your generosity is too much. It isn't fair for me to take from you and give nothing in return."

"If things were different, wouldn't you do the same for me?" she reasoned, and I knew I'd hurt her, even if that wasn't my intention.

"You know I would," I muttered, "and I know that, just like I am, you'd struggle with it."

"Yeah, I'd struggle, but I'd expect nothing less. We're sisters," she stated staunchly. "Sisters have each other's backs. Plus, what the hell are you going to do? You're pregnant, you'll be getting tired in the afternoons soon and—"

"Pregnant women work, Lily," I said dryly, amused by her declaration. "They manage to get through morning sickness in the afternoon during a business meeting as well, all while keeping their homes clean and sometimes caring for more than one kid at the same time. There's no reason why I shouldn't be one of them."

"Why would you take a job away from someone who needs it?" she countered, and I growled under my breath.

"That's fighting dirty."

"That's the truth. You don't need the money. You're not a spendthrift, so I won't even have to give you that big of an allowance—"

"Oh my God! That's enough, Lily. I can't handle this conversation right now. I'm not thirteen—"

"No, I know you're not, but you're potentially a mom, and you have to think of that kid. Anyway, I've already told you that the Sinners want your help. You can work for them as a favor to me. You're living with me at the moment, and food isn't an issue. If the father doesn't want anything to do with you, then there's no reason to worry. We can raise the baby together."

My lips curved at that. "Like a commune baby?"

She snickered. "Yeah. I don't see why not. The baby can grow up knowing what pedicures are while fixing bikes in their spare time with Link—"

My heart clutched at the thought. Damn, I was really nuts if I thought that sounded like an epic idea.

Raising a baby with Lily? Knowing that Link and his men would protect it, even if Sin wouldn't?

Heaven.

Because I didn't entirely trust heaven right now, uneasily, I argued, "I'm not trained."

"Only because you quit school. We both know you could—"

I rolled my eyes. "Don't be jealous."

"Of your 4.0 GPA without you even having to open a book?" She snorted. "Bet your damn ass I'm jealous. Anyway, they need you. Whether or not you're officially trained, those women need you more than you will ever know, Tiff. Fuck, what they've been through?" She shuddered. "You're the only help they'll get too. It's either you or nothing. I've been building up the courage to get you involved with them for over a month, but I've just been too nervous to."

I reached up and rubbed the back of my neck. "I still don't understand what they're doing there—"

"It's complicated."

"You're telling me."

As far as I could figure out, two of the women weren't 'technically' there. As in, the authorities weren't aware of them. They knew about one woman, and she was the one who'd gone to the cops and was the reason Donavan Lancaster was flitting around Asia trying to evade arrest warrants and extradition orders. It was like something out of an action movie, where the man I'd known pretty much all my life was the villain.

Surreal didn't cut it.

"They need you, Tiff. Working in a restaurant, in a store...you're not going to be helping anyone. Sure, you'll be earning an honest buck, but that money could be going to someone who actually needs it, and you won't be helping three people who my family destroyed. Please, Tiff. Please? Do it for me?"

Her tone wasn't wheedling. It was filled with an urgent need I couldn't hide from, one there was no avoiding. I stared ahead, seeing a future open before me that I'd never anticipated. There were two reasons I'd stopped training as a therapist. One because of politics, and two, because I couldn't do it.

Literally.

I got too involved.

It wasn't...

Fuck, it just wasn't healthy. *I* wasn't healthy with it.

My education had been derailed, but I was too self-aware to fail to realize that being a therapist wasn't good for me.

Yet, equally, she was right. Why wouldn't I do something to help women who'd been hurt by the men in Lily's family when it was within the realms of possibility? If anyone deserved for me to try, it was her. She gave and gave, and at the moment, all I was doing was taking.

And for that reason, I knew she deserved for me to be honest with her. "Lily?"

"Yes, sweetheart?"

"Sin's the father."

Her brow puckered. "Sin? The brother who was—"

"Shipped off so that Nyx wouldn't behead him? Yeah." My tone was a mixture of dry and tortured. "That sums it up."

Her shoulders straightened. "Well, this changes things. I'll speak to Rex."

My lips twitched at the thought of little Lily shoving her nose in club business and bullying Rex, the Prez.

I'd taken in a lot when I was at the clubhouse parties. Watched dynamics, studied interpersonal relationships, learned things that the bikers probably wouldn't have anticipated me picking up on...

There were secrets in that clubhouse, but then, weren't they everywhere?

My life was riddled with them, Lily's too.

The thought had my heart twisting as I stared down at the hand which I'd covered my belly with. "We'll get through this, won't we, Lily?"

"Of course we will." She smiled at me, and her love for me shone through.

I reached out with my spare hand, slipped my fingers through hers, and whispered, "Thank you."

She squeezed me back. "No thanks necessary."

SEVEN

SIN

SCRUBBING the back of my neck with a handkerchief where sweat had gathered, I stayed as still as I otherwise could in the tree where I was sitting.

It wasn't the most ridiculous position I'd ever been in for the club, but this was on my own time and dime.

I had a purpose.

I wanted to go home, and the fucker in the house opposite me was my means to an end.

Nyx had two weaknesses.

Giulia was one of them, and the other?

The bastard in front of me, who didn't deserve to live.

I'd been here for three hours, just waiting on him to make a move. With none of the connections I was used to hitting up in NJ, I was having to track this bastard in a truly old-school way.

It was a pain in the ass, but it'd be worth it to get back to West Orange.

I deserved to be here. I'd left my post, had left Giulia in danger, and the only reason I wasn't fertilizing the compound grounds was because I had proof.

Proof that my woman had been messed with. Of course, said woman didn't know she was mine because I didn't have time to claim her officially before I rode the fuck out of Jersey with Nyx baying for my blood.

The thought had my jaw popping to the side, and I carefully eased the cramp in my foot as I stretched it out.

The dick was supposed to have left an hour ago, but he was still here. I'd cloned his phone, so I knew his plans had him heading out tonight, but he hadn't specified a time. If he left it any longer, he'd be leaving tomorrow instead of tonight, which would ease into my new duties at the clubhouse.

Hissing at the inconvenience, I watched as, slowly, the dick got himself ready to leave.

When he finally pissed off a half hour later, the cramp in my foot had turned it numb, and when he roared off into the distance, unaware that I was tracing him, I hopped down from the branch that had become my bench and winced when I almost dropped to the ground.

Ignoring the pins and needles which instantly bombarded my extremities, I hustled into the shadows and walked to the front door. Kneeling, I picked the lock, crawled into the house, and closed it up behind me the second I could.

I wasn't here just for shits and giggles. I'd been watching him go into that damn safe every night for the past three weeks I'd been tracking him, and last night, I'd finally seen his combination.

I knew what was in there, but I needed the proof. Needed something to give to Nyx to make him forgive me. Ohio might be great for the chapter of the Sinners who lived here, but it wasn't my place.

I was an East Coaster, born and bred, and being in the middle of the country was only making me antsy. I needed to go home, and I didn't want to lose a fucking limb in the process.

With a grunt, I unlocked the safe and trained my flashlight on my phone into the dark cavern of the strong box.

Shuffling through the different files, I came across the material I'd been seeking, and once I had it confirmed, I switched off the flashlight, not needing to see another fucking picture, and connected the call to Rex—the first time I'd spoken with him in weeks, because I was well aware I needed to earn my place back home. He'd already gone above and beyond for me by not kicking my ass out of the MC, telling Nyx he'd sent me to Oklahoma and not Ohio to save me from his wrath. Last thing I wanted was to waste his time too.

"You already know the answer if you're asking if you can come home," was his greeting. "Nyx ain't nowhere close to forgiving you."

Pulling a face at that, I told him, "He will be. I found him a toy."

Silence echoed in my ear, then he muttered, "Might not be enough, bro."

"I know, but I had to try, didn't I?" I rubbed my chin, hating how fucking good it felt to be talking to him. Shit, I missed my family. This fucking exile sucked. It was, I also realized, a testament to my feelings for

Tiff that I'd go through this shit for her. My voice turned gruff as I muttered, "I'll send you his name and details so Mav can confirm the kill order is just, and fair warning, if Nyx doesn't take out the trash, I will."

"That bad?"

I could almost imagine my Prez's brows rising at my statement.

He knew I didn't get my hands dirty unless someone deserved it.

"That bad," I confirmed. It was sickening, but I was insensate to the images I'd just seen.

The first time I'd ever come across that shit, back when I was younger, I'd actually puked, and it was the only time the brothers wouldn't rip me a new one for being a pussy.

Our business was more than just the usual. We dealt in blood, we dealt in protection, and no one would ever thank us for it, because no one knew we were behind the eradication of these sick fucks.

But, numbed as I was, my stomach still snarled uneasily with what I'd seen in the fucker's folders. I'd make him pay for every single picture. And if Nyx got involved? There was nothing he wouldn't do to reap vengeance on the fucker's soul.

"I'll tell him. Wait to move on his word."

"I will."

He disconnected the call without another word, and I replaced everything in the safe as I'd found it. With all the fucker's documents restored to its original neatness, I locked it up, then retreated to the outside once the door was closed too.

I left the place like the specter I was and headed for my bike.

I'd seen the message waiting on me, and while I wanted to reply, I knew that would be beyond stupid.

I needed to get out of here, away from David Faudreaux's house and subdivision. The second someone saw me, I'd be implicating myself in the investigation when he was eliminated.

For that reason, I retrieved the kickstand and put the bike into neutral before rolling my hog down the road.

It took me a while, and each goddamn step felt like it took twice as long, but by the time I was at the unsecured entrance to the housing estate, where the noise from the highway shielded the kickstart of my ignition, I rolled away and back to the Sinners' compound.

Ohio wasn't for me. Sure, it was great and all that, but it just wasn't my place. My home was in the Northeast.

Everything was just that little bit different. The smell, the way the people were. They were actually nicer, but I wasn't used to it, and I missed home.

I missed her.

I didn't think I'd be that pussy who'd get sentimental about his girl, but I kind of felt like a soldier who was on a deployment. I'd been there back in the day, and I could honestly say that I missed Tiffany more than I'd ever missed my bitch of an ex.

The only consolation was that here, sand wasn't getting in every crease of my body—how the fuck it got in my asscrack with all the gear I'd had to wear back then, I'd never know—I wasn't being shot at, and I didn't have to kill anyone.

Not technically, at any rate.

Shit was starting to go down with the *Famiglia*, that much I knew, even if the council in Ohio kept things to themselves. I'd lost any ranking I'd earned with my exile here, but while even the average brother was kept out of the loop, we'd all learned that the Hell's Rebels down in Texas had declared unofficial war on them, as had the Five Points, and since we were tied to them, that meant we technically were as well.

The Italians were sleazy fucks, trading in flesh and bone, selling women like they were property, and now the Russians were at war with them too? Nowhere was going to be safe for very long.

The prospect of Tiffany being in danger didn't sit well with me, but there was fuck all I could do about it.

Fuck. All.

That killed me, but it made me haul my ass. I could have drowned myself in easy pussy the second I made it down here. Nyx held long grudges. He was the meanest motherfucker I'd ever met in my life, capable of things that would make a Spanish Inquisitor look soft-core, and I'd known, the second I heard that Giulia had been attacked, my life was on the line.

I felt like a pussy for leaving with my tail between my legs, but the truth was, I knew my brothers. And I got it. If I'd set a guard on Tiffany and they left their post when she was attacked? I'd want blood too.

But instead of feeling hopeless, instead of accepting my fate, I was working toward getting my ass back home.

It was either that or bring Tiffany down here.

And I really couldn't see her in Ohio.

New Jersey was a come down for her, even though she never said anything. I mean, I could just tell she didn't like West Orange, and though it was my home, I got it. I'd been born and bred in Manhattan, Five Points' territory, so I knew what the sparkle of the city that never slept felt like.

But also, it was no home. Not for me anyway. Still, Tiff and Podunk, Ohio? Nope.

It was an option, but it was one I'd prefer not to take.

I had a gut feeling she was pregnant.

Why?

Because life sucked sometimes, and kids always had a habit of popping up when the timing was never ideal. You picked that up really fast when you lived in an MC for as long as I had.

And what could be worse than my being in another fucking part of the States, forced to stay here at risk of Nyx giving me a Colombian necktie, while a half dozen of the nation's criminal underworld were at war?

What a perfect time to bring a new life into the world, huh?

Of course, that was just my gut talking, and my gut had been known to be wrong. But the pill and then the drugs? She'd puked all over herself, several times until there was nothing left in her, and she ate like a bird anyway. If that morning after pill stuck, then it was a miracle.

As I rode past a cornfield—I'd never seen so much fucking corn in my fucking life—I pulled into the clubhouse.

A party was raging, and I'd skipped it to go monitor Faudreaux. To be honest, I wasn't in the mood.

Back home, I was the life and soul of the party, along with Link, but here? I was a miserable bastard, and I felt sorry for the fuckers who called me brother and had to deal with my sorry ass.

It didn't help that I was cutting back on the booze, and that was mostly because I'd known I was drinking too much. Socializing, being friendly, and enjoying a party didn't come natural to me. I needed the lubrication to fully enjoy those kinds of things, so without a bottle of tequila lining my stomach, I wasn't going to appreciate shit. If anything, at the moment, I was maudlin as hell, and I had the feeling alcohol would only make that worse.

With that in mind, I gave a mock salute to the Prospect manning the gate and drove around to my digs.

Because I was, technically, a visitor, until I earned my place here, I wasn't staying in the clubhouse proper. I preferred that though. These people weren't my people. They were my brothers, and I'd die for them and kill for them if need be, but they weren't family.

I knew that wouldn't make much sense to most folk, but only those of us in the life could understand the mentality we had. We were united against the Man, and the Man might change from time to time, but we remained as one.

Rubbing my chin the second I was off my bike, I grabbed my shit and ducked into the bunkhouse.

It wasn't unlike the Sinners' place, where there were small bunkhouses that a visiting chapter could crash in, or that unexpected guests like Giulia and her brothers who were newly patched in Prospects could stay at until they proved themselves or found some digs of their own.

Here, it wasn't as nice. Sure, those bunkhouses were old-fashioned and filled with shit from another era, but they were better than the row of beds that made me feel like I was staying in a POW camp, especially since shower curtains were the only partitions we had as some semblance of privacy.

I'd been here before on a long run, and it had sucked back then, but now that I was here on a semi-permanent basis—I refused to look for extra accommodation because that would be admitting defeat—it was even worse.

The only consolation was I slept at one end, and the only brother, a guy called Brakes, who shared with me took the opposite end.

When I saw Brakes was absent, I strode toward my bunk and pulled out my phone.

The scent of mildew was in the air, and it was tinged with perfume that told me Brakes had either been boning someone in here earlier, or a club snatch had been waiting on my bunk for me to return and had grown bored with my absence before fucking off.

They didn't get that I wasn't interested, and the truth was, it still blew my fucking mind that I wasn't.

Rubbing a hand over my jaw, scratching at the stubble, I pulled out my cell and opened the message app.

Tiff and I had been in communication since Rex had exiled me down here for my own safety, and while that made me feel like a pussy again, I'd prefer to be on Al Qaeda's radar than Nyx's.

Yeah.

Fucking Nyx.

Good thing I loved him like a brother and understood his fury with me, or I'd have needed to shoot his brains out before he got to mine.

With the app open, I saw Tiff had sent a few more messages since I'd taken off from Faudreaux's place, but so had Rex, and because I knew my fate rested in whatever he had to say, I opened that one first.

Prez: *We'll be riding in the next couple of hours.*

I fist pumped the air, knowing quite well that if Nyx was satisfied with my pedo haul, I'd be home sooner than anticipated.

And that was a good thing, because Tiff's final message?

Didn't bode well.

Tiff: *We need to talk.*

Fuck.

EIGHT

TIFFANY

I STARED AT MY CELLPHONE, which was ringing in one hand, then switched my focus to the stick I'd peed on a few hours ago which, after dousing it in Purelle, had been sitting on my nightstand ever since.

I still couldn't believe what it was telling me.

I really was pregnant.

There'd been two sets of two different kinds of tests in the bag Lily had brought me, and because she was a thorough PITA, that made sense. I'd used them all, and not a single one of them had been negative.

They were all different brands, too, some seeking early pregnancy—which was just stupid considering Sin had been gone eight weeks—another just a regular test, one set digital, the other not.

Whatever the stick, it was happening.

This was happening.

I was going to become a mother.

Unless I didn't.

Unless I—

Could I do that?

Rip out Sin's baby from my womb?

I was an advocate of pro-choice. A woman had the right to do whatever the fuck she wanted with her body, but how could I have an abortion because the timing wasn't right?

It was our fault. We'd fucked up by having sex bareback. Twice. Each time, I'd done the stupid thing and grabbed the morning after pill, but apparently, it hadn't worked.

My cell rang again, and I stared at the picture of Sin and me in bed that flashed on the screen as he called me for the third time.

I'd texted him earlier, needing to speak, but now? I wasn't even sure what to say.

Ever since he'd gone to Ohio, I'd been keeping shit from him.

So much shit.

I didn't even know why.

We'd been dating for longer than Lily and Link had, but I'd kept it a secret.

Why had I done that?

I felt like a real bitch, because a part of me knew I'd kept him as my dirty little secret. Almost like I was too good for him or something, but I wasn't.

Sin was a good man.

Sure, he was rough and ragged around the edges, but he was good.

Sure, he rode for an MC and he killed people and dealt drugs—

Okay, so that made him sound bad, and I guessed he was.

But then, what was Donavan Lancaster? What had Luke Lancaster been?

I shivered at the last memory I had of that bastard—him laughing as he squeezed my tit to the point where it was bruised days later after I crashed my car.

I didn't remember how I'd crashed it, didn't remember even scratching it. Just remembered waking up in Sin's bed feeling like I'd been hit over the head with a sledgehammer, with memories of Luke's hideous laughter echoing in my ear.

Because he'd come when Luke had texted him, pretending to be me, he'd lost everything.

His place at the MC, his home—okay, while that was still his property, he was stuck in Ohio, so it wasn't like he could goddamn use it, was it? But he'd lost his friends and family, and even worse, he'd lost their respect.

If there was any consolation to this mess, it was that he was keeping me a secret too.

I'd learned that when he'd had no alternative than to ride to Ohio for the long term.

I'd almost expected that would be the last I'd hear from him, even though he'd told me how solid we were, but when he'd arrived, he'd called me, and every day since, he'd called me.

He texted me every morning, too, and I texted him every night before I climbed into bed.

Fuck, I was so confused.

Why had we been so secretive if we were starting to feel more for each other?

None of this was turning out like it was supposed to.

I was supposed to get married to someone from the country club, we'd have a big party full of people who we hated and who hated us, and I'd be drinking too much vodka by the time I hit thirty, my kid would have his christening pictures in the fucking papers, and at that point, my husband would have boned every secretary he'd ever had.

Now?

Everything was on its head.

The phone went silent only to ring again, and when I stared at the picture of us, I saw the happiness in my face. In his too.

It felt like a long time since I'd been like that.

Since I'd felt that way.

Sure, a lot of crap had gone down, but was it because he'd been ripped away from me?

My feelings for him were complicated. He'd started off as a challenge, then as something I'd known my family wouldn't approve of, and then...?

Then what?

More.

That was the only answer I had.

And now, somehow, he was my baby daddy. Jesus, I was turning into someone from *Teen Mom*. Yeah, I knew that made me sound like a snob.

I blew out a breath, then hit connect on the phone.

"At fucking last, Tiff. Jesus."

His gruff voice made me sit up higher in bed. Something about it always set my nerve endings alight. In an odd way, he reminded me of home, and it prompted me to ask, "Were you raised in New York?"

It was definitely odd that I didn't know that already, when I'd been 'seeing' the guy for just under three months, but hell, there was other stuff to talk about than his accent.

"Yeah."

My brow rose at his curt answer because, in his own way, he was very patient with me. "Whereabouts?"

"Hell's Kitchen."

A sigh whispered from me, one that was filled with a vague sense of homesickness. "I used to live near there."

"I can guarantee you didn't live anywhere near where I was raised."

His dry tone had me questioning, "That bad?"

"Yeah. No princess like you would have been allowed near that shithole."

If anyone else called me that, I'd have told them to fuck off. But Sin? In his own way, yet again, he treated me like a princess. Everywhere except between the sheets.

It had been a long time since we'd fucked though, and I was getting tired of him treating me that way. I liked all his edges. Liked it when they bumped up against me.

When he was angry? Jesus. The memory had me flopping back against the sheets with my eyes close to rolling back in my head. Christ, he was hot when he was angry. And angry fucks with him left me walking bowlegged the next day, but damn, it was worth it.

I bit my lip, wishing he was here, wishing he could fuck me and help me forget about stuff, but it was time to confess.

And not just about being pregnant.

"Sin?"

"Yeah, angel?"

I was no angel, but he seemed to think I was. "I haven't told you something."

His gruffness raked up against me, making me feel even guiltier. "I know you haven't. What's put that sadness in your voice, darlin'?"

"D-Daddy died." Tears bubbled up in my eyes, like they were forged from a hot spring or something. They hurt, and the sobs that longed to claw out of my throat were painful enough that my chest ached from the pressure.

"He died? What the fuck? Why didn't you tell me?"

His bark had me rolling onto my side. "He killed himself."

A sharp breath escaped him. "Oh, angel, I'm so sorry. Why did he do that?" He inhaled deeply. "When?"

The when was harder to answer because I'd stayed silent when I should have opened up to him. "Because we're broke," I whispered.

"You're broke?" he almost shrieked that, his surprise coming down the line loud and clear.

"Yeah." Rolling onto my back again, I raised my arm and covered my eyes with it. "He couldn't deal with it, so he took the easy way out." If I sounded bitter, then that was because I was.

Mom was many things, a pain a lot of the time, selfish at others, but hell, she hadn't left me. She was more prideful than Daddy, and riding out the shame would devastate her, but it drove me insane to think that I didn't know my father at all. Because if he couldn't deal with the aftermath of his fall from grace, then he wasn't the man I thought I knew.

"I'm sorry, love."

Four letters, and they were like a warm embrace around my heart.

I wanted him to love me, I realized, and it figured the timing was shitty for me to have that epiphany. It'd look like I only wanted that because I was carrying his baby, but the truth was, I figured I'd been wanting that from the start.

That first night, when he'd finger fucked another woman in my presence, when he'd thought he could treat me like her? I'd seen him for the prize he was—no, I wasn't insane in thinking he was a prize—and I'd wanted to conquer him.

You didn't vanquish a man like that by being a slut.

You showed him you were different.

And I was.

He was too.

Sure, he wore a cut that proclaimed him an outlaw. He rode a bike for a living and, I had to figure, they did illegal shit to pay the bills, because I'd seen him come home with blood on his hands more than once when I was staying at his place, but for all that, he was special.

He didn't care if I didn't wear makeup every day, and if I wasn't dressed up in designer gear, he didn't even notice. If my nails weren't manicured, he wouldn't make a comment about me not taking care of myself. He didn't expect me to be anything other than Tiffany, and it was weird, but I actually knew who 'Tiffany' was around him.

It said a lot that the highlights of my future in my mind were becoming an alcoholic as I tied myself to a man who'd have cheated on me with every secretary in his employment.

With him?

I saw a different future, a future that, with Dad's death, suddenly seemed plausible.

He'd have made me marry up. Though he let me get my own way, and though he'd never force me down the aisle, I knew that if I wanted his approval, and I did because I was a Daddy's girl and that was how Daddy's girls worked, I'd have to marry someone he thought was worthy of me.

Sure, it hurt that the man who was 'worthy' of me would ultimately treat me like shit, but still, that was how our world worked.

But Sin's world didn't.

And that was so incredibly freeing. I was seeing it in the flesh with Lily and Link. Being around them helped me so much without them even knowing it, because I saw what it was like to date a biker out in the open.

Lily could swear, she could wear sweats. She didn't have to always be pristine, and I'd even seen her sitting with her back against her chair in Link's presence, which meant she could actually chill the fuck out with him near. I mean, I wasn't that bad, because I hadn't been 'finished,' but that Lily felt that relaxed around him? It was clear she felt no worries that he wanted her, warts and all.

She said what she wanted without fear of repercussions. Passive aggressive bullshit wasn't a thing, because you said what you meant and that was it. No take backs or other crap.

I'd seen that, felt that, when I was with Sin.

And in all honesty, I wanted more.

I wanted him.

For real.

The thought was a revelation, but I knew I'd treated him shittily along the way. And for all that, he considered me his princess or his angel, he'd kept me under wraps too. I didn't think he'd been cheating on me, not even when he'd been forced to go to Ohio, but maybe I was wrong.

Just like I was wrong about my daddy.

"You've gone quiet on me, angel."

"Yeah, I guess I did," I whispered, moving my arm from my eyes so I could stare up at the ceiling that had a fancy chandelier in the middle. It was beautiful, lots of spun glass that reminded me of candy in pretty wrappers twirling around a domed light.

"What are you thinking?"

"You don't want to know."

"I won't let you break things off with me."

That gruff tone of his made a reappearance at that, and while my brows lowered, wonder filled me.

He didn't want to break up.

Relief made me whisper, "I wasn't even thinking of that."

"You weren't? A woman texts you and tells you, 'we need to talk,' you have to figure she's about to break things off."

I shook my head, even though he couldn't see it. "No. That wasn't my intention. I just have a lot to tell you is all."

"Like your daddy dying and you suddenly being poor?"

"Yeah." My bottom lip trembled at him spelling things out for me. Not because it was cruel, but because it was like reality was hitting me square in the face.

"This why you've been quiet on the phone the past couple of weeks?"

"Yes."

"You going to keep stuff from me in the future?" A hint of a warning appeared in his tone, cascading through the words like a promise. A promise I didn't mind giving him.

I knew he was asking, without saying it, for whatever else I'd been hiding.

I got the feeling if I told him now, there'd be no repercussions, but if I held out on him again, there would be.

While I didn't know what they might be, the prospect didn't annoy me. It was only fair. I'd been stupid by keeping this from him, but in my defense, I'd been in denial.

If he'd been here, things would have been different.

As it was, he was in another state, far away, and I was having to deal with things all alone.

It didn't make up for me being secretive, but it was the only answer I had as to why I'd acted the way I had. Sure, it was shitty of me, and there was no excuse, but God, we all made mistakes that bit us in the ass later on, didn't we?

My throat clutched as I thought about telling him the other stuff.

"I can hear your breathing, Tiff," he said softly. "It sped up. What's got you so scared, princess?"

"Everything," I whispered.

A rumble escaped him. "I can feel that. I'm sorry he did that, Tiff."

"Me too." I gulped. "I'll tell you the details, I promise, just not tonight."

"No, I know you will." That was him telling me I wouldn't be able to keep stuff from him, and again, it was merited. "But what else has you nervous?"

"Mom can't deal with being poor, and Lily said she'll support us—I shouldn't let her, but what am I supposed to do? I can't keep Mom like she's used to being kept, and Lily said it herself. It's terrible, but it's true—if Mom can't buy the random crap she wants, she'll do what Dad did."

"She's not a child, Tiff."

"She is!" I argued mournfully. "Daddy kept her that way. He kept her like a butterfly, always hopping around for the next flower. He wanted her like that. I don't know why he did, maybe it made him feel needed, but she's not going to be able to change."

He hummed. "She has to know what's going on."

"She does. She's having to go bankrupt too."

"Jesus."

"Lily said that if I got a job in a diner, it would be taking money from someone who truly needed it, and I don't because I have her. She's right. It would, and I really don't want to work in a diner. I know it's bad for me to admit that, but I really don't—"

"You can say all the bad stuff to me, angel. You know I won't judge you."

His words made me feel both relieved and kind of young, and because I appreciated neither, I muttered, "You think I'm spoiled."

"No, I don't think it, I know it, but you're not as bad as your mom, which I'm grateful for."

I grumbled, "I'm definitely not that bad. Anyway, Lily suggested I do some work for the Sinners."

"Like what?" he asked warily.

"Lily suggested it, Sin," I replied dryly. "That means she doesn't see me sucking dick for my dinner."

"Not unless it's mine," he growled, and the rumble made my belly do somersaults.

Because I didn't want to encourage him or that line of conversation—I wasn't averse to phone sex, but I didn't need things to devolve just yet—I murmured, "She says the hostages her brother and father kept need a therapist."

"Huh," he replied. "Why the hell didn't I think of that?"

My eyes flared at his response. "You think I could do it?"

"I know you could." He sighed. "Gotta admit, Tiff, I like the idea of you getting intertwined with the Sinners. They're my family."

"I know."

"I'd like them to become yours."

Clenching my eyes closed, I whispered, "I might be bad at it." I knew how important the MC was to him—what if I fucked things up?

"You're good at everything you put your mind to. Apart from serving dishes, of course." He snickered, and I blew a raspberry at the ceiling as he stated, "You're not doing that menial stuff anyway. I like those hands as soft as they are—"

"Don't think with your penis, Padraig!"

He huffed. "I knew I shouldn't have told you my name."

My smile was smug. "I have ways of making you talk."

"Apparently, I need to work on mine so you don't keep this shit bottled up in the future." He grunted. "That wasn't cool, Tiff."

"No, it wasn't," I agreed. "I'm sorry, Sin."

"It's okay."

"It isn't," I countered, "but I was just feeling overwhelmed."

"I should be there," he ground out, "and I will be. I'm working on it."

I sat up excitedly. "You are?"

"You didn't think I was just going to stick my thumb up my ass and sit around, waiting for Nyx to forgive me, did you?"

My brow puckered. "Well, not when you put it like that."

He laughed. "Nope. I've been busy. I'll be home soon."

Throat tight, I whispered, "That a promise?"

"Yeah, angel," he said. "That's a promise."

A shaky sigh slipped between my lips at his words, and I whispered, "Padraig?"

"Yeah?"

I couldn't blame him for sounding wary, but I just couldn't tell him he was about to be a father by calling him Sin. Sure, it was his road name, but this was a special moment.

At least, I hoped it was.

From this conversation alone, I knew that any insecurities were in my head and I was projecting them onto him, which gave me the courage to admit, "I'm pregnant."

NINE

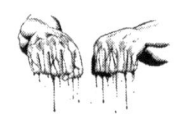

GHOST

I SAW Tatána eying the cutlery in my hand, and it instantly made me feel guilty.

I understood why Giulia refused to let her have knives and forks anymore, but it felt weird eating with plastic spoons all the time, and she still eyed them like they had potential.

I understood that she wanted to die

There'd been times in that pit where I'd wanted to die too. Where I'd felt like death would be a welcome respite from the nightmare I was living, and while the physical reminders were growing faint, mentally?

We were messed up.

Tatána more than most.

I wasn't sure why.

I mean, there wasn't a measure on whom the Lancaster men had hurt more. It wasn't a competition. But we'd all gone through the same war, and to be honest, I'd been in that damn hole longer than she had.

She was fragile though.

Fragile enough to end it all, and she'd tried several times since we'd been saved.

I was almost annoyed at her. Sure, things weren't ideal, but they were brighter than they'd been before, and considering that had been hell on earth? I figured she was being greedy asking for more.

Our captors were either dead or on the run. I was getting justice for us, we had a brotherhood of men who were willing to fight on our behalf—

Of course, things were different for me.

I had Maverick.

Even if I didn't really.

Shyly, I eyed him as he spooned up some of the soup Giulia had brought us to eat.

All of us were mobile by now, and our physical wounds, while not exactly pretty, were mostly healed. That meant we had more freedom and motility, and Tatána was using her new liberation to try to end it all. But our better health was why we were sitting at the table where, before, we'd eaten in bed. I was glad, though, because it meant Mav got to sit with us.

He ate with a grace that surprised me. He picked up his napkin after each bite and wiped at the corners of his mouth. His shoulders didn't hunch over his bowl like some of the guys I'd seen around here. If anything, he sat up straight in his wheelchair, even though it was awkward with the armrests getting in the way of the table.

He was beautiful.

And, mad though it was, he was my husband.

I still had to pinch myself when I thought about that.

I was a wife now.

I mean, I was a shitty one.

I hadn't shared more than a peck on the cheek with him, and I knew he'd proposed only to provide me with some security in the upcoming days.

It was likely I'd be deported back to Ukraine, but that was okay. That was...well, it wasn't okay. That was a lie. I was here for a reason, here to find my sister, Katina, but the truth was, I wasn't sure if I'd be good for her anymore.

She'd lost all her family and was stuck in the welfare system, but was that better than being with a woman who'd been...

I blew out a breath.

What they'd done to me didn't define me, I knew that. I did. But sometimes, it was hard to remember that.

Hard to see myself as anything other than their victim.

Their fuck pig.

Cum slut.

A piece of shit for them to use as a human toilet.

My stomach churned at the remembered insults the Lancasters had hurled at me as they tortured me in all the ways a woman could be tortured.

A hand covered mine, surprising me with the contact.

I jolted back, but then I saw it was Maverick, saw his scarred fingers blanketing mine. He was squeezing me gently, his gaze on our joined hands like mine was.

Feeling even shyer now, I peered at him from under my lashes, and whispered, "Sorry."

"You were back there, weren't you?"

How could I lie to him?

I knew he understood.

Maybe not in the same way, but I knew something had happened to him, something back when he was a soldier. There was a reason he had so many scars, why his eyes were haunted with shadows that matched my own. He was in a wheelchair for a reason, and from what Giulia had told me, he never left the compound.

Ever.

But he had for me.

And I'd seen him that day when we'd gone to the town hall first, and then off to the police station second. He'd been white, shaking, but he'd held up.

For me.

A man didn't do that for no reason, did he?

He didn't see me as just a victim, because if he did, then he wouldn't have faced his fears to help me beat mine.

I twisted my hand around in his grasp, and when he pulled back, I grabbed hold of him quickly, spearing my fingers through his, bridging the gap, and holding him close.

Tatána made a disgusted noise, and I knew it was at my response to Mav, before she surged to her feet and shuffled back to her bed. Amara shot me a look, her eyes loaded with shadows as she cast a weak smile my way before she returned her attention to the soup we were eating.

"It's like a mausoleum in here," Giulia grumbled from the doorway as she strolled in.

She was a little harsh, a lot ballsy, and very outspoken, but I liked her.

Maverick did too.

Although, I got the feeling he liked what she did to his brother, and if a man like Nyx could be tamed, I wasn't sure I wanted to know that particular side of Giulia, which was capable of making a man like the MC's Enforcer happy.

She was unfailingly kind to us, though, and went out of her way to make us foods she thought would increase our appetite.

Even if Tatána was a bitch in return, she tried.

"Don't have much to say," Amara said and I translated as the other woman shrugged as she returned her attention to her soup.

Giulia rolled her eyes at me, and I had to smile. She treated me differently. I didn't know why. Because I belonged to Maverick now? Because I was grateful where Amara and Tatána were the opposite?

I had no idea, but I had the feeling we could be friends, and I hoped so. I hoped that was possible before I was sent back to my country.

Maybe we were already friends, and I just didn't know it. I kind of hoped so.

Giulia was new to the clubhouse too. Or, that's to say, she'd been raised here so she knew everyone, but she didn't know them *now*.

"The soup is delicious," I told her with a warm smile. "Thank you, Giulia."

"My grandmother's was better."

Amara's comment had me frowning at her. I didn't care that the others couldn't understand because she spoke in Ukrainian—I was still pissed at her rudeness. "Your grandmother isn't here, as far as I can tell."

Amara scowled at me, but she ducked her head and focused on the soup her grandmother had 'supposedly' made better.

Giulia snorted, though. "Thanks, Ghost. I take it Amara isn't impressed with my soup."

My fists clenched with annoyance at the other women's consistently ungrateful attitudes.

"It is very delicious. Makes me think of home."

Maverick's hand tightened around mine. "This is your home now."

I shot him a wary look. "We both know that's not for sure."

"It fucking is," he groused, and Giulia slapped her hand on his shoulder. "Don't swear in front of them."

I laughed, unable to stop myself. "I'm afraid that ship has already sailed, Giulia."

"The fuckers are pigs."

I snickered at her cursing. "I swear too."

"Do you?" She tipped her head to the side as she twisted Tatána's chair around and straddled it like she was a boy.

Her mannerisms were like that of a tomboy, but it made her easier to be around.

Maybe because she wasn't like the women I'd spent far too much time with in that pit, or like the Lancaster men who'd bought us like we were animals. No, Giulia was different. Most of the people at the clubhouse were. No one fit in the real world, but here? They'd found their niche. It comforted me to think that maybe I'd found mine too.

Amara and Tatána could find theirs also if they just lowered their defenses some.

Sure, we'd learned the hard way that people couldn't be trusted, but I refused to live my life being a closed door to the world.

Look what had happened to me because I'd tried…I was married.

To an American.

Who was willing to fight for my right to stay here.

My mind boggled.

"What did she say?" Giulia peppered.

"That her grandmother's soup was different," I murmured, trying to be more diplomatic.

"What would make it more like your grandmother's soup, Amara?"

That Giulia continued to try astonished me. Her patience wasn't infinite, but she persisted, and I had to give her credit, because I wasn't sure if I'd be as generous.

"Less onion," Amara muttered to me and I translated. "More salt. More sour cream."

"A squeeze of lemon juice," I added softly, my lips curving as I thought about the last time I'd made borscht. "I'll help you the next time you make it."

Maverick wrinkled his nose. "Can't you make something that isn't purple?"

My smile grew bigger. "But the color is so pretty."

"Mav doesn't like beets," Giulia explained with a giggle.

My brows lifted. "Then why do you eat it?"

He cut the other women a look, and my heart melted.

It literally melted.

My fingers tightened on his to the point of what I knew had to be pain, but I didn't care.

He was trying to gentle them.

Trying to get them used to men again.

It was working as well. No other men could come into the room without them flinching or panicking, but slowly but surely, they were trying to reintegrate us. Nyx and Link popped in every now and then, and every day, someone dipped their head around the door to ask if we needed anything.

Tatána tended to scream, and Amara huddled in her bed, but I always replied.

The poor man, whoever he might be, didn't deserve that welcome. It was enough to give someone a complex.

"You can show me how to make something American," I suggested to Giulia. "Something truly American, then Maverick will like what we eat."

He laughed. "Get her making Jell-O Salad. That'll blow her mind, Giules."

My brows rose. "A salad? With jelly?"

Giulia's nose crinkled. "It's just a dessert. I'll show you meatloaf." She nudged Mav in the side. "Mav loves that."

His smile turned bashful, and the hard lines of his face softened up some, making me wish I had the right to reach over and trace my fingers over them.

I mean, I did, technically. But we weren't man and wife in anything other than name.

Was it crazy that I wanted to work toward a point where the 'name only' part wasn't true anymore?

Something about him... I felt safe with him. I hadn't felt that way for a long time, not since my grandmother had died. Even then, there'd always been the fretting and worrying over what would happen with her inevitable passing. Of course, whatever I could have imagined was a thousand times less than what had happened, so the prospect of Maverick being my guardian?

My protector?

It was enough to keep the demons at bay, and there were many.

Thousands of demons haunted me, terrorized me. Waited to grab me with their clawed fingers and drag me into hell once more.

I tensed, and like he knew I was back there again, he gently pulsed his fingers around mine, reminding me he was there.

My savior.

He'd repel them. I knew he would. He kept his own held back, so why wouldn't he be able to show me how to do it?

"I've got news."

My eyes flared at Giulia's tone, which came at a bad time, considering my mental diversion. But I was used to her throwing random pieces of information at us. We weren't very good at conversation and, for the most part, she ended up in a one-sided chat, but her tone had changed some.

"What is it?" I asked, anxiety starting to scratch at my reserves.

Giulia was rarely serious. Never somber.

"Nyx and I are going on a run tomorrow."

My brows lowered. "Oh, is that all? Where are you running to?"

"She doesn't mean that kind of run, Ghost. She means a long run."

"You mean like a marathon, Giulia?" Amara queried with interest, and I scowled at her. She understood more English than she let on, but never spoke and always allowed me to translate for her.

Still, her question had me wondering too, so I repeated, "You mean like a marathon?"

Giulia laughed. "No, it means I'm going on the back of Nyx's bike for a long ride."

"Why don't you call it that then?"

"It's just what it's called. Anyway, I won't be here for a few days."

The sudden tension in the room told me how we all felt about that.

Amara and Tatána didn't treat her as they should, rarely speaking to her in anything other than broken English, but I knew that to them, Giulia represented safety.

She'd been there when we'd been removed from that pit, when we were at death's door. She'd stayed with us past the doctor's treatments and visits, and she'd been here, helping us, feeding us, protecting us. Our mother hen.

Though I had Maverick, even I felt panicked.

Giulia knew things about us no one else did.

"You come back, yes?" Tatána whispered, making Giulia twist around to face her.

"Of course, I am." She cleared her throat. "*Tak.*"

Tatána looked like she'd seen a ghost, and it was clear she didn't believe Giulia.

"Would you even care if I didn't come back?" she questioned, no bitterness to her tone, more surprise than anything else.

I translated. Sure that they understood, but just to be on the safe side.

"*Tak!*" Amara cried with more emotion than I'd heard from her in weeks. The last time she'd sounded like that...

Well, I didn't want to think about it.

Callused fingers pried at my digits, and I blinked, wincing when I saw how hard I'd been digging my nails into Maverick's hand. "Sorry," I whispered miserably. "I didn't mean to hurt you."

"Takes more to hurt me than that. Just wasn't comfortable." He twisted our fingers so we could stay connected without his hand being in the line of fire of my nails.

"It won't be for long," Giulia reassured us, but nope, it wasn't working.

"How long?" I inquired huskily.

Giulia shrugged. "I don't know. We were supposed to ride out this morning, but I knew I had to tell you—"

My stomach twisted. "You'll be back before the week is out?"

"I don't know," she admitted, and her tone was genuine, so I knew she wasn't lying. She really didn't know. "But there's someone who's just arrived who wants to help."

"Not that Lily *suka*."

I scowled at Tatána. "It isn't her fault she's related to them—"

"No, it isn't," Giulia interjected sharply. "And I won't hear of you disrespecting a brother's woman, do you hear me?" She pointed a finger at me. "Translate every fucking word of that, Ghost."

Tatána's mouth tightened once I had, and she swung her head to the side to avoid Giulia's glare.

"It isn't Lily, although Lily is here too. It's her friend."

"A friend of hers is no friend of ours," Amara muttered in Ukrainian, prompting me to kick her under the table.

"That's not fair."

"Nothing about this is fair," she complained, scowling at me as she reached down and rubbed her shin.

"Tiffany is a therapist. She's come here to try to talk with you."

I winced when, after translating, and with a burst of energy that I hadn't known she was capable of, Tatána leaped off the bed and pulled an honest-to-goodness tantrum.

As she screamed and wailed, her fists banging against the walls like she was an oversized toddler, I flinched when her shrieks hurt my ears.

"Apparently, being honest wasn't the right approach," Giulia muttered, viewing the spectacle with wide eyes.

Unaffected, Mav snorted as he picked up his spoon and sampled more purple soup. "Ya think?"

TEN

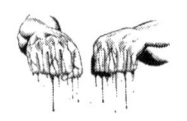

NYX

BLOOD WAS ON THE HORIZON.

I could almost scent it, and it made the long ride down to Ohio more than worth it.

Especially with my Old Lady at my back, her arms wrapped around my waist, her body curved into mine like she was born to be there.

Only fitting because she was, and she kept on proving it to me. To the rest of my brothers too.

We'd been riding for hours, and she hadn't bitched once.

Not fucking once.

This was her first long run, but she was taking it like a trooper. I knew her ass had to be killing her, and when we arrived at the bunkhouse, I knew she'd need muscle rub. I had it packed in my saddlebags, because I was well aware how that initial ride felt after nine hours on the back of a hog, and I also remembered the shitty digs where we'd be spending the next few nights.

As I rummaged through the possibilities of more comfortable accommodations, some that included us going to a hotel, I discounted that thought, because we would be returning to our room covered in blood, and that wasn't something a receptionist needed to see, was it?

Just imagining the screams was enough to make me smirk at the road ahead.

But I'd have to figure out something, because no way in fuck was I sharing one of the grody-ass beds in that damn bunkhouse this chapter had for visitors' use.

Because this was my fight, my war, I led the way at twelve o'clock instead of Link, our Road Captain. Rex was at ten past, and Link at ten to. Behind, we had Steel and one of Giulia's brothers, who was riding in a cage in case she couldn't manage the return journey riding bitch.

Not that I had told her that.

I appreciated my dick staying where it was, thanks.

As fate would have it, though, dawn started to illuminate the road ahead, a few glimmers of light making it easy to spot the sign for our turn off, and since the highway was dead, I sped up, my brothers around me doing the same. The wind whipped at our bodies, and I laughed when Giulia let out a whoop that was audible even over the roar of the engines.

Exhilaration flooded me, knowing that she loved this as much as me. I never thought I'd find someone who got me like she did. Who'd love the same shit as me.

And though it killed me, though the reasons behind it made me want to castrate Lancaster's corpse, that she wanted to shed blood too?

We were truly soulmates.

If I'd ever doubted it, her energy at that moment affirmed it entirely.

She let out another loud holler, one filled with a joy so pure, you wouldn't know our reason for driving nine hours straight.

Her effervescence had us speeding up, revving the engines harder as we fed her enthusiasm.

As always, my brothers had my back in this, and my grin grew only wider as we eventually had to slow for the turn off.

When we made it to the clubhouse twenty minutes later, the sudden silence as we killed our engines was enough to make my ears ring.

I pressed my hand to her thigh, rubbed it slightly, and asked, "You doing okay?"

"Hell fucking yeah," she replied, and she even bounced on the seat, making the hog creak.

My lips twitched, and I directed, "Come on then, skippy. Move that sexy ass of yours."

She did as she was told, climbing off the bike with only a little moan as she cocked her leg high over the seat. When she was off the hog, I raised my arms over my head, yawned, stretched, and then climbed off too.

When I was standing beside my machine, I kicked the stand down, then turned to face her.

One second she was there, the next, she was in my arms, her legs around my hips and her hands linking at the back of my neck.

I grabbed her ass, propped her up, then gave her the kiss she was asking for.

Sinking into her mouth was like going home. It didn't matter that we were nine hours from the place we lay our heads and called our clubhouse, she was it.

Home.

I never thought it'd happen for me. Never thought it was something I wanted or even merited, but now that I had her?

She was just that perfect amount of fucked up for it to make sense that she was mine.

When she tangled her tongue with mine, thrusting hers back and forth like she was having sex with my mouth, I patted her ass and managed to pull back.

"Note to self, long runs make Giulia horny."

She clenched her thighs around me. "Fuck, yeah," she rasped, making me laugh.

"Come on, you two," Rex said around a yawn. "You're the only ones stoked to be here."

Snickering, I turned around with her in my arms, not letting her down, because though she'd clearly enjoyed the journey, I knew she had to be exhausted.

"Where are we sleeping?"

"Sorted it out with Butch. You're staying in his Road Captain's room."

Giulia tensed. "I'm not sure what's worse. That his name is Butch or that I have to worry about how clean the place is."

I chuckled. "Butch is cool." Sort of.

"Yeah? Should have picked himself a better road name."

"Since when do we pick our own road names?" Rex retorted, arching a brow at her.

Her mouth worked at that, then I realized she got the picture because she muttered, "Wait, none of you had any say in it?"

"Nope."

Link shook his head.

Steel shrugged. "No."

She eyed me, but I hitched a shoulder too. When the cage with her brother in it rolled up along the driveway, she muttered, "I wonder what he'll get called."

"Jackass?" Link suggested helpfully.

Hawk wasn't the most popular person around the clubhouse. His attitude stank, but he was a good brother. Whatever anyone asked of him, he did it and did it well, his face was just sourer than a toothless hag sucking on a lemon.

"Lemon," I tossed out, making my brothers laugh, because they knew where I was coming from.

"He isn't always a jackass," Giulia defended, making us snort.

"Had a personality transplant, did he?" Steel groused.

"No, Mom died," she pointed out softly, sadly, and as one, we all grimaced.

Before we could get into more shit, the door to the clubhouse opened and Butch ambled out, yawning as he tugged on his cut.

He strode over to Rex, and the two slapped each other on the back after they shook each other's hand.

Butch made the rounds, leaving me and Giulia until last. When he reached for mine, he eyed Giulia's tattoo on her throat, squinting at it before he shook his head.

"Never thought I'd see the day you'd take on snatch permanently."

With her wrapped in my arms, I felt the instant her body began to vibrate with anger.

She was many things, but slow to rile wasn't one of them. Before she could bite him, or worse, headbutt him, making me grateful I still had a hold on her, I retorted, "Miracles happen. Giulia meet Butch. Butch, this is Giulia."

He barely spared a glance her way, his lack of interest in her evident.

Stupid dick.

"What's the story behind your road name?"

My brothers tensed up—I literally felt all our dicks crawl inside our bodies at her tone.

I wasn't sure why I put up with her crap, but mostly, she amused me, and I got her logic.

At this moment, she was pissed at being labeled as 'snatch,' and I didn't blame her. The trouble was, in our world? That's what she was. Even though she was my Old Lady, to some of the old fucks like Butch, she was pussy, and brothers always came before pussy.

My brow puckered as I wondered if that was true for me, but when I uneasily recognized that it wasn't, that if it came down to taking a bullet for Giulia or for my Prez?

It'd kill me, and the guilt, in the aftermath, would destroy me, but I'd save Giulia every fucking time.

Wanting to make amends, but unsure how to make up for not defending her, I didn't soften things up or smooth them over like I should.

"He pulled a Coyote Ugly on a woman," a voice called from the door. I turned to it, and saw Peggy, Butch's Old Lady, standing there in a practically invisible negligee, revealing a body I didn't need to look at because I'd seen it way too many times to count. Not because I'd fucked her, but because Peggy was an exhibitionist who liked to screw at parties. "The chick's sister came after him. Massive dyke. Beat the shit out of him. Hence, Butch."

Giulia hummed. "Because he wasn't butch enough to take that woman on?"

Peggy beamed at her. "Exactly."

"You're not supposed to call lesbians dykes."

Peggy scoffed. "Political correctness left the building the second you passed through the gate."

Giulia's grunt was irritated, but it was quiet enough for only me to hear it.

"You got legs, sugar? Or you going to let our resident King of Darkness walk you around like a baby?"

Under her breath, and for my ears only, she muttered, "Please tell me you didn't fuck her, because I may have to scoop out her eyeballs—"

"I didn't," I reassured her quickly, and guilt speared me some more because, fuck, how shitty must it be for her to come face-to-face with pussies I'd fucked before her?

I knew, for a fact, that I'd want to kill any of her other lovers if I came face-to-face with them.

"My ass hurts," Giulia reasoned, and I hid my smile in her throat by making a show of kissing it.

"Pounded it hard last night, did he?" Peggy commiserated, and her passive aggressiveness had my shoulders bunching. I wasn't sure if she was trying to make friends with my woman or if she was trying to be a bitch.

From Giulia's tension?

I picked up on the fact that she didn't think this was an overture of friendship.

While Butch was the Prez of this chapter, the way it worked in the Satan's Sinners MCs was that the original chapter's council ranked higher than the other presidents.

As Enforcer, second only to Storm, the VP, after Rex, I was higher ranked than her Old goddamn Man.

I'd never pushed shit, though, never wanted to come across as a dick, but I would now.

For Giulia.

"Rex says you've turfed out your Road Captain for us?"

Butch grunted. "Yeah. And he ain't happy about it."

I scowled at him. "Well, it's your fucking job to make sure he doesn't bitch. If I hear any crap from him, you know what will happen—"

"Hey, calm down, Nyx. Jesus. It's his room. Of course, he ain't happy about being kicked out!" Butch retorted, but his eyes were wide because he wasn't used to catching shit from me.

I scowled *harder* at him. "Then you need to think about sorting out your shit pile of a clubhouse, because fuck only knows when we'll have business down these parts now that routes are getting narrower."

His jaw hardened. "You telling me how to run my fucking club?"

"That's what I'm fucking telling you."

"Jesus, I thought an Old Lady would have calmed you the fuck down. Sugar, you ain't sucking that dick of his enough—"

He didn't get the chance to say another fucking word before my hand was around his throat. I had enough strength to hold him in place, but not to keep Giulia hooked around me at the same time. Not when Butch started struggling.

Unsurprisingly, Peggy didn't even squawk at the sight of her Old Man being choked, but Giulia, God love her, hopped down and hissed, "Butch, you don't have to worry about my Old Man's cock. It's in good hands, but just because you're happy with your bitch of an Old Lady showing off her goods to the rest of the fucking nation, doesn't mean we're the same."

Rex snorted at that, and when I cast him a look, I saw he had his arms folded across his chest, taking in the show like it was a fucking dinner theater.

That was Rex's trouble.

I entertained him. And Giulia? Together we were better than the Marx brothers for him.

My thumb dug deep into Butch's throat, getting to the soft tissue. My attack had shocked him, or he'd have defended himself more. As it stood, he wasn't focused on offense, just concerned with scrabbling at my wrist, trying to get free.

I let loose when Rex whistled at me under his breath. I wasn't his fucking dog, but at the same time, I knew I could be pretty rabid in certain circumstances.

Butch pretty much folded over, grabbing at his throat as he choked and coughed, sputtering as we stared at him.

"The fact that your men haven't come out here to defend you tells me a lot about how you're running this place," Rex commented casually, and Butch, not a complete and utter prick, recognized the tone.

When Rex was like this, he could be more dangerous than me.

Sure, it was in a different way, because Rex shed less blood than me, but that didn't mean he wasn't lethal.

Butch's life, his position here, rested in Rex's hands.

The brothers owed him their loyalty as a Prez, but they answered to Rex first and foremost.

It was why he had his road name.

Rex was a king among the MC world, thanks to the legacy his daddy had left him. Bear didn't have the diplomacy his son had, and in Rex's paws, I knew our MC would grow over time. Bear had known that too.

"They're all too pissed from last night."

The voice had me tensing, even as I snapped, "Thought you told me that fucker was in Oklahoma."

Rex shrugged. "Oklahoma is a lot fucking farther than Ohio. Didn't want you killing the bastard and regretting it later."

My mouth tightened as shit shuffled together, making sense to me now. "You found the fucker we're taking down?"

"Yeah."

Despite my annoyance with my Prez and with this dick, I was pleased to know Sin was here when none of the others were. Rex ran a tighter hold on his men, even if it didn't seem like it, and that Sin was awake when the others weren't? It was a good sign of the difference in discipline among us.

"Sin," I rumbled out a gruff greeting. Giulia tensed some, and I realized she hadn't recognized the voice. Now that she had, now she knew, I figured she was back there.

Back to that night that had changed everything.

"Nyx." I could sense the wariness in him, and that was because he was a smart man. He knew he was on my shit list.

His gift to me would be one step toward home.

I rubbed my jaw as Giulia curled into me, and I slung my arm around her shoulders and hauled her closer, knowing where Sin's presence had taken her.

That hour that had turned everyone's world upside down.

"Butch, fuck off inside. I'll be using your office while I'm here," Rex informed him, and Butch, having stopped being an idiot, scurried away, dragging Peggy with him when she squawked her irritation at him.

"We need to talk," Rex said calmly. "Giulia, you need to go to bed—"

"Fuck that. No one knows who the fuck she is here—"

"She has your brand on her," Rex retorted with a scowl.

"If they're all fucking drunk, they won't care. I need to intro her before I let her loose around these halls."

Giulia sniffed. "I can defend myself."

"Yeah, you can, but I ain't putting you at risk," I countered with a growl. I wasn't going to slam her confidence, but neither was I going to let her put herself in danger. If she'd been stronger, Lancaster would never have gotten the drop on her. "It can either wait until the morning, or we can talk with her present."

Link cleared his throat. "Whatever it is, Giulia knows more than she should anyway, Prez."

I dipped my chin in thanks at him, and when Steel concurred, "She's solid, Rex. You know that," I reached over and slapped his shoulder in gratitude.

Rex huffed. "It isn't that I think she isn't solid, dumbfucks. It's that I'll get shit if I start letting bitches in on club business."

"Then we talk about it tomorrow—"

Rex rolled his eyes, but Sin spoke up, "It's okay, Rex. It's time they knew."

"Expect salt in your coffee tomorrow for lumping me in as a bitch," Giulia threatened, but I heard the tension in her voice. She was on edge, even if she wasn't entirely joking about the coffee shit.

Rex huffed, but he didn't say another word, just strode toward the clubhouse and walked through the doorway Peggy had been leaning against like a whore from an old-school bordello.

He strode in like he owned the place—oh, wait, he fucking did—then headed down the hall to Butch's office.

As we followed him, I ignored Sin for the moment, content to have my brothers at my back as I shuffled Giulia forward. She had her thumb tucked into one of my belt loops while my arm was still around her shoulder.

As we walked, she mumbled quietly, "Thank you."

Didn't take a mind reader to figure out what she was thanking me for. "Shouldn't have to thank me. He shouldn't have said what he did."

She tapped my butt with her hand slightly, not in a teasing way, but in a soothing one.

My lips quirked up at the touch, then they flared into an outright grin when she muttered, "I thought our clubhouse was a shithole."

Giulia had made it quite clear that she didn't approve of the standards of cleanliness in the clubhouse. The clubwhores hated her for more than just the fact that she wasn't afraid to break noses if required, and she had them actually cleaning for their supper now.

"Peggy sure as shit isn't you when it comes to keeping the place clean," Rex agreed, as he wandered into Butch's office.

Her nose crinkled at the sight of the dust everywhere, and that was nothing compared to the furniture, which looked either like someone had been fucked to death on it, or just fucked or just stabbed... I really wasn't sure myself. Red and white splattered on it in a way that made me pray it was excess paint from the walls and ceiling.

Wryly, I advised, "Don't touch anything, or, alternatively, touch everything and I'll disinfect you later."

She snickered, then found a space at the corner of the desk she evidently wasn't entirely disgusted by. She grabbed a tissue from the box on the side of the desk, and while those tissues might have been innocent enough, I really didn't want to tell her that he probably used them to wrap his used condoms in. Well, I figured that was why. Maybe he didn't give enough of a fuck to do even that.

Deciding not to tell Giulia about any of that particular thought process, I cleared my throat as I slumped in front of the desk when Rex had taken a seat. At my side, Link propped himself up by leaning against my chair, Steel sank onto the sofa, and Hawk trudged in only for Sin to tell him, "The bunkhouse is outside. Turn left at the front door, carry on walking, and you'll see the building. Brakes is probably still asleep. If you wake him up, he'll fuck you over in the morning."

"Used to that with you bas—" Hawk caught himself, quickly swiveling on his heels and hauling ass to get out of the office before he could get into any shit with us.

Once Sin closed the door behind him, Rex murmured, "I think Sin has something to say to you Giulia."

I was surprised she hadn't gone to slap him for what he'd put her through by being a shit guard, but if anything, at Rex's words, her shoulders huddled up, and she folded her arms across her chest.

The defensive posture didn't suit her.

I was used to her headbutting shit, not her hiding from a situation, but where Luke Lancaster was concerned?

She was still fucked in the head.

Take, for example, the fact she kept wanting me to chase her, pin her down, and fuck her—like I was taking her choice away.

I didn't like it. Hated it, actually, but what the fuck was I supposed to do?

My job was to give her what she needed, and if that was how she was going to try to find control in a situation she couldn't control, then that was what we'd do.

"Giulia, you have to believe me, I'd never have left if it wasn't urgent."

Scowling at that, I half sat up, prepared to smack the shit out of him for his bullshit, but Rex raised a hand. His eyes promised retribution if I didn't control myself, and because I wasn't used to seeing that, was pretty much used to him letting me do whatever the fuck I wanted, I froze in surprise.

"I got a text from my woman," he rasped. "She'd been involved in an accident—"

"What fucking woman?" Steel groused, but I could hear his anger too. He always had my back, and in this, there was no difference.

"She's mine, even if she doesn't fucking know it yet," he countered uneasily, hunching his shoulders much like Giulia had. "She texted me telling me she was in an accident and that she needed my help.

"When I got there, she was drunk out of her skull. At least, that's what I thought at first, and I was fucking furious. But she was acting weird, had puked everywhere.

"It wasn't right. Something was wrong, and when I tried to talk to her, it was like..." He blew out a breath. "She couldn't move. Couldn't function. She didn't stink of booze, and I knew there was no way in fuck she'd have been able to send me those texts she had—"

"What's your point?" I snarled, not appreciating his delay in apologizing to my woman.

"She was drugged."

My mouth worked at that, but Giulia questioned, "She'd been raped?"

"No. I took her home, looked after her, and when she woke up and didn't remember anything except for one thing..." His jaw clenched. "Well, you'd already dealt with the bastard, so I didn't have much chance to get some vengeance."

Her eyes widened. "Luke Lancaster drugged your woman?"

"Who the fuck is this goddamn bitch?" Link snapped, evidently as agitated as the rest of us. That took a fucking lot, considering Link was beyond laid back.

"Tiffany Farquar."

For a second, I knew we did nothing other than just gape at one another.

Then, when we'd processed that, Giulia asked again, "You're sure he didn't rape her?"

"No. She only remembered him touching her..." His face tightened with anger as he waved a hand at his chest. Didn't take a genius to figure that one out either.

"Wait, so..." Steel sat up, scowling as he slowly verbalized, "You mean to tell me that Lancaster drugged your woman to...feel her up?"

"No. He did it to get me away from Giulia. He must have known we were seeing each other, and he knew I'd leave my position to help her. Nothing else would have made me leave Giulia, Nyx. You have to believe that."

"I thought you'd gone to the strip club," Giulia muttered uncomfortably.

"No! Fuck, Giulia. As if I'd do that. I know I was getting out of hand, drinking too much before—but I knew what you meant to Nyx. Fuck, I know it now. I'd never have let either of you down if it wasn't urgent."

"You could have fucking called," I muttered, unwilling to totally relent.

"I was panicking," he admitted.

I scowled at him, my dubiousness clear. "You? Panicking over snatch?"

"Is Giulia a snatch to you?"

"No," I said slowly, and if anything could have resonated with me, it was that. If Sin felt that way about Lily's friend, then fuck.

Hadn't I just admitted to myself that if it boiled down to it, I'd save Giulia over Rex?

Jesus.

"You kept this fucking quiet," Link pointed out. "Hell, I don't think Lily even knows. If she did, I figure she'd have told me by now."

"You always did keep too many secrets," Rex observed pointedly, his brows high as he focused on Sin.

"What the fuck does that mean?" I demanded, but Rex wasn't having any of it.

He stated, "I sent him here because he deserved it. He left Giulia, left his post, let us down. There are many 'should have dones' in this scenario, but it's time Sin comes home."

Before I could say a word, Giulia murmured, "Sin?"

"Yeah?" he asked warily.

"Is she okay?"

"Yeah. He didn't hurt her. I think his intention was to get straight to you." He grunted. "She's pregnant."

My mouth dropped open—and I wasn't the only one. Rex looked stunned too.

"The kid's mine," he declared defensively.

Rex sniffed. "That wasn't the part that stunned me," he said with a roll of his eyes. "How far along?"

"Around two months."

"You speak to her?" Link questioned.

"Fuck's sake, I know she's kept us a secret, and I know I did that too, but damn, I'm not lying about this—"

"You have to understand that this comes as a surprise to all of us," Link pointed out diplomatically. "As far as many of us knew, you were—"

"Footloose and fancy free," Giulia interrupted, her tone dryer than a bag full of salt, and that she could find some amusement in this situation made my tension lower.

Sin snorted at her joke, and the others chuckled, me? I just reached forward, grabbed her hand, and tugged her onto my lap.

"You need to come home then for sure," Giulia agreed, but her eyes were on me. I could see forgiveness in her gaze, and even though I got it, and even though I was glad he hadn't just gone AWOL to watch a fucking show at the strip joint, I wasn't totally happy.

He'd fucked up.

Majorly.

And so had Rex.

"Why is this the first time I'm hearing about any of this shit?" I ground out.

"Because you've been focused elsewhere. We've had more important things to be dealing with," he answered, but he was unapologetic. "But now's the time to move on. If Giulia can accept that, then you need to as well."

I huffed out a sigh.

Didn't look like I had much of a goddamn choice, did it?

ELEVEN

SIN

IF YOU'D EVER TOLD me there'd come a day when I was happy to become a dad, I'd have told you to fuck off.

Kids and I didn't gel.

And ever since I'd teamed up with Nyx on his quest to rid the country of as many pedophiles in as many painful ways as possible, the desire to have children had been dampened even further.

It was probably why, however, Faudreaux got to me more than most now.

My woman had my baby in her belly.

The thought still blew my mind.

Her small voice on the phone, the way she had to psych herself up to tell me...it all fucked with my head.

We'd had a weird relationship. Secretive, closed off, but close nonetheless. We'd shared a lot in the time we'd been dating, and while some of it was DNA, not all of it was.

There'd been times when we'd just been. I'd bought a fucking hammock for us, for Christ's sake, because I knew she loved my yard, and I liked seeing her happy.

I knew she took that godawful coconut milk in her coffee, and that bedhead actually looked good on her.

I knew she loved *Sponge Bob*, even though she'd never admit to it— it was always on my 'Recently Played' list on Netflix, and I sure as fuck didn't watch it—and I knew she was lost, uncertain of which way the future was going to take her.

Funny how fate had a way of taking control of things for you.

I already knew from her texts and the quick call we'd had earlier, before we'd snapped up Faudreaux, that today hadn't worked out that great. She was supposed to help the captives the club had saved, and apparently, it hadn't gone well. Tomorrow was another day, though, and she hadn't sounded upset about them rejecting her help. If anything, I'd sensed some resolve about her.

Like she knew she was needed, and even if they didn't want that help, they were going to fucking get it.

Just the thought made my lips twitch, because she was so goddamn obstinate, and she didn't even see it.

A scream shattered my thoughts—as a truly haunting scream should do—and I cut a look at Giulia, who was standing there, watching Nyx at work.

I wasn't sure why he was letting her watch. Had no idea why she was here.

He said she had anger issues.

I mean, I knew that. Jesus, didn't take someone with a fucking degree to figure that out. Christ. But still, she was standing there, trembling.

Link hovered nearby like he was there to shield her if shit got too bad, but any regular person would shiver at the sight of what their man was capable of.

I mean, there was knowing someone was insane, and then there was seeing it with your own fucking eyes.

Personally, I was used to it.

And I got it.

I wasn't one of the old-school brothers like Steel, Link, and Rex were. But I'd been around long enough to know what fucked with Nyx's head. We were brothers, and even if I'd let him down, that wouldn't change. Sure, he'd be pissy with me for a while, but we went too far back.

I'd run from home to New Jersey because my ma had told me my dad was a Sinner, and whether or not he was, she'd never told me his name, and I hadn't given a shit. I'd just wanted to get away, so I'd gone to West Orange. Bear had heard my story, hadn't turned me away, and I'd patched in as a Prospect when I was sixteen years old. I'd never have enlisted if things hadn't derailed and I needed to get out of the country. Fast.

I tugged at my cut, one of the few things I valued, and knew that I'd take it off for Tiff. That was what she meant to me. I wondered if Nyx felt the same way for Giulia, and if he was about to have his heart broken because he'd revealed too much, too soon. They'd barely been together before he was letting her see this, and that wasn't smart.

Not in my opinion anyway.

I leaned back against the wall as Nyx sliced and diced Faudreaux. The images Nyx had taken from his safe were on the floor around us in shreds, no part visible anymore. That was how tiny the pieces were, and he was making Faudreaux eat them.

The bastard was sobbing with each gulp, but Nyx had pulled some fucked up shit with the guy's dick. He'd created a tourniquet around it, and every time Faudreaux bitched, he yanked that tourniquet a little tighter.

Absentmindedly wondering if his dick would fall off, if that was even possible, I watched as Giulia flinched when the pedo fucker let out a particularly high-pitched scream.

Nyx had gone around behind him, and fuck only knew what he was doing to the naked piece of shit.

Rex pulled a face at the noise, but returned his focus to his phone. Link just looked stoic—like this wasn't how he wanted to be spending his night, but for Nyx, he'd have his back. Steel was the only one with his back to the cunt. He had his eyes wandering around the warehouse we were using, making sure no bastard came in.

This was Sinners' territory, a Sinners owned warehouse, but still, with the squealing this fucker was making, we needed to be watchful. Even though the chapter used this place with this purpose in mind, caution was always warranted when you were torturing someone.

Giulia took a step forward, shakily moving toward Link. Nyx hadn't let her see the pictures, and I couldn't blame him. Though Mav had confirmed Faudreaux deserved to die, Nyx had quickly glanced at one because he didn't believe in trying a man without proof, and what he'd seen had made him go straight to level one on the map of torture—the tourniquet.

Dick territory.

That was when you knew what he'd seen was really bad.

She muttered something to Link, and he arched a brow at her but handed her something.

She moved toward Faudreaux, who, seeing her and evidently believing she was the weakest link, took the opportunity to plead, "Please! Help me! Stop this—I didn't do anything—"

"Guys like you never do anything, do you?" she rasped, her voice low. Her words haunted. "You just take. You don't care who you hurt, what you leave behind." She bowed her head as she stared at the scraps on the floor. In between them all were some old-fashioned pieces of film. The sepia brown foil could be spied between all the flecks of photos. She bent down, picked up a piece, and remarked, "Do you know cellulose is highly flammable?"

I tensed at that, and with my experience with explosives, I knew where she was going with that question. Rhetorical it fucking wasn't.

Her tone was wooden, kind of. At first listen. Then you heard the fucking layers behind it.

Jesus, she was just as bad as Nyx.

Loathing and disgust throbbed through every word, seething at such a level that she sounded almost toneless.

I cast Rex a look, wondering if he was going to put a stop to this, but he'd peered up with interest now.

Sick fuck.

Hell, we all were.

The irony being, of course, that as a Sinner, I'd killed more when I was in Iraq than I had running for the club. And the few deaths I'd helped perpetrate as a Sinner was with Nyx and the crew as we helped Nyx avenge his sister.

I peered around the warehouse, wondering if it would withstand a blaze, but I didn't have much time to think.

She stepped closer to him, managing to move around puddles of blood, piss, and vomit, then she grabbed the tourniquet, tightened it until his mouth opened in a scream, and shoved the film into his mouth.

He tried to spit it out, but Nyx had made an appearance by now. He'd grabbed some duct tape, and he rolled it around the bastard's head, from chin up to his crown, keeping his mouth locked tight forever while ensuring the cellulose stuck out, quivering with each move he made.

When it was done, he turned to Giulia, and asked, "You know it might explode?"

A whine escaped Faudreaux, who promptly pissed himself.

Again.

"I think that's what the fucker deserves, don't you?"

"You sure?" Nyx inquired, his tone conversational. Like he was asking her if she was ready to get a dog or something. Maybe asking if she wanted Italian or Mexican for dinner.

Not, ya know, asking if she was okay with setting fire to someone.

She shrugged her shoulders as she stared at him. "He served time?"

Rex cleared his throat. "Two stints. The first for possessing child porn. The second was for child rape."

She tensed, and I knew that'd just signed his death warrant.

But then, I'd signed that the first time I'd settled on him as my act of contrition for Nyx.

"Some fuckers just need to burn for their sins," she muttered, then she raised the lighter up high, let it hit Faudreaux's eye level, and flicked it so the flame burned.

As Faudreaux began to struggle, she let the flame touch the cellulose.

The next thing I knew, Nyx had shouldered her out the way and was hauling her out of the warehouse toward the door.

The rest of us didn't stick around either.

When we hauled ass outside, Rex huffed. "I'll get Butch onto the sheriff. Make sure he knows to keep his blind eye turned away from this Podunk shit pile."

And as he pulled up the call, the rest of us wandered over to our bikes to the happy soundtrack of a man burning to death.

When my mind turned onto the kid in my woman's belly, only one thought crossed my mind—it was a good day to be alive, because that sick fuck in there? He was incapable of hurting another kid, thanks to us.

TWELVE

TIFFANY

"THEY HATE ME."

I snorted. "It isn't about you."

Lily winced. "I mean, I know it isn't."

"Then what's the problem?" I shrugged. "They don't have to like us for us to help them. In fact, it's better if they hate us. At least that's them reacting. Them choosing to do something, rather than being passive."

Lily frowned at me, but I got that. She wasn't used to being disliked, and the women in the bunkhouse were definitely not fans of her.

She sniffed. "Why aren't you upset?"

"Do you want me to be?" Then, before she could get snippy with me, I laughed. "Babe, you can afford a far better therapist than me, so if you need to be liked, go and discuss it with them."

She narrowed her eyes at me. "Bitch."

I grinned, finding this funny, even though it really wasn't. "But you wuv me anyway."

She wrinkled her nose as she sank back onto the sofa. "Sadly, that's true."

"*Sadly*, I wouldn't sit on that sofa."

That was pretty much where my story had begun with Sin.

Me, sitting there, feeling totally out of place, feeling like a frickin' Martian amid Earthlings, while a dude I now knew was the VP got slurped down like a popsicle by a club slut.

Somehow, this was our world now.

She pulled a face and darted off the sofa like it had cooties.

Hell, it probably did.

I hid a grin, because she wouldn't appreciate it, then suggested, "We need to take over a room or something."

"Giulia claimed the kitchen."

"That has to be clean, right?"

"I'd hope so."

Making a gagging noise, I let her tug me down the hall.

I'd only been at the clubhouse for parties before now, and had never gone wandering around the place to figure out the lay of the land because, well, did I look stupid?

Only Christ knew what actually went down in this building, and I really didn't want to find something out that would necessitate a hole in the head being my next go-to style.

I mean, I didn't think they'd kill me, not now that I was carrying Sin's kid, but back then? Who knew?

When we bypassed the bar with its whole sex den vibe—even though it looked pretty innocuous, like a biker version of Cheers, apart from all the extra DNA splashed everywhere—and headed into an industrial-looking kitchen, I almost sighed with relief when it was not only empty, but scented of lemons.

"Parallel universe," I muttered under my breath.

Lily laughed. "Yeah. Pretty much."

"Can you believe this is our world now?" I asked, verbalizing my thoughts as I stared around the place, looking down the hall to where other rooms were filled with rowdy bikers and women whose purpose was to fuck the men and do their laundry.

"I don't know, I guess it's weird, but I don't associate Link with it somehow."

"How can't you? He's on the council, isn't he?" Christ, I knew what these words meant now. Sin never went into details about the club, but I knew the vocab. Knew he wore a cut, that the council watched over the MC as a whole, and the brothers could vote for stuff in church.

Lord above.

"Yeah, but he's Link."

"What's that supposed to mean?"

Another shrug was my answer, but when I frowned at her, she explained, "What he does here, what he does with me, two separate things entirely."

"You know they do illegal stuff, don't you?" I questioned warily, not wanting to rupture the shiny, happy picture she had going on there, but hell, she needed a dose of reality if she hadn't figured that out by now.

She rolled her eyes at my question, which actually filled me with relief. "Tiff, I managed to figure that out on my own. I'm a big girl now, you know?"

I grinned at her. "Smartass."

She dropped a curtsey—and you just knew that shit was authentic, because she'd gone to Switzerland to finishing school and everything. "I try."

"I'll just bet you do."

Her nose crinkled, and something about it had me tipping my head to the side. When she started to move toward the fridge, I grabbed her hand and said, "Hey. You okay?"

She bit her lip, which was an instant giveaway that she wasn't, then she stared down at the counter rather than at me as she traced her fingers over the veins in the marble. "Me and Link haven't, you know..."

I blinked, because no, I didn't know. And from her bashfulness, I figured we had to be talking about the one thing that made no sense.

I knew what the bikers were like. I'd seen Link in action unfortunately. Of course, that was before Lily was even a twinkle in the guy's eye, so I wasn't going to hold it against him forever, but still...

He was no angel. Certainly no virgin.

"You mean, you haven't gone on a date?"

Because that, I could dig. It made sense.

Bikers didn't do dates. Sin had told me that, but I'd been intent on keeping things awkward for him.

Hey, you had to keep a guy like him on his toes!

"No, nothing like that. I mean, we haven't had sex yet."

"You haven't?" I squeaked, my eyes bugging out, because if she'd told me the Virgin Mary had visited her dreams last night, I'd have found that easier to believe than what she was telling me right now.

"No. We've done stuff, but not that."

Well, that was good to know.

Usually, we talked about everything, but I hadn't told her about Sin, and she hadn't told me about Link, not until later on.

It figured that we could both be secretive where we chose, but still, this felt different.

This felt...

Like she was using me as a therapist and not just a friend.

Or a complex mixture of the two, maybe?

I dragged her over to the nearest stool, pushed her onto it, then propped myself up. "You sure you want to talk about this here? The walls have ears."

She laughed. "Everyone's asleep, and you know it."

"True." It was only ten AM, and that meant everyone was still sleeping off last night's revelry in the bar.

I'd only happened to see that because Lily had been late in picking me up from here, and when I'd wandered in and seen a ménage going down on the pool table, I'd gotten a little waylaid watching.

Hell, it was better than tuning into a porn flick!

The memory didn't really turn me on that much because I wasn't into sharing. And Sin? No way in fucking hell would I share him.

Maybe he'd be down for it, what with the way they all shared their bitches and shit, but me?

Nope.

With another guy, I might have been down to experiment, but with Sin, I knew I had to lock him down tight if I wanted something serious with him.

And I actually did.

I wanted this kid to be raised with his daddy in the house, not living two streets over because his momma had caught said daddy with a clubwhore.

The image wasn't one I'd thought to ever picture in my head, but that was how it worked. Not just in this world either. Mine too.

Cheating happened everywhere. I mean, I knew my parents loved one another, but I wouldn't have been surprised if Mom was banging the pool boy and Daddy was fucking his secretary.

Was I happy about it?

Nope.

The prospect upset me, but I knew that loyalty and faithfulness weren't two things that went hand in hand. Not all the time, at any rate.

I mean, they should, but this was the real world.

They didn't.

And I wanted them to with Sin. But what Lily was telling me kind of blew me away, because it was the opposite of what I was thinking.

Link, who was a horn dog, hadn't had sex with his woman yet. She was branded, for God's sake. In the eyes of the club, she was his Old Lady. I mean, it didn't take a marathon of *Sons of Anarchy* to figure out what that meant.

"What's going on, Lily?" I asked warily, confused and taken aback all at the same time.

"I find it hard to talk about."

"I'll just bet you do," I muttered. "Because how you haven't hopped onto Link and ridden him like he was his Harley, I'll never know."

Her nose crinkled again. "Hey, he's mine. Have lascivious thoughts about your own biker."

I grinned at her, happy she was good with me teasing her. "Oh, trust me, I do. Alllll the time."

She huffed. "I can't believe you kept him from me."

"You kept Link from me too."

"Only because I didn't think you'd approve."

I arched a brow at her. "Exactly."

"Oh. Yeah, you're right. This world is different than ours, isn't it?"

"I don't think that's a bad thing," I replied earnestly, because although it was weird, it wasn't technically bad. "Ours isn't all that great. At least here, if you want to shoot someone, you can."

"We'd prefer no blood on the floor."

The squeaking of wheels should have given away Maverick's presence, but if anything, he whispered into the room like he had wings.

The pair of us jolted, turning around to see who'd joined us, and when I saw it was Maverick, my tension lessened some.

I'd prefer to come face-to-face with a brother than a clubwhore.

Especially that bitch who I knew had a thing for Sin. It was the same slut I'd seen him fingerbang that first night, so I wasn't predisposed to like her anyway.

Daisy, I thought her name was.

Or Dinky?

Who the fuck knew?

They all had stupid ass names, that was for damn sure.

"Even if we clean it up really well?" I joked, because Maverick was a brother I understood.

He was damaged, and he wasn't ashamed about that.

One night, when we were in bed together, Sin had told me he'd served overseas. That had come as a surprise, because I'd never have pegged him as a veteran, but he'd said that some men came back all right, and others came back like Maverick.

At the time, I'd wanted to ask him what his definition of 'all right' was, but coming across Maverick, learning about him and his ways, it was easy to see how someone like Sin would be uneasy comparing himself, and his state of mental and physical health, to a man like Maverick, who was injured in more ways than were actually visible.

According to Sin, Maverick hadn't left the clubhouse in years except for once—to marry one of the 'women' and to take her to the cops to rat out Donavan Lancaster.

That was it.

And that he'd done that? Hell, it told me quite clearly what he felt for the woman they called Ghost.

I'd met all the captives yesterday, but only briefly because one of them had been having a tantrum like she was two.

I wasn't all that surprised. No, I wasn't totally trained as a therapist, but I'd seen a lot, heard a lot, read a lot. Back at college, I even had a mentor who'd shared some of the dubious experiences he'd had when he was first starting out and had been assigned to a prison where he'd helped the prisoners come to terms with all kinds of stuff.

That Tatána was acting out, as well as the fact that she kept trying to off herself? She definitely wanted attention.

She'd get it too.

From me.

In spades.

But the truth was, I could only help them if they let me in, and thus far, no dice. They'd barricaded us out today, in fact. I'd heard some arguments going down in the bunkhouse though, in a nasty, Baltic language that made it sound like they were verbally stabbing each other—

"They'll let you in now, by the way," Maverick muttered, when he rolled over to the fridge.

"Huh?"

"I said they'll let you in now. It took me and Ghost to calm Tatána down. She pushed her bed in front of the door and wouldn't even let me in, but we managed to talk her into opening it up."

"How did you do that?" Lily asked curiously.

"With a lot of persuasion," he said drolly, then he picked up a bottle of juice, opened it, and drank straight from the container.

When he was done, he stuck the bottle on his lap and turned to us with a neat move that made it look like the wheelchair was on a motor, but it actually wasn't. There wasn't even a squeak either. It made me wonder how he'd learned to be so sneaky, and what he picked up on by being that way...

"I'll come over with you, introduce you better. Giulia didn't do that good of a job yesterday. She shouldn't have said shit."

"I don't like lying to people," I told him candidly.

"No?" He grinned. "Then you must get screamed at a lot."

"You'd be surprised how little it happens."

His lips twitched again. "Come on, let's get this over with. The sooner they know it's happening and come to terms with it, the better."

I shot Lily a concerned look, because I knew she wanted to talk to me about her and Link not having had sex yet, but she turned away and started toward Maverick.

I guessed that was the end of that conversation, but we'd be talking about it later. That was for damn sure.

I mean...she'd just turned my entire belief system on its head, and I was glad about that. So fucking glad, in fact, because hell, I didn't want to think that if you didn't put out one night, your boyfriend-slash-partner would go and find it with someone else.

And here?

They had so many other someone elses who'd all drop to their knees or spread their legs the instant these guys snapped their fucking fingers.

My brow puckered at the thought, though, because while most men didn't have access to easy pussy like the bikers here did, wasn't there always someone out there who'd fuck your man when you weren't looking if they were out there trawling for sex?

My brain was whirling as I stepped out of the clubhouse and back into the yard.

Sin had wanted me to become a part of the club, a part of his family, he wanted me to be in his world, and I got the feeling that when he made it back home, whenever that would be, he'd make me his Old Lady.

I thought about the brand I'd seen on Lily's wrist.

It was a big step getting someone's name inked on your skin, but hell, wasn't it a big step having someone's kid too?

Just as permanent.

I was grateful when we made it to the bunkhouse and found the door open. I really needed to stop thinking so much. I was all up in my head, and to be fair to Sin, I was probably getting things wrong. It wasn't his fault I came with preconceptions about men—not bikers, just men in particular. Lily had, strangely enough, helped. She'd not only fired up my curiosity, but she'd given me some hope too.

In silent thanks, I reached for her hand before we crossed the threshold and gave her fingers a squeeze.

She arched a brow at me in question, but squeezed back.

"Thank you for being you," I told her softly.

Her eyes flared wide, but a softness came into them that made my heart turn into a puddle of goo. "That's a lovely thing to say," she whispered.

"I mean it." I curved my arm over her shoulders.

There was a reason Lily hadn't had sex with Link yet. The guy was hot, and I'd seen him in action—he knew what to do with his dick. I didn't think the clubwhores were playing around with their orgasms either. They were loud and proud, and whenever Link had—well, ya know—they'd been more vocal than ever.

So, he was cute, had the skills, and fuck, he loved her.

He loved her so much, it was like looking at a Hallmark advertisement with a biker filter over it. I mean, he wasn't obvious about it. It wasn't like they were glued to the hip, but he was protective of her. Defended her. Made sure she was taken care of—Christ, his checklist before they'd gone on that long run yesterday had been crazy.

She'd had to promise to call him last night as she went around the house checking that all the windows were closed!

So whatever reason she had for not giving into him, for doing other stuff with him but not that? I knew it was bad.

And her dad and brother had held the women in front of me as hostages. Sex slaves.

Fuck.

Had they touched her too?

It seemed likely.

And she'd never told me. I'd never known.

What a shit friend I was.

Even as nausea made me feel sick to my stomach at the prospect, I came face-to-face with three women who looked at me with a variance of hatred and concern.

I knew they didn't want to talk to me.

A lot of people didn't want to talk to therapists.

They didn't know I wasn't a shrink for real. But I'd been one final away from graduating, and if I'd done them, I'd have been sailing into my masters.

Even if I was nowhere near fully trained, I was all they had.

We could get through this together. Learn together. Help them help themselves together.

"My name's Tiffany," I introduced myself, tilting my head to the side as I murmured, "I know you're Amara, Ghost, and Tatána." I grimaced. "I also know Ghost has to translate everything so this might take some time."

Ghost had moved over to Maverick's side, and the way she hovered close to his chair, not touching it, warmed my heart.

She saw him as a protector, that was clear, and I got the feeling it had been a long time since Mav had felt that way, had anyone see him that way, and I knew she'd be good for him.

The pair might even heal each other. Wouldn't that be a miracle?

Unfortunately for me, Ghost had the kindest expression on her face, and even she looked dubious.

Tatána eyed me as though I was scum on her shoes, and Amara shot intermittent glares at me before she glowered down at her feet.

That was nothing compared to how they viewed Lily either.

But the truth was, after what she'd said? I kind of wanted Lily to stick around.

I wanted her here too.

Not necessarily to hear the details of what her family had put these women through, but for...

Hell.

Was she one of her brother's victims too? Her father's?

I needed to know as much as I didn't want to know.

I'd always thought her dad was scary, and Luke had been that strong, silent type. Until I hit eighteen and realized he was creepy too, I hadn't figured out that he gave me vibes that were the opposite of what my Lelo vibrator gave me.

I plucked at my bottom lip as I pondered how to broach this particular topic, but before I could say a word, Lily cleared her throat.

"I know you hate me, I know you think I'm one of them. One of the Lancasters." She filled her voice with the loathing she felt for her family, and I reached over and pressed a hand to her arm, trying to imbue the touch with strength.

I wanted her to know I had her back.

Always.

No matter what.

"Well, I hated my family as much as you did."

Though she'd been translating for the others, afterward, Ghost scowled at her. "You can say that now—"

"No!" Lily barked, her tone sharper than I'd ever heard it. "You can think this is cajoling—"

"Don't think they even know what that means," Mav said wryly.

Lily glared at him, but carried on, "You can think what you like about my reasons for telling you this, but I'm telling you, whatever hatred you have for him, them, I share. My father killed my mother."

I froze. Whatever I'd expected her to say, it wasn't that.

"What?" I whispered, and she shot me a tortured look.

"He did. He pushed her down the stairs."

We'd all known her mom had a drinking problem...

"I know what you're thinking. He pushed her down the stairs and just told everyone she was drunk. I saw him do it."

In the background, the Ukrainian translation a hum that was like white noise, I saw Ghost and Amara start to fidget. Even Tatána's hate-filled scowl had lessened some. There was confusion now, like she was trying to judge whether or not Lily was lying.

"Why did he kill her?"

Amara. Well, Amara through Ghost.

Lily shot her a look. "He wanted her money. She was the rich one, and he wanted to control every aspect of her fortune."

Amara frowned after Ghost explained the situation to her. "You very rich?"

"Yes. My mom was incredibly rich. Old money. My dad wasn't. He came into it. We only just discovered how." She tipped her chin up. "For a very long time, he raped me." Her jaw worked, and I stared at her, taken aback by the confession, and even as everything inside me screamed for her, I saw Maverick's surprise, Ghost's and the other women's too.

"When you child?" Tatána asked quietly in broken English, before she whispered something to Amara in Ukrainian.

"Yes," she admitted. "And Luke used to do things in front of me too. He killed a maid once." She gulped, but her eyes were clear of tears, her face free of expression. "I know you want to hate me. I know you want to lump me in with them, but I'm not like them. I'm not saying I'm like you. I'm not saying that you weren't treated a thousand times worse, and I'm not even comparing my life with yours, because what they did to you was so heinous that I wish Giulia could kill Luke a thousand times over.

"And I wish like hell that the Sinners could get to my father, that they could set a thousand hungry dogs onto him and I could watch him be torn to pieces. I don't even tell you this so that you can feel sorry for me.

"I just don't want you to think I'm like them. I'm not. Please, don't think I am."

With that, with those torturous words uttered in a broken voice, she turned on her heel and started to walk out.

For a second, I was frozen, totally bewildered by what she'd said, then I was kickstarted into gear when she softly closed the door behind her.

Two thoughts hit me. One, I needed to go to her.

The second?

"She's as much of a survivor as you are, and if you can't see that, if you don't think she deserves more than to be labeled a Lancaster like her horrendous brother and father, then—" I blew out a breath, speechless, but before

I could get angry at their lack of reaction, forgetting that they probably didn't understand a damn word I'd said, I jumped into action. Pushing open the door, I rushed outside and found her leaning against the bunkhouse wall, the sobs she hadn't allowed herself to set free were now coming in waves.

Her cries, her misery, her heartache, tore at my walls until I didn't have any.

Until I vowed that we'd never have any secrets between us ever again.

Before she could say anything, argue or back off, I moved over to her, tipped her upright so she was no longer folded over, and forced her to let me hug her.

She was so tense, so taut, that it felt like she was brittle. Enough to shatter.

And suddenly, it all fit.

Why Link was so protective of her. Why they hadn't had sex. Why, when we'd been at the funeral and she'd been out in the open, the bikers had surrounded her like she was a precious treasure.

Not only was she that to Link, but she was as much of a victim as these women here—just as much of a survivor—and for people such as they? They needed to know they were protected.

Shielded.

I knew, point blank, that no one would ever touch Lily again.

No one.

Link would make sure of it.

And I was so thankful for that.

So fucking happy that the tears that poured from me were both a mixture of relief at that thought and an outpouring of misery too.

Misery for her.

"You should have told me," I whispered in her ear, and she sobbed even harder, clinging to me, her face damp against my throat, her body heaving against mine.

Everything inside me felt raw, cut open, because I wanted to heal her, but I knew I wasn't good enough to do that. Which meant I wasn't good enough to heal the women in the bunkhouse either...

What fucking use was I?

Christ.

I squeezed her tighter, needing her to know she was loved. That she was my sister, that we were in this together, and then, something insane happened.

People pressed around us.

Slim bodies, with too bony arms slipping around our waists, huddling into our sides.

Tears that belonged to neither of us dampened our clothes as the three women from the bunkhouse stepped into the light and embraced one of their own.

Because Lily was precisely that.

One of them.

And suddenly, I knew what a killing rage was, because if Donavan didn't die a miserable death? I knew my soul would never be at peace again.

THIRTEEN

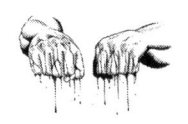

MAVERICK

I'D KNOWN. Sure I had. Link had told the council, but him telling us and seeing it in the flesh? Seeing the outpouring of hurt and misery and vulnerability?

Yeah, that was different.

Seeing Lily's suffering was night and day compared to Link sharing the minimal details to keep her privacy contained.

When the women went out to comfort her, after the sounds of her sobbing filled the small building, I knew they'd taken a giant leap forward.

But for me?

I wasn't sure what to do.

I really wasn't.

I knew what hatred was. I did. I knew what it felt like, knew how it could consume. But what I felt for Donavan Lancaster outweighed that.

I thought it even measured up to what Nyx felt for the sick fucks he slayed.

Because I was at a loss of what to do, how to think, what to feel, I reached for my cell phone.

I'd contacted Lodestar before, had tried to get her to come into the fold to help us out, and while she'd given us key information that was pivotal in getting Lancaster back on US soil, she'd gone AWOL shortly after.

I knew what she was like. She had projects that took her all over the country, projects that involved her doing illegal shit, that necessitated her becoming a ghost. Even if I wanted her to respond, I knew it wasn't always possible.

So, when I texted, I didn't expect a reply, even if I really fucking needed one.

Me: *Lode, I need your help. Please.*

I sure as fuck didn't expect her to answer almost immediately.

Lodestar: *Yeah. Sure. I'm on my way to the compound. I'll be there tomorrow. I need your help too.*

My brows rose at that. I'd never known her to need anyone's help.

Me: *What kind of help?*

Lodestar: *Somewhere to stay.*

Me: *What have you done?*

I mean, I didn't really care, but I needed to know what shitstorm she was bringing to our door so I could prepare Rex.

Lodestar: *Can't really talk about it on unsecure channels. I'll be bringing someone with me. Someone wanted.*

I frowned at her response, but I shrugged, because it was worth dealing with that to have access to someone of Lodestar's skills.

The truth was, I needed her to find Donavan Lancaster's exact location so we could work on the channels we owned to bring that bastard back to U.S. soil.

He needed to be here. Not so he could spend his life in jail, but so he could truly know what it felt like to hurt as he'd hurt his daughter, as he'd hurt my woman, and Tatána, Amara, and every other female he'd used and abused in his miserable life.

Lodestar: *That going to be a problem?*

Me: *No. But if you were heading this way anyway, you should have given me a heads-up.*

Lodestar: *Haha, yeah, because that's what I do on the regular, right?*

My lips twitched, even though nothing about this situation was funny.

Me: *True. You know you could normally crash here without any expectations, but the truth is, I want you to find someone for me. If you're down with that, you're welcome here for as long as you want.*

Lodestar: *Someone cool?*

Me: *Someone cool without a doubt.*

That was our codeword for someone who needed to die.

Lodestar: *Even more fun. See you tomorrow.*

Me: *I'll get one of the bunkhouses made up for you.*

Lodestar: *Thanks. Two beds.*

Mav: *Done.*

With that, I switched to Link's texts.

Me: *How far are you from home?*

That he saw my text straight off told me he was either at the other chapter's clubhouse or they were on the road and had stopped off for food.

Link: *We'll be setting off in the morning. We're done. Giulia got a little overzealous. Almost had the fire department on our asses.*

My lips twisted in amusement.

Me: *Knew Giulia would be a thirsty wench when it came down to it.*

Link: *Ha. She and Nyx sure know how to work together.*

I grinned at that understatement, but it slowly slid from my lips as I replied.

Me: *You need to know that Lily told the other women what she's been through with her dad.*

Link: *Fuck. You're kidding me.*

Me: *It's okay. Well, that sounds crazy, because nothing about this is okay. Still, Tiffany is with her. So are the other women. They're comforting her.*

Link: *That's a big change from yesterday. I can still hear Tatána's screeches in my ears.*

Me: *Yeah. But she broke down. I think they realized she's one of them.*

Link: *Fuck, I hate that.*

Me: *I know, man. Trust me. I do.*

Link: *Do you think I should grab a flight home?*

My eyes widened.

Me: *And leave your bike there?*

Link: *Can replace that shit. Can't replace her.*

I gnawed on my bottom lip, wondering what the right response was. I didn't want to interrupt the little powwow that was going on outside, because I knew from experience how healing something like that could be.

But I needed to know from the horse's mouth what she wanted.

Me: *Two minutes.*

I wheeled over to the door and saw just how much the women were clinging to each other.

It was enough to make me feel odd inside, because it was so genuine, honest, and earnest, and it made me wish that I'd had that when I was home from the sandbox.

Sure, I'd had my brothers, but the truth was, we were men. Men didn't do shit like this. That was why we needed a woman, a strong woman, at our side.

They gave us this.

They gave us the softness to counter the hard shit we came across in this life.

I wasn't sure how, considering I knew my wheels hadn't made a squeak, but Ghost's head popped up the second I was in the doorway.

She stared at me, and I stared back, and without saying a word, she did what she'd never done before.

She moved over to me, away from the hug that was going down a few feet from me, and plunked herself on my lap.

It could have been weird, because it was the first time she'd ever done that, but it wasn't. Why? Because she turned her face into my throat, curled into me, and started crying.

Instantly, my arms went around her, and I buried my face in her hair.

I felt my eyes prickle with tears. For her, for the others, for Lily. For my fucking self, selfish prick that I was.

I hugged her as tightly as she hugged me, aware this was the closest we'd ever been to each other.

The closest we might ever be.

The thought had resolve hitting me, and I knew that if Lodestar truly was on her way and didn't get diverted—a distinct possibility, especially since she knew I wanted a trade for her shelter now—that I'd have her doing something else.

Creating a past for Ghost.

Making a file for her, filling it with bullshit, anything to make it look like she deserved to be here. That she had the right to stay as my wife.

I wasn't sure how we'd do it, what we could use to make it happen, but there were ways and means. If anyone knew that, it was me. False certificates to make her look like she could work here and bring something to the country, maybe even a padded bank account so it seemed like she could support herself... Shit like that mattered to ICE.

I hugged her tight, and when my cell buzzed, I wanted to ignore it, but I knew what Link was like. He'd call if he thought something was wrong, and where his woman was concerned, nothing was right at the moment.

I muttered in her ear, "Do you think she needs Link?"

"He's in Ohio," Ghost whispered back, tears in her throat, making each word soggy.

"He said he'll fly back."

"But I thought your bikes were important to you."

"What has Giulia been telling you?"

She sniffled. "The truth?"

I grinned despite myself. "Not about marathons though, huh? Long runs, my ass."

When she slapped my shoulder teasingly, I knew we'd turned a corner, especially as she scoffed, "A long run is a marathon."

"Not in this world," I teased. "But yeah, when a man finds his Old Lady, one he'll brand and be happy about branding?" I hitched a shoulder. "Seems like he'll be willing to leave his bike behind."

I guessed it sounded pathetic, how important a bike could be to us, but that was the life. It was more than just two wheels. It represented freedom.

Peace.

It was our way of flying down the highway. Our hogs gave us wings.

Fuck, I missed mine. Some days, I missed it so badly that it was like a visceral ache, but I always discounted the misery it caused me to be without my ride by thinking about the truth of my situation.

Said situation, however, had changed.

I had Ghost now.

Even if it wasn't like Link and Nyx had their women.

I had her.

"Is marriage so different than being an Old Lady?" she inquired gently, and though I was no idiot in the brains department, I didn't need to be a genius to understand why she was asking.

"Yes," I answered her softly. "Being an Old Lady means more to the club."

"But not the government?"

"The club? The council? That is our government. They're the only laws we really listen to."

"So why did you marry me?"

"Because you need Uncle Sam on your side," I said wryly. "The club doesn't give a fuck if you're Ukrainian or from goddamn Saturn. So long as I want you, that's all they care about."

"Do you want me?" she asked quietly, so quietly that I almost didn't hear her.

"You know I do, Ghost," I whispered. "Wouldn't have wifed you if I didn't. And wouldn't be working hard to keep you here if that wasn't true."

I let my hand drift over her shoulders, and when she didn't flinch, when she didn't jerk away like she'd been scalded, I rested it against the small of her back, wanting her to feel the connection.

Figured she did, because she questioned, "What if I'm not—"

"You don't have to finish that sentence. We take this at your pace if you want that from me. I mean, that is, if you want that from me."

"I do. I want to be your wife," she admitted, stunning the shit out of me.

We'd never actually talked about this before. I'd just proposed because I wanted her to stay here, to be safe. I wanted her to know that she could speak out against that fucker who had hurt her and that she'd get justice.

But I wanted her.

Fuck, I did.

I wasn't sure why when she was an itty bit of a thing. All bones and blonde hair.

She needed more than she'd been eating, that was for sure. Ten thousand plus calories a day, more like, but she resembled a porcelain doll who was slowly turning into a real woman the more she was around me and Giulia, the more time she had to heal.

I wanted that real woman more than Geppetto had wanted Pinocchio to be a real boy.

Biting my lip at the thought, I muttered, "Then we'll take it one day at a time. Okay?"

Nodding, she whispered, "I'd like that."

My phone started ringing, spoiling the fucking moment, and the sound had the other women jolting in surprise.

When the song came on though, Lily was the one who peered at me.

"Link?"

I almost smiled that she'd figured it out. "Rough Sex" by Lords of Acid was the song we all set for Link.

Mostly because he was the Lord of Acid himself.

"Yeah."

"You told him?" she asked, mouth wobbling.

"Had to, Lily," I admitted sheepishly. "You're his Old Lady. I'd want to know if Ghost was hurting."

Ghost tensed on my lap, but I didn't look at her as she peered up at me with big, wide blue eyes.

Lily frowned but nodded. "You can tell him I'm okay."

"He wants to know if you want him to fly home?"

She reared back at that, her head almost thumping into the wall. "Really?"

I smiled at her. "Really."

Her brow puckered, but she maneuvered her way throughout the tangle of arms and bodies from the other women, and murmured, "Give me the phone, please?"

I passed it over to her, and she hit connect, "Baby, I'm okay."

When she wandered off some, I ignored her conversation, even though giving her my phone made me antsy, and instead, I looked at the group who was over by the wall, each of them looking wrecked.

"Are you going to talk to Tiffany?" I asked them all, but no one in particular though.

"I don't think I'm good enough to help," Tiffany whispered. "I mean, I can't...can I? How can I help?"

"You think we is hopeless?" Tatána inquired, her voice filled with sadness.

"No. I'm just not fully trained for this." Tiffany's voice was small, miserable. "I quit school. But I thought I could help, only I don't think I'm good enough for you. You deserve the best but—"

"You helped already," Amara interjected softly through Ghost's interpretation.

She shook her head. "No, Lily helped. I didn't do anything."

Tatána reached over, cupped her shoulder, and in broken English said, "Maybe we help all of us other, and you watch us over?"

She bit her lip. "I'd like that, if you would."

I shot Ghost a look, interested to see if she'd talk to Tiffany or not, but she wasn't focused on the conversation. Instead, I saw that she had a funny look on her face, one I could actually read, and I felt no compunction in admitting to her. "If I still had a bike, I'd leave it and take a flight home to you."

She sucked in a sharp breath at that, and enjoying that I'd confounded her, I grinned, then reached up and tapped the tip of her nose.

"Now, I have shit to do, ladies," I told them when I saw Lily was wandering back, my cell in her hand. "Can I leave you to play nice for an hour or two?"

They were all somber, all far too sorrowful, staring at me with soulful eyes, but they nodded, and though it might not seem like much, it actually felt like a big step forward.

The biggest step?

Getting Lodestar here, getting her to find that fucker so we could slay him.

Sinner style.

Fuck, that was a day I couldn't wait for.

FOURTEEN

SIN

LINK WAS antsy to get home, and I couldn't blame him.

He was fiddling with that fucking rosary of his like the damn thing wouldn't break, and if he jiggled his goddamn foot much more? I was going to kick it out from under him.

Still, for all that he was annoying me, I got it.

Fuck, I did. I wanted to get back home as much as he did.

"I know you want to get back," Rex was saying patiently, "but we still have things to tidy up here."

"The fire department looked the other way," I grumbled. "I don't see what the holdup is either."

Rex narrowed his eyes at me, but I scowled right back.

"I haven't seen my woman in a fuckuva long time. You bet your ass I want to be on her the second I'm home."

At my words, everyone in the office stilled, then Nyx turned to me with a raised brow, and muttered, "Shit. You're going to brand her, aren't you?"

"What about my statement made you think that?" I rumbled, my brow puckering as I stared at him with irritation.

"The fact that you just admitted you haven't boned anyone since you got here."

"I never said that," I countered.

"You pretty much did," Steel muttered, eying me up like I was a fucking alien or something.

Because I wasn't thinking straight, I ground out, "Just because I'm not stupid enough to let my woman get away from me for free pussy—"

Steel's eyes flashed. "Fuck you."

"No, thanks, don't know where the fuck you've been."

"Children!" Rex grated out. "I don't need this right now, do you hear me?"

I shrugged, but folded my arms across my waist. "It's not that fucking crazy that I might have found someone I actually like, is it?"

"She's pregnant, you want to brand her, and apparently haven't cheated on her since you got here months ago. That means the brother who'd fuck the bunnies at least three times a day has turned into someone completely different."

Nyx's words had me shrugging.

"You didn't touch a drop last night either," Link pointed out.

"So it's a crime for me to be a better man, is it?" I snapped.

"No," Rex murmured, his tone soothing, "but you have to deal with the fact that these guys are learning about all this in a very short space of time. They've gone from thinking you were a shithouse for leaving Giulia stranded to go and watch one of the strippers get naked, to suddenly becoming pope material."

I snorted at that. "Nothing about me is a pope. I'm still all sin."

Link pshawed. "Yeah, yeah."

That had me grinning, because even though I was a twisted fuck, I was among my own kind here. Sinners? There was a reason we'd made a family among our brothers. It was easy to do that when you were with people who were like you.

"We're traveling down tomorrow," Rex stated, steering the topic back to the one at hand. "We can't change that. Not when we have to clear up the mess we made last night."

"Not much of a mess considering the department is in our pocket."

"We left the chapter short a warehouse."

"The fucking thing didn't burn down," Nyx muttered.

"No, it just gutted it." Rex rolled his eyes. "We're here, and that's final. Anyway, I want to see if Butch needs ousting."

"He does," I confirmed. "He's lazy, doesn't get shit done, and I'm pretty sure Peggy has a hold on him that none of our council would appreciate."

Rex groaned at that. "What do you mean?"

"If Butch is too busy fucking, she'll order the guys around and they listen."

"That's not a crime," Steel reasoned. "Giulia does the same thing."

"When it comes to cleaning the fucking kitchen," I retorted. "I'm talking about runs. She knows about shipments and shit. What's in them, where they're going. Details we keep among the brothers. Hell, some of the council probably don't know as much as she does."

"You think she's acting in his stead?"

"Wouldn't be surprised. He's more interested in the sex and booze. Pretty sure he's got a coke habit."

"Fuck," Rex spat, and I knew why. Sinners weren't allowed to sample the wares.

It was the number one rule.

Fuck who you wanted, drink how much you needed, but drugs? Nope. Back the fuck away, or take off your cut and get another job.

Link groaned. "Fuck, we'll be staying longer if we need to find another Prez."

"What about Storm?" Nyx suggested softly.

I blinked at that, surprised by the proposal. "Storm's *our* VP."

"Shit job he's doing of that when he's soaking himself in drink and pussy like he's waiting on his funeral."

"He's been like that since Keira left," Link agreed. "But I don't know if it would be wise to bring him down here."

"Might be good to give him the option. Rex, your hold on the Sinners is absolute. His job is pretty much unnecessary unless you're on a run, and you don't do that anymore. Not much anyway. This is a one off, let's face it."

Rex rubbed a hand over his chin. "Fuck, this is a big deal, Nyx. I mean, shit, he'd be leaving his woman and baby girl behind."

"Like he isn't doing that already?" Nyx shrugged. "I'm just saying it's an option. He's a good man when he isn't being a fuckwit."

"Does anyone know what happened between him and Keira?" I asked.

"By the sounds of it, one of the bunnies told her that she gave Storm a BJ while she was pregnant," Nyx muttered.

Rex grunted. "Fucking dumbass."

Yeah.

Dumbass was the word.

That was the trouble when the women weren't in the life. They didn't get how it worked sometimes. I mean, it didn't work like that for everyone. Giulia would have Nyx's dick on a platter before she shared it, and he was a possessive fuck anyway. He'd kept things to one bitch at a time for as long as I'd known him.

Link?

I mean, I'd assume he'd be loyal to Lily, especially as he was antsy as fuck to get back to her now. Like, I'd never seen him be that way with anyone else, so I figured it must be love.

And for me?

Well, I hadn't fucked anything, not even my fucking fist unless Tiff had talked me off over the phone since I'd come over here.

Maybe I was made like Nyx.

I'd been loyal to my ex. She'd been the one who cheated on my ass, something I only found out when I got back from deployment. And since then, I'd never been committed to anyone. But they were right. I might not have said the words, but I'd be branding Tiff.

Whether she liked the idea or not.

Rex scratched his jaw where stubble had gathered, then muttered, "Wonder if I could get them all to come down here together. Fresh start?"

"Could set things in motion. Might pull his head out of his ass actually having to work, you know?" Nyx mused, and I knew why too. Nyx was the only one who could talk Rex into shit. Not even Storm could do that.

The two were tight.

But more than that, they trusted each other and had the other's back. I'd noticed it before, but because I was, essentially, in a council meeting where I'd never had that before, I hadn't seen it.

Church was different.

That was the council telling the brothers what was going down. Sure, we had some say in shit, could vote on certain matters, but most things were pre-decided by the council for the good of the club.

"I don't think that's fair," Steel muttered. "Storm does a lot at the chop shop and for the strip joint."

"Getting drunk and watching pussy strip ain't good for our business. Still," Nyx mused, "ain't saying he's a shit VP. If anything, he's the opposite. He's too good to waste as Rex's VP, especially when there's a position opening up here."

"There's time," I pointed out. "Butch and Peggy aren't running the place into the ground."

"Not yet. If he's high as a fucking kite, though, then things will change soon. There's always a fine line between a hobby and addiction."

"He's functioning, is all I'm saying. If you want to put things in motion, then the option's there."

Rex eyed me, staring at me like I had shit on my face or something.

"What is it?"

"If Storm takes the job, there'd be a position on the council."

"No shit," I replied drolly.

"Before this fuck up with Giulia, I'd have thought you'd be a good fit for it. Especially since you had stopped drinking so much."

"Shit-faced ass," Steel muttered, and I flipped him the bird.

"Fuck you," I retorted, but there wasn't much heat to the words. He was right. I'd been soaking my liver in tequila. Still, I cut Nyx a look, and he wasn't glaring at Rex for the suggestion, neither was there death in his eyes when he looked at me.

"You'd have a problem with that?"

"No."

One word.

Never let it be said that Nyx was prone to rambling.

I looked at Rex. "If you think I could—"

Rex pursed his lips. "Nyx would be promoted to VP. He's pretty much that anyway. You worked with him on security. Would make sense for you to take his place as Enforcer."

Despite myself, my throat choked at that. "You being serious?" I'd never have expected to come out of this with a promotion, but fuck, this was insane.

"Yeah, I'm being serious, but only if Storm agrees to be Prez down here." Rex tapped his fingers against the shitty desk chair. "I can't see it myself. He's too fucking lazy to move, but we'll see."

"It would be a solution. Needs to be someone from our club to keep things in control here."

"You want the role?" Rex asked Nyx, his tone serious.

He shook his head. "I'm no Prez."

Rex pulled a face. "No. You're too fucking headstrong with this war you're fighting." He sighed as he pinched the bridge of his nose. "Steel, what about you?"

He arched a brow. "Me?"

"Yeah, only one fucker called Steel."

"If Storm doesn't want the job, I'll think about it, but I think he'll take it. The fucker isn't happy, and he's being a dick right now, but he's a good brother. Maybe this is the kick in the ass the bastard needs."

Everyone nodded, because he wasn't blowing smoke up our asses. He meant it.

And it was the truth.

Storm had been a good brother before he'd fucked up his life.

Sometimes, in our world, it was easier to think you could have the cake and eat it too.

He had a wife at home, a kid, then he thought he could fuck whoever he wanted without there being any repercussions?

He'd learned otherwise, but the shitty thing was, he'd messed it up for his kid as well.

More than anything, that pissed me off.

I knew what it felt like to come from a broken home. It sucked, and when it was unnecessary? It sucked even more.

"Okay, at least I know what I'm doing. Once I've smoothed shit over with Butch and helped him figure out how to patch things up at the warehouse, we'll ride tomorrow. Be ready. It might be in the early hours. Fucking hate this place and those goddamn bunkbeds."

Nyx snorted. "You should have tossed Butch out of his room."

"What, and wake up with Peggy's mouth around my dick?" Rex shuddered. "No thanks."

I laughed. "She's been sniffing around you something fierce."

"Shame I've never wanted to fuck a barracuda."

Link chuckled at that. "We all know that's bullshit."

Rex frowned. "Huh?"

"Rachel." He arched a brow. "She's a barracuda."

Rex huffed, but his eyes turned thoughtful. "You're right. Never thought of her that way though."

"Yeah, well, it's a day for firsts," Nyx said dryly, and fuck if he wasn't wrong.

FIFTEEN

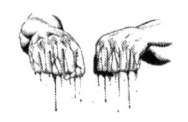

SIN

"MOTHERFUCKER."

The word slipped from me the second I rounded the corner into the kitchen and found Butch in there with a clubwhore.

Dray was pretty cool, all round, but the fact that she was sniffing the shit on the table while Butch boned her was a fucking no-no.

And that Butch was condoning it? That he'd probably bought it for her?

Fuck.

I scrubbed a hand over the back of my neck, and for the first time, I was unsure what to do.

I'd seen Butch sniffing marching powder up his nose before, wiping away white trails on his nose, but that was *before*. I was uncertain of my place here. I had to fit in.

I had no place in this chapter, and with my future on the line, Tiff's too, I'd been unable to say shit.

Now?

I was potentially going to be the Enforcer for the NJ chapter of the Satan's Sinners.

Enforcers didn't hide around fucking corners wondering what the fuck they should do.

Nyx wouldn't hesitate to smash the bastard's skull into the table, and while I definitely wasn't as insane as Nyx, I'd earned my name for a reason.

"The fuck are you doing?" I snapped, striding into the room.

Dray squealed, and the straw she had up her nose went flying, as did a lot of the powder. Her wail was neither orgasmic nor in surprise at her being caught—it was outright distress at the powder's flight.

Butch shot me a grin, and from his eyes alone, I saw he was high.

The dumbfuck knew the rules. Christ, it wasn't like there were many.

No drugs.

Mostly because it fucked with business. We were a hedonistic bunch. It wasn't often we were denied anything pleasurable, but drugs? Caused shit.

Plus, Bear had put the rule in place back when his VP had gotten hooked on meth. It had sent the fucker loopy. Could still remember Prince shoving the barrel of his fucking gun into his mouth and blowing his brains out—not just because it had been a disaster for the club, but because I'd been a Prospect at the time and I'd had to clean his fucking brains up off the floor.

I grabbed Butch by the back of the neck and shoved him down into the table. As his head collided with it, he growled at me, "What the fuck?"

He shoved Dray aside, and she went flying onto her knees, then he turned to me, dick out and flopping in the breeze, his fists raised.

One hit to the nose, and he went flying, joining Dray not only on the ground, but in a sprawl. He fell onto her, their heads colliding, knocking her out. He was out for the count seconds later, and that had nothing to do with the cocaine he'd been snorting.

A whistle sounded from behind me. "Long time since I've seen you do that."

I cut Rex an irritated look, since it was clear he'd been watching me, waiting for me to act. "You could have waded in. I have no rank here."

His grin was dry. "Wanted to see what you'd do. Can't have my Enforcers pussying out on situations like this one, can I?"

My nostrils flared. "I'm not your Enforcer."

"Not yet." He sniffed as he peered down at the Prez. "Ain't looking like Storm has that much of a choice now, is it?" He wandered over to Butch, kicked his foot. "Was looking for him anyway."

"Why?"

"Peggy."

The name had me snickering, but he shook his head at my amusement. "She's been a bad girl."

"You gonna spank her?" I joked.

"No, she'd like that. You're gonna do it for me." The menace on his face told me he wasn't asking me to cheat on my woman for that skank.

My mouth dropped open, and unease slid around my veins like a snake hopped up on Red Bull. "I don't hurt bitches."

"She ain't a bitch."

Brows lifting at that, I cut a look at Butch. "If Peggy's a he, then Butch will be the one who'll want to slice and dice—"

"No," Rex interrupted, rolling his eyes. "She's snatch, devious snatch at that."

I arched a brow. "Spit it out. I don't hurt snatch unless—"

"The bitch is a traitor. And we all know that traitors have no gender."

"The fuck did she do?" I rasped, anger starting to filter into me, overtaking the unease. We all loathed traitors, but Old Ladies who betrayed the club earned a special place in hell.

"Maverick went digging after I told him what you said—that Butch is a junkie."

"What did he find?"

"A fucker that was trashed by the Five Points for snitching with the *Famiglia*—"

"Jonny O'Byrne?"

Rex's brows lowered. "How do you know that?"

"Mary Catherine told me." I shrugged. "Her mother told her O'Byrne had gone missing." I grunted at his look, knowing what he was thinking. Wanting to avoid that particular minefield, I groused, "She told me about O'Byrne."

Rex frowned. "Why would she do a thing like that?" he asked as he waded over to where Butch and Dray were snoring on the floor like they'd just finished fucking instead of the rude disruption they'd both had.

"Because I knew him."

"How?"

"He was in my class." The fucker had been a prick back then too. My lips twitched. "He used to bully me."

Rex's eyes widened as he lowered himself beside Butch and rolled him onto his side so he could access his pockets. "He used to bully you?"

"I was a lot smaller. Barely fucking ate. You saw the state of me when I landed at the Sinners' compound back then."

His mouth grew taut. "Fucking bitch of a mother."

"Yeah. I'm not so small anymore."

"Not so much," he said with a laugh.

"The fuck are you doing?" I questioned, as I watched him start to rifle through the other Prez's pockets.

"Looking for his wallet. Sure as shit ain't groping the ugly fuck."

I snickered as I leaned back against the wall. "Go on. You were talking about Jonny O'Byrne."

Rex hummed. "Guess what Peggy's surname is."

Irritation washed through me. "Motherfucker."

"Yeah."

"How related are they? I don't remember him having an older sister at school."

"Cousins." He cut me a look. "We both know what we'll do for family."

My nostrils flared at that, but I just said, "What did she do?"

He wafted a hand. "Betrayed us. Fucking traitor." When he finally grabbed Butch's wallet, he opened it as he got to his feet and shoved shit on the table. "And this fucker let her get away with it."

"You think he was involved?"

"He had to be."

"What did she do?"

"Mav got into her phone, read her text messages. Jonny would ask her to pass on messages to Sinners in the local prison. You remember last year when that big bust went down in Cincinnati?"

"The gun haul?"

He dipped his chin. "*Famiglia*."

"The haul or the reason it was busted?"

"Haul. Twenty of their men were dumped in the local penitentiary. *Famiglia* has been using O'Byrne as a go-between, getting their men perks on the inside. Easing shit for them until they can get home. Through Sinners who were instructed to protect them by fucking Peggy."

My brows lowered. "You have to be shitting me. Guns? Crossing state lines? They were in there for the long term."

Rex's mouth turned into a sneer. "Exactly. A budding long-term, long-distance relationship. All without my or the council's sanction."

As he flipped through the guy's wallet, he muttered, "I just wish Maverick had found all this shit out before we had our little church earlier."

"Why?"

Rex smirked at me. "So everyone could catch a glimpse of Butch's pencil dick."

I snickered, then walked over to the downed man. Kicking him onto his front to hide said pencil dick, I looked over at Rex as he commented, "That had to feel good."

"What?" I asked warily.

"Getting back to your roots."

That had me wincing. "I don't like my roots."

"You can't avoid what you are." Rex cocked a brow. "We both know that."

"Which makes me the son of a slut and a motherfucker? Yeah, great."

Rex sniffed. "You know I'm talking about the fighting."

"Ain't you always where we're concerned."

"Fucking waste," was all he said.

"I'm too old for that shit now."

"Maybe on the circuit, but not for the MC. You've been wasting yourself as a lackey. About time you rose through the ranks. Just fucked up this is how you had to go about it."

"You're only saying this because—"

"What? Favoritism?" Rex sniffed. "Yeah, you don't know me at all if that's the case. You're a fucking strong brother. Your loyalty to the MC is without question. I think that's what made shit hard on Nyx. Aside from the boozing, you never let the club down. That means a lot."

I shrugged. "Had to defend my woman."

"Yeah, I got that back then, and I get it now. But still, you were sneaky about it."

"I had my reasons."

"Don't we all." Rex pursed his lips, evidently pissed at how unforthcoming I was being.

He'd never understand why I'd done what I had, never get it because I'd never say a word—he was right where that was concerned.

Even though I'd been spawned from two disloyal cunts, I was loyal to my core.

Rex, surprising me, grabbed his knife from the holster on his shoulder, then wandered over to Butch, crouched at his side, then proceeded to dig it in Butch's throat at the same time as he grabbed the bastard's head and dragged his head back.

Butch came awake with a squawk.

"Put your cock away. We have business to discuss."

Butch's movements were slow. From my hit, from the drugs in his system, but also because he was a slow fucker anyway. How the hell he'd made Prez here, I'd never know. This chapter had voted him in though, and Rex was pretty democratic—for a knife-wielding autocrat.

When Butch finally shoved his dick away, Rex ordered, "Punch him again."

I obeyed, smashing the fucker's head back into the tiled floor with enough of a bounce that his mouth dropped open wide as he fell into unconsciousness again.

"You woke him just to make him put his dick away?" I inquired wryly.

"You're the one who's about to carry the fucker to the bunkhouse. Be grateful I'm so thoughtful."

I snorted. "Thoughtful? The fucker weighs over two hundred pounds."

"You telling me you've gone soft since the last time I saw you?"

I shifted out of the crouch. Kicking Butch into place, I leaned down and hauled him over my shoulder in a fireman's hold.

"You always were built like a bull."

"You say the sweetest things," I mocked.

"It's a gift," Rex retorted dryly.

He opened doors for me, steering me out of the ramshackle clubhouse that made our place back in West Orange look like a palace.

When we veered outside, striding toward the bunkhouse where our chapter was staying, we passed no one. Not a single fucking soul. And even though most brothers got up late, the ones who didn't have regular jobs at MC owned businesses at any rate, four in the afternoon was late for us.

"The fuck is going on in this place?" Rex growled. "Where is everyone?"

"They all have jobs."

"Jobs?" He scowled at me. "For the MC?"

"No. For other places. Lots of garages, some factory work."

"What the hell? Why?"

"No money coming in."

Rex's nostrils flared. "That does it. Storm ain't got a say in it. He's coming down and sorting this shit out."

"Why?"

"Because if the funds are low, so fucking low that brothers are having to go out to work—then why are the accounts that Butch sends me showing that the MC is ticking over?"

And that was a question I couldn't answer.

Rex's mouth turned down at the corners as he stared at the fucker on my shoulder. "He'll give us some answers before the dumbfuck finally does something useful with his life."

I cut him a look. "Feeds some pigs?"

Rex scowled ahead. "Exactly."

SIXTEEN

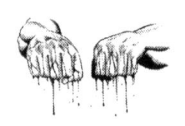

TIFFANY

ME: *I miss you.*
    Sin: *I never thought you'd admit to that.*
    Me: *Why?*
    Sin: *You're pretty close-mouthed when you want to be.*
    Me: *Ha, says you.*
    Sin: *Yeah, I guess that's calling the kettle black.*
    Me: *Ya think?*
    Sin: *Okay, okay, I admit it. I think we need to work on that though.*
    Me: *You're probably right.*
    Sin: *No probably about it. You didn't tell me about your dad, angel. That's bad.*
    Me: *I know. I'm sorry.*
    Sin: *Why didn't you? Didn't you think I'd care?*
    Me: *Fuck, I don't even know. Not really.*
    Sin: *Yeah, if you think I'm going to accept that bullshit answer, you really do need to remember what it's like with me.*
    Me: *What? That you take no bullshit?*
    Sin: *Lol, yeah. See, you do remember.*
    Me: *I remember you're a pain in my ass.*
    Me: *Figuratively and literally.*
    Sin: *I can't wait to fuck your ass again, babe.*
    Me: *I can't either actually. Ooh, what have you done to me?*
    Sin: *Aside from destroying that bubble butt for good?*

Me: *LMAO. I can still shit with it.*

Sin: *Good to know rofl.*

Me: *You're never, and I mean, ever, shoving pool balls up there though. Hard pass.*

Sin: *Pool balls?*

Me: *Yeah. Don't pretend like you didn't see the same shit I did at the party where we met.*

Sin: *Ohhhh. Yeah, I remember. One of the clubwhores...*

Me: *Exactly. My rectum is a pool ball free zone.*

Sin: *I can deal with that lol.*

Sin: *TBH*

Me: *TBH...?*

Me: *TBH, what? You can't go all silent on me now.*

Sin: *Sure I can! After what you pulled? I can play that card for years.*

Me: *:P I have ways of making you talk, remember?*

Sin: *Lol, send me a picture of your pussy. I can't wait to taste it. That'll get me to open my mouth.*

Me: *Fuck. Don't talk about my pussy until you're in the room and can get me off.*

Sin: *Tired of your hand, baby?*

Me: *I can almost hear you rumbling that in my ear.*

Sin: *If I was there, you'd hear a fuckuva lot more than that.*

Me: *Christ, I'd love that.*

Sin: *Me fucking too.*

Me: *How long until you're home?*

Sin: *Should be tomorrow.*

Me: *Good. Phew.*

Sin: *Should have been back today, but we had club business to sort out.*

Me: *I'm going to learn to hate those two words, aren't I?*

Sin: *Club business? Maybe. I'll use them a lot. But...and it's a big but, I can't imagine your daddy sharing all the nitty gritty of his work.*

Me: *No, but if I'd been a boy, he probably would have.*

Sin: *So glad you don't have a dick, angel.*

Me: *LOL. Me too!*

Sin: *It's not that great being a man. Sure, the whole pissing standing up thing is kinda cool.*

Me: *Kind of cool? Penises are so much more sensible than vaginas. Especially if you like concerts.*

Sin: *Porta potties are shit whether you stand up or squat.*

Me: *Fuck you. I might dare you to squat over a porta potty the next time we're near one, and you can see how gross they are.*

Sin: *You dare me, I'll have no choice but to accept the dare.*

Me: *I like a man who stands by his word.*

Sin: *That's why you've liked me since that first night.*

Me: *I certainly felt something.*

Sin: *More than you expected?*

Me: *I think we both know the answer to that.*

Sin: *How do you feel about the baby?*

Me: *It's unexpected, and I'm pretty sure I'm going to be a shit mom, but fuck, I can only try to be the best I can be, right?*

Sin: *You go in with that attitude, then totally. That's all anyone can ask. I think every expectant mom and dad thinks they're going to be shit. We just have to try to be better.*

Me: *Look at us, acting like adults.*

Sin: *We kind of have to, babe. You're pregnant.*

Me: *No shit.*

Sin: *Lol. When's your first appointment?*

Me: *I could have gone today, but I waited.*

Sin: *Why?*

Me: *For you to come with me? I mean, I can rearrange it, but, I dunno. *shrugs**

Sin: *Thank you. <3*

Me: *Really?*

Sin: *Yeah. I didn't expect you to wait, if I'm honest.*

Me: *Why not?*

Sin: *I don't know. I figured you'd be one of those women who liked to do shit on their own.*

Me: *Maybe I would have before.*

Sin: *Your dad dying...it's opened up a door for us, hasn't it?*

Me: *I hate to admit it, but yes. He'd never have approved, and I don't know if I'd have been strong enough to go against him. Damn, that makes me sound like such a wimp.*

Sin: *It makes you sound young. In this world, you have to take what you want, Tiff. Don't let anyone hold you back. Including me.*

Me: *Including you?*

Sin: *Yeah. I mean that. You know how I feel about you.*

Me: *No. I don't. Not really.*

Sin: *You do. You just aren't ready to admit to it yet, and that's okay. When I'm back, things will change. But I'm not a dinosaur.*

Me: *You're pretty old. Lol.*

Sin: *But sexy with it?*

Me: *Evidently, or you wouldn't be my baby daddy.*

Sin: *Lol. True. Fuck, we're having a kid.*

Me: *Yeah, I keep having those moments.*

Me: *Sin?*

Sin: *Yeah.*

Me: *I promise...even if Dad was still alive, I wouldn't have had an abortion or anything.*

Sin: *Thank you.*

Me: *You don't have to thank me for that, yikes.*

Sin: *I don't think you realize how grateful I am that you told me that.*

Me: *Maybe not. But I mean it. I would never have done that. And I'd always have told you.*

Me: *It kinda puts things into perspective though.*

Sin: *How so?*

Me: *Well, my life would have changed whether or not things went down the way they had.*

Sin: *Explain.*

Me: *Daddy would have probably cut me off.*

Sin: *I don't think so. He loved you.*

Me: *Exactly. When people love you, they do weird things to protect you.*

Sin: *Sadly, that's true.*

Me: *I know. I'm so smart for my age.*

Sin: *Lol. Don't be bratty.*

Me: *But it's what I do best.*

Sin: *LMAO. You do a lot of things real well, angel. Not sure if being mature is your best life skill.*

Me: *Oooh, that sounds interesting.*

Sin: *Not as interesting as what you were saying. Carry on. I think you need to get this off your chest.*

Me: **sighs* I just mean...well, Daddy would have cut me off, Mom would have had a few tantrums with me because she wouldn't understand why I was doing what I was doing, and everything would have changed regardless of us losing it all or not.*

Me: *Honestly, I almost wish that was true. At least he'd be alive. At least I wouldn't be wondering if there was something I could have done to stop him from being so stupid. I can't believe he committed suicide.*

Sin: *I want you to stop thinking of it that way.*

Me: *Which way?*

Sin: *'Committed.' Like he was involved in a crime. He was obviously depressed, Tiff. Probably lost and scared.*

Me: *I think that's what I can't forgive. Was money that important to him? Did his reputation mean so much more to him than I did?*

Sin: *No, sweetheart. He loved you. That's all you have to remember.*

Me: *Easier said than done.*

Me: *I don't even have my degree, Sin. I know how things work, but even I'm at a loss. There's so much to becoming a psychologist. I was only at the start of my education.*

Sin: *Do you think you'll want to go back to school to get your degree? Maybe head in that direction?*

Me: *Is that an option?*

Me: *I mean, I'd kind of like that.*

Sin: *I can keep us well fed and with a roof over our head, Tiff. Not saying you could live like you did with your daddy, but we can have a good life.*

Me: *Really?*

Sin: *I might be in line for a promotion, and if I am, things will get better still. I might think about putting in an extension on the back of the house.*

Me: *Why? It's plenty big enough as it is.*

Sin: *In case we want two.*

Me: *Oh.*

Me: *Fuck.*

Me: *Really?*

Sin: *I told you a long time ago that you and me will never be nothing, Tiff.*

Sin: *Glad I'm coming back just to remind you of that.*

Me: *Thank you, Sin.*

Sin: *For what?*

Me: *Being you.*

SEVENTEEN

SIN

THE NEXT MORNING

TIFF: *Fuck.*
　Me: *Lol, what is it? It's early for you, isn't it?*
　Tiff: *I think this is what morning sickness feels like. Either that or I ate something bad last night.*
　Me: *What did you eat?*
　Tiff: *A sandwich. I wasn't very hungry. After the way things went down at the clubhouse? Yikes, no way was I ready to eat. I only had the sandwich because Lily said I had to.*
　Me: *She's going to be a tyrant through this pregnancy, isn't she?*
　Tiff: *Lol, yeah, I think so.*
　Tiff: *TBH, I'm going to let her be. Maybe if she uses me as a project, it will help her.*
　Tiff: *Did you know about her dad? Luke?*
　Me: *No, but I shot the shit with the guys last night. They kept me in the loop. I'm sorry, love.*
　Me: *I knew about the women, but not about what they did to her.*
　Tiff: *I'm ashamed of myself for not spotting the signs.*
　Me: *Don't be nuts. You weren't born a therapist.*
　Tiff: *She's my best friend. Christ, we're like sisters. But she was being abused for all that time, and I never picked up on it?*
　Me: *You were a kid for most of that time, angel. Stop being so hard on yourself.*
　Tiff: *Easier said than done.*

Me: *Ain't that the story of everyone's life.*

Tiff: *True.*

Me: *How did yesterday go, anyway? You wouldn't really talk about it last night.*

Tiff: *Badly. But good too.*

Tiff: *I never expected for Lily to admit what she did, but when she opened up? The others let her in. It was touching. Sad, but beautiful.*

Me: *I hate that fucker.*

Tiff: *Me too. I wish he was dead like Luke.*

Me: *It's something to think about.*

Tiff: *It is?*

Me: *You're in a whole other world now, babe. Just leave it to us.*

Tiff: *Shit. Right. Yeah.*

Me: *You scared?*

Tiff: *No.*

Tiff: *I just realized something is all.*

Me: *What?*

Tiff: *Our kid will be one of you.*

Me: *You will be soon too.*

Tiff: *I guess.*

Me: *Lol. Don't turn snooty on me now.*

Tiff: *I've seen what goes down in that bar, Sin.*

Me: *Can't judge the whole club on that. We're a family, you know that. We protect each other. That's what matters.*

Tiff: *You also fuck each other.*

Me: *Lol. Clubwhores are a different thing.*

Tiff: *Will you still sleep with them?*

Me: *I'm surprised you asked.*

Tiff: *Why?*

Me: *Because if you'd asked me and I was home already, I'd spank you for that.*

Tiff: *Oooh, did I make you mad?*

Me: *You know you did.*

Me: *Ain't fucked anyone since the last time I slid into that delicious cunt of yours.*

Tiff: *I really shouldn't like it when you get all gruff on me.*

Me: *Gruff's one way of phrasing it.*

Me: *Pissed is another.*

Tiff: *I'm sorry. I didn't mean to make you mad.*

Me: *No, you never do.*

Me: *I'm gonna go.*
Tiff: *No! Sin! Please don't.*

TWO HOURS later

ME: *I'm on the road. We should be back for three.*
Tiff: *Are you still mad at me?*
Me: *Disappointed.*
Me: *Did you fuck someone while I was gone?*
Tiff: *Holy shit! Is that why you're mad?*
Me: *Maybe. If you think I'm fucking anything that moves, maybe that's you projecting it onto me.*
Tiff: *Fuck that. I'm not a cheater.*
Me: *Neither the hell am I.*
Tiff: *You've gone to a place you might have been stuck in forever. I wasn't sure what was going on with us.*
Me: *I was always either going to get my ass home or bring you down here.*
Tiff: *What?!*
Me: *You read that right.*
Tiff: *Well, why the fuck didn't you tell me? Sin, I'm not the only one who's shit at communicating. You never said dick about me moving to Ohio.*
Me: *Because I didn't think you'd be open to the idea, but if my plans didn't work, I wouldn't have let you get away.*
Tiff: *Fuck, is it bad that I like that?*
Me: *Why is that bad?*
Tiff: *I'm supposed to be a feminist.*
Me: *Lol.*
Tiff: *It isn't funny!*
Me: *You want me to go caveman on you?*
Tiff: *Maybe. *gulps* What does that involve?*
Me: *Probably what you're already used to. My dick is so ready to slide home, angel.*
Tiff: *Oh.*
Tiff: *Shit.*
Tiff: *Why do you always say that kind of thing?*
Me: *That a complaint?*

Tiff: *No, but now I'm horny. And I thought you were mad at me, so my body's all restless.*

Me: *Lol. I'll settle your body the second I get back. And I WAS mad at you. Let's not beat around the fucking bush, angel.*

Tiff: *I'd never cheat on you.*

Tiff: *Ever.*

Tiff: *But my life, my world, is different than yours. Yours has women who'll service you and won't even care if you're married or not.*

Me: *I can't argue with that, because you're right, but it's down to each man to say no, isn't it?*

Tiff: *Yeah, it is.*

Tiff: *But you can't blame me for being nervous.*

Me: *Yeah, I can. If you think you're not special to me, then that's an issue. Like I said, I'll be home soon, and we can sort things out then.*

Tiff: *Should I be scared?*

Me: *Lol, your pussy should. My cock is aching something fierce.*

Tiff: *God, when will you get here?*

Me: *ASAP, doll.*

Tiff: *Thank fuck.*

Me: *I missed you.*

Tiff: *You already know I missed you. I did. I'm not good at talking about this stuff, but I'll get better with time. If you want to hear it that is.*

Me: *Of course I do.*

Me: *I have to go, the guys are calling me, but I want you to know something.*

Tiff: *Sure. What is it?*

Me: *I was married before. Back when I was new to the Forces. It didn't last.*

Tiff: *Oh. Christ. You were married?*

Tiff: *Why didn't it last?*

Me: *Got back from deployment, my first one, and she'd been cheating on me.*

Tiff: *Shit. Sorry, Sin. Even if I'm glad you're not with her anymore and you're mine.*

Me: *Does my heart good to know you think that way, angel.*

Tiff: *I won't do that to you. I'm not like that.*

Me: *I hope you're not.*

Me: *I don't intend on letting you get away from me, Tiff.*

Me: *But I won't be like Storm. He's a dumbass. Lost his woman and his kid over it, so I'm going to be straight up with you.*

Me: *If a clubwhore comes on to me? I'll tell you, because they're catty bitches and they'll share it either way. When I tell you, I don't want you fucking thinking about whether I'm telling the full truth or not. You hear me?*

Tiff: *I hear you.*

Me: *Good. I'll be honest with you, and I expect the same in return.*

Tiff: *You'll get that. But I don't think I have to worry. I'm dating a nasty biker. I think I have a big fat 'no entry' sign on my forehead coming my way.*

Me: *Lol. Yeah, but still, there's always a way to lie to people.*

Me: *I don't want that with you.*

Tiff: *I don't want that either.*

Tiff: *I'm sorry I made you worry.*

Me: *Yeah, you did. I thought you weren't like that—then you were weird this morning.*

Me: *I'll be so fucking glad when the only reason I have to text you is to ask you to pick up something from the store or to tell you when I'll be home.*

Me: *I want to be able to fucking look you in the eye when we talk about important shit.*

Tiff: *I suggested vid calls back in the day.*

Me: *No privacy. Not letting anyone catch a glimpse of you.*

Tiff: *You're a lot more possessive than I thought you were.*

Me: *That going to be a problem? If it is, say so now because I'm only just getting started.*

Tiff: *It's not a problem.*

Tiff: *But hurry home, yeah?*

Picture received

Me: *Fuck. I want those juices all over my fucking mouth.*

Me: *Get you hot thinking about me being all possessive over you?*

Tiff: *Yeah, it did. It really DOES.*

Tiff: *Sin?*

Me: *Yeah, baby.*

Tiff: *Be safe?*

Me: *Got someone to worry about and someone who worries about me now, angel. I'll always be safe.*

EIGHTEEN

LODESTAR

"KATINA, if you ask me one more time, I might scream."

She snickered. "Are we there yet?"

When I let out a holler that turned into a wail a banshee would be proud of, she started pissing herself.

Not literally.

Thank fuck she was past that phase.

There'd been a few times, right at the start when I'd fostered her, that she'd been a bed-wetter, but I was proud we were past those days. Phew. They'd been kinda gross.

Okay, more than that, they'd been a lot gross.

I wasn't sure what she'd expected though, way back then, but I thought someone might have hit her for pissing the bed. She'd been shaking when she'd woken me up to tell me, and that we'd gone from that to this?

Her laughing as I screamed in the car?

No lie, I thought I'd done a really fucking great job.

When she started slapping her knee, I stopped screaming and grinned at her when she let out a final hoot.

When she asked, "But, really, Star, when are we gonna get there?" I rolled my eyes, and she saw that plain as day because she was staring at me in the rearview mirror.

"I told you it was a long drive."

"Yeah, you did." She grimaced, then something had her perking up. "Can we really go to New York?"

"Yeah, not right away." As in, not this year, not with the fucking Irish Mob breathing down my neck, but she didn't need to know that—both the time or the reason why. I'd only just figured that shit out too. aCooooig for a username? The Acuig Corporation. Five Points... I'd bitten off more than I could chew for once. "We need to set up a base here first," I muttered, after I cleared my throat.

She squinted at me. "Are you in some kind of trouble?"

"Why do you say that?"

It was really hard not tugging at my shirt collar, because Christ, kids were better investigators than the cops.

They really got into the nitty gritty of shit, and when they scented blood, they never fucking let go.

I huffed out a sigh. "How can I be in trouble? I'm a virtual assistant."

She snickered. "Yeah, you keep on telling yourself that."

"Have you been snooping?"

"It's not snooping if you leave the computer on, is it?"

"I never do that, so you must have been snooping."

"Well, it was a bunch of letters and numbers and stuff." And stuff.

Malboge.

Ha.

She could be a better bloodhound than the FBI, but she couldn't read that level of coding.

Not yet, at any rate.

I peered at the odometer, the gas gauge, then the GPS, and told her, "We'll be there soon."

"Now you're answering?"

"Yeah, because we'll be there soon. Plus, we need to be there soon, because I can't afford to keep you with snacks on this trip."

She sniffed. "I haven't eaten that much."

"You've eaten me out of house and home."

"You can afford a Porsche, so I figure you can afford a few quesadillas here and there."

I grinned at her, loving that she never took any of my shit. "You're going to like it where we're going. They're your kind of people."

"They are? Who are my kind of people?" she inquired, frowning at me.

She was a pretty kid. All blonde hair, long arms, and short legs. I mean, she looked like an alien, kind of, but I figured when she grew into her limbs, she'd be cute.

As it stood, her face was doll-like, and I knew if I took her to Manhattan, some fucking model agency would pick her up and put her on their books.

She was that level of weird that designers liked on their catwalks.

I stared into her clear blue eyes and told her the truth. "They're good people. But they might have a few scars here and there, might utter one too many swear words, but they're friendly if you let them be."

That was a bit of a reach. But hell, the bikers were good with kids. I knew because they were a family, even if that family usually had parties that would make a Roman orgy look tame from time to time.

I mean, it wasn't like the kids were frickin' invited to those fuckfests.

Jeez.

"They might not like me," she mumbled.

"Of course they will. Just, ya know, don't be too honest with them."

"What do you mean?"

"I've already told you. You can't tell people if they have a zit. I mean, they have to know. It's their face, right?"

She sniffed. "If there's a big fat zit on someone's nose, I'm telling them. I think it'd be mean not to."

"Is it kind to make them feel embarrassed?"

"No, I guess not, but I'm trying to save them from embarrassment in the long run."

I sighed, because fuck, we'd had this conversation so many times. The kid wondered why she found it hard to make friends when she was so honest—it was painful to behold.

Like the other day, before the shit had hit the fan and we'd had to go AWOL, I'd worn a really nice pair of shorts and a great tee to take her out to the movie theater.

I went downstairs, headed for my bag, and she said the forbidden words: "Your butt looks big in those shorts."

Even now, I cringed at the memory.

I was used to her, though, so I hadn't been offended, and I'd told her, "My butt doesn't look big, it looks thick. Yes, there's a difference."

Shaking my head at the memory, I grinned when the GPS told me we were almost there.

For someone who was relatively smart, and a veritable genius with computers, I found it incredibly difficult to navigate. As in, I was terrible at it.

As in, I could get lost in a fucking supermarket.

So that the GPS was bleating at me to get off at this turn? I was a very happy bunny.

We'd taken three days to do the nine-hour journey because she kept getting car sick, and I was so tired of being on the move.

The trouble was, if she sat in the front seat, she didn't get sick. If she sat in the back, she did.

The last thing I needed was for us to get stopped by the cops considering, she was, ya know, technically kidnapped.

I mean, she didn't know that, but we weren't supposed to cross state lines without approval from her social worker, and I'd done more than cross the damn line, I'd gone over to the East Coast.

I figured there'd be all kinds of alerts on me by now, so I'd been taking back roads.

Worth it.

We were there, nearly home free. I'd had to burn another identity, but I wasn't about to let her go back into the system, not when it had fucked her around already.

When we made it down the road to the clubhouse, I saw the Prospect on the gate, and climbed out of the car when I pulled off to the side of the road.

"Stay here, this might take a while."

"Why?"

"Because I said so?"

"Yeah, that never works."

I turned around to look at her for real, instead of just in the rearview mirror, and muttered, "I need to speak with one of the guys."

"I can't believe we're going to a biker's clubhouse. This is so cool."

Yeah.

Cool.

I pulled a face. "You didn't tell anyone, did you?"

"What? That we crossed a gazillion state lines?" She was too smart for my good, and her smile told me that. "Yeah, I didn't tell anyone. Not that I have anyone to tell," she muttered.

"Well, we're going to work on that for the future, aren't we?"

She huffed. "I guess I can try."

"You'd better try. These guys are nice, doll, but they're not that nice where you can talk mean to them and tell them they look fat in their jeans."

She grinned, but when I just stared her down, she ducked her head. "Okay, I won't."

"Good. Even if you think it's going to hurt their self-esteem if someone else picks up on it before you, or teases them about it, you don't say anything, okay?"

Not until I could get her into some martial art classes or something where she could stop anyone from bitch slapping her.

"Okay," she muttered.

"What are you going to do now?" I questioned.

"Stay here and not get out of the car?"

"That's right."

Thinking I'd pinned her down, I walked off. When I strode over to the gate that was a boring, unpainted steel with straight up and down bars, I saw the Prospect wander over to the middle, his eyes on my legs, which were as thick as my butt.

He didn't care that they were, from the looks of the grin he shot my way.

I grinned back, then greeted, "Hey!"

"Hey," he rumbled, and I'd admit, he was a cutie pie, and I'd totally have boned him if I was his age.

But that ship had long since sailed. He looked to be about twenty-three, and while he'd be a nice sojourn, I didn't intend to fuck up the sanctuary I was bringing Katina and me to by fucking some dude and making shit awkward.

I had a kid to think of now.

I was a momma. Sort of.

I mean, I didn't tell her to drink milk and shit, but I did tell her to do her homework, so I figured that had to count.

Right?

"I'm looking for someone."

His brow arched. "Me? I've been waiting all my life for you."

I grinned. "Does that ever work?"

His wink told me that it didn't. "Sometimes."

"Wellll, in this case, no, not you. Maverick? He's on the council. I need to speak with him. He agreed to let me stay here a while."

His brows rose at that, and I knew I'd told him a lot of information that very few would know.

Maverick was a ghost too. Had been ever since he'd returned from overseas. Most people weren't even sure if he'd survived the blast that had stuck him in a wheelchair, and truth be told, I was one of the people who'd worked hard to bury his identity, because I was a good friend like that.

He pulled out a cell phone and told me, even though he couched it as a question, "Just give me a second?"

"Of course."

I watched as he wandered up the driveway, talking on his phone as I checked out his ass.

"He's cute."

"Thought I told you to stay in the car. How do you even know what cute is anyway?" She was eight, for God's sake.

"I know what cute is because I have eyes." She tutted. "And he went away, so I can come and talk to you."

"The theory being that you'll dash away the second he comes back?" I snorted—like that was going to happen. "You think I was born yesterday?"

She beamed up at me. "Yes, because you're soooo beautiful."

"And I look that young, huh?"

"You totally do."

I curved an arm around her shoulders. "You're precocious, you know that, right?"

She hummed. "I prefer the term 'blunt.'"

"Precocious," I repeated.

When the Prospect, who I recognized as such because he was wearing a cut with a Prospect patch on it—I was a smart bitch sometimes—turned back around and saw me with her, he froze. But when he came back to life again, he moved over to the gate and opened it up for me.

"Thanks!" I called out, even as I returned to the car with Kat at my side.

When she hopped in the front seat—I didn't tell her off because there was no point now—I slowly crawled up the driveway, being careful because it was tight and my Porsche was wide, and there were little white pebbles that lined the strip of asphalt.

The sight amused me, even if it was actually practical. I'd noticed this shit about a lot of MCs. The women tended to pretty up the compound without the men really even noticing, so it meant that there was really girly shit going down, and the guys didn't say jack because it just floated over their head.

I'd learned a lot from the Old Ladies I'd come across in my time.

It was better to do than to ask, because if you asked, you could be refused. Mostly, whatever you were asking your man for wouldn't even register in their minds, so what was the point in chancing a refusal in the first place?

There was an MC down in Texas where the Prez's Old Lady wasn't in charge—God forbid that in a 'man's' world—but she definitely held sway. There were all kinds of pretty shit in the compound. A kind of gazebo thing, a firepit, lots of flowers and stuff.

It wasn't to my taste, but it certainly made the grim buildings the compounds usually consisted of look less like a prison camp, and boy, did some of them need *Queer Eye* to make these places presentable.

When we rolled past the pebbles that had been painted white—by someone who deserved a medal, because that must have been boring as hell—I parked up in front of the building.

It wasn't as ugly as most, but it sure as fuck wasn't pretty. Looked like something Stephen King would write about, and because King would find it suitable, I liked how gritty it was.

I was, however, glad we wouldn't be staying inside it. Mav had said as much on the phone yesterday when we'd texted one another, but I had confirmation because the man himself was outside the front door, waiting on us.

When we climbed out of the car, he arched a brow at the sight of the kid with me. I knew when I'd told him I was bringing a guest, the last thing he expected was for that guest to be a child.

My lips twitched as his jaw dropped before he started glaring at Kat like he fucking hated her or something.

For a second, I wasn't sure what the hell was going on with him. Mav knew how to hide his expression, for fuck's sake. And as far as I knew, he'd never had any problems with kids before.

Of course, that was before he'd almost had his dick blown off—

"How can a kid be wanted?"

I tipped my chin up, guilt hitting me because I was bringing a lot of shit to their door if the cops came looking for her. "I took her out of a bad situation."

His mouth narrowed, before, softly, he asked her, "Is your name Katina?"

It was my turn for me to gape. "How the fuck did you know that?" I scowled at him just as hard, just as mean, before I demanded, "Kat, get back in the car." When, of course, the little shit didn't obey, I moved so I was between her and my ex brother-in-arms, and snarled, "Have you been spying on me, you fucker?"

"No," he stated grimly, "I've been looking for her too. So I know she's in the foster system in fucking Ohio. What the hell have you done, Lodestar?"

I lurched back, prompting Kat to stumble and huff as she fought her way around me. "You've been looking for Kat? Why?" As far as I knew, she hadn't even been lost...not until I took her away from Ohio, I mean.

"Her sister asked me to find her," he said, and Kat whispered brokenly, "Star?"

When she huddled into me, her body turning as tiny as her voice, I glared at him harder.

Kat was vulnerable, delicate. Sure, she was getting stronger, and her attitude was twice her body weight, but fuck, this was not the way to go about shit.

"This is just cruel," I snapped at him. "I've been on the hunt for Alessa ever since Kat came into my life."

He blinked. "How did she?"

"You said it yourself—she was in the foster system." I tipped my chin up. "I decided it was time to become a mom."

His eyes flared wide at that, but not with amusement or surprise, just outright horror. "Star, if anyone wasn't made to be a mom, it's you. Do you remember to feed her and shit?"

"I'm not a dog," Kat said with a sniff, sounding more like her ballsy self.

He wriggled his shoulders. "Christ, this is not going down how I thought it would." He reached up, pinched the bridge of his nose, and muttered, "Katina? I'm sorry. I should have introduced myself better, but you look so much like Ghost, I mean, your sister Alessa, that it's crazy."

"Ghost?" I echoed with a frown.

"Yeah, it's her nickname."

"Some fucking nickname. Bet Link picked it."

Mav chuckled. "You'd be right."

"Always was a charmer." I sucked in my cheeks. "Anyway, care to share?"

He raised his hand and stunned me by waggling his fingers, revealing a wedding band. A goddamn wedding band. "Ghost's my wife."

I gaped at him again. "Shut the front door."

His grin was a combination of wicked and sheepish. "It's true."

Christ, did Ghost know what the fuck she was getting herself into?

Mav was into...

Well.

Okay, I didn't know, exactly, but there'd always been rumors about him in our unit.

Fuck.

And Ghost had to be fragile too. Could a woman who'd been bought and sold like a piece of meat at a market be anything but?

Still, I knew the years had changed Mav. He'd not only matured, thanks to the passing of time, but as a person, being injured, going through his PTSD, and dealing with his agoraphobia, it had altered him.

I hoped for Ghost's sake that it was for the better.

"This is surreal," I muttered gruffly. "I don't like coincidences."

"Maybe it's destiny," Kat murmured, staring at Mav with wide eyes. I tensed at the word, and tensed even more when she whispered, "That's why we came here, Star. Everything had to happen the exact way it did, or we wouldn't be here."

"Why did you come here?" Mav inquired, head tilted to the side as he rolled toward us.

The sneaky fucker—those goddamn wheels of his were quieter than soft soles.

I eyed him as he moved toward us like he was on a chariot or something, and muttered, "Need to lay low for a while."

"You've put Kat in danger?"

I stiffened, but what could I say? His tone made me want to punch him in the fucking face, but also, he wasn't wrong.

I had put us both in danger.

For myself, I could deal with that. I was used to living in hot water. My feet were pretty much made of asbestos now or something. I was so used to it, they could feel the flicker of a flame but never be burned.

I was even more used to being on the run.

But with a kid? Shit was different. I mean, she definitely cramped my style, but it was worth it.

I loved the little shit.

Sure, she gave me crap, but fuck, with her, I wasn't lonely.

And Mav could go suck his own cock.

I was a good mom.

Not a very responsible one, but I was good.

She'd stopped pissing the bed, hadn't she? That wasn't because I'd waved a magic wand.

"I've been on the hunt for Alessa," I told him. "Might have ruffled a few feathers along the way."

He dipped his chin. "Makes sense." Mav cut Kat a soft look. "Sorry if I scared you before, Kat, I didn't mean to. It just came as a massive surprise."

She ducked her head, and shyly whispered, "I bet."

"Would you like to meet your sister?"

That had her peering over at him. "I haven't spoken to her in years."

Years.

Fuck.

That was how long Ghost had been locked away.

It still messed with my mind.

Apparently, it messed with Mav's too, because his eyes nearly bugged out at that. "Years?"

She shrugged. "Yes. Do you think she'll like me? I've changed a lot."

Squeezing her arm, I told her, "She's going to fucking love you, kid.

You're awesome. Just don't tell her she's got a zit or anything, and you're good."

I ignored Mav's confused look, enjoying Kat's little nervous giggle. I was used to soothing her though, and fuck...

Would she not need me now that she had her sister?

Christ, this was not going down how I thought it would.

This was all that fucker aCooooig's fault.

I'd gotten us into the shit with the Five fucking Points to find Kat's sister, but as much as I hunted her down, I felt like I'd never find her.

It was worse than a needle in a haystack—it was a goddamn nightmare. Especially as every folder I seemed to open revealed more home truths that would take years to dig through.

So, for all that to have been in vain, but to be here and to have found her? As easy as this?

Christ, maybe Kat wasn't wrong. Maybe it was fate.

"C-Can I wash up first?" Kat requested timidly, sounding the exact opposite of her usual self. "I don't want her to see me all messy from the drive."

"Why not? That's how you usually roll, kid," I teased her.

She shoved me in the side, making me laugh. "I do not look messy all the time."

"No, just most of it." I stuck my tongue in my cheek when she huffed, and as I cast a glance at Mav, I could see him analyzing us both.

It pissed me off. Enough that I glared at him, which only had him smirking at me.

"Sure, but you know she's going to be so happy to see you whether you're messy or not, right?"

Well, that was a good answer, so I didn't need to stick a whoopee cushion on his wheelchair seat the next time he got out of the damn thing.

Coyly, Kat smiled at him, so I got us moving. Moving back to the trunk of the SUV, I grabbed our bags—my one, her four, kids and all the shit they carried, man—and dumped one with her for her to pull. The other I tossed at Maverick, which he caught and stacked on his lap. The other two I rolled along as well when he started to wheel over to the bunkhouses.

This place didn't get better for keeping, but Christ if I wasn't glad things had turned out the way they had.

Everything happens for a reason...or so they said. I just didn't want to think about what the next step was, because losing Kat?

Wasn't just going to suck, it was going to hurt.

Really fucking badly.

NINETEEN

TIFFANY

"GHOST?"

When I peered over my shoulder at the doorway, spotting Maverick sitting there, I arched a brow at him in surprise.

For the second day, he'd left us alone to talk things through, and while we hadn't particularly made massive progress into anything particularly therapeutic, per se, I actually felt like it was more important they just get used to us. My professor called it 'building a rapport.' Getting to the hard stuff would take weeks. With their pasts? Maybe months.

I hadn't been bullshitting yesterday, I meant it when I'd told Lily that they didn't have to like us. Active, strong emotions, be they negative or positive, were healthier than apathy.

But still, in this instance, having properly spoken to them all now, I got the feeling they'd do better with us on a friendlier scale.

Just looking at how they'd brought Lily into the fray was good for both her soul and mine, I thought.

She wasn't on the outside looking in. If anything, I was. She was seated between Amara and Ghost, and Tatána, with Ghost's running translation, would glower at me if I asked her anything that made her tense, even if it was something as simple as my asking her if she wanted to tell us anything about her abusers.

I'd tried to help today, just to dip my toes in the water, but had been rebuffed several times. I figured it was a learning curve, one I was happy to take, one I was happy to adjust to suit them and their needs.

But Mav's face?

I got the feeling he was about to fuck with my best laid plans.

He looked nervous.

Kind of...anxious actually. More than nerves were at play. Which from a man like him? Put me on edge.

Ghost, who apparently had extrasensory hearing to go with her name, had already turned to look at the door before Mav had even gotten a word out, and was frowning at her husband.

"What is it?"

He gnawed on the inside of his cheek a second, then muttered, "It's good news."

"What is?" She half stood up. "News about Donavan Lancaster?"

He raised a hand. "No. About your sister."

She gaped at him. "Katina? What about her?"

"It's a fucking coincidence is what it is," he muttered, rubbing the back of his neck, "but she's here."

"Here?" Ghost reared back in surprise. Couldn't really blame her. Since yesterday, I hadn't picked up on that much from her, but she'd told us her reason for trying to come to the States. "In West Orange?"

"No. Here as in here at the compound."

She raised a shaky hand to her mouth. "No. Don't tease me."

"Since when do I tease you?" he rumbled, his eyes darkening. "She wants to see you, Ghost, but she's nervous."

Ghost gnawed on her bottom lip. "She won't want to see me looking like this." Her hands settled under her so she was sitting on them, but it was clear to anyone with eyes that she was gripping onto the chair like that would glue her to it.

Maverick's face softened. "Oh, sweetheart, she said the exact same thing. She'd just been on this long ass drive, and she looked ragged around the edges. She wanted to look her best for you."

Ghost gulped, and her eyes started to water. That was all I saw before she ducked her chin and hid her face behind her hair. "I-I don't want her to see me like this."

"Like what?" I asked softly. "Looking beautiful?"

Because she was. Even if she had a few scars on her face, on her wrists, and even more hidden beneath her baggy clothes, she was gorgeous.

With bone structure that any model would be jealous of, and the biggest eyes that made her look like some kind of pixie, especially with her short hair.

All the women had that, and I knew it was because they'd had to have their hair shorn.

I mean, I didn't know all the details of their situation, but it figured they'd had lice or something living in their hair.

But still, she was beautiful.

And I needed to make sure she knew that.

"If she knew what you'd been through, all she'd see was that you're a survivor," I whispered gently, hurting for her and wishing I could make things better.

"I'm not a survivor. I just let them do—"

"You didn't have a choice. Sometimes surviving means making a decision that will keep you alive. We're not all fighters. We're not all born to take charge of a fight and dominate it. Sometimes, we just have to bide our time and wait. You did that. You're here, you're alive, and Luke isn't. Donavan Lancaster, when he's caught, will be in jail for the rest of his life. No, he won't be in similar conditions as you were, but he'll suffer too."

Ghost shook her head. "I don't want her to know about that."

"She won't. She doesn't," Maverick inserted. "I asked the woman with her."

"Woman?" Ghost repeated. "Who's with her?"

"Her foster mom." He shrugged. "She was coming here to visit with us because we need her help, but she brought her kid with her. Turns out it's Katina. The second I saw her in the flesh, I knew she was your sister. She looks just like you." His eyes pretty much had hearts in them as he stared at her.

I wasn't sure if he even knew how much he mooned over Ghost, and I shot Lily a look to see if she picked up on that, and from the rueful twist of her lips, she saw it too.

Maybe Amara and Tatána did as well.

The only one who didn't?

Ghost.

Fucking typical.

Why was that always the way? Why did everyone else see how someone felt about us, while we were totally blind to it?

The rumble of motorbikes slalomed into being behind us, and Lily and I tensed up—all day, bikers had been coming and going from the clubhouse, as was their way, but we were waiting.

Link and Sin were supposed to be coming back, and I knew we were both more than ready to see them. Especially after our texts. I wasn't sure if he was still mad at me, and I didn't want him to be. I wanted to just... God, I wanted nothing more than to be in his arms. No artifice, no playing around.

Just us.

Earnest.

Honest.

Real.

For the first time in forever.

The notion sent chills down my spine and made me want him here even more than I already had, which was saying something.

Still, my responsibility was to these women. They needed me, and I wasn't going anywhere until they were ready to quit for the day.

We weren't doing like group sessions or a therapy circle, mostly we were just talking, and I was trying to get them to open up.

Yesterday and today had been eye-openers though. Learning the little they'd shared was enough to give me a nightmare for the rest of my life.

It blew my mind how I'd eaten at the same table with Luke and Donavan. How my parents had dinner parties with him, how our families had been in business with one another.

I'd never thought they were capable of doing what I'd learned, and yet, these women were living proof of it.

Worse still, I'd never picked up on him forcing himself on Lily.

What kind of fucking therapist was I?

Jesus, no wonder I'd thought it best to pull out of school.

Fuck.

I mean, I'd known she didn't like him. That she thought he was a control freak, but I'd always just thought she let him do that.

If my daddy told me to eat a certain breakfast, I'd have told him where to get lost.

Lily had always seemed so cowed...but I'd never imagined it was for the exact reason it was.

Guilt hit me, as it kept on doing whenever I thought about how long I'd known her and her family, and how I'd failed her as a friend.

She didn't look at me with hatred though. She didn't hold it against me. If anything, she was still supporting me. Still thinking nothing of allowing me and my mother to live with her, even though Mom was being a royal pain.

I reached up and tugged at my bottom lip as Lily whispered, "Link told me he was looking for Katina. Seems a shame that you asked him to find her and she's found now, but you don't want to see her."

"I do want to," Ghost snapped, for the first time raising her voice. "But I don't want her to see me as this..." She released a shaky breath. "She's too young to know, she can't possibly understand—"

"Say you sick," Amara suggested, and because she was a woman of few words, even when Ghost was translating, we all turned to her in surprise. "What?" she questioned uneasily. "Is only suggestion."

Ghost gnawed on her lip. "Maybe. I could say I was ill, that would work for how thin I am."

Mav scowled at that. "I don't like it. Feels like you're wishing shit on yourself—"

"She was ill for a while," Lily reasoned. "I know the club was concerned about you pulling through after they found you."

Ghost wriggled her shoulders. "No, I like it. I think it will work."

"Will you see her then?" I questioned gently.

"Yes, if I can tell her..." She reached up and gingerly touched her head. "Maybe she won't think anything of it. Maybe she'll think it's fashion or something." No one answered, because we knew she was talking to herself. Something that was confirmed when she got to her feet without waiting on us to say anything and walked over to Mav. "Will you take me to her, please?"

He reached for her hand. "Of course."

I watched as she squeezed his fingers before she muttered, "Can I push you?"

I'd never seen anyone push Mav. He always did it himself. He didn't have a motor or anything on it, just his hands on the wheels.

His arms bunched up, and I could see on his face that he didn't want to, but he mumbled, "Sure."

Ghost blew out a relieved breath, and I figured she was wanting to do something with her hands, wanted to focus on something else.

Her nerves filtered through the room, making it cloying with just how anxious she was—pretty much a parallel to how Maverick had been when he'd wheeled himself into the room.

As they walked away without a backward glance, we stared at them, all four of us watching them leave.

"I hope go well," Tatána rasped.

"Me too."

"*Tak.*"

"I do too."

We all shared the sentiment, even as we turned back to each other.

The bunkhouse was small, made up of grody furnishings that'd been new back in the sixties or seventies, but the pieces, while ugly, were comfortable. I was sitting on a weird leather armchair, Tatána and Amara were on a sofa that Tatána usually slept on, and Ghost and Lily had been on one of the dining room table chairs.

I wouldn't say we were lounging. If anything, it looked like a strange AA meeting, but we were starting to gel, and I was glad for that.

Maybe I'd never be able to help them fully, but I could do something by just trying to get them to open up.

Had to have faith, right?

Although, without the main translator here, that was going to be damn hard. I knew they understood *some* of what I said, but if I asked anything complicated, they just stared at me blankly.

And by complicated I meant more than a single question with a few words.

Amara cleared her throat. "Men back."

I frowned at that. "How do you know?" The room had no window in it, but even though it was stupid, her words had me itching to get up and go look for Sin.

She shifted her shoulders. "I heard bikes." Her accent was so dense it was hard to understand her. "Link bike. When arrive, bike make noise." She whistled, mimicking the sound.

Lily frowned. "A whistle?"

Amara nodded. "Yes. Small." She whistled again.

"I'd best tell him, because I think hogs are supposed to roar not whistle," she commented wryly, making me laugh.

That they babied their bikes was a given, and we shared a sheepish grin, because somehow, we'd stopped being with guys from the country club who jacked off to thoughts of Lamborghinis and Ferraris, and were now with anal-retentive fools who spit polished their bikes for fun.

"We're not done here," I pointed out when Lily went to stand up.

Tatána mumbled, "Tired. Need sleep."

Frowning, I asked, "Are you sure? We can stay." We wouldn't accomplish much with a language barrier that was deeper than the Mariana Trench, but I didn't want them to think we were cutting and running the second our men showed up.

"Giulia home." Her eyes lit up, before she shrugged. "Food. Eat."

Amara's eagerness was pathetic to behold—not for the food, but for the fact she wanted to see Giulia but couldn't admit to it.

Sorrow filled me, as did a surge of sympathy. "I'll get her to come and visit with you when we see her."

Amara perked up, her eyes still gleaming. "Thank you."

I nodded as I got to my feet, and though I wanted to dart off like Lily did, I couldn't.

Wouldn't.

I needed to take this slowly.

I hadn't seen him in months.

Fuck, but it felt longer than that.

As I rounded the bunkhouse, which looked out onto the fields around the clubhouse, not onto the building itself, I made it to the driveway where a cluster of bikes were indeed gathered together.

I registered Sin's bright black beast instantly. It had black and silver flames licking the body, which made it gleam like it was a mirror or something.

Lily was already with Link, her legs around his waist and her butt in his hands as he stared up at her.

They were both laughing, and the sight of them together did something to me. Relief and hope swirled about inside me as I hoped, for her sake, that Link could help heal her wounds.

He seemed like a good man, like good people, even though I knew, to decent society, he wasn't, and maybe that was what Lily needed.

Someone with dark edges, but whose soul could fit hers. Like two jigsaw pieces, no?

I bit my lip as I cast a look over Rex and Nyx and Steel, noticed Giulia was missing, then I found him.

He was turned away from me, talking to Nyx.

He was tall. Fuck, when had that happened? I mean, I knew he was, but seeing him standing by all those super tall, hot guys rammed home just how big he was.

It seemed like he'd been working out in his absence too, because he was larger than before. His cut kind of looked small, and the back seam definitely strained. Oh man, he was like looking at trouble with a capital T.

But he was mine.

And the kid in my belly?

His.

A shaky breath escaped me, and it was so stupid to feel so nervous that I felt pretty much like a dick, but my emotions were all over the place. The last time I'd seen him, things had been normal.

Now?

My world was upside down, and the only thing that was stable was him.

He represented far more to me than he could ever know.

My dad was gone, my mom was being weird, my world was on its ass, and we had debts coming out of us worse than bad lobster at a fish restaurant.

I was grief-stricken, pregnant, trying to help women who'd been held captive, and my best friend had just admitted that, for years, she'd been sexually abused and psychologically tortured by her family.

In that moment?

I totally understood Lily's mindset.

And while I wasn't her, while I wasn't exuberant, and while Sin wasn't used to me doing shit like this because I was terrible at the whole PDA thing, I could no more stop myself from running over to him than I could stop the tears from pricking my eyes at the sight of him.

Link saw me, said something, and Sin twisted around to face me. When he did, his eyes turned dark, stormy, and he moved forward, not as fast, but we collided.

And it was like the Big Bang happened.

He grabbed me hard, hard enough to hurt, his arms around me like fucking concrete as he held me against him. My legs were up around his waist after I leaped at him, and he clung to me as much as I clung to him. I gripped him tightly even as our mouths smashed together in homecoming. He had a beard that tickled the heck out of me, and normally, I'd have complained, but God, I didn't even care. It just felt so good to have his lips on mine.

I pulled away, mumbling, "So glad you're home early."

His groan as I kissed him again sent need soaring through me, hitting me in the stomach with a force that was close to painful. Enough to hurt. But in the best possible way. I sank into him, knowing he'd hold me, that he'd support me, that he'd always have my back, because he was that kind of guy.

He was a sequoia. Timeless, endless, his roots deep, his calm eternal.

I needed that.

More than I ever imagined needing a man this much.

When he thrust his tongue into my mouth, the move surprised me, because it was such an act of claiming in front of his brothers that I almost tensed before I had no alternative but to melt into him.

Seemed like we were tearing down the shroud of secrecy in one fell swoop, and I didn't have it in me to be sad about that.

Daddy was gone. Mom was in another universe. If I wanted to be with a biker? Who was going to judge me?

The people who were supposed to be close? The family and friends who hadn't attended my father's funeral?

Yeah, fuck them.

I wanted Sin more than I wanted anything, more than I'd *ever* wanted anything.

He was mine.

And I was going to take him.

TWENTY

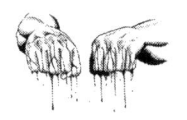

SIN

THE FEEL of her fucked with my head.

I was gone for her. So fucking gone that I was only just realizing it.

I knew, without a shadow of a doubt now, that if this crap with Faudreaux hadn't worked, I'd have hauled her ass down to Ohio, because there was no way in fuck I could have been without her longer.

Call me pussy whipped or call me a man who recognized solid gold when he found it, I wasn't going to let go of her.

I wasn't.

And it had nothing to do with the baby in her belly. If anything, that made me happy. I was nearly fucking forty. If there was ever a time to have a kid, it was now.

Never thought I'd be having it with a woman who was twenty-three, but my dick was smart. Probably the smartest thing about me.

It had seen her, scented her out, and knew prime pussy when it saw it.

My lips twitched at the thought, because I knew she'd slap me if she realized I was thinking crap like that, but fuck, it was heaven to be around someone who wouldn't take my shit anymore.

I squeezed her as I kissed her, loving the feel of her in my arms, before I tore my mouth from hers and ground out, "You ready to go home?"

"W-What?" she stuttered.

She flickered her gaze to the others, but I tutted and said, "Nope, you know what I'm talking about."

"Your place?"

I shook my head, not only at the words but her shy tone. Fuck, what had happened to my woman since I was gone?

Tiff wasn't shy.

She was loud, proud, and fucking dangerous to know.

Of course, dangerous in the real world was a relative thing.

On the scale of danger, I was a ten and she was a one, but that mouth on her? Always unpredictable.

"Our place," I rasped, suddenly glad I'd invested in the property because that meant my kid could grow up in that old house with the woods in the yard and all that land to roam in. He'd have everything I didn't—space, freedom, parents who gave a fuck. Now that I was back, he'd be safe here in the town, and my rep would precede him in several states around us.

Fuck, I needed to brand her.

I needed to make sure she was safe too.

Being the club's Enforcer meant a pay rise, plus a higher taking of our hauls, but to be honest, that came with a shit ton of more danger too.

I wasn't averse to that. It was no more danger than I'd been in back when I was deployed, but the truth was, I needed it. If Storm was languishing by having no real role in the club because Rex was Type A with the Sinners, then so was I.

I was goal oriented and a hard worker. There was a reason it'd been easy to drown my problems in the bottle.

It was something to do.

Until she'd come along.

I didn't think she knew how much she'd changed my life without even trying.

It had all happened so smoothly.

From a one-nighter to a few hookups to becoming a regular thing.

I wasn't even sure how it had happened.

Couldn't pinpoint the moment when, suddenly, I'd wanted to wake up with her hair in my face in the morning, blunt razors on the vanity because she'd used them on her legs, and weird froufrou vegetarian shit in my refrigerator because that was what she liked.

She pulled back to nip my bottom lip, then as her fingers entangled in the beard that was on its way out now that I was back with her, muttered, "Do you still have a room here?"

That she was as desperate for this as I was shouldn't have come as a surprise. She kept up with me like the sleek ride she was, but the notion of fucking her here?

Man, the possessive bastard in me didn't like the idea of anyone hearing her come, but they'd know whom she belonged to.

And the clubwhores?

They might figure out I was taken without shit getting nasty.

So, without another word, I grabbed a firmer hold on her ass, and ignored my brothers as they howled at me with laughter.

Rex called out, "Your room is still empty. Good fucking thing, huh?"

I didn't reply, just carried on kissing my woman, moving down to her throat so I could look over her shoulder and suck on her hotspots as we moved. Last thing I needed was for us to go flying over the doorjamb or tripping up.

When I was inside, there were some cheers and jeers at what we were doing, but she didn't shy away from it, which surprised me.

I knew how private she could be.

Did this mean something to her?

Was it her way of staking a claim in a place that mattered to me?

I shouldn't have liked that as much as I fucking did.

My dick hardened even more within the tight confines of my jeans, and she moaned, rocking her hips back and forth against its thickness as we maneuvered up the stairs toward my room.

When I pinned her against the wall on the upper landing, she reached up and stuck her tongue in my mouth. I almost choked on how good it felt, then as she tongue fucked me, I ground into her, loving how she turned to goo in my arms.

"Need you inside me," she rumbled, pulling back to pant the words against my lips.

"Nowhere else I want to be, angel," I rasped, knowing my eyes were dark and hard in response to the soft light in hers.

She melted against me even more, confirming what I already knew—her feelings were deep.

I just needed to work on making her at ease with them.

She'd had a weird relationship with her family, but fuck if I could judge. Mine was the weirdest out there.

I hitched her up again, loving how her sleek legs clung to me, then moved us down the hall to where I slept.

When I peered inside, I was glad to see that all my shit was still in there.

Had Rex put it all back or had things just never been moved?

I'd have thought Nyx would trash it all, so it made me wonder if he'd had Prospects move stuff around.

Either way, I didn't care, was just grateful everything was pretty much where I'd left it.

The notion of taking her in that bed didn't sit well with me.

I'd fucked a lot of bitches on that mattress, and she wasn't a bitch.

She was going to be my Old Lady as well as the mother of my kid.

I wasn't sure if she knew what I was thinking, but she muttered, "I need you to fuck me, Sin."

My eyes flared wide at her words.

"I need you to make me scream, I need every fucking bitch in this clubhouse to know you're taken. Do you hear me?"

My tongue felt thick in my mouth. "I hear you."

"After this, we'll burn the bed," she told me, the words hoarse as she peered into my eyes. "But fuck if we'll do that yet. I need you."

"I need you too, angel," I whispered, then I pinned her to the wall again, only this time, I urged her legs to slide down so she was standing on her own feet.

When she was, she leaned back against the wall as I reached for her pants—neat little shorts that covered her to mid-thigh and not the butt hugging stuff she tended to wear around my place. I fiddled with the button and muttered, "Ain't never seen this pair before."

"I'm trying to be professional with the women," she answered.

"I like them. Secretary chic."

That had her snickering. "Better than the short shorts?"

"Time and a place, angel," I told her with a grin, as I slipped my hand down the front of her shorts. When I twisted my arm so I could rub the front of her panties, I groaned at how wet she was.

"All this for me?" I demanded.

"Only for you," she whispered back with a depth that stunned me.

I stared into her eyes and saw emotions she'd never let me see before.

She was all over the place. Mostly, I could see that. She'd lost weight, her cheeks were gaunt, and when she'd hurled herself at me, I'd noticed she looked a bit haunted. Kind of like she'd expected A, B, and C from her dealings with the women, but was getting G, F, and Z.

Considering what she was discussing with them, what she'd learned from Lily, and how her father had died? I thought she was holding up well.

But seeing her staring up at me? I knew she'd changed.

For the better.

She'd always been guarded before, but something had flipped the switch.

I could never be happy about how that had happened, but it relieved me that I wasn't going to have to go full caveman on her ass like I'd warned in our last texts.

I slipped my pointer finger over her panty-clad folds, and muttered, "This is my cunt, isn't it?"

She gulped.

I knew she had a fondness for that word. Got her engines revving faster than my hog started up.

"Y-Yeah, it's yours."

"Say the word," I purred. Knowing that got her even hotter.

She sounded like her tongue had turned into a slug or something in her mouth as she mumbled, "My cunt is yours."

"I want all those fucking juices drowning me," I grated out, the words harder than my touch.

She reached up and set her arms on my shoulders even as she dug her chest into mine. "I want your cock inside me. I've been dreaming about it."

"You get yourself off?"

"Not many times. Usually when I talked with you on the phone."

That had me grinning at her. "Good answer." I tapped her clit, happy when she made a keening sound like I'd been rubbing her off for minutes instead of seconds. "No more touching this little cunt without me around, hmm?"

She licked her lips. "What if I'm horny?"

"Then you ask me to suck you off. I'm more than willing."

Her pupils turned to pinpricks. "What if I fingered myself in front of you?"

"I'd be agreeable to that kind of show."

She sighed. "I like that you don't want me to be a doll."

"No. I definitely don't. I like you to be what you are—all woman."

She bit her bottom lip. "It feels good being able to be myself again. You only want me to be me. I like that." She rubbed herself against me like a cat would before her arms slipped tighter around my neck and she whispered against my mouth, "My cunt feels empty, Sin."

I pressed a quick peck to her mouth. "Not for long." I put pressure on her clit before I murmured, "Stand up straight so I can get you nekkid."

She snorted, but did as bid, slumping against the wall like she was drunk or something.

I slid my hand out of her fly, reached up and sucked my fingers clean, our gazes connected all the while, grabbed her pants, and dragged them and her panties down at the same time.

Then I moved to her blouse. Another prim little thing with a faint pinstripe, and I began to unbutton it. When I saw she wasn't wearing a bra, I arched a brow.

She had big tits, and though she'd go bra free at my place, she didn't leave the house without them.

"You said you were coming home today," she admitted with no shame.

I grinned as I cupped the heavy weights in my palm. Fuck, I'd missed these.

"Gonna titty fuck you at some point tonight."

"So long as you get me off first, I don't give a shit," she muttered with a moan as I fondled the peaks of her nipples, and her answer had me holding back a laugh.

When I eyed her body, looking for changes, I'd admit to being disappointed when I didn't see any.

Her tits weren't bigger, she didn't even have a pooch or anything like that.

Then, I gently pinched her nipple, and when her face pulsed with pain, I realized why.

Reaching down, I laved said nipple in apology, and her hands tore through my hair, gripping me there, keeping me in place.

"Sensitive, hmm?" I mumbled against the bud, laughing when she arched into me the harder I sucked.

A squeak escaped her, telling me it was borderline painful, but after I jammed my thigh between hers and she started riding it, I grinned and carried on sucking.

When she screamed, I didn't stop, and neither did she. Her hips rode me faster than a bucking horse, until, out of nowhere, she went limp in my arms.

Brows high, I pulled back and saw how her face was slack.

"Well, that's a fucking first," I muttered under my breath, as I saw she'd passed out.

Fuck. I didn't even know women could do that, and especially not from having their nipples sucked.

Humming, feeling stupidly proud of myself, I picked her up and moved around the room to the side where there was an armchair, which I placed her on.

The space was simple. TV on the wall, table underneath it. A bed, two nightstands, two odd lamps on them, and then two dressers for my shit. I kept most of my stuff at my house, but I had some games here and shit tucked in the dresser for when I was bored.

Moving over to one of them which had, once upon a time, contained sheets, and thankfully still did, I made the bed.

It'd been a long time since I'd made a bed. The clubwhores tended to do that, even in the other chapter, so it took me longer than it should have, but by the time I was done, I twisted around and saw she was watching me.

Her legs spread.

Her fingers between her fucking thighs.

Tongue cleaving to the roof of my mouth, I had to smirk because she was a little fucker.

"Thought I said no touching yourself."

"You never said anything about me not being able to do it when you're in the room."

"In the room and watching," I clarified.

She shrugged and hitched one leg on the side of the armchair, revealing a cunt I'd been dreaming about for months.

She sank back into it and began to finger fuck herself.

My jaw tightened to the point of pain as I started to strip out of my jeans before dumping my cut and Henley on the ground after I'd toed off my boots.

She carried on teasing me, and I regretted putting sheets on the fucking bed—that was what I got for being a gentleman.

The second I was naked, I strode over to her, fist on my dick as I whacked off a few times.

The tip was wet, seeping pre-cum, and when I was close enough, she moved forward, sitting up, and took the tip between her lips.

She sucked me clean, sucked me off some, but I knew I'd blow my load way too quickly if I let her play. Just the feel of her was manna, but to know she'd carry on was a mind fuck.

I grabbed a handful of her hair, pulled her head back, and muttered, "Another time. Gonna come too fast as it is."

She smirked at me, and I wanted to fuck her until she was too exhausted to smirk again. But...

"You okay?" I asked, concern hitting me when I thought about her passing out.

"Little sleepy."

"You've never done that before."

Her gaze quickly cut to the wall beside the door where she'd just exploded into unconsciousness. "Time for firsts, I guess. Not going to complain. That was intense."

I hummed, reached down, and hitched my hands under her arms until I could drag her into a standing position.

She moved, flowing into me like she was a dancer and we'd been training together for years.

How had I only known her for less than four months?

It felt unreal, impossible. One moment, I'd never known her, the next? She'd been at a party, watching me. Watching me do stuff I was ashamed she'd seen, because if I'd seen her doing stuff like that, I knew I'd never get the image out of my head.

That she might feel the same way actually pissed me off and made me want to make amends.

I just wasn't sure how.

The only way I thought I could do so was to make my claim on her so fucking evident that everyone knew to back the fuck off me in future.

Sure, I was trading a lifetime of varied pussy for just the one, but she was worth it.

Why have a sample of middling cunts when you had a platinum snatch waiting for you at home?

I moved us back, holding her close as I flopped onto the bed.

When she crawled over me, her cunt instantly settling atop my dick, I knew she was as hungry for me as I was for her.

She didn't even fucking wait.

No more foreplay, nada. Just grabbed my cock, slipped the tip inside her, and rolled her hips down until we were joined.

When she'd stopped panting, and my eyes were uncrossed, she rested her hands on my shoulders and muttered, "I thought you'd be angry about the baby."

That brought me down to Earth with a bang.

I placed a hand on her stomach. "Why?"

"Thought you'd think I'd trapped you. I didn't. I did everything I was supposed to do."

Jerking a shoulder, I told her, "And the kid still came to be. That tells us something."

"It does?"

"That she's going to be a pain in the ass."

Her eyes softened. "What if it's a boy?"

"Then we'll butt heads."

She grinned. "You'll do that if she's a girl too."

"Yeah." I swallowed. "Never thought I'd be a dad."

"Why?"

"Made sure of it. Never trusted no bitch before."

"You trust me?" she breathed.

"You're not a bitch," I corrected her softly, well aware she didn't like it when I used those kinds of words.

I had me a feminist on my hands, and while that was absolutely fucking hysterical, I wasn't about to piss her off when my dick was in pussy heaven.

"You gonna ride me or talk me off?" I demanded.

"I can do both." She grinned at me, then whispered, "When you'd call me and you'd ask me to talk about stuff to get off, I'd lie there and I'd finger fuck myself."

"I know you did. I heard."

"Didn't know I always took those calls with a butt plug in though, did you?"

Eyes flashing, I reared up at that. We both moaned at the change in position, but I was the first to come down from it, and I spread her ass cheeks apart and fingered her rosette. "You like it?"

"Loved it," she said thickly. "I'd fuck myself with my finger, and with the other hand, I'd fuck myself with that."

"You know I'm going to want to see that, don't you?"

Her pussy fluttered around me. "Figured as much."

"Fuck, now I want to fuck you there," I complained.

"You can. Later," she promised, her eyes wicked. Then she hitched herself higher and began to ride me.

Giving me exactly what I needed, feeding her own fire too.

She let her head fall back as she started to rock harder, faster. Her hands came up, one to cup my shoulder, the other to grab a firm hold of her tit.

The second she did?

Fuck, it was like she detonated.

I wasn't sure if tits were always that sensitive, but she'd been tender there before. I'd never been able to gnaw on them without her squirming under me—in a bad way. Now? It was like night and day.

I groaned as her cunt tightened around me, literally sucking the cum from my balls. I wasn't about to complain either.

Fuck.

She ground down on me again, then screamed when I sucked her other nipple between my lips.

Her orgasm was loud, hard, and fast. It fucked with my head how quick she was to explode, and even as I wanted to carry on, to ride this out, I knew I couldn't.

Storms flared behind my eyes, lights flickered like I was in the Polter-fucking-geist, and when I came? I came hard.

TWENTY-ONE

GHOST

WHEN KATINA'S hand was tight in mine, I smiled at her, even as I felt nerves flutter to being inside me.

I wanted to be strong for her, but she looked so like Mama that it was hard not to cry. Hard not to think about what Mama would say to me, knowing what she did about me.

Katina was still unaware of all that, but it was like looking into my mama's face, so it made me feel bad. So bad.

I wanted to be as innocent as I'd been the last time I'd spoken to Katina on the phone, but that wasn't possible.

And I had to accept that.

We were in the kitchen of the clubhouse, where her foster mother was making her a sandwich because Kat got something Star called 'hangry' around five in the afternoon.

I wasn't entirely sure what that even meant, but to be honest, I was just happy she was here.

That I could look at her.

That she was safe.

I honestly thought she was better off in Star's hands than mine. Evidently, the state had picked her out a suitable parent, and the truth was, I wasn't suitable.

I was a wreck.

I wanted her, I wanted to know she was safe, and I wanted to be close by, but I knew I couldn't be what I had once been, and that broke me.

It truly did.

"What's wrong? You look sad."

I felt sad. But I couldn't say that. How could I tell such a young child all that?

I rubbed my stomach instead, and muttered, "I'm just hungry."

"Star makes the best PBJ sandwiches ever."

Star snorted. "I don't." The older woman sounded jovial, teasing, but the look she cast me over her shoulder was wary, concerned.

I got the feeling she was worried I'd take Kat away from her, and that made me feel so much better.

Star loved Kat.

That much was clear, and it made me so happy to know that. So happy because if I ended up being returned to the Ukraine, then I knew Kat was in safe hands.

"I'm not used to PBJ."

Kat's nose crinkled. "How can you not be? It's like, sooo good."

"I'm not from the same place as you," I reminded her with a smile. "I speak good English, but I grew up with things that are very Ukrainian."

Kat tipped her head to the side. "Like what?"

"Didn't Mama show you?"

Kat shrugged. "Nope. She usually made things that were very American."

I arched a brow at that. "Really? What like?"

"I don't know. Just things like meatloaf, you know? With gravy. I loved that when she made it. She used to do a really great mac and cheese too."

"She used to make me that as well." I smiled at Kat. "Did she ever make you *trisky pechinka?*"

"Nope. I don't even know what that means."

"I'm surprised. She used to love that snack."

"What is it?"

"It's basically cod liver on little toasts. Most people buy the toasts, but she used to make them herself."

"Why?"

"She liked baking."

"Mom? She hated baking!" Kat denied with enough vehemence that I raised my spare hand and said, "It's okay, Kat. She must have changed in the time she was in America."

Kat blinked at me, then bit her bottom lip. "Why is your voice so husky?" she blurted out, then she quickly peered down at the counter like she was scared of my answer.

What was I supposed to say to that though? I was bought and sold like a piece of meat, raped and tortured, made to endure things no living being should have to endure and through it all, I screamed until I lost my voice?

That wasn't something I could tell my baby sister, was it?

"I just have a sore throat," I said huskily, but my gaze drifted to Star, whose eyes were loaded with sympathy.

She knew.

She knew about my past.

A surprised breath soughed from my lips, as I found myself wondering if that was liberating or not.

"Katina?" Star asked softly. "Are you ready for your sandwich still?"

My sister hunched her shoulders. "Yes, please."

Star reached over and scrubbed a hand over Kat's head, mussing up her ponytail. Kat grumbled, made a big show of sorting out her hair, then made a bigger show of getting off the stool to go and wash her hands.

Star laughed, then said to me, "Kat likes to remind me I'm a heathen."

"A what?"

"Star forgets things."

"Like what?"

"Basic human hygiene," Kat muttered.

"As if. I brush my teeth three times a day, thank you."

"You just forget to turn the dishwasher on or clean the floors every day." Kat snickered. "What about vacuuming? And you never brush down the walls. Ever."

Even though my brows rose at that, because *who brushed down walls?* Star rolled her eyes. "I have a life. I have better things to do with my time than clean the walls."

"Tidy house, tidy mind," Kat stated sagely, and I just knew she'd heard that from our mom.

That was what we said in the Ukraine. Well, the literal translation, at any rate.

I didn't remember Mama being particularly house proud, but it sounded like she'd changed a lot when she had Kat.

Star placed the sandwich in front of my sister, and almost shyly placed mine beside hers. "It has banana in it. That's why Kat likes it. She loves bananas."

"Thank you," I told her, and I meant it.

I also wanted to tell her that I wasn't intending on tearing my sister away from her. I could see that was her major concern. It was clear to me, in fact.

Maybe not to anyone else, because Star had a very good poker face, but I knew what that meant.

The best poker faces hid the worst secrets. The deepest feelings.

My heart almost ached for Star, who'd fallen for my little sister, even though she evidently had an attitude problem.

Not that I minded, but I knew if she'd been raised with my grandmother, she'd probably have boxed her ears three or four times during this conversation.

Watching my sister, I reflected on the fact that I wished, for Kat's sake, she'd known our grandmother, but I was also glad she'd never know what it felt like to have your ears pulled on as punishment.

It was only a meager means of castigation, but I didn't like the idea of punishing children that way. It was old-school.

Reaching for the sandwich, I took a bite and recognized that mine was much different than Kat's. Hers oozed jam and squishy banana. Mine had a lighter layer of strawberry preserves and a few thinner slices of banana.

"This is lovely," I enthused.

Star grinned. "You got the adult version."

A man walked into the kitchen, shirtless, and scratching his chest, and I reared back in surprise.

He was big, tall, very muscular—like most of them. Only, I'd never seen him before.

Though there were still some women I didn't know, I recognized all the men's faces from watching them out of the window to my bedroom. They visited us as well, asking us if we needed anything from the big house, and while the gesture was kind, it was mostly to get us used to them. To stop Tatána from screaming every time she saw a strange man.

Yes, it got very wearing for me too. I couldn't even imagine how annoying it was for the bikers to have these three strange women on the property and for them to all flinch whenever they approached.

Star didn't suffer the same nerves as me however. She raised her hand for the man, who slapped it back. "Sin, my main man. How's your tight tush faring?"

So, *this* was Tiffany's man. I eyed him with interest, because he was raw around the edges where she was anything but. Cultivated, classy, elegant. All words that described her, but they didn't describe him.

Then he grinned at Kat, a conspiratorial smile that had me understanding Tiffany's appreciation of a man who... I didn't know him, but I rarely had to know someone to *see* them. There was violence in Sin's nature. Of course, that sounded silly when I was in the kitchen of an MC. All the men were violent. Maverick as well.

But Sin?

I felt it seething beneath him like a volcano with torrents of lava just waiting to erupt.

Though it put me on edge, his smile, his kindness eased me as he told Star, "Not sure you're supposed to talk about tushes in front of kids."

Kat scoffed, "I know what a tush is, and..." She peered around the counter. "Yours is very nice."

The man, Sin, snickered, but I whispered, "Kat! That's incredibly rude!"

"Kat *is* rude. It's like her USP."

"USP?" I echoed, confused even more now.

"Yes. Unique selling point. It's how she is. More attitude than sense." Star cocked a brow at my sister. "Didn't we already have this conversation about watching the words that fall from our lips?"

Kat huffed, but then stuffed her sandwich between said lips.

Sin grinned and replied, "Who is Kat anyway?"

"She's my foster daughter," Star answered proudly, and her pride surprised me.

Sin hummed. "Huh. Didn't think that would be your thing."

"It isn't," Kat inserted helpfully, now that she'd swallowed. "She's a terrible mom, but she's a really great sis—" Her eyes flared wide as she broke off guiltily, then she froze, cut me a look, and hunched her shoulders. "Sorry, Alessa."

"Don't be silly," I chided her gently, not wanting her to be upset over something so natural.

After all, we were tied by blood, but she didn't know me. I didn't know her either.

Not at all.

And by the sounds of it, we'd known two completely different mothers. Even if they'd been the same person, she'd changed.

So, we didn't have that to relate to either.

Because *my* mama hadn't been particularly house-proud...

Star questioned, "Heard you're back from Ohio. Didn't realize. I'd have hit up that clubhouse instead if I'd known."

That she changed the subject made me grateful, even if I was curious about her knowledge of things.

As far as I could see, the men shared nothing with women.

Well, nothing except for saliva and sexual fluids.

I'd seen things through the window that they probably didn't know about, and truth be told, it was reassuring to view.

Maybe it surprised me at first, but I'd done worse. Had worse things done to me. Only there was no shame attached to what they did together, and that was wonderfully refreshing.

I cleared my throat to dispel the memories, then I watched in surprise as a woman who was definitely not Tiffany came squeaking into the room.

She had on a pair of very high shorts and a barely there halter top, and she plastered herself to Sin's chest.

She squeezed him tightly and almost climbed him like he was playground equipment or something.

"Sin!" she squealed, her voice as high as her shorts.

"Dammit, Tink, fuck off," he rumbled, trying to untangle her hold on him, but she was like an octopus, she clung to him better than a fly to a spider's web.

He managed to shove her off, though, and she pouted up at him. "What? No greeting?"

"No. No greeting. I told you before—we're done. I'm not doing that anymore."

She heaved out a sigh. "I thought you weren't being serious!"

"I was being very serious." He grunted, then peered at Kat, Star, and me who were all watching with interest. "I've got a woman now."

"So?" She tucked her fingers into the waistband of his jeans and tugged him to her. "That's never stopped a lot of brothers before."

"Yeah. Well, it's stopped me." He sounded firm, vehement, and when he reached for her wrist, at that moment, Tiffany walked in.

My brows rose at the sight of her taking everything in with a calm that surprised me.

She walked over to Sin, who only just saw her, then slammed her hand down on the woman's wrist. She instantly shrieked, "What the hell? Who are you?"

"I'm his woman, bitch. You touch what's mine, and I'll break your nose next time," she snarled, surprising me even as my lips twitched in amusement.

She came across as such an elegant person, with her tailored clothes and neat hair, and the way she stared at the world as though she could read it like it was a book—but still waters ran deep. Perhaps she was better suited to this Sin than I thought.

I hadn't liked her at first, but neither had I disliked her. I'd been predisposed to be unappreciative of the way she was being brought in, trying to help us get back to normal, but there was no normal for us anymore, and it annoyed me that she might try to whitewash everything that had happened.

But she hadn't done that.

If anything, the two times we'd spoken, it had been more like us hanging out, just being women of similar age with similar backgrounds.

Odd, but nice.

Nothing to be angry over.

Still, to see her so fired up? Unusual, but it was a nice insight into the woman herself.

Tink reached up with her non-injured hand and clasped her nose. "You wouldn't dare."

"Try me," she snapped, but Sin grabbed a hold of her shoulder and dragged her against his chest. When he slipped his arms around her waist, he muttered, "It's all good, angel. She knows now. And Tink, you'll tell all the others what's going down, won't you?"

Tink scowled, then peevishly slammed her heel into the floor like a child. "It's not fun here anymore. Link and Nyx won't play, and now you?"

"Play? What the fuck are you? Five?" Tiffany spat. "Grow up and go screw some men who aren't committed to other women."

Tink stormed away, and though Tiffany stayed riled up like a porcupine whose spines were erect and ready to attack, Sin murmured something in her ear that had her relaxing slightly.

She moved away though, headed for the fridge, and grabbed some stuff out of it like she had the right to be there.

As far as I could discern, the kitchen, and its contents, were fair game. It made me curious as to who bought everything, as to who did the shopping too. I'd hate to have that thankless job, although I could probably do that without messing up.

We needed to start pulling our weight around this place, that was for sure. We couldn't live off the brothers forever and not repay their many kindnesses to us without doing something in return.

As I pondered that, Sin watched Tiffany open a container of yogurt, even as Star cleared her throat and said, "Hey! I'm Lodestar, but you can call me Star."

Tiffany peered over her yogurt and muttered, "I'm Tiffany."

"I'm Kat," my sister chirped.

Tiffany smiled. "Nice to meet you."

"Nice to meet you too. That was sooo cool what you did with her wrist. If I had a boyfriend and a lady tried to touch him, I'd do the exact same thing."

"You don't need to worry about that yet," Star inserted dryly.

Kat, her tone serious, questioned, "Have you met Kyrian yet?"

"No. Who the hell is he?"

Sin laughed at Star. "He's Junkyard's kid. What is he? Nine?"

Kat hitched a shoulder. "So? I'm eight. I like an older man."

"Katina, you shouldn't say things like this. You're far too young."

Kat sniffed. "No, I'm not. He's my soulmate," she declared dramatically.

"Soulmates?" My brows rose. "Do you even know what that means?"

"It means our souls are friends, silly." Kat huffed. "Anyway, if any of the other girls touch him, I won't be happy. Now I know what to do."

"Thanks, Tiffany," Star muttered ruefully. "That's all I need is some pissed off biker daddies coming to beat my ass because Kat's learned how to karate chop from you."

Tiff hunched her shoulders. "Sorry." She cleared her throat. "Katina, violence is never the answer."

"You've never played a video game, have you? Violence is always the answer."

"No, it isn't," I countered.

"What video games are you playing?" Star ground out. "Christ, I only let you play Pokémon Go!"

"Pokémon can be pretty violent," Sin reasoned, but I knew he was joking, because his eyes were alight with humor. Goodness, even Tiffany's were.

"Exactly. And have you heard Justin Bieber's songs? He's always in pain when he talks about love. Love is violent," Kat said dreamily.

Star sighed. "I need to take away your tablet."

"No! What will I watch YouTube on?" Kat yelled, loud enough to make my ears hurt. "That's so unfair, Star!" Before I could say a word, before Star could, Kat leaped off the stool and stormed off.

Until she returned, grabbed her sandwich, huffed at us all, and made a swift retreat to wherever it was she and Star were staying.

Or where this Kyrian kid was.

"She has quite a temper on her, doesn't she?" Sin observed.

Goodness, that was an understatement.

"She has control issues," Star confirmed, but her gaze was puzzled. "I mean, I can't stop her from listening to the damn radio."

"Kids are growing up fast these days," Tiffany pointed out.

"Too frickin' fast," Star complained with a grimace. "I'd best go and check on her," she muttered to no one in particular, before she scurried away.

When she left, without a backwards glance to me, I cut Tiffany a look. She was watching me too, and I knew what she was going to say.

"Are you okay?"

I tensed. "Not really." Replacing the sandwich on the plate, the two bites I'd taken already congealing in my stomach, I watched as she drifted over to me.

Sin placed his hand on her waist though, tugging her back into him, and though she tensed up at first, she blew out a breath.

"I'm not mad at you," she said, and I was confused, because at first, I thought she was talking to me.

"No. I know you're not," Sin replied calmly.

"I'm just mad in general."

My brows lowered. "You should be mad. She touched him inappropriately in front of a child."

Tiffany growled under her breath. "These women have no decency."

Sin shrugged. "It's kind of what they do."

"Doesn't make it right."

"Don't try to counsel them," Sin warned. "I don't need the brothers on my ass because you're taking away their daddy issues and they stop putting out."

Tiffany sniffed. "It's gross."

"That's the life." Sin tapped her on the side. "Don't worry about it. It won't happen again." He bent down, pressed a kiss to her shoulder, then told her, "I'm going to get my shit together, and then we'll ride out in, what, twenty minutes?"

Tiffany smiled at him. "That's good with me."

He didn't notice as he walked away, but her smile was strained.

I tipped my head to the side. "Are you okay?"

"Would you be?" she replied gruffly, her eyes on her yogurt, even as she leaned on the counter opposite me.

"No, I don't think I would be," I responded gently. "This life...as he called it, I don't think it comes naturally to you."

"It doesn't, but my world isn't open to me anymore either. Lily, the only person I care about aside from my mom, isn't interested in that world now that she's with Link. But the truth is, men cheat in every world, don't they? Doesn't matter if they're in an MC or not."

"True." I dipped my chin. "I just think it's more blatant here."

"You've seen..." She cleared her throat. "Things?"

"Yes. Through the window. I like to look out of my room at night onto the compound."

Her head tipped to the side at that. "Why?"

"Because there are some foxes who drift out when it's late. I like to watch them."

"And inadvertently catch a glimpse of some free porn?" Tiff pursed her lips. "I'd have thought that would trigger you."

"No. It's a free exchange. What's to trigger me?"

She hummed at that. "That's interesting."

"Is it?"

"Yes." She smiled. "It's good though. Means that, eventually, if you want to be with Maverick, things might not be a problem for you."

I frowned at that. "I can't..."

"Can't, what?"

"Can't think about a future with him. I'm pretty sure I'll get deported soon, even though I'm married to him."

Her brow furrowed. "I have to figure that these men don't follow the regular rules of the world." She patted my hand. "I'm sure Maverick earned his name by fair means and foul, Ghost."

"What does Maverick mean? I thought it was just a name."

"It means someone who goes out on a limb to do things. Who goes the extra mile, you know?"

My brow puckered as I thought on that, then I commented, "Okay, I think I understand."

She patted my hand again. "These men earn their nicknames, Ghost. Maverick is as Maverick does. I get the feeling, from the way he looks at you, that he wants you. I don't think he's going to let anything come between you and him. Certainly not the U.S. government."

Unease filled me. "I don't want him to break any laws for me."

She snorted. "Honey, that's what a one-percenter club does. Laws were made to be broken." Her shoulders wriggled like she was uneasy. "It's new to me too. I'm not going to lie. Aren't we raised to follow all the rules? Told to honor, respect, and obey the law at all costs? Then, here, these guys are doing the exact opposite. In fact, they do whatever they damn well choose, but we care for them anyway."

"You care for Sin?" I asked quietly. "Very much?" I tacked on, when I thought about her response to the clubwhore touching her man.

"Very much. More than I thought I was capable of, to be truthful."

I frowned. "Why?"

"In my circle, we didn't marry for love, even if it might look that way on the outside."

"You love him?"

"I'm on my way to it." Her cheeks gusted out. "I'm pregnant."

"With his baby?" Somehow, that didn't surprise me. Sin had held her with tenderness, even when she'd been pretty angry at the situation in which she'd found herself.

"Yes."

My lips curved into a genuine smile. "I'm pleased for you."

She winced. "I'm scared."

"Of what? Losing the baby?"

"No. Of being a mom." Her nose crinkled. "I'm not good with kids."

"I don't think anyone is ever ready for a child. You get used to it very fast. It's not like you have a choice."

She laughed. "That's very pragmatic advice, Ghost, thank you."

"No problem."

She reached over and patted my arm, saying, "Ghost, if you ever need to talk, I'm here."

"As a therapist?"

"No, as someone who'd like to be your friend." Her smile was—I could think of only one word to describe it—brave. "My dad lost everything, our livelihoods, all of it went down the toilet, and I learned along the way how few friends I actually have."

"We're in the same boat," I admitted. "I don't think the other women like me."

"Which other women?"

"The ones like Tink."

She sniffed. "Well, I don't like them either."

"Tell Giulia that you, how did Katina say it, karate chopped Tink's hand. She'll be fast friends with you in no time."

Tiffany's brows raised at that. "Really?"

I grinned as I thought about how bloodthirsty Giulia was for one so small. "Oh, without a shadow of a doubt."

TWENTY-TWO

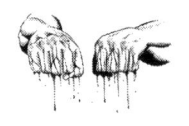

TIFFANY

THIS WASN'T MY HOME.

Not really.

He'd called it 'our place' before, but it hadn't been. It was his. It still was. But damn, it felt good to be back here.

Nothing was how I'd have decorated, but everything matched and felt right in here. The way he had the massive armchairs instead of a sofa to watch TV on, the modern kitchen and stove that, somehow, helped me not burn things. The squeaky front door screen, and the wooded copses that I could see from the kitchen window.

"Where are you?"

I snorted. "Not that many rooms for you to look in to find me," I hollered back.

"Saves me time."

"You're all about efficiency, are you, hmm?" I called out, then, when he made an appearance in the living room, I waved a spatula at him, a part of me still taken aback by how swiftly he'd shaved his beard off. His cheeks were as smooth as a baby's butt now, where before he'd been all lumberjack —surprisingly cute with it too. "I'm making something to eat," I informed him.

He arched a brow, but his interest was clear. "What are you making?"

"Quesadillas." I didn't wait for him to reply, just twisted on my heel and returned to the stove.

I'd stacked pesto with cheese to make a delicious quesadilla—I'd already eaten one while he was doing whatever had taken him so damn long in the garage.

Of course, I knew that was his way of giving me time to cool off.

I didn't blame him.

I didn't.

But the rage that had filled me at the sight of that bitch touching him?

Irrational.

Mostly because she'd been the one I'd seen him finger fuck that first night.

I winced at the memory, hurt filling me, even though it wasn't his fault.

I knew that.

That was why I considered these dumb feelings irrational, because I wasn't about to get jealous over women in his past, not when I had men in mine. Sure, not as many people as he did, but some.

I was no innocent, and I didn't want to be. I sure as hell didn't want him to be inexperienced, because what he could do with his body was beyond epic, and it made me cream my panties when I thought of all the stuff he'd learned along the way.

Lessons that came to my benefit.

But I was still riled up, still on edge, and he'd known it.

It pissed me off though, because I'd missed him so fucking much, and a few hours after he was back, I was spoiling shit.

The thought had me downing the spatula and putting my hands on the counter to grip them.

My temper wasn't that difficult to rile, but I was a very sensible person, preferring to rationalize something rather than argue for the sake of it.

But these emotions were complicated. These feelings inside me were hurt and anguish and fear for the future.

I was going to get fat.

Trixie, Dixie, Lixie, whatever the fuck her name was, well, she wasn't going to get fat, was she?

Me? I was about to blow up like a balloon.

Why would he stay with me then?

Christ, I really needed to not be so insecure. Not only was it fucking unsexy as hell, but the truth was, I wasn't this person.

Not usually.

The trouble was, I was vulnerable.

In more ways than just the situation with Sin. My family was decimated, and now, for the first time, I was falling for a guy who could have any pussy he wanted in the clubhouse.

But I wasn't this woman.

This pansy assed moaning cow who took shit lying down.

Earlier, I'd smacked that bitch's hand, and I'd do it again. They'd learn, and they'd realize that I wasn't going to let them touch my man without paying for it.

Him too.

The thought solidified in my gut, a bit like the first quesadilla I had in my stomach, and when he approached me, I didn't turn around, just let him slide his arm around my waist. Of course, he surprised me.

He grabbed the tip of my stubby ponytail and tugged it all the way back so that my head rolled on my neck and I was peering straight up at him.

"When did you get so tall?" I asked him softly, before he brushed his lips over mine from that angle—looming over me like Lurch from the *Addams Family* or something.

His lips moved. "You only just noticed? Damn, my pride hurts."

"Yeah? I can elbow you in the gut. That'd hurt more."

"Yeah, you could, but you won't."

"Why won't I?"

"Because you know I'll fuck your ass and spank it—"

I moved my elbow, getting ready to dig the pointy bit right in his gut, but when I did, he grabbed my arm and laughed. "Feed me first, woman. I haven't eaten in hours."

"You mean pussy juice didn't sustain you?" I granted him a mock gasp. "I'm stunned."

"You can't survive on pussy juice and cum." He sighed. "I researched it when I was a kid."

"As far as I remember, from the scientific world of Facebook, there was a meme floating around with all the calories and nutritional info on jizz."

"Babe, hate to break it to you, but as fine as this ass is, and as much as I want to bone the ever-loving fuck out of you, I ain't gonna be able to sustain you on cum."

I snickered, unable to stop myself, and because my head was rocked back the way it was, the snicker came out as a weird snort. When he let go of my hair, I let out a raucous chuckle, as did he, because that snort? Meme worthy.

The pair of us laughed our asses off, but as we did, his hands were on my hips, my ass nestled against his front, and truthfully?

I'd never felt closer to a guy than I did right at that moment.

Unable to stop myself, I turned around once I'd stopped giggling, nestled into him, and on a sigh, apologized, "I'm sorry for being uptight."

Like usual, when I thought he'd rub salt in the wound or get mad, he didn't. His calm retort soothed me in ways he'd never know. "You're not. It's a big adjustment." He shrugged, then reached up and tugged on a strand of my hair that had fallen loose from my ponytail with his tussle. "You handled yourself brilliantly."

"I did? I could have really hurt her wrist."

"I said no. She could have backed away, but she didn't. Now she knows otherwise. Law of the jungle in that clubhouse, angel. Remember that, and you'll be okay."

"That seems harsh."

"It is. Hard life, but we're a family too." He reached up and bopped me on the nose, his eyes filled with a kind smile that made me feel like my heart was being embraced. "And I wasn't necessarily talking about you. You're different."

"I am? How come?"

"Because you're not a clubwhore. You're my baby momma and you're gonna be my Old Lady."

I swallowed at that, and my eyes narrowed as I stared at him, trying to burrow into his gaze, figure out what he was thinking.

And what I saw had hope filling me.

I sank into him, trusting him to support me.

"You mean it?"

"Of course, I do. Was going to brand you as mine, even before you told me you were pregnant. Was just waiting until I could get home."

"Or haul me down there?"

"Yeah, or haul you down there." His lips twisted. "I knew you wouldn't have liked Ohio, so I didn't focus on that as an end result. Knew you'd want to be close to your family and Lily too, so I figured out a way. It's done now, and I'm home to stay."

I swallowed back all the emotions that were flooding me and, finally, I had no choice but to just rest my forehead against his pec and whisper, "I want you to be my Old Man too."

"No teasing?" he jibed, but it was tender. Not mean. "No joking around?"

He knew I tended to ease uncomfortable or awkward moments with humor, but nothing about this was either of those things.

It was perfect.

This was his way of getting down on one knee and asking me to marry him.

Though I wanted to blame them on hormones—I wasn't sure if you could do that when you were only two months pregnant though, and shit, I really needed to get some books on pregnancy—my eyes pricked with tears.

But they felt good.

Different than the ones I'd been shedding since Daddy had died.

I released a shaky breath, feeling his support, his strength, and let it sink into me.

No, we hadn't had the most orthodox of starts, but that didn't mean we couldn't have an unorthodox ending. A happy one. And that pretty much summed us up.

Happily.

Ever.

After.

TWENTY-THREE

LINK

"YOU'RE WHAT?"

My lips twitched as I stared at the woman, who sat like she had a bunch of ice cubes in her ass, as she shifted on her feet like she was going to stand.

Tiffany had straightened her shoulders, and even though Sin was still slouched back against the dining chair like I was, I knew he'd leap into the fight if necessary, but it wasn't necessary.

From the chatter whispering through the clubhouse, Tiffany had the balls to stand up for herself.

I was glad too. Sin had made a reputation for himself, one that was almost as strong as mine. I was surprised that he was willing to stick it through with Tiff, but I was glad for both their sakes.

They said a playboy was impossible to reform, but it depended on the woman who they chose to take to their side.

I knew for myself that you could glut yourself on pussy without it ever surpassing only the physical.

I hadn't even fucked my Old Lady yet, and damn, every time she made me come?

It was like my brain was boiling inside my skull.

Sure, the thought was gross, but that was how it felt.

Like I was almost dying. Like every part of me was being rattled up in some kind of pressure cooker.

It was so bad—well, so fucking good—that I was nervous about when I finally did get inside her, because sweet fuck, I wasn't sure whether I'd survive or not.

Still, what a way to go.

"You can't be serious," Laura whispered, her voice going from loud to quiet as she stared at her daughter.

"I'm deadly serious."

"You're pregnant too? Dear God, what is this? Some kind of gag? Are you doing this for TikTok, dear?" She fluttered back into her seat. "Yes, that's what it is, isn't it? You're playing a joke on me. A, what do you call it? A prank?"

"No, Mom, I'm not," Tiff said softly, but the hurt on her face was clear. "This isn't a joke. I love him, Mom, and nothing you do or say will change that."

Sin grunted. "Damn, Tiff, you didn't think I'd like to hear those words for the first time when we were alone?"

When he could bone her.

I snorted at the thought, and merely grinned when he glowered at me.

She bit her bottom lip. "It's the truth, doesn't matter where I say it or when or to whom. But Mom needs to understand that this isn't a rebellion, this isn't me acting up because of Daddy—"

"Dear God, what he'd say about this!" Laura whispered, sounding so dramatic that I thought she actually belonged on one of those high regency drama shows.

I sometimes caught Lily watching it on Netflix, but she always switched it off really fast.

I swear, she acted like she was watching porn. Of course, I'd have been interested in watching that with her.

Humming at the thought of eating her out while she watched porn, and wondering if that would trigger her, I switched my focus onto my woman, who was watching the interaction between mother and daughter as though it was a match at Wimbledon.

She was concerned.

I could feel it across the table, and I hated that, enough for me to reach forward, snag her hand in mine, and murmur, "Excuse me, Laura, but this is unnecessary. Your daughter has brought her partner over to introduce you to him, she didn't bring home the plague."

Laura's nostrils flared, and as she'd done since she arrived, she carried on as though I didn't exist.

As though I wasn't real.

Yeah, it was starting to wear really fucking thin.

"Tiffany, you can't just—"

"Can't just what?" she spat, her hands slapping down against the table, hard enough to make the silverware rattle. "It's my life, and it's not like anything is the same as it was anyway."

"Your father must be rolling around in his grave."

"You dare bring him up when you didn't even have the decency to attend his funeral?" she snarled. "Anyway, if he's doing the horizontal tango underground, that's on him. He should be here."

"If he was, he'd disown you."

"I know he would," she whispered sadly, miserable enough to make me pity her. "That isn't news to me."

Laura's nostrils flared, and just when I thought she was about to cry, she didn't. Instead, she swept up to her feet in a cloud of Chanel No.5, and a dress that probably cost a fortune but made her look like she was dressed for an office function in the twenty-one hundreds, and headed out of the room.

Lily blew out a breath, drawing my attention her way. "That wasn't too bad."

I arched a brow. "That wasn't too bad?"

"She's a drama queen," Tiffany confirmed. "That actually went quite well in comparison to her past explosions."

My brow arched even higher, because though it hadn't been particularly explosive, it certainly hadn't been good for my or Sin's egos.

Saying that, it figured that the in-laws wouldn't approve of their child taking up with a biker.

We were bad men.

Sure, we might have hearts of gold when it came to our women, but when it came to business?

We were bloodthirsty, and we took what was ours.

I reached for Lily's hand, which she'd fisted on the table, and squeezed. "You okay?"

"Of course. It's not me who's shaking," she rasped sadly, her gaze on her friend, even as she twisted her hand in mine so we could lace our fingers together.

Something about her, and it was something that developed the longer I was with her, was so fucking seamless. It was as natural as putting one foot in front of the other. Or taking a gulp of air and letting your lungs absorb the oxygen. It was natural to hold her, natural to want to fix shit for her, and even more natural still to want to kill for her.

I'd slay a thousand of her demons if it meant protecting her.

I figured she knew that too because, slowly but surely, she was gentling around me. I'd touched her ass last night by mistake when I was eating her out on the hall floor—I hadn't been able to wait a goddamn second longer. I'd burrowed my hands under her butt and had used my grip on her to pull her ass cheeks apart and tug her into me so every part of her was accessible.

Yeah, that was a big step. A massive step, and I didn't think she even fucking realized it.

But I did.

I knew it, and it made me proud and excited simultaneously.

We were getting somewhere, and when we reached the end destination?

Heaven. Absolute fucking paradise.

I was waiting on her letting me inside her for me to propose. Not because wifing her hinged on me getting laid, but because that was the moment when I knew she'd let me in.

All the way.

And then, when I was staring deep into her eyes, she'd know this was it for us.

This was us. Against the fucking world.

Maybe I was being a pussy, and I should just bite the bullet and propose tonight. But I wanted her to want me that way. I wanted her to let me in, because the second she did, I knew there was nothing between us. Nothing that would ever make me wonder if she was in it for the protection or the—

She didn't deserve to bear the brunt of my insecurities, yet either way, I knew I'd wait. Until all the other white noise was gone, until the bullshit was shoved aside, and when she took me in, let me have all of her, I'd know as much as she did that we were done. I was hers, and she was mine.

Forever.

Tiffany broke into my distracted thoughts by shoving her plate away.

We'd barely started eating our meal before Laura had questioned, "Is it truly necessary to eat with these two gentlemen?"

Only, she'd imbued the word 'gentlemen' with so much distaste and loathing, we were pretty much aware that, to her, we were fucking cockroaches.

Not that I gave a shit, of course, but Lily and Tiffany minded.

I'd admit it had been worth her being a cunt just to see their reactions to her words.

If we had any fear that our women looked down on us—which mine only did when she was riding my fucking face—it had been blasted out of the water.

That snooty bitch didn't get away with shit before Lily had snapped, with enough vitriol to make Laura blanch, "Laura, with all due respect, you are a guest in my and Link's home. Please be aware of that before you're rude to him again."

Sure, it wasn't the same way Giulia might have responded, by breaking the bitch's nose, but hell, for my woman? She used words, not violence.

I liked that.

Fuck, I might get her to talk dirty to me later just by being all fancy-like.

I almost smiled at the thought, until she muttered, "What are you looking so cheerful about?"

I grinned at her. "Nothing."

"Yeah, looks like it," she retorted, but her lips were twitching, and in her eyes? Happiness. Fuck, that floored me every time I saw it.

Once upon a time, I'd have thought nothing of dragging a bitch onto the table in front of Sin and fucking her, and while I really wanted her here and now, every bit of Lily was mine.

No other fucker could see her, share her, hear her, or smell her.

I didn't share Lily.

Her cheeks grew pink at my prolonged stare, but I was okay with that.

She needed to know what I felt for her. What she did to me.

I knew it strengthened her, made her feel more powerful. Hadn't she come running over to me and leaped into my arms like that was her natural place yesterday?

I mean, it was, but this was the chick who'd almost been as uptight as Laura Farquar.

If I'd ever imagined a day where she could let loose to that extent, it hadn't been outside the clubhouse, in front of my brothers, at the compound.

I knew she was still nervous there, and I didn't blame her. A lot of funky shit went down around it, and that wouldn't change. The clubhouse never changed. Didn't matter how many Old Ladies made an appearance, things always stayed the same.

Well, maybe Giulia had the power to change things. It depended on if Nyx became VP and how long Rex took to claim Rachel.

"At least she knows now," Lily was saying, her voice soft as she tried to soothe Tiffany.

She scowled at her though. "She's going to be a pain in the ass. More so than usual."

Lily shrugged, but the gesture was more helpless. Like she knew Tiff was right and didn't have a way of making shit better.

As far as I could tell, how Richard Farquar hadn't divorced the bitch years ago was a miracle.

She'd yet to leave the house, and somehow, every day, even though she knew she was going fucking bankrupt, and even though it was my woman bankrolling her, boxes turned up. Big fuckers. She was spending a fortune that wasn't even hers, so if this was her moderating herself?

Christ, no wonder Farquar had dug himself into shady business deals just to get his neck out from under the flood.

Grunting at the thought of how stupid the prick must have been to let her ride roughshod over him to the extent where he got into bed with a fucker like Donavan Lancaster, I muttered, "What's she going to do? Order more stuff off QVC?"

Yeah.

The queen of snoot loved shopping TV.

Sin chuckled. "She buys from the shopping channels?"

Tiffany's cheeks burned. "You're kidding me. I told her to stop doing that last week."

Lily frowned. "I think she asked Conchita to put the mail in the kitchen until you went out."

"Fuck's sake," Tiffany muttered, before she raised a hand and rubbed her eyes. "I'm not even sure what to do about her."

"Nothing you can do," Sin replied, but his hand stroked over her shoulders, and he squeezed one of them hard enough to make her moan before he gave her a little massage, working his thumbs into the back of her neck.

She arched upward like it felt good, and it amused me to think that the sight did nothing for me.

Now, if Lily had done that, my cock would be hard as a pike.

"I have to do something. It's Lily's money, not mine."

"I can afford to buy the shopping channel, Tiff. She isn't going to bankrupt me."

Tiff reached up and pinched the bridge of her nose. "Who's the fucking mother here?"

"Not yours. I mean, Laura's brilliant when it comes to needing to know what to do with your hair, or wondering what to wear to the governor's ball, but for real life stuff? She isn't exactly trained for it, is she?"

I cocked a brow at her. "No? Do you have to be trained for real life?"

Lily stuck her tongue in her cheek, making me laugh. "Yeah, you do. She's like a legit Southern belle. Reared to flit around and stuff."

"You can't hear the accent," Sin pointed out, his tone curious.

"No, she had elocution lessons when Daddy told her it was bad for business."

Sin gaped at me, and hell, I couldn't blame him.

"Your father made your mom go for speech therapy because it was bad for business?"

"I never said he couldn't be kind of an ass. I loved him, but which part of me telling you that I knew he'd throw me out for being with you didn't you get?"

"That's a shitty father. I'm not going to be like that," Sin vowed. "And even if that kid in your belly has a Romeo or Juliet pining for him, we're going give them the benefit of the doubt."

"You say that now," I remarked dryly, "but when they're older, and they're starting to want to fuck bikers like us, you're going to change your fucking tune."

Sin winced. "Okay. Maybe. Shit. We need to have a son, angel. Can you arrange that?"

I snickered, so did Lily and Tiff. "Unfortunately for you," Tiff replied, "your little soldiers are the ones who make that decision."

"Christ. Then I'm fucked. My dick led me astray until it pointed at you."

Tiff snickered at that, but she smacked him on the shoulder, and somehow, I knew shit was going to be okay for them, even if Sin was going to have the most expensive mother-in-law from hell, one who literally thought he was trash.

I felt bad for him, and I felt bad for the fact that I didn't have any in-laws to worry about, but when I watched Tiffany climb onto the back of Sin's bike, I snagged my arm around Lily's waist and said, "You gonna put your money where your mouth is?"

She peered up at me. "What money?"

I mocked her earlier pose, where she stuck her tongue in her cheek and pulsed. "That."

She grinned. "That was the visual for tongue in cheek."

"Looked like a blowjob to me. Either way, you gonna do it?"

Her eyes narrowed. "Will you let me do something?"

Her gaze got all intense, I'd have been a fucking fool not to. "Sure."

"It might take me a while to build up to it."

"You got it."

"You might not like it."

I snorted. "Lily, sugar tits. I got it. You can have your wicked way with me." I spread my arms wide open. "All this is for you to play with."

She giggled like I'd wanted her to, then she grabbed my hand and insisted, "Come on then. Let's get started."

I'd have been insane if my dick didn't get hard, so when I followed her upstairs to our suite, the rooms we were going to expand to take up more space—because this place wasn't massive enough—I flopped onto the bed, arms wide once more, and waited for her to do as she wanted with me.

I stared up at the ceiling, gazing at nothing as she moved around, but not because I didn't want to see, because I did. I really wanted to see.

Curiosity killed the fucking cat, and only the answer brought Link back and all that shit.

But, truth was, I didn't want her chickening out on me.

Every step forward where she expanded her horizons was a step in the right direction.

Something plopped onto the bed, and I rocked my head to see it.

When I saw a bottle of lube, a string of anal beads, and a butt plug, my eyes widened and my heart accelerated.

I knew, point blank, this shit was not for her.

I caught her gaze with mine, and muttered, "You sure?"

"You wanted it before, and we haven't done it yet." Before I could say a word, she was starting to unfasten the zipper on the side of her body.

I never thought I'd date a woman who'd eat a meal in a bodycon dress just for a regular midweek evening dinner, but yep, that was my life now.

As was this fucking mansion with a bedroom which my grandmother's old house could have fit into three times over.

When the material slipped off her, revealing her tits and no panties, my nostrils flared.

"Should have warned me, sugar tits."

She grinned at me. "There'd be no fun in that, would there?"

Tongue cleaving to the roof of my mouth, I started to kick out of my boots, then I jumped up and dragged off my jeans and tee. I wasn't wearing my cut, mostly because I was at home, and as it hung on the back of the door that meant I was naked and so was she.

"Wow, you're so hard," she murmured, her hand coming to shape my cock.

"Bet your ass I am," I rumbled, my head falling back as she began to jack me off.

I sighed as she picked up a rhythm that I'd taught her, one that was what I needed. Just that pinch of pleasure with a bite of pain. She didn't think anything of it when I'd taught her to dig her nails in around the base of my shaft, and she didn't think it was weird when I asked her to pull hard on my balls.

The joys of fucking a virgin.

They were blank canvases, and they would do whatever you taught them.

Perfection.

I was leaking pre-cum by the time she finished, and when she asked, "How do you want to do this?"

I could hear her nerves.

Couldn't blame her. She was weird where her ass was concerned—naturally—and this was the first step down a path I knew she registered was going to change things for us.

Without saying a word, I rolled on the bed and stacked my hands under my shoulders, my knees under my hips.

The sight had her breath hitching, and when she touched my ass, I got the feeling this wasn't going how she imagined, but I liked to get to the good shit fast.

Sure, I could kiss her, make her come, make her relax, but I knew my Lily.

She didn't want that.

She wanted to pull the Band-Aid off.

Next time, we could do stuff differently. Work up to the play, but now? She wanted to get it over with, and I wanted her to fuck me.

Damn, I loved this shit.

As I wondered if there was ever a day when she'd peg me, I felt her hand slip down the crack of my ass. When she did, it made the hairs at the back of my neck stand on end, and I shuddered, loving the tender touch.

It was so different from mine that my body responded to it on a different level. Her nails scraped over the inner curve before she tugged them apart, digging both sets of her claws into my skin.

She hissed at whatever she saw, then she rubbed over the pucker of my ass.

My balls drew up, my cock leaked some more, and I went down onto my forearms, because the touch of my woman's finger on my butt?

Fucking paradise.

I shuddered when she reached for the lube and poured it down my crack, and I shivered when she pushed the tip of her finger in.

I could feel her nail, and it wasn't the best sensation, but because I liked the bite of pain, and because it was her, I knew I could come so easily it was ridiculous.

Groaning when she pushed her finger into me more, I felt her flex it inside me.

I turned around, peering at her under my arm, and saw her face.

She was white, blanched, her skin sheened in sweat like this was a trigger for her, but also, she licked her lips like she wanted to taste me.

Of course, that made me want to fucking groan because had I known this was on the cards, I'd have gone and fucking showered first.

Just the thought of her rimming me was enough to make my cock weep some more.

Fuck.

I groaned when she bit down on her bottom lip, and for all that I could see she was nervous, and a little out of it, I also sensed she liked it.

I spread my legs wider, and she hissed out a breath when my dick swung back and forth between my thighs. The next second, she had my balls in her other hand before she slid her fingers down to my cock, tugging as she jacked me off in this new position.

Fucking hell!

I groaned when she removed her finger, but the pressure of the anal beads being inserted into me had me shuddering once again. She pushed some in, then would pull it out right to the smallest ball before making me take it all.

I knew, right then and there, she'd googled this stuff, because she didn't act with hesitation.

None at all.

If anything, she was in control, which surprised me. Especially since I was the opposite of in control. I was already covered in sweat, and my muscles were twitching like an electric current slalomed through it from time to time, and when she shoved her finger into my ass when the beads were in deep and started jerking it around, I knew she was trying to find my prostate. She wasn't doing it right, but I wasn't going to argue over technique when this felt fucking amazing.

The notion she even wanted to *try* to find it made me bury my teeth into my forearm, because the truth was I didn't want to make a whimper, didn't want to utter a sound, because if I did, my pleasure sounds might be similar to her pained ones when her father had touched her, and that was the last thing I wanted.

I groaned when she sped up her pace, and how I didn't explode, I'd never know.

She pulled it out, tossed the beads on the floor with a splat, and suddenly a plug was there.

It wasn't little, definitely not a starter, and I guessed we should have had a conversation about what I could take, because this was too small, but it still felt like heaven as she pushed it in.

Then, it didn't matter, because she was between my legs, lying on the bed, and her mouth was around my cock.

"Fuck!" I groaned, and I began to sink into her lips like I was sinking into her cunt, except I knew I had to be careful when I was feeling anything but.

I shuddered as I slowly thrust into her, but she only let me do that a handful of times before she started tugging on the little ring pull at the top of the plug.

The intensity of the moment made fucking fire blaze along my retinas, and though I could hear her starting to gag slightly, I was lost to everything as she carried on fucking my ass, pushing the plug into me, harder, faster. Digging it into me as deep as it would go, all while I fucked her lips.

When I exploded, I heard her gag for real, but even though I should have rolled off her, I couldn't, didn't. I was blind. Endlessly seeking the pleasure only she gave me as I sank between her lips, wanting all she had to give.

When I sagged down, my upper body smashing into the mattress, only then did I realize what I'd done. I jerked onto my back, terrified that she'd be cowering, crying, but I saw her laying there, sputtering still, only her eyes were half closed and her hands were between her legs.

The sight had my nostrils flaring as I watched her finger fuck herself.

Miracles happened, because my cock hardened again, especially when my body reacted to the presence of the plug, and I grabbed a firm hold of it around the base as I moved toward her, shifting myself between her legs, and sought out my home.

She didn't tense up, didn't even freeze, if anything, she breathed with delight as the tip burrowed between her lips.

And I knew, then and there, I could slide home.

I could.

It would be bliss.

Heaven.

What wouldn't be? The hell that'd come after when I took from her when she wasn't ready.

So I backed off, even if it killed me, and instead of sliding into her, used my dick to get her off. Within seconds, she was creaming around me, tempting me again, but I evaded it.

I had to.

I wasn't about to fuck this up. No way, no how. Respecting her boundaries, gaining her trust, helping her to embrace change were three ways I'd made her fall in love with me. And Lily's love? The only thing in my world that I couldn't live without.

TWENTY-FOUR

TIFFANY

THE POUNDING music didn't bother me.

I actually liked it.

The chatter and hollers of a bunch of men who were way past drunk? It amused me.

The sluts dancing on the pool tables? The ones with their mouths full of cocks I didn't need to see? The ones with all their holes stuffed full?

No such luck. Funny? I wasn't feeling it.

"You need to let it go," Lily yelled in my ear, as she grabbed my hand and tugged me into the makeshift dance floor.

I let her, only because she was smiling at me, and fuck, this was one of my favorite songs.

I had no idea how Anna of the North had managed to make her way onto an MC's playlist, but I wasn't about to complain.

We passed a crowd of men and women, some dancing, some I knew, some shooting the shit, some unknown to me. I spotted cuts and patches, people from West Orange who weren't brothers here, and I saw the Prez, who caught my eye, stared at me contemplatively for a second, before he cut me dead—not that I minded. He wasn't a man to be messed with, and I knew my attitude could sometimes piss people off, which told me *someone* had been telling tales about me.

As Lily raised my hands, I forgot about them all as we started dancing like we used to back in college before I'd fucked things up by doing the right thing. Knowing I wasn't the only one feeling nostalgic, we grinned at each other, the heavy, pulsing synth-beat sinking into my bones, as we let our hands drift down the other's arm as we twirled around.

The music cut off, switching onto something more hardcore, then I heard Sin and Link snarl simultaneously, "Switch back to the other fucking song."

I laughed, and Lily's giggle made my heart warm.

When "Lovers" started up again, the gentle tinkling sounds that morphed into a dance beat which made the tension in my neck and shoulders disperse as I lost myself to the music, I didn't even care that our men had caused the focus to shift onto us, I just fell into the song, dancing to it like we were twenty again, not ever so ancient at twenty-two and twenty-three.

The song grew louder, and I had to figure Link or Sin had turned up the volume.

As we moved around each other, I wondered if they considered it sexual. It never had been before. If anything, we'd done it to be able to dance at nightclubs without any guy trying to elbow their way in and make us dance with them.

I hated it when men did that, Lily too—for reasons that were obvious to me now—so we'd started dancing together, and to be honest, without anything loosening my nerves thanks to the baby, I needed her to back me up.

As the song came to an end, I wasn't surprised when Sin and Link approached. A different song shifted onto the speakers, not so heavy rock, but neither was it electro-pop. I'd never heard it before, but it let me fall into Sin's arms and sway with him before the beat started to surge, and writhing against him felt like more than just a requirement, but a necessity.

As I moved against him, I loved how his hands held me. They gripped my hips, held tight to my body so that there was barely any distance between us. The beat, though edgy, made my pulse soar, and I could feel the heat inside me from dancing turning into the heat that always arced between us.

His boner was there, digging into my hip, but he didn't move us away or off the dance floor. Didn't try to make me more aware of it by saying something crude.

He just let me feel it.

Let me know what I was doing to him.

And I loved it.

As I stared into his eyes when the song reached a fever pitch, I saw his feelings for me, but I felt them too.

I felt it in how he touched me and held me, how he danced with me and how he acted around me.

I never thought I'd be treated with such respect from a biker, more than any other man I'd known, but that was why stereotyping sucked. Why it meant shit. Because Sin was the best man I'd ever known.

I dug my hands into his hips in return, grinding into him as I danced, then as the music died, he reached down, pushed his face into my throat, and kissed me there, making me shiver.

His mouth moved over to my ear and he nipped the lobe. The feel of his cock suddenly became a temptation, but before I could reach between us, take advantage of how few inhibitions there were in this place where people were outright fucking in public, he rumbled in my ear, "Can I get you a drink?"

Before I could pout, Lily dragged me from his arms, and Sin let her with a raised brow and a smirk that had me grinning at him. I waved and turned into Lily's hold, letting her drag me across the floor and over toward the hall that led to the kitchen.

The bar wasn't that much better at night than it was in the day. The darkness didn't hide the multitude of sins that came from furniture that had been used for fucking one too many times, a bike that somehow was perched on the wall, lots of shitty, black leather sofas, and a crap ton of stools that I never saw anyone sitting on.

The floor was gross—my feet were sticking to it—and there was a haze of smoke in the air that, surprisingly enough, was all tobacco and not weed.

When we made it into the kitchen, passing two dudes who were boning one chick, I groaned my disbelief which had Lily shaking her head.

"You're a prude," she accused.

I scowled at her, then I opened my mouth to deny it, but maybe I was. "I didn't think I was," I replied slowly, and I knew I surprised her with my honesty, because she blinked at me a few times before she edged away from me and headed to the fridge.

When she threw a bottle of lemon tea at me, I snagged it, opened it, and then took a sip. It was hot as hell in the bar, and dancing with her then Sin had only raised my internal temperatures to a dangerous degree.

"You have to get over it," she repeated, as she'd done when she dragged me over to the dance floor earlier.

"Get over what?" I hedged.

"The clubwhores. It's just a part of the life."

I scowled at her. "You know how wrong that is, don't you?"

She snickered. "Umm, yep. I figure I do. But I don't get why it bothers you so much."

"It doesn't."

"Yeah, it does." She pulled a face, then pointed to it. "Do I look like I'm sucking lemons?"

I stuck out my tongue at her, knowing she was saying that was how I looked when I was glancing around the place.

"The feminist in me is dying inside."

Lily shrugged. "You think mine isn't? But it's not down to us, is it?"

"They want us to come here more often. Take part in more of the parties... It's either look like that and get used to it, or not come at all and create a divisive line."

"They're not going to appreciate it," Lily warned. "You just look like you're thinking you're too good for this place."

My nose wrinkled. "That isn't the way of it at all."

"She's right." The voice was deep, rough, and I turned to behold Steel. I didn't know him, but then, I didn't know anyone here really. Not even Link, and I'd eaten dinner with him and stayed at his and Lily's place, for Christ's sake.

I didn't greet him, seeing as he hadn't greeted me. Instead, I hitched my shoulder. "Well, I'm not looking down at you."

"Just the whores?" He hummed at that. "I can see that."

"If you can see it, then what's the problem?"

"It ain't gonna change whether you like it or not." His smirk was the opposite of Sin's. I wanted to slap him, not kiss him. "You think you're the first Old Lady to disapprove—"

"I don't care that you're fucking them," I grumbled, taking another sip of my drink. "I care that they let you bastards treat them like shit."

Lily huffed. "Way to make friends and alienate people, Tiff."

I cast her a look before I stared Steel down. "I don't care if you like me. You like Sin, and that's what matters. You have to know that I want what's best for him, and as his friend, his brother, that's all that should matter."

Steel squinted at me for a second, then he slowly nodded before he, too, went to the fridge. Only he didn't pull out a Coke or a beer or something normal for when there was a party going on, he grabbed some yogurt.

Some fucking yogurt.

I stared at the container for a second, surprised by his choice, but when he popped the top and began to spoon some of the concoction into his mouth, I felt my own begin to water.

Not at him, but at the yogurt.

Fuck.

Out of nowhere, I was starving.

Pushing past the pair of them, I headed into the refrigerator and looked at the contents.

I'd never seen as much food as I had at this place, and considering how many men were here and how many were fed on a daily basis, it fit, but still.

When I found the containers of yogurt, I snatched one, but then, beside it, I saw a big package of bologna.

Normally, just the smell of the pork and garlic was enough to make me dry heave, but if my mouth had watered at the yogurt, that was nothing in comparison to the bologna.

I stared at it so long, Lily ducked into the fridge with me and mock-whispered, "Are you scared to come out or something?"

Biting my lip, I forced my thoughts away from the processed meat and forced myself to stay content with the yogurt.

I was a vegetarian for environmental reasons, and it had been a long time since I'd had anything with meat. The sudden desire for that crap had me hunching my shoulders with guilt.

I tried to cut out dairy for the same reason, but I wasn't as hard on myself with that. Doing without turkey bacon was hard enough. No ice cream? Ever? Yeah, that was far too painful a loss.

When I retreated from the refrigerator, I'd admit, my mind was on the bologna, so when Steel groused, "You were saying?"

I just blinked at him. "Huh?"

He scowled at me. "Is Narnia through there or something?"

I scowled back at him. "You have a shitty attitude."

"Takes one to know one," he retorted, but he was grinning at me as he said it.

I huffed, then thought back to what we'd been discussing before yogurt and gross meat—I really had to ram that home—caught my attention.

"It's not right for them to live the way they are."

"And who decides that? Them or you?" Steel rumbled, as he stuck the spoon in the yogurt container and began to stir it.

"Them," I muttered, my mind still on the fridge.

Lily elbowed me in the side. "So what's the problem?"

"My problem, not theirs." I heaved a sigh.

"Are you okay?" She reached up and pressed the back of her hand to my forehead. "You feeling well?"

I scowled at her. "Yes, I'm fine!"

"You don't normally give up an argument that easily."

"Well, this is different."

Steel tipped his head to the side. "You scared of me or something?"

I snorted. "No."

Lily huffed out a laugh, but I knew my bluntness had always amused her. I could be diplomatic, but these weren't diplomatic times.

"Then why did you go silent? You don't think I can keep up with you or something? Just because you're a fancy fucking doctor—"

Well, that had exploded out of nowhere.

I raised my free hand and told him, "Hey, I'm not a doctor. I didn't finish my training. Hell, I didn't even get my masters, certainly not my PhD—"

Steel's mouth tightened. "Then why did you stop arguing?"

"Did you want me to argue with you?" I countered, confused as to what the problem was here.

When I shot a look at Lily, I could see she was just as confused, but she shrugged, evidently unsure where Steel's irritation came from. She knew Steel and the rest of the brothers as much as I did—not a lot. Considering Donavan was an enemy of the MC, maybe it made sense that they'd kept her at arm's length until Link had outright claimed her as his. While this wasn't my first party like it was hers, it was the first time I'd been here as Sin's woman, and it figured that I'd be making a shitty impression from the get-go.

Steel's cut declared him as the Secretary, and that he was on the council told me he had clout here.

I.e., I shouldn't piss him off.

Seemed that memo had hit my brain a little too late to be of use to me.

I cleared my throat. "There's bologna in the fridge."

He scowled. "Huh?"

"There's bologna. In the fridge. I want it."

"So? Eat it."

"She's vegetarian."

"Oh." His gaze drifted to my stomach, and he grinned, with none of that smugness that made me want to punch him in the face. "Can't believe Sin's going to be a dad."

"No? How come?" These guys all did enough of what it took to get someone in the frickin' family way, that was for sure.

"Said he'd never put a kid through what he'd been through."

I tensed. "What did he go through?"

He eyed me warily, and I knew he was measuring his words. "Ma didn't feed him half the time. When he showed up here, he was half scrawny and half stacked."

My brow puckered. "Why?"

"Used to fight for food."

Was this guy the king of one-liners or something?

"He used to fight for food?" I repeated, feeling like he was speaking to me in Mandarin.

Steel rubbed his neck. "He was poor. Did what he had to in order to survive."

Lily's hand grabbed mine, and as she squeezed, I felt like my heart was doing the same.

God, Sin's childhood had been far worse than I'd expected.

That I'd been blessed was a given, and in the face of Lily's treatment, I knew it had nothing to do with wealth and everything to do with love, making me so goddamn grateful for my parents.

Even as pain for the loss of my dad hit me, even as pity filled me for my man, even as the need to make up for his past hit me square in the soul, he appeared, rounding the corner, his gaze darting left and right like he was looking for me. Link was behind him, and as he homed in on Lily, Sin moved toward me.

When he eyed Steel, who was back to eating the yogurt, he arched a brow at me. "All good?"

I nodded, even though it was a lie. "Yep, all good."

Steel's glance my way was knowing, but I ignored it and him, and turned into Sin, who looped his arms around my waist.

"It get too hot in there for you?" Link questioned me, surprising me because he didn't speak to me that much.

I wasn't sure if that was some unspoken rule or something. Sin barely spoke to Lily either. That would have to change if that was the case though. Lily was my best friend, so that meant Sin and Link were about to spend a ton of time together.

"Yeah, and I started getting hungry."

"You get eating then," Sin directed, moving away to snag me a spoon from the dishwasher. As I popped the lid on my yogurt, I listened to Link ask Lily, "You doing okay, sugar tits?"

I rolled my eyes at the endearment, even though I saw the little sparkle in Lily's gaze from it.

She needed someone like him. Somehow raw and crude, but warm and open, giving. Someone who'd be patient, and someone who knew what he had and was appreciative of it.

"It's more sexual than I expected," she answered with a small laugh. "But it's all good."

I snickered at that when she shot me a look. "You mean you didn't expect grown ass women to drop to their knees when a brother snapped their fingers?"

"No, it did come as a shock."

"So why were you giving me shit about it?" I complained.

"Because whether I like it or not, they're going to keep on doing it, and I want—"

When she broke off, her cheeks turning pink, Link pressed, "Want what, love?"

"The brothers to like me," she admitted sheepishly, hunching her shoulder at the confession.

Though it was slightly to take the attention off her, just as I'd been doing since high school, it was also the truth as I stated, "I don't care if the brothers don't like me."

Sin snorted out a laugh. "That doesn't surprise me."

Steel arched a brow. "You catch more flies with honey than with vinegar."

"How apt that you consider yourself a fly," I retorted sweetly. "I don't care if you don't like me, because I am who I am," I clarified. "And Lily, you rock. If they don't like you, then tough shit. I like you, Link likes you, and Sin likes you. That's all that matters."

Her lips twisted in a smile, but I saw, deep in her eyes, that she liked my words. "Thanks, Tiff."

I winked at her. "Got your back, babe. Always."

When Sin pulled me into his arms, I went with ease.

"You got mine?" he rasped, his tone deep. Soul deep.

With as much ease as I'd fallen into his hold, I stared up at him, my heart in my eyes, and told him the truth.

"Always."

TWENTY-FIVE

SIN

"WHAT THE HELL ARE YOU DOING?" Tiff squeaked as I opened the door, then, after closing it, I leaned back against it.

I shrugged. "Keeping you company."

She scowled at me as she scooted her knees close together. "Pissing into a cup isn't something you need company for."

That had me snickering, but I kept staring straight ahead. "You been in here long enough that I was starting to think you'd jumped out of the window."

"I can't pee on command." She winced. "I'd ask you to do it, but that would defeat the purpose."

"Yeah, just a little," I told her, amused as fuck. "I didn't know you were a nervous pisser."

"I'm not."

"Well, the fact you've been in here twenty fucking minutes says otherwise, babe."

"It hasn't been that long, has it?" I turned to look at her just in time to see her eyes widen with horror. "No, it can't have been."

"It has." I tipped my chin to the side. "You doing okay, angel?"

She blinked at me. "Of course."

"Nervous about the baby?"

"Maybe." She crinkled her nose. "This just makes it all real."

"Was real before," I pointed out softly. "This isn't going to change things."

"Just feels more formal, I guess." Tiff huffed out a sigh. "I know it's silly."

"We're all entitled to be that when we're growing humans."

"Do it on the regular, do you?" she teased, making me grin at her. We shared it for a second, the spark of lightning that always pinged between us starting to sputter into being, even if she was sitting on a toilet in a doctor's clinic.

"Yeah, I make it a habit," I teased back, my lips gently sloping back into a soft smile. "I'd pee for you if I could. Just don't think the doctor would be interested in what my hormones had to say."

"Shame." She heaved another sigh. "I should have drunk more this morning."

"You drank a lot of tea," I reminded her.

"Should have drunk double that. Maybe I wouldn't be having issues now." She bowed her shoulders, hunching over as she stared at her feet. "Never thought of myself as a mom."

"Never thought of myself as a dad."

"I could see you as a dad," she murmured, her gaze still on her feet. "You're very affectionate." Her cheeks blossomed with heat as she peeked up at me. "You always make me feel loved." She ducked her head again. "Protected."

"You'll always be safe with me."

"I know." Her lips twisted. "That's what makes this craziness bearable. Never saw myself as a mom until you. Now it's happening, but it's just…it's going to be really soon, isn't it?"

"Yeah, it is, babe. Only woman I could think of having kids with is you. Whether it was now or ten years down the line. Although I'd be an old fucker by then."

"Everyone would think I was your sugar baby," she joked, and it made me smile to see her being chirpier. More like her real self.

"I could deal with that. To be fair, angel, everyone already thinks that." I laughed. "Or maybe they thought I was yours. You were a lot richer than me."

"'Were' being the keyword there." She winked. "I can deal with that. You're a hunk."

"A hunk?" I sputtered.

"Yeah. You know it too. Those come to bed eyes? Yum." Her grin at my discomposure widened. "You should see the look on your face."

"There's a mirror over there—is it worth me moving?"

"No, if you move closer, you'll be nearer to me on the toilet." She covered her face with the hand that wasn't holding the plastic cup. "I can't believe you're in here."

"I can't believe you're *still* in here."

"You try peeing in a cup."

"You think I've never had to take a piss test before?" I barked out a laugh. "Angel, you know you're tangling with a biker, don't you?"

"This is the perfect time to remind me you've been in jail," she mumbled with a huff.

"Only on misdemeanors." I smirked at her. "Pinkie promise."

"I'll bet." She rolled her eyes. "I don't mind if you have, but let's not tell Mom?"

"Agreed. She has enough of a problem with me as it is."

She gulped. "Oh."

"Oh?"

"I think I can go now."

"So go," I prompted with a shrug.

"Eww! No way! Go outside. I'm not peeing with you in here."

"You've used the bathroom when I was in the shower before," I retorted, amused by her logic.

"That was when you were in the shower and the running water covered the noise of me using the bathroom," she hissed, wafting her hand at me. The cup went flying, of course, and she moaned.

"You know I'm going to be in the room when you're giving birth, don't you?" I reasoned, as I strolled forward and grabbed the container before I passed it over to her.

She snatched it with a mumbled, "Thank you."

"Don't you?" I reiterated, wanting her to know I wasn't messing around.

"I know, I know," she retorted with a huff.

"Good. And along the way, when you're as big as a house, I'm going to have to help you shave your legs and shit."

"Yeah, that'll be *then*. As it stands, I still have standards, let's not break them until I'm desperately in need, hmm?" She grunted. "Like now? As in, get the hell out while I can still have control over my bladder."

"If I was a dick—"

"Which you're not," she growled, her cheeks turning pinker than before.

"No, but if I was, I'd stick around just to prove a point."

"What point would that be? That you *are* a dick?"

I winked at her, but as I twisted around to open the door, I stated,

"Nope, to prove that every part of you belongs to me, and nothing we do, nothing we have, could ever be that gross..."

With that, I left her, giving her the privacy she needed which, to be honest, I got. I just wanted her to know I was there for her.

No matter what.

I'd seen Keira, Storm's Old Lady, back when she'd carried Cyan. The stuff he'd done for her back then had blown my fucking mind. I'd never thought I'd find someone whose hair I'd hold back when they were puking from morning sickness. Never thought I'd be the kind of guy to find fucking ice cream at three AM because she desperately needed it.

But it just proved that the imagination was limited. Because the second you found that one woman who just made things click, you'd do all that crazy shit and more.

In fact, you'd look forward to it.

And if that wasn't insane, I didn't know what was.

TWENTY-SIX

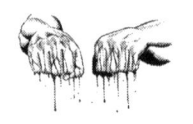

TIFFANY

"THANK YOU."

He shot me a look. "For what?"

"For being there today."

His lips curved into the sweetest smile. "You're crazy if you'd think I was going to miss that."

"No, that's the reason I waited. I knew you'd want to, but I mean thank you for wanting that. For being that way."

He tipped his head to the side. "You don't have to thank me."

"Yeah, I do. I'm grateful, and it's only right you know that. That's how this works, doesn't it?" I said softly. "Communication?"

"It is, but you're going to break my fucking heart, angel, because I know why you're thanking me."

My brow puckered. "What do you mean?"

"You're comparing me to your daddy."

"I'm not actually," I told him, not angry because I understood his logic. "Mom never got pregnant again. Not as far as I remember anyway. And the two times she was in the hospital, he pretty much camped out in the ward with her."

He hummed. "Ah, so you're grateful I'm like him?"

The question had me snickering as I leaned over and slipped my fingers over the fade at the back of his neck. "Babe, you're nothing like my dad."

"Thought little girls married their daddies."

My nose crinkled. "That's a very simplistic way of looking at things, but yeah, we have a tendency to seek out mates who are like our earliest representatives of gender roles."

"What does that mean?"

"Did you never get a crush on your mom when you were small?"

He snorted. "Fuck no. When I was little, I knew she was a cunt. That opinion didn't change much over the years."

My heart hurt for him. "I promise I'll be a good mom."

He grabbed my hand and tugged it onto his lap. We were seated on his sofa, Netflix was playing my favorite—*Disenchantment*—and I was curved into him, my attention more on him than the show.

He'd been a star today. I'd been freaking out in the bathroom when he'd barged his way in, and he'd made me smile, calmed me down, and somehow helped me provide the sample the doctor needed. He'd been there for the sonogram, held my hand when the doctor had confirmed I was nine weeks pregnant, and we'd just...

Fuck, we'd just been together for it all.

I hadn't expected it.

I mean, I didn't know what I expected, I guess. Just not that.

For him to be a biker.

For him to be squeamish or something. Or maybe belligerent when the doctor had to roll in another piece of equipment when the first sonogram machine didn't work.

Aside from stereotyping, I wasn't even sure why I thought that. He was a biker, therefore he was arrogant?

I knew better than that.

I knew Sin.

He was a hard ass in business, but I felt sure that he was never that way to people who didn't deserve it.

"What's going on behind those pretty eyes of yours, hmm?"

I sighed when I pushed my face into his palm. "Nothing."

"Don't lie, angel. It's okay."

"What is?"

He grinned. "You didn't expect me to be like that because I'm a biker."

I wanted to deny it, but I couldn't. I moved away from his hand and smushed my face into his shoulder. "I'm sorry. I'm such a bitch."

"Naw." His lips twisted, showing me his lack of offense at the insult I'd given him. "You're just not used to me and this life yet."

"But I am. I totally am," I rasped, guilt hitting me even more at his understanding. I mean, I was so glad he wasn't angry or offended, but that he wasn't made me feel worse. Rightly so, too, when he'd always treated me the same way—like I was precious.

"You're used to *me*. Not me as a biker." He shrugged. "I get it. We were insular back in the beginning, now the club's coming more into our world. You're hearing shit, seeing it too, stuff you don't like... I get it."

"I know you're not like that though. That's why I feel like a bitch and why I'm so grateful. You were so good to me today, Sin. So good. I wouldn't have expected that from anyone, but you gave me that. I'm fucking this up, but I just wanted to say thank you for being you." Recently, I'd thanked Lily for the same thing, but losing Dad? It put things into perspective.

The ones who stuck around, even if you were a pain, deserved appreciation.

"Well, it's not like I can be anything else," was all he said before he kissed the crown of my head. "Not unless you're into role play. That I could do."

I snickered, grateful he was teasing me and hadn't taken offense. I wouldn't have blamed him if he had been insulted. "Oh yeah, what would you want me to dress up as?"

"Not sure you want to hear the answer to that," he rumbled, and when I slapped his stomach, he snickered as he curled upward into a sitting position, frickin' *guffawing* all the while.

"What the hell is so funny?" I demanded, chuckling with him just because he was so tickled by whatever he'd been thinking.

"My first thought," he sputtered, and I eyed him in surprise because his face was bright red from laughing so hard.

"Oh man, you have to share it with me now."

"P-P-P-Princ-cess," he managed to snort out. "F-F-Fionna."

I gaped at him. "The princess from *Shrek*?"

"Yeah." He started wheezing, and when he flung himself back against the sofa, I just carried on gaping.

"You have an ogre fetish or something?"

I snickered when he roared some more, wondering what on earth was going on with him. Jeez, had he been sniffing laughing gas or something?

My lips started twitching at the sight of him though because, fuck, it was contagious. I'd never, ever, *ever* seen him like this before, and damn, the reason why hit me.

He was happy.

Happy.

God.

Even as I started to laugh with him, my eyes grew wet with tears.

It made me happy that *he* was happy, and damn, I figured that meant I knew I was in love for real, because that was the best feeling in the world. Everything was in perfect alignment with us both to the point where he could laugh like this, be free with me like this, and that filled me with a joy so pure I knew I'd never felt it before.

I'd had relationships before, but men had never made me feel like this. My ex-boyfriends were all probably starting their careers, the lot of them as white collar professionals, but not a one of them would have come with me to the doctor's office like Sin had today.

If anything, they'd have shepherded me for an abortion. Hell, they might not have even given me the money for it.

But this man, this beautiful, beautiful man, wanted this child we'd made together. He wanted it so much, he was excited for it. His eyes had shone with joy at the sight of the heartbeat on the screen, and he'd been calm personified when we'd been waiting in the corridor for our appointment, easing my nerves exponentially just because it was so restful being with him when I was so on edge.

Everything about him was tailor-made for me, and that meant that I might have been born a rich kid, daddy's girl princess, but in my heart?

I was a biker bitch because I was *this* biker's bitch.

My lips curved, pleased by the thought, and when Sin finally started getting himself back under control, I had no choice but to launch myself at him.

This biker daddy of mine deserved more than just a verbal thank you for rocking this fucking hard, and I wasn't afraid to show him my appreciation with more than just words.

TWENTY-SEVEN

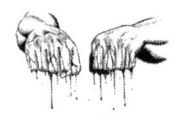

SIN

I LOOKED around the spare room, eying up all the boxes that housed shit I'd collected over the years and, rather than feel horror at the prospect of emptying them, I kind of felt excited.

Yeah, surreal.

But this?

It was going to be the baby's room.

Fuck, there was gonna be a kid in here in the future. Seven months were nothing, they'd pass in the blink of an eye, and soon, there'd be a mini Tiff or a mini Padraig roaming around.

The thought fucked with my head, even as it made me happy. It was a good kind of fucked up, which I knew didn't make that much sense.

It was weird how the world was still spinning, but inside this house, I was happy in my world. *With* my world. A place that Tiffany was now a part of.

I'd known we gelled before my exile, but getting back here only confirmed it. We slipped seamlessly into each other's lives, moving around one another like things were choreographed. She was the easiest 'roommate' I'd ever lived with. Even if she was messy where makeup was concerned.

I leaned against the doorjamb, trying to visualize where the furniture would go. I didn't know much about babies, but I knew they needed a shit ton of stuff. Back when Cyan, Storm's kid, was born, he'd yet to be promoted to VP, and he'd complained about how expensive shit was.

Money wasn't a problem, but I knew we'd need to go shopping. The prospect of which didn't exactly fill me with fucking glee.

I rubbed my chin as I thought about the details, then I felt her slip up against me, sliding her arms around my waist as she asked, "Whatcha thinking?"

Her breath made my back heat up where she'd pushed her face against me, and it felt fucking good. I loved that she wasn't nervous about holding me. About coming to me.

Some days, I felt like we'd been born this way.

There'd been none of the shit I'd seen my brothers go through with their women. No stupid arguments, no crazy 'play hard to get.' We'd just clicked. Straight from the start.

I'd say it was fate or some shit like that, but I wasn't sure a fucker like me deserved that. I was a sinner, born and bred. I'd done shit that meant I didn't deserve a woman like Tiff at my back, but she'd found me, and it wasn't like she'd let me go.

"Why did you think we were over when I was in Ohio?" I inquired softly.

"That's what you're thinking about?"

"No, but it just came to me."

She sighed. "Most men don't do long distance well." Her shrug had her tits digging into my back—definitely wasn't going to complain about that. "That's without the clubwhores and stuff you guys have on tap. I just never imagined you'd—"

"I'd what? Wait for you?"

"Yeah."

"We need to work on your self-esteem."

She fell silent. "Huh?"

"We need to work on your self-esteem," I repeated, "because it says a lot about you that you don't think you're worth waiting for, angel."

She didn't reply, and I didn't say a word either. I wanted that to sink home. Then, of course, I felt the wetness on my shirt, and I knew she was crying. When I went to turn around, she didn't let me. She squeezed my waist tighter, pressed into me deeper, and whispered, "I love you."

"I know you do." I sucked down a breath, preparing myself to say it for the first time, only, when I did? It came out easy. None of the discomfort I'd expected as I told her, "I love you too."

Fuck, see? This was how we worked. Sliding against each other, rippling around one another.

Was this what it felt like when you'd found a soulmate?

It had never been this easy with my ex-wife. Ever.

"I missed you."

"Missed you too."

"When you were gone, the world was going to shit, but you were still there. I kept expecting you not to answer the phone when I called. Every day, when you did, it filled me with hope. I didn't want to lose you, and I thought I had."

"You didn't. I'm going nowhere. What we have, Tiff, you have to see it's special."

She cleared her throat. "I just didn't know if you knew that."

"I'm not an idiot," I grumbled gruffly.

"Never thought you were. Just thought you were a man."

I snorted. "I'd make you pay for that, but then I have a few brothers who are dicks, so I get it."

She squeezed my waist. "You gonna tell me what you were thinking about before I turn into more of a cry-baby?"

"Just where we should put a crib and shit in here." When I felt more tears leak into my shirt, I muttered, "Tiff?"

She whispered, "Just ignore me."

Confused, I grabbed one of her hands and gently slipped my fingers through hers. "You okay?"

"Yeah, I think I just fell more in love with you is all."

I snickered at that. "I think I can deal with that."

"Good."

TWENTY-EIGHT

TIFFANY

I EYED HIM, then I eyed the sandwich. Then, heaving a sigh, I turned my attention to the yard where we were both sitting.

"Why do you keep huffing?"

"No reason," I muttered, shoving a carrot stick into my hummus.

Hummus was like my favorite food. I considered it a whole food group of its own. That was how much I fucking loved it.

But here? Now?

It was nothing compared to the ham in Sin's sandwich.

What the fuck was going on with me?

I glowered at the hummus and contemplated tossing the carrot stick into the yard for a bird to eat or something. Then a thought occurred to me. "Do birds eat carrots?"

Sin paused. "I dunno. I've never thought about it before. Google it."

"Nah, I was just thinking out loud."

"Dangerous brain you've got there."

My lips twitched. "Says you with your Princess Fiona fetish."

He grinned at me, his eyes twinkling. "I already told you it was before she turned into an ogre."

"Yeah, right. That's what all the men say." I winked at him. "I need to invest in green face paint."

He snickered. "Save yourself the trouble."

I pouted. "Killjoy."

Nudging my shoulder with his, he asked, "You okay?"

"Yeah. I'm fine. Today was rough is all."

"Why?"

"Tatána was just talking about the journey over here. They were in a truck for eighty hours after they landed in the States. No air, no toilets, no goddamn water.

"It was tough to hear. Really hard for Lily as well." I grimaced. "Poor Ghost had to translate every word too. Nightmare."

"I'm sorry, sweetheart."

"No, it's okay. I needed to hear it, but it was just difficult, you know?" I winced. "Fuck, not as hard as what they endured."

"Hey, you don't need to qualify that. I understand."

I leaned into him, silently thanking him for being, well, *Sin*. To me, he might as well have been called Saint, because he was like the Tiffany Whisperer.

"How did you earn your road name?"

He tensed. "Why do you ask?"

His tension almost made me wish I hadn't asked. Hissing, I muttered, "That bad, huh?"

"Maybe."

I eyeballed his ham sandwich which he had hovering in midair because I'd asked the question when he was about to take a bite. "Just a little hint?"

"Seven deadly sins," he mumbled.

"Huh? What about them?"

"It was when I got back from my final deployment. They said I was all seven of them."

I arched a brow. "Really? That's it?"

"Yeah." His cheeks were red, so I knew I was getting the edited version, but I was okay with that. At least I had an answer. I didn't need to know about all the sins he'd committed—didn't take a rocket scientist to figure that shit out.

He wasn't a scout leader, for Christ's sake. He was a biker. He traded in blood and secrets.

What surprised me the most was why that didn't bother me. It wasn't like I had a bad moral code or anything. I'd always been law-abiding before, and it wasn't like he'd corrupted me...

Had life done that?

I mean, I'd fallen for him way before my world had collapsed, but I'd seen things along the way. Learned shit. Nothing was as peachy as it seemed. Ever. And being rich? That usually came at someone else's expense.

Even Dad had been a dick on his way to the top. I knew the labor unions had been sniffing his ass because they claimed he wasn't paying his workers enough overtime—and that had been when he'd been constructing Orange Hills, the subdivision in West Orange that would be his final project.

Life wasn't black and white, and the blur between wasn't always gray either. That was too simplistic a view on things.

"You mad?"

"That you have a past? No."

"Why you looking at me like I've grown horns then?"

"You haven't. I'm just wondering why it doesn't bother me. I don't *know* the shit you get up to—"

"And you never will, Tiff. You know that, right? Some shit I just won't be able to tell you."

"I figured that out along the way," I said wryly.

"Good. I don't do it to be a dick. I do it to protect you."

Was that the case? Or was it a means of stopping my view of him from being tarnished?

Maybe it was both.

"I don't know what you did that brought you back home, Sin, but I'm glad you did it."

His eyes darkened, and not in a way I was used to. Anger spiked those dark chocolate orbs, making me wonder who it was aimed at. "Me too, angel. Me too."

I reached for his hand when he dumped his sandwich on his plate. I felt like a real bitch for checking the trajectory, watching the ham tumble out of the bread thanks to the fall, then I muttered, "Didn't mean to drag up the past."

"You didn't. Just..." He blew out a breath. "Never mind."

I wanted to offer to be an open ear for him, but I knew he didn't want that from me, so I cleared my throat. "Sin?"

"Yeah?"

"I know the answer to this but...the Sinners don't trade women, do they?"

He snorted. "I'd be mad at you for even thinking to ask me that question if I didn't know what Tatána had been talking about. It's only natural you'd ask, but no, we don't."

"I mean, I did know that, but I just wanted to confirm it."

He reached over and bopped me on the end of my nose. The move made me sneeze of all things, which had him chuckling like I'd told the best joke in the world.

Sheepishly, I grinned at him. "I think it was the mustard. You must have some on your finger." He stuck said digit into his mouth and licked it clean. When he did, this time, his eyes darkened in a way I was totally used to.

Need unfurled in my core as I watched him suck on his finger, and within seconds, we were both dealing with one of the deadly sins...

Lust.

TWENTY-NINE

TIFFANY

TWO DAYS LATER

AS I WALKED over to the clubhouse, I peered at the Prospect beside me.

You'd never think he was a glorified errand boy by looking at him, what with the mohawk and all the tats down his throat, but that's what he was.

He'd come to tell me that once I was done with the girls, I needed to go speak with the Prez, and because being the messenger wasn't enough, he was even escorting me to the clubhouse itself.

So, yeah, I'd settled on 'girls' as my collective term for the women back in the small bunkhouse I'd just left behind.

Why?

Because I had to give them a name.

They were so fucking young that they were practically girls anyway, and beyond that, I couldn't think of them as what they were—captives. Ex-hostages. They were survivors, but as a label? Yeah, that didn't work.

Although maybe it should.

Maybe I could make it a thing.

Either way, I wanted to get used to a different name, because I wanted the bikers to start calling them that too.

We needed to help them move on, and letting them rot in the shadows of their past was only going to remind them of what they'd been through.

So, yeah, girls was what I'd settled on, and it was apt that Rex called me in to speak with him because I needed to talk to him anyway.

Not only about that, or about what he wanted to discuss, but a few other things too.

While I was kind of nervous because I knew what the Sinners were capable of and he was their leader—a leader they actually loved, which was always clear to see whenever Sin talked about him and his leadership—so that meant he condoned every single act of violence, every single broken law, and everything that kept the Sinners out of the lines of regular society.

I knew I'd be a dumb fuck not to remember all that.

When I made it into the clubhouse, like most of the time in the late morning, it was quiet, because everyone was still starting their day.

The guys had drifted off to their jobs—I knew because I'd heard the bikes start up and rumble as they left the compound—but the clubwhores? Still sleeping.

Bitches.

I hated them.

And it was a stupid hate, because it was a collective word too.

Just like captives.

They were whores for the club, but that was taking away the whole truth of what they were.

I didn't like that I hated them. Didn't like that they got to me so much, but the truth was, hate didn't have to be sensible.

I didn't know them, but I didn't have to, to know that I disliked what they did.

Not just because I thought it was shitty how they allowed themselves to be treated, but because they let the guys cheat on their Old Ladies with them.

I was sure some of them were great—they couldn't all be bitches, after all. Maybe one had anxiety and another had a really amazing singing voice, but I had no desire to get to know them. Because what they stood for did not gel well with my own personal ideals.

So, yeah, I sniffed at the thought of the sluts being in bed still, and when we walked past the stairs and I saw one of the doors open, with a quick glimpse showing me Trixie Dixie Lou on her back, naked, with the sheet half off her, snoring away? I wondered whose marriage or relationship she'd ruined that night.

The Prospect reached around me to shut the door, and when I cocked a brow at him, he didn't look at me.

In fact, now that I thought about it, he hadn't looked at me once.

Why was that?

My brow puckered, and I thought about asking him, but we made it down the hall to the end where he knocked on the door.

When a deep voice called out, "In," the guy pushed opened the door and wafted me inside.

All without looking at me.

I turned to watch him go, saw him trudging down the hall, and shook my head at him.

"Who the fuck's there?"

The low voice growled at me, but I wasn't scared.

I mean, I hadn't dealt with worse criminals, but I'd sure as hell dealt with a lot of important people over the years.

Lily wasn't the only one who'd had a semi-public life. I'd dealt with politicians and governors just like she had. Only difference being that Dad hadn't sent me off to finishing school.

I knew why too.

He would have.

But he loved me.

He liked me close.

It was why, when I'd gone off to college, he'd been glad when I dropped out. He liked me to be home.

I bit my lip at the thought, at the memory which speared me to the quick.

It was easy to think badly of him now. So easy to think of him leaving us behind to deal with the shit he'd left us in, so easy to think that he'd be that unhappy with my being with Sin that he'd toss me out, but I knew it wouldn't be forever. He'd do something to help me. He couldn't have stopped himself.

He loved me.

I was a daddy's girl for a reason.

He'd always shown me that love, and I actually thought that was why I was so mad, because he had left me when he'd said he'd never do that.

I'd known it was a promise he couldn't keep, but death of natural causes and suicide?

Two different things entirely.

I sucked in a breath as I stepped into the office, asking, "Do I smell of shit or something?"

Rex's head popped up at that. He'd been bowed over a laptop, glaring at the screen, but when his gaze drifted down me, he grumbled, "Fuck, we got ourselves another Giulia."

I snorted, because Giulia's reputation was preceding her. I hadn't even had that much of a chance to get to know the woman, but it was clear she had an attitude problem she was famous for.

I didn't mind being thought of as a Giulia number two, but I didn't want them to lump me in with her forever.

I was Tiffany.

With all my flaws and good sides to my nature too.

"I might not be willing to take any of your shit, but I'm not Giulia. I'm Tiffany." I strode over to him, hand stretched out. "Pleasure to meet you."

He eyed my hand, then he looked at me before he reached out and cautiously shook mine. Like he was expecting me to pull out a weapon or something.

Told me how often he shook hands, that was for fucking sure.

As did his punishing grip which, when I winced, he instantly softened.

He pulled a face. "Fuck, sorry. "

"No worries. Guess you're used to pissing contests when you shake hands, huh?"

His lips twitched. "Yeah, or something like that." He tipped his head to the side and offered, "Take a seat." When I did as he asked, he murmured, "I should have spoken with you the day you first came to speak to the—"

He cleared his throat, and it was perfect timing actually. Hadn't I just been thinking that? About how weird it was to think of Ghost, Amara, and Tatána as a collective but not know what to call them?

"Girls," I propped.

His nose wrinkled, and I had to admit, at that moment, he was cute. I mean, I was Sin's all the way. Sin was sleek, where Rex was rough, but hell, I could appreciate a good-looking man who knew how to fill out a pair of jeans, couldn't I?

Wasn't like I was offering to spread my legs for him.

The thought almost had me snorting, but instead, I watched him grimace at me, as he asked, "Girls? Really?"

"What would you prefer we call them?" I countered dryly. "I mean, we have to call them something, and I ran into a similar issue. I think we should get used to that, because then they'll be able to integrate more."

"You want them to integrate? With us?"

"Yeah, I don't see why not. It's not like they have anyplace else to go."

He scowled. "Tiffany, I mean, Tiff? Do you have a preference? Sin calls you Tiff."

"Yeah? He calls me lots of other names too."

Rex snickered. "Yeah, I'll bet. Never thought I'd see a woman who could tame him, but it seems like you have."

My back stiffened at that. "He isn't a house cat."

His nostrils flared. "No shit."

"You know what I mean. I haven't done anything—"

He raised a hand. "Sorry, I didn't mean it that way. I just meant that his ex did a number on him, and it messed him up."

"He told me she cheated on him," I muttered, knowing it was bad that we were talking about this, but also understanding that Sin probably wouldn't talk about it himself, so if I could pump Rex, then it would be for the best.

"Yeah? He told you that?" His surprise was clear.

"He told me a lot of things. Like that it was during his first deployment."

Rex's brows rose. "He told you he was in the Marines?" He whistled under his breath. "Fuck, he *is* serious about you."

Though it warmed me to think about that, to think that Rex thought that, I just shrugged because the truth was, after a few coming to Jesus moments since his return to Jersey, I knew he was serious, and I didn't need his Prez to confirm it.

"Sin's dad was who she cheated on him with."

Rex's statement had my eyes flaring wide. "Are you kidding me?"

"Do I look like I'm the kind to kid around about shit like that?"

"No." I scowled at him. "No wonder it messed him up."

"Yeah, it did. Especially as... I shouldn't be telling you this stuff, I'm just surprised is all." His lips twisted. "Surprised and happy."

"You are?"

"Yeah. I mean, I want all my brothers to be happy, but Sin has a special place in my heart."

He had a heart?

Jesus.

Although, that was being mean.

Hadn't he brought the girls to the compound? Wasn't he feeding them after he'd spent a fortune on getting them back to health? Wasn't he letting them stay, even though they were back on their feet physically?

I tugged on my bottom lip with my teeth before I asked, "Why?"

His head tilted to the side, but he smiled. "He didn't tell you that, though, did he?" His hum was clear. "He's a secretive shit. Not always a bad thing in a world like ours." He rocked back in his chair, and the thing creaked under his substantial weight, but once he'd done it a few times, it fell silent, like it knew the score.

Whether it creaked or not, Rex wasn't going to stop rocking.

"You can't leave it like that," I complained when he didn't say anything else.

"Sure, I can. I'm the Prez. I can do whatever the fuck I want." His eyes darkened, and I knew that was a threat, but because he didn't compound it by being physical, I knew he was only telling me to tread carefully. "Sin's secrets aren't only his to tell. That's why he kept his mouth shut." Rex's top lip quirked up in a smile. "You just made me happy that he'll be getting a promotion soon."

Utterly confused, I gaped at him. "What?"

He wafted a hand. "Talk to him about this. Tell him I said it was okay to talk about Grizzly."

"Grizzly?" I repeated dumbly, feeling no wiser when he just nodded.

"Anyway, that isn't the reason why I brought you here. I wanted to tell you that whatever you see on the compound stays on here, okay? You're Sin's, and that gives you some leeway, but if you betray him, if you betray us, that isn't something you want to do. Do you hear me?"

The gravel in his tone made such a swift appearance that it had my back straightening, but what was I supposed to do? Argue? Ha. Not going to happen. "Yeah. I understand."

He dipped his chin.

"Did you warn Giulia or Lily like that?" I queried softly.

"Giulia was raised in the club. She doesn't need to be told to say shit about the MC to outsiders. Lily's up to her neck in crap without me telling her to keep her fucking trap shut. You, on the other hand, are different."

"I am?" I questioned warily, wondering what shit Lily was in, and why she hadn't told me about it.

"Yeah. You are." He leaned up and scratched his beard. It wasn't fully grown out, just like straggly stubble, which made me think he'd shaved recently and it was itchy.

"Why?"

"How much do you know about your dad's business practices?"

"Not a lot." I sucked in a breath. "I just know that he lost everything. The IRS froze all his assets and—"

"Sure they did. But I've been looking into things, you know, because you're Sin's bitch, and because Lily is tight with you. Your daddy's money wasn't coming from a clear-cut source, and I'm curious about that."

"A clear-cut source?" I repeated, wondering what that even meant.

"Yeah. We've been tracing where Donavan Lancaster was funding shit, and because Lily's left things open to us, we have a wide avenue of data to maneuver through. He wasn't funding your father with his own money. Someone else was directing the money through his corporations."

"Do you know who?"

His lips twitched. "Wouldn't have brought you here if I didn't."

I gulped. "Why isn't Sin here?"

"Because he wouldn't want me talking to you about this, he wouldn't want me scaring you. Shit, I don't want to scare you, but I need to know what you know before I let him do something fucking stupid."

My hands tightened around the armrests, clenching down to the point of pain. "Stupid?" I whispered, more nervous than I had been at any point during this conversation.

"Yeah. Stupid. Like wifing you."

"Wifing me?" I squeaked, rocking back into my chair. Why did marriage sound like such a terrifying prospect when he phrased it like that?

"Yeah. Propose, the whole white dress and tuxedo shit." He rubbed his scruff again. "I know that's what he's got planned. Can see it in his eyes. The bastard's fallen hard for you, and despite it all, I'm glad.

"He deserves to be happy. Fuck knows he had a shit enough time of it growing up."

"He told me about some of it." Some wasn't enough though.

I felt like a broken record, but crap, the information he was dropping on me was both fascinating but torturous because, like Steel, I knew he wouldn't tell me more, wouldn't give me the details I needed, and Sin? Though I trusted him, I knew he was quiet by nature. The life and soul of the party when he had a couple of tequilas in him, but on the regular? He wasn't a talker.

He wouldn't share things easily.

It would take time and patience, a lot of it, for him to open up. Or maybe it wouldn't. Not now. Things were different. We were openly together. No secrets. Him and me against the world... Perhaps he'd changed to reflect that?

If I thought telling Rex that Sin had shared something of his past with me would get him to open up, I'd been dead wrong about that.

"I just don't want him getting hurt. Long story short."

"And you think I have the power to do that?"

"The man left his post for you, Tiffany. He lost his place here, he lost his brothers' respect, and all without saying shit to them about why and how. I don't know why he did that. I don't know why he wanted to keep it quiet."

My jaw tensed. "I asked him to."

He narrowed his eyes. "Why?"

"Because, in the end, it didn't matter."

"Sin wouldn't go to the cops over it, even though Giulia was dragged through the mud...and Luke's intent would have proven that he went there premeditatively to hurt her." He pursed his lips. "Protecting you over her. Over Nyx. Why would he do that, do you think? Why would you put Giulia through that?"

Guilt wanted to spear its way into me, but this wasn't on me. It was on Luke. My tone was hard as I told him, "I had no proof that Luke drugged me. No proof that he'd even been the one to send the texts. My screen was cleaned so there weren't even any prints—Sin checked. He didn't rape me. Didn't hurt me aside from groping me hard enough to make me aware it was him who'd drugged me. It wasn't like I was covered in bruises to show the cops. How do you think that would have stood up in court? How do you think the cops would have taken that? Any member of staff at the Lancaster's could tell them I drank too much.

"I was driving intoxicated, Rex, without the drugs." I stared him down. "You tell me what me coming forward would have done."

"Oh, I don't know, a little thing like reasonable doubt on Luke's character?"

I scoffed, "Reasonable doubt? In the face of a man like Donavan Lancaster's propaganda campaign to make him look like Jesus reborn?" I hooted, even though nothing about this situation was funny. "He'd have dragged me through the mud too, and while I could have dealt with that, I know how cops treat assault victims."

He narrowed his eyes. "You've been assaulted in the past?"

"Almost. I keep having near misses." My smile was false. "Aren't I the lucky one?"

"Explain."

"One of Daddy's business associates decided to come onto me." I turned my face away from him. "I was reminded that women shouldn't wear such short skirts if they don't want to inspire that kind of reaction in a man." I tightened my lips. "Then, back in college, I-I—"

"You what?"

I tipped my chin up, refusing to be ashamed of what I'd done. Refusing to feel badly when my intention had been pure. "A professor attacked a student. She wouldn't come forward, so I did it for her. I didn't drop out of school because I was flighty."

"The authorities found out?"

Shrugging, I answered, "Yeah. Obviously, I did it after the fact. But the girl, a friend..." My voice turned choked as I thought about Octavia. Beautiful Octavia with a laugh like a song and a smile that made anyone smile in return. So fucking smart. Such a fucking waste. "She killed herself soon after, and she'd told me everything when she was drunk one night. I used it against him and it backfired." I sniffed. "*That's* why I didn't come forward. I'd put myself on the line for any woman who needed me, but do you really think the police were going to listen to anything I had to say? With my reputation?

"I'm not an idiot. Neither am I scared to come forward when I think I need to, but there was nothing I could do in that situation. Nothing that wouldn't cause more shit to fly, and none of it in Lancaster's direction. If I could have, I would have. You bet your ass I would have nailed Luke to the cross, but this is 2020, not 3020."

Rex's top lip curled, but he didn't say anything on that subject, not whether he agreed or didn't, whether he was disgusted by my silence or not, then, I realized, he already knew. He'd known all of that because he'd looked into me, just like he said he had. He'd been waiting to see if I'd speak out about the situation.

"Sin protected you, Tiffany. All without knowing you're pregnant too, I guess, because I know he'd have said something to me before I shipped him over to Ohio."

I gnawed on the inside of my cheek, even as I let my hands dig into the armrests of the seat I'd taken. The office wasn't as grody as I'd have feared, but it was old-fashioned. More like this was his dad's domain or something rather than his.

But whether or not the decor screamed nineties, he didn't. He screamed power.

It flooded the room in a way that made the hair on the back of my neck tingle.

Danger.

I felt it.

Knew to be wary of it.

Jesus, I'd never felt the likes of it before.

Not even around Donavan and Luke Lancaster, and holy fuck, look at what they'd done.

My tongue felt like it was superglued to the roof of my mouth before I whispered, "I told him recently. Just before he came home."

"So he went to bat for you without knowing you were carrying his baby?" He arched a brow. "That seem like something you'd do for a woman you didn't give a fuck about?"

"No."

"Exactly. So I know he's in way over his head, and I get that. I'm glad for the fucker, like I already told you, but I need to protect him, no matter what the cost."

My eyes flared wide at that, and though my instinct was to leap to my feet and run for the hills, I didn't.

I stood my ground.

Because even though I never imagined myself being married to a biker, being his Old Lady, and having babies that wore 'My daddy's a Sinner' onesies, that was my life.

My choice.

And I wanted it.

I wanted that life so fucking much, I'd fight this bastard for it. I wouldn't let him scare me into running from something I actually knew I wanted.

Yeah.

Me.

I knew what I wanted.

And sure, it'd be nice to finish college and to be able to do something that helped people like the girls, but I wanted to be Sin's.

Yeah.

I did.

I really fucking did.

I wanted to be in bed with him every morning when, before he woke up, his feet started rubbing against each other as his body began to prepare for the day ahead. I wanted to see him stare at my coconut milk-laced coffee with distaste, even though he'd been the one to make it for me. I wanted to watch him laugh over some stupid YouTube video that he strong-armed me into watching—Mr. Beast. I had no idea why I loved watching those vids, but I totally did now that Sin had dragged me into the mix. I wanted to watch him with our kid, wanted to see his eyes darken when he realized we'd made this person together.

The only aspect of being a parent that didn't terrify me was knowing Sin would be at my side.

He was competent at life. I wasn't. I was spoiled and restless, aimless for years, used to being cosseted, even if that cosseting fell short of the mark sometimes. Sin had graduated from the school of hard knocks, and I figured that would help our child in ways I'd never be able to.

But yes, I wanted all that. And more. So much more.

Because with Sin?

I was Tiff.

Not a Farquar—be that a Farquar broke or rich. I was me. And he seemed to like me. In fact, he loved me, and I loved him for that.

I loved this world where a man would bring me in to make sure that I wasn't fucking Sin around. I loved that, if a man tried to hurt me, Sin would go to war for me—he'd have killed Luke if Giulia hadn't already done the deed for him. He'd told me that himself one night when he was still in Coshocton. I loved that I could hurt someone back if they tried to hurt me.

Our world was filled with violence, but we were in denial about it. We were held back by laws that protected no one. This world was a different one. I could dole out what was reaped upon me twofold in the form of a biker who'd shed blood in my name.

Sin was all I wanted and more.

So I grabbed a tight hold of the armrests and ground out, "Okay, what do you want to know?"

He arched a brow at me. "What do you have to tell me?"

I squinted at him, wondering what he wanted me to divulge. "I don't know. Daddy shared next to nothing with us about his business. He wanted us in the dark."

"You never heard any conversations on the phone, or snuck up on any business meetings?"

"Never. Even when he was talking with Donavan, they always tended to do it with no one around, and, also, his office was a safe room."

Rex's left brow arched up at that. "It was? Why?"

"We were rich. He was paranoid. And that was where the safe was, I guess."

The chair started squeaking again as he recommenced rocking. "Carry on."

"So, when he shut the door, you couldn't hear anything. That was how his meetings went down."

He studied me, and I could sense he was trying to discern whether I was bullshitting him or not, but I actually wasn't. I knew very little about my father's business, because he'd liked it that way.

When I was around twelve, I could still remember him joking about how I'd be taking his place on the board of directors when I'd graduated college, then something had happened. Something had changed. He'd gone from saying I could do anything I could set my mind to, to saying I was a woman and a woman's place wasn't in the boardroom.

Fuck, that still had the power to irritate the ever-loving crap out of me. Dad had been flawed. Didn't mean I didn't love him and miss him.

"Have you heard of Fuoco Corp?"

I frowned. "No. Should I have?"

"They're the front for the Fieri family. You have to have heard of them.

I know for a fact the Fieri family and Donavan were in business together, and that your dad went to school with them."

Though I understood what he was saying, only two words registered. "The front?"

"Yeah. The. Front."

"But I don't understand. Yeah, I know the Fieris. I know Gianni. He's a creep. I only met him like—" I shrugged. "A year ago or something. He was at one of Donavan's parties."

"Well, whether you know him or not, your father certainly did." He rubbed his chin. "And I wasn't only talking about Gianni. He's the son. Benito—Gianni's father—he's the one your dad went to school with."

My brow furrowed as I processed where he was going with this. "When you say 'front,'" I rasped, "you mean like...organized crime, don't you?"

Rex nodded. "Yeah, that's what I mean."

"You're saying my dad was involved with the..." I blew out a breath. "Mafia?"

"Exactly."

My throat felt like someone's hands were around it. "And the IRS wasn't involved?"

"No. Not at all. It was the mafia," Rex told me dispassionately. "They pulled the lines of credit on your father, and because they are who they are? It's no wonder your father took the easy way out. You think we're bad people? I can see it in your eyes when you look around the place, but you can guess again when you think about the Fieris. They're scumbags, and coming from me, that means more than you know."

My world had crashed around my feet when Daddy had died, so there was nothing left to crash, but that didn't mean I wasn't astonished.

I slumped back in my chair, grief and confusion warring with fear as I stared at the Prez.

This place wasn't my place yet. It was Sin's though, and with time, I knew it would become mine too. I wanted that. I did. But at the moment, I was still an outsider, and Rex was reminding me of that.

Painfully.

I could feel my body seizing up with tension as I rasped, "Why are you telling me this?"

"Because I wanted to know if you knew how your father's business was funded."

"No. I didn't."

"I can see that for myself now." He hummed under his breath. "Was your father close to Donavan?"

"I-I guess. I'd never have said...well, I didn't know they went to school together. They played golf once a week. I thought they were on friendly terms because of how close Lily and I were."

"That's interesting, don't you think?"

"Yeah, I do. But he really didn't share anything with us on that score, very little about his past or anything like that."

"Why didn't you question that? You don't seem like the sort of woman who wouldn't ask questions. You evidently aren't afraid to make waves."

That had me scowling at him, but I guessed I wasn't, and he was right. But also, neither was I the kind who questioned my entire childhood.

Parents were how they were. Kids didn't change their personalities that dramatically—Dad had always been closed off to a certain extent, and what hadn't been closed off was his love for me.

"Did you stop to wonder why your dad didn't regale you with tales about his time in college?"

Rex snorted at my question. "Pop didn't go to college, but I figure you're right." He huffed out a laugh. "Okay, I believe you."

Even though I knew how important his judgment was, I still muttered, "King Solomon has spoken."

"You should be grateful I have." He narrowed his eyes at me. "If I find out you're lying—"

"I'm not! I have no reason to lie!" I snapped. "Frankly, I'm pretty pissed that I'm getting the third degree when I haven't done anything wrong." And I hadn't.

No, I hadn't come forward after Luke had died, but with little to tell the authorities that wasn't going to have me laughed out of the police station, it wasn't like there was much I could do.

"Did you trap Sin?"

I gaped at Rex. "Are you kidding me?"

"Do I look like I'm having a ball here?"

My nostrils flared in hurt anger. "No. I didn't trap him. I had no need to trap him."

"Good, that's all I needed to know. Got a special hatred for women who trap men with kids, and I know Sin feels the exact same way, seeing as he was one of 'em and it didn't work out." He firmed his lips. "You should talk to your baby daddy before the sprout appears, because there's shit he should tell you."

Why did that statement feel like an olive branch? I released a soft breath as I calmly stated, "I remember—Grizzly."

He nodded. "Grizzly. You can go now."

I glared at his dismissal, which made me feel like I was back in school, but I got to my feet and strode out without a backwards glance. I hated that my heart was pounding in my ears, and that I felt all hot and flustered.

His interrogation had been unexpected. I hadn't known his reason for wanting to speak with me, but I figured it had to do with the girls, so to get blindsided that way?

I rounded the corner and went to the only place I knew where very little sex went down—the kitchen.

Hiding myself in the pantry, which was stocked full to the brim, I rested my back against the wall and closed my eyes.

Since his death, things had been a nightmare. A walking nightmare. But now? It was a thousand times worse.

My dad had been up to his neck with the mafia.

The motherfucking mafia.

And he'd been friends with Gianni Fieri's father—Gianni was the creep I remembered from the Lancaster's party a while back. Dad had made us all go to a fuck ton of parties, but that one had been particularly drab.

The way Fieri had looked at Lily?

Just the memory sent chills down my spine, and I knew Lily had felt it too.

Something had happened, some kind of insider trading I thought that had put Fieri away, but in all honesty, I couldn't remember. Just knew he was in jail, because Dad had happened to mention it to Mom over dinner a while back, and I was glad about that now, even if I hadn't thought all that much about it at the time.

I was, all of a sudden, happy that Lily sported that tattoo of Link's on her wrist. I knew what it meant—she was his, and the MC? They'd go to war for her.

If Fieri was mafia and Donavan Lancaster had been in business with him...

God.

Maybe 'war' wasn't selling the kind of shit we were in short.

"What did you get us involved in, Daddy?" I whispered to the stacked shelves, racking my brain for anything that might have clued me in... Then, I thought about the day when everything had changed *before* Dad's death.

When I'd found Mom and Dad arguing after the news had hit about Donavan.

She had to know something, didn't she? I reached for my cell, but when I put the call through, she ignored it.

Like she'd been ignoring me since I'd told her my being pregnant wasn't a TikTok prank.

Lost, uneasy, confused, and scared, my heart was still pounding in my ears as I headed on out of the pantry, and when I walked into the main thoroughfare and saw Sin hugging another woman?

Let's just say that was the cherry on the fucking cake.

THIRTY

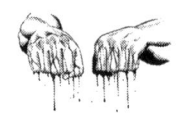

SIN

I FELT the hair stand up on the back of my neck when Tiffany approached.

I'd never been so hyperaware of another woman in my entire life, but it was like something about her got to me in a way I'd have figured was insane if another brother had told me about it.

It'd been there that first night.

I'd felt her watching me from the start.

A brother had pointed her out, pointed out her candid stare, but I'd known.

I'd sensed her.

And what did men do when they were feeling on edge?

They fucked up and pulled stupid shit.

Like fingering the club snatch in front of the woman who made you aware of her without having shared two words.

Tiffany came across as strong and confident, and I knew deep down she was, but the life made her nervous.

And I got it.

I'd be a fucking moron not to. So her finding me this way?

Not ideal.

I pulled back from Mary Catherine with a soft smile, and murmured, "MaryCat, I have someone to introduce you to."

Tiffany's steps had been soft, soft enough for me not to hear her presence, but I was still a Marine, even if I'd long since lost my uniform.

I'd heard her.

I'd know her tread anywhere.

She sloped in at the toe on her right foot, which made her heel squeak just a tad when she walked.

Undeniably hers.

But even though I'd known it was Tiff, I'd felt her first, and I also felt her bewilderment and hurt.

I twisted around to face her and called, "Tiff? I want you to meet MaryCat."

Tiff's eyes were wide when she met Mary Catherine's, and from the size of her belly, I knew she was suddenly feeling a lot more secure. The fact MaryCat had a tattoo sloping down from behind her ear, soaring under her chin, and ending on the side of her jaw in a flower caught her attention too.

Within the tattooed petals, her Old Man's name was visible, even if it was cleverly shielded in the shading, and I watched her shoulders droop with relief.

I guessed I should be irritated at her lack of faith in me, but ironically enough, I wasn't. I was glad. Not because I wanted her to feel vulnerable or insecure. Not because I was a dick who wanted my woman to be scared and on edge about my loyalty to her.

But because it meant she cared.

She fucking cared.

She wanted me so much that it hurt her to think of me with another, and in my world, that was important. It meant something. Not just with the sluts who wandered these halls, sharing themselves with any brother who tugged them onto their laps, but as it had been with my ex.

I knew it would take time for both of us to open up around each other. We'd been together a while, I guessed, long enough to make a baby, but whenever we'd been together, it had been our little secret.

That mattered.

It meant we'd never been around other people before. I'd never been claimed by her, and she'd never been claimed by me.

Everything was changing, so we might as well be starting fresh.

I'd told her the truth though. If someone touched me, I'd tell her, just because I knew what the bunnies were like—spiteful bitches who wanted to become Old Ladies, and when a brother wouldn't brand them? They got bitter.

Nasty.

Twisted.

Not with the brothers who'd put them in their fucking place, but with their women.

And sometimes there were battles a man couldn't fight for his woman. Sometimes, in this life, they had to go to war on their own, all while knowing you had their back and that you'd fucking kill anyone who dared to hurt them.

But rep, position, posturing, and all that shit was important here. Dominance mattered. Survival of the fittest played as big of a part here as it did in evolution. Darwin would get a boner every time he walked through the clubhouse's doors.

When MaryCat tugged on my cut, I shot her a look and curved my arm over her shoulder, even as I held out a hand for Tiff.

She wandered nearer, looking confused and uncertain, but I immediately cleared shit up by saying, "MaryCat is my sister."

Both women tensed.

MaryCat because I'd never said those words out loud before.

Tiff because this was the first time she was hearing I had a sister.

I didn't even care that Steel was sitting in the kitchen, spooning up Cheerios from a massive bowl, and that he sprayed a mouthful out onto the counter.

Didn't pay any attention to how Storm choked on the bite he took of his sausage biscuit.

Didn't give a shit that Nyx braked to a halt on his way out of the gym toward the kitchen.

No, I didn't care.

Because it was time.

Time people knew.

So I jerked my head out of my ass, aware that I'd been keeping secrets for too long, and muttered, "MaryCat, this is Tiff. She's my Old Lady."

"What the fuck? You're related?" Nyx groused, his scowl ferocious, even as he tempered it some when he looked at MaryCat.

The irony being, of course, that her dad was a fucking Five Pointer. Nastier cunts than him were hard to find.

He suited our mother.

She was as much a cunt as he was.

Just like she'd pushed me into running off to find my real father, who wasn't much better than her, she'd pushed MaryCat into finding me...when she'd inadvertently fallen for one of my brothers.

MaryCat was the reason the Five Points and the Sinners had a deal going on. Of course, no one knew why she'd come, just that she had, and because that was what women did—hung around the place—no one had thought to question where she was living or what she was doing.

Tiff's mouth worked as she finally accepted my beckoning hand, but she managed to get out, "Is, I mean, who...I mean... Hi?"

I snorted. Tiff was a smart woman, but I loved her greeting. She pinched me on the side, and muttered, "Shut up, you. I can't believe you're telling me this here."

"Had to tell you at some point. This was good enough."

Steel, from across the kitchen, demanded, "Why the fuck didn't you tell anyone else? I took a bullet to the ass for you last year."

I snickered at the memory. "Not your business."

"But it is now?" Nyx grumbled, as he peeked his head into the fridge and pulled out a bottled protein shake.

"It's Tiff's business, and I don't want to keep shit from her."

Steel scoffed, "Fuck's sake. You guys are turning into fucking pussies on me. First Nyx, then goddamn Link, and now you? What the fuck?"

I didn't bother arguing, but I didn't have to—Nyx strode over to him and punched the fucker's arm. Hard enough for Steel's eyes to bug.

"Shut the fuck up, dick."

Giulia snickered, and I twisted around to see that she'd wandered in with a big bag of what appeared to be dirty laundry. "You tell him, Nyx."

Steel flipped her the bird in between rubbing his arm. "Giulia, two words—"

"Wuv you?" she mocked, grinning at him as she dumped the laundry down. "I swear, you fuckers are so worried these guys are turning into pussies. Why? You want to fuck them?"

Steel's eyes bugged out harder than they had when Nyx had punched him in the shoulder.

Me? Nyx? We bust a gut laughing.

MaryCat even joined in with her soft, tinkling laugh, and Tiff smirked as she relaxed deeper into me. Storm, as per usual, watched us like we were on a docusoap, but even his lips twitched.

Trust Giulia to set the atmosphere on the right track.

When she moved over to the fruit bowl on the counter and picked up an apple, she cast a look around us and asked, "There a reason we're all standing here like something from a sitcom?"

"I was just introducing my sister to Tiffany."

Giulia frowned. "Your sister?" Then her eyes drifted over to MaryCat, and I saw her gaze alight on the tattoo. "Huh. I don't think we've met before."

MaryCat's smile was shy. "I don't really come to the compound that much. Digger doesn't like me here—"

"Can't fucking blame him," Giulia rumbled. "Not around these dicks. Not with a face like yours." She whistled under her breath. "You're beautiful."

MaryCat lurched back in surprise. "Umm, thank you."

Giulia shrugged. "Got eyes, don't I? I mean, babe, you're so fucking cute, I wish I was gay."

Nyx snorted. "I'm glad you're not."

She shot him a grin. "Don't worry, baby, I love your Terminator dick more."

Steel rolled his eyes. "This is what I'm fucking talking about."

"Shut up," Nyx and I said simultaneously, the pair of us shooting him a warning glower before we grinned at each other.

"Well, it's a pleasure to meet you," Giulia chirped at MaryCat, before casting a wary look Tiffany's way. "Everything okay with Amara, Ghost, and Tatána?"

"The girls are fine," Tiff replied huskily. "They miss you."

Giulia's nose crinkled at that. "Girls? They're not girls."

"What else should I call them?" Tiff countered wryly.

Giulia huffed. "I'll be over there in a short while. I just needed to get my head back on straight after our run."

Nyx wandered over to her, hauling her into his side as he dipped his chin and pressed a kiss to her head. He didn't say anything, but then, he didn't have to.

Tiff and MaryCat wouldn't understand, but we did.

The first kill—and that fucker Lancaster wasn't a kill, that was self-defense—was always a tough one to deal with, and that was only right.

Didn't matter if the cunt deserved to die, it was still hard on the soul, because by ridding the world of that evil, you were taking some of that evil into you. Corrupting yourself to make the world a better place.

I squeezed Tiff's waist, both overjoyed and weirded out by the fact our kid was in her belly, and looking forward to feeling her up when she was as big as MaryCat.

"Well, when you can. Amara really missed you."

Giulia shook her head. "She has a weird fucking way of showing it."

Tiff said, "Makes sense. You're their safety net."

"How so?"

Steel grunted. "You know how when animals are born they, like, imprint on their mothers?" He dropped his spoon in the bowl of cereal, making milk splatter on the table.

Storm jibed, "You're the mother hen."

Giulia's nose wrinkled, but Nyx was the one who chuckled. "Of all the fucking answers you two could come up with, you bring up fucking poultry?"

"Better chickens than fucking snakes!" Steel growled back.

"He has a point," Storm said with a laugh.

"Do snakes even imprint?" MaryCat mused, curious to the last, and somehow, that was the most ridiculous question I'd heard all fucking year, and I couldn't stop myself from laughing.

When the others joined in, Tiffany was the last to follow. She eyed us all like we were fucking Martians before, her lips twitching, she caught the laughter bug and let it swallow her whole.

It was good to see her lighten up, to loosen up among my brothers, my family. This was all alien to her as well, so it would take time.

But time was all we had.

Me and her?

We were it for one another.

She didn't have to recognize it for me to know it.

A man didn't wait nearly thirty-eight fucking years to have his heart cleaved to another only to give up easily.

Yeah, this was a strange environment for her, yeah, her family situation was fucked up, but we'd get through it.

Together.

Because that was the only constant that mattered.

Her. Me. United as one.

And baby made three.

THIRTY-ONE

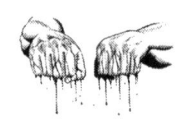

SIN

THE FEEL of her arms around my waist on the back of my hog was a sensation that wasn't going to stop giving me a boner for a long time to come.

And riding a bike with a boner wasn't ideal, that was for fucking sure.

Still, I'd deal with it, because it felt epic as fuck to have her with me.

To have her at my back, at my side.

"Sin?"

Her hollered screech reached my ears, as did the way she tensed her fingers around my waist. I pulled over, indicating the second I could, and when I came to a halt, she murmured, "Can we ride past my old place?"

The request surprised me, but I did as bid, taking us the long way around West Orange to reach her house.

The subdivision where her place was located epitomized the word 'swank.' I didn't like it. I preferred shit to be more real than a place where the roads were lined with fucking palm trees.

This was goddamn NJ, not LA. The sheer ecologically unfriendliness of the place was a testament to corporate America not giving a shit about the land we lived in, but hey, not my monkey, not my circus.

As we pulled up to the manned gate, an older guy approached in a security uniform. He eyed the bike, then me, then his gaze softened on Tiff and, without a word, he raised the gate for us to enter.

Each house on the six-dozen strong estate was a mansion and belonged on an old-school episode of *Cribs*. Massive gates and long driveways were pretty much all you could see except for the roofs that peeped through the filigree lacework rails.

The streets were beautifully lined, not a pothole in sight, and I was sure that a bird wouldn't dare to fucking shit on the sidewalk, not without fear of being shot.

It was inauthentic and extravagant, but that was nothing compared to her place.

When we approached, she tugged at my waist again when we were around twenty feet from the gates, telling me, I figured, to stop here.

"I'm surprised the security guy let us in."

"I was kind to Leonard when his wife was sick," was all she said, before she fell silent as she looked at a house that had once been hers but now wasn't.

By comparison, my place was a shithole, but she seemed happy there.

Not once had she even suggested she spend the night at Lily's. Neither of us had said anything to indicate otherwise, but yeah, she'd moved in with me. After this palace, while it wasn't my thing, it had to be a come down.

Unease settled heavily on me, and then I stopped it in its tracks.

There was no point in second-guessing her reasoning for anything. She wanted me. And she kept on showing me that.

"You okay, angel?" I rasped when we just sat there, idling. I didn't mind, but her arms around me were tight, and her face was burrowed into my shoulder.

"I-I miss him."

It was a whisper.

A hurt, pain-filled whisper.

"I wish I could bring him back for you, sweetheart," I replied softly, reaching down and covering one of her hands with mine.

"He wasn't perfect. No one is. But I-I just can't..." She sucked in a breath.

"You can't what?"

"I don't know what's happening."

My brow puckered. "In what sense?"

"Who's Grizzly?"

I tensed. "Who the fuck told you about him?"

"Rex. When he asked me if I was some kind of—Christ, I don't even know. A gangster's moll or something."

The tension in me surged to a fever pitch. "He spoke to you without me there?"

She clung to me when I tried to turn around to face her, but she kept her nose burrowed in my cut. "Don't. Please."

"He had no right to talk to you without me there," I growled. "And sure as fuck not about Grizzly."

"Who is he?"

"Why did Rex think you were a gangster's fucking moll?" I snapped, unable to moderate my tone, even though she was upset.

I'd smash the fucker's face in.

"Because Donavan Lancaster went to school with Benito Fieri, who, according to Rex, is mafia." She sucked in a breath. "Turned out my father attended college at the same time with them."

"You didn't know that?"

"No. Never. He never talked about the past."

"Ever?" My brows rose in surprise.

"No. Never," she hissed. "Do you not believe me either?"

"No, of course not! I'm just surprised."

"Yeah, well, if I thought about it myself, then I'd be surprised too, but that wasn't how he worked."

"How did he work?"

"He focused on the present. On the future. He believed in goals," she mumbled, her tone telling me she was in the past. With her father. Not here with me. "The irony being that he'd have a daughter who had no idea what to do with herself."

"You knew. You just weren't ready to make the decision," I told her firmly.

"Maybe." She laughed. "Maybe not. Every step I made took me away from what I thought I wanted, and now I'm here." A hum escaped her. "Funny how things turned out better than I ever expected."

Despite myself, that hit me square in the fucking feels. "What kind of goals?" I mumbled, not only because I wanted her to keep talking, it was only now that I recognized we hadn't mentioned her father once since I'd returned home—how goddamn selfish of me was that? What a fucking prize I was—but also because I had no desire to talk about fucking Grizzly.

"Sometimes it was to own a certain watch or a car, another time it was to have a head office for his company in every state."

"Christ. Every state?" Jesus. I'd known the bastard was rich. But that fucking rich?

"Yeah. That was before the downturn though. When I was a kid, like, when I was twelve? We suffered a lot of losses, but we got through them."

She gulped. "I think that's why it made it so hard when he didn't even try to fight through this one. He was like that. Always striving for more."

"Sometimes it gets tiring, always striving."

I knew that from my own past. Fuck, just wishing for a day when Mom wouldn't forget to put food in the refrigerator had been exhausting.

"Maybe. I guess I'll never know why he did it," she said mournfully.

"Did he leave a note?"

"Not that I know of. Mom didn't tell me if she found one."

"She found him?"

"Yeah." Her gulp said it all, and when she changed the subject I let her. "Rex said that his company was funded by the Fieri family, Sin. It's crazy for me to think that could be true."

"A lot of corporations are fronts," I told her. "It's not that surprising."

"My dad wasn't like that." She made a scoffing sound. "Or at least, the dad I thought he was didn't seem to be like that."

Because she sounded like she was on the brink of tears, I muttered, "Grizzly is Rex's uncle."

She tensed. "Rex's uncle? Why would he want me to talk about him with you?"

I pulled a face at nothing in particular as I muttered, "Because he's my father."

"What? You're Rex's cousin?"

Blowing out a breath, I groused, "Unfortunately. Grizzly and I never got on."

"Start at the beginning."

"I don't get why the fuck he was talking about this shit," I snapped, determined that I really was going to beat the shit out of my Prez when I got my hands on him.

"Maybe because it was important?"

"It isn't. Rex and I don't tell anyone. We never have, and we never will."

"How come?"

"It's how I want it. I don't want to get any perks for being blood—"

"He doesn't help you out more than the brothers?" she queried doubtfully.

"No. The only time he has is with the Ohio situation. Fuck knows what might have happened if Rex hadn't listened to me."

She squeezed me. "I'm sorry."

"Not your fault. That fucker's fault. It's all right now. I'm back home, you're with me, and that cunt is waiting on a crypt. Exactly how it should be."

Tiff burrowed into me as she inquired, "Why didn't you and your dad get along?"

"Because I didn't know him. Not until I was older. Mom wasn't the best parent in the world. She was a selfish bitch then, and she's still one now, but she's morphed from being a trashy slut into a trashy wife. I wouldn't be surprised if Mary Catherine's father divorces her soon for a younger model."

She winced. "That's a little harsh."

"No, it ain't. I knew what she was when I was a kid, and I know it even more now. Just because she's stopped whoring herself out for cash doesn't mean she isn't still doing it with her husband. He might be a high-ranking officer in the Five Points, but that doesn't mean she ain't still his whore."

"You hate her?"

The long-held bitterness that had kept me under control almost all my life froze up inside me at the question, then I figured I was the man I was today because of that slut. So I relaxed and thought about it. Thought about how good it felt for her to hold me. How good it felt for my future not to be solely focused on the MC. How good it felt to know I might be the MC's Enforcer someday... All those things were made possible because of how my past had forged me.

So, I released a breath, expelled the poison, and sucked in some fresh air that wasn't tainted with hate.

"I actually don't. I did. I'll admit that. I fucking loathed her for a long time. The shit she made me listen to, the shit she did, the way she'd treat me? Throwing shit at me when I was little. Now? I know she was a fucking kid herself."

"She had you when she was young?"

"When she was fifteen."

"Jesus."

"Yeah." I blew out a breath.

"Grizzly was eighteen when he met her, but even though he was young, he knew what she was, and he also was as much of a dick back then as he was before he died."

"He died?"

"On a run," I said dispassionately—about his death, not about the lie I just told her. If she knew the truth? She'd never let me near her again. I'd lie to her about nothing else except for that bastard's death and my involvement in it.

"Oh."

That summed it up.

I cleared my throat. "I remember Grizzly from when I was really young, like his visits when I was just a brat, but it's very faint. I almost forgot about him until she mentioned that my father was a Satan's Sinner because he stopped coming around when I was maybe seven?

"One day, I got sick of being her fucking punching bag, sick of her never feeding me, sick of me having to steal shit just to get by, for having to fight for every mouthful of food, and I left home. Ran away to NJ, found the clubhouse, and almost pissed myself as I walked up the driveway when the Prospect let me in."

"I'm surprised they did. Thought they'd ask who you were."

"I'm my father's spitting image."

It was her turn to clear her throat. "Well, I'm sorry for your sake, Sin, but not for mine. You're a beautiful man."

My nose crinkled. "Shut up. Men aren't beautiful."

She snickered, and the sound of her laughter during such a heavy conversation was music to my goddamn ears. "You're totally beautiful. A rose by any other name—"

"Still sends ants up your nose."

She froze. "Huh?"

I laughed. "If you sniff a rose, ants come out of the petals, crawl up your nose, and enter your brain."

"I need scientific proof of that theory," she retorted.

"Will a Google search be enough?" I joked, making her snicker.

"Go on though. You were saying?"

I heaved a sigh. "They recognized me. All of them did, but they were the older crowd. The last generation. Lot of them are dead now, and what happens inside the club stays there."

"You mean they never told their kids who you were? Christ."

I shrugged. "Nothing to tell. What the fuck does a bastard kid have as any importance? Lots of them around. I was no different. Sure, I was related to the Prez, but again, so what?"

"Did they take you in?" she asked after a few seconds.

"Still here, ain't I?" I muttered awkwardly, because that wasn't down to dear old Dad. Nope. That was down to Bear, Rex's dad, and the MC's last Prez.

"You enlisted for a reason. A lot of young kids do that because they're looking to find a home."

Maybe it was pussy assed of me to do it, but I reached for her hand once more, entwined my fingers with hers, and said, "Yeah? Well, the Marines weren't no home. This is my home. You, me, the kid. Us."

A shaky sigh escaped her, and she sank into me like I was all she needed in this fucking world. "Yes. We are."

"We don't need mansions. We don't need—"

"You don't have to finish that sentence," she whispered. "No, we don't need any of that stuff. I never imagined I'd have someone like you, Sin. Someone who'd want me for me. Who'd want to be with me because I'm Tiffany and not just Tiffany Farquar. It's... I'm still trying to get my head around it if I'm being honest."

"What's to get your head around, Tiff? You're fucking awesome."

"Takes one to know one," she countered wryly, but I heard her smile and knew she'd liked what I had to say.

"You know that first night?"

She hummed under her breath.

"I knew where you were. At all times. I saw Storm beside you, and I didn't like it. Not when he pulled his fucking cock out, not even when he just took a fucking seat.

"I saw you wander around the MC, all wide-eyed and watching shit like it was a science experiment.

"I didn't like it. I liked your ass, but I didn't like how you were fucking staring at shit as though it was too good for you." I sucked in a breath. "Then you goddamn smirked at me. And it fucked with my head. You fucked with my head. It's what you did from the start—"

"And what I'll do until the day you die," she purred, twisting her hand in mine so she could lace our fingers together.

I had only one word to say to that.

"Amen."

THIRTY-TWO

SIN

THE NEXT MORNING

"THE FUCK IS YOUR PROBLEM." When I shoved Rex in the shoulder, hard enough to make him fall back, I knew it was a mistake, knew it, but it didn't stop me from fucking doing it.

Rex's eyes flared wide with warning, and the stillness he was renowned for made him look like a goddamn puma on the verge of pouncing. "You got a problem?"

"Damn fucking straight I've got a motherfucking problem. You think you can speak to my woman without me there? The fuck, man?" I snarled at him, but I wasn't a fool.

Even in the haze of rage, I wasn't going to get in his face now I'd gotten a good lick in. I wasn't averse to having the shit kicked out of me, but I was averse to Tiff having to see it and having to look at the fucking shiners every day for a couple weeks.

His jaw tensed, before he snapped, "The only reason I'm not going to make you kiss your own ass right now is because you came to me in my office."

I was so mad at him I couldn't see straight, but I didn't have a fucking death wish.

Not only would that bring Rex's ire to my shoulders, but Nyx's too.

I tipped my chin up. "Your momma didn't raise no fool."

That had him bellowing out a sigh as I dropped Rene into the conversation. "Motherfucker."

"Yeah, I am right now. Except I'm fucking the *future* mother of my goddamn kid, Rex. The fuck were you thinking loading that shit on her? Treating her like she's the fucking enemy?"

He reached up and scraped a hand over his chin. "You're not the Enforcer yet, Sin."

I heard the warning.

I wouldn't be the Enforcer if I didn't back the fuck down.

"Since when have you known me to back off when something needs to be said? How the hell would you feel if I'd approached Rachel, got her all riled up and questioning shit, and all while she was carrying your kid?"

Rex's glower lessened after I mentioned his Achilles' heel. "I'd want to make you eat your balls."

His admission had some of the tension seeping from my shoulders. "E-fucking-xactly. Why the hell did you approach her without me? I'm her Old Man, Rex. You come through me with this shit."

"Ain't branded her yet."

"Fuck you," I growled, furious at the statement. "She's pregnant."

Rex scowled. "So? Even more reason to brand her."

"You can't get ink when you're pregnant, dumb fuck."

"Watch it, Sin," he snapped.

"What's to fucking watch? Can't make my Old Lady my Old goddamn Lady because she's pregnant." I flipped him the bird. "That mean she ain't entitled to the same protection as Giulia?" When I arched my neck, thrusting my chin at him, his answering scowl didn't make me back the fuck off. "You and I both know if you'd pulled that shit on Giulia, Nyx would be more than in your goddamn face over this."

Rex's temper settled at my retort, and he grunted, "Didn't know that about pregnant women and ink."

"Yeah, I see that," I retorted. "But she's mine. Do you fucking hear me? I claim her here in front of you, and the second she can get ink, I'm getting her ink."

"A doctor told you she can't? She isn't—" He shrugged his shoulders. "—trying to get out of it?"

"No," I raged, fury making me feel like steam was surging out of my pores. "What the fuck? I'd ask if you didn't like her, but I don't give a shit if you do or not. She's mine, Rex. Do you fucking get that?"

Rex's jaw tensed but he raised his hands. "I get that."

"So what's the problem?"

"Nothing. I just didn't know the score. That's all."

"Well, now you fucking do. What's this shit about Fieri, anyway? You should have talked to me about this first."

"Yeah, you're right. I should."

"I'd have lost everything for her, man. If anyone knew that, it was you."

"And that was why I had to protect you."

"From her? I don't need protecting from her." I shook my head. "Here's me trying to make her see the MC as my family, and you just go and knock shit back for me."

"I'm sorry, Sin, I didn't fucking know, all right? I can see you want to wife her, but brand her? That's another thing entirely."

Typical—didn't think there'd be much asslicking by way of apology from this fucker. I was damn lucky to have gotten what I did.

"You should have spoken to me about Grizzly as well. That entire fucking conversation you breached all kinds of boundaries."

"I was preparing her—"

I narrowed my eyes at him. "We agreed. That shit would stay in the club."

"And it will. She needs to fucking know you've got a temper on you."

"Why? You were hoping to scare her off? Make her back away? Make up your fucking mind. Either she's bad news for me or I'm bad news for her." I clenched my teeth. "Not only will I never fucking hurt her, she's carrying my kid. You wanted her to run off? Take my kid from me? I won't be like my fucking father. I want to be in my kid's life, do you hear me?"

Rex, brave bastard that he was, approached the lion in his den and moved toward me. He put a hand on my shoulder, then, when I didn't snap it off, he put the other there too. I knew I was breathing like I was a bull in the middle of a fucking fight with a matador, but that was how goddamn enraged I was.

Not only had he disrespected Tiff, he'd disrespected me. He'd told her shit I wasn't ready to tell her, and worse of all, he'd told her shit that scared her without making sure I was in the loop first.

"I hear you, and you will be. That wasn't my intent," he told me softly, not stopping until my forehead was butted up against his. "We're family, whether or not you like to hide from it. I want what's best for you."

"She's what's best for me," I rasped. "Fuck, she's the only good thing in my goddamn life."

Rex argued, "That ain't true."

"Yeah. It is." I let him see the whole truth and nothing but the fucking truth in my eyes, and when he did, I whispered, "Yeah. Been hanging on by a fucking thread for a long goddamn time, cuz. Too much drink, too much sex. I can't deal with this shit without her, man."

His hand tightened about my shoulder. "Fuck."

"Yeah. Fuck." A breath rattled from my lips. "Don't scare her off."

"I won't. I was trying to protect you. She's in deep, and you didn't know it."

"Neither did she," I rasped. "She didn't know shit until you tore her eyes open."

Rex winced. "I'm sorry."

"Not enough," I replied, honestly. "She's my woman. Just remember that."

"I ain't likely to forget," he rumbled. "Not now."

A sigh heaved from me. "Good. Now, what the fuck is going on?"

"Lodestar and Maverick keep uncovering clusterfucks," he muttered. His forehead pushed into mine, not aggressively, like he was reminding me we were blood. I appreciated it. When he pulled away and scrubbed a hand over his hair, tugging at the ends like he wanted to tug it off by the roots, I watched him as he strode over to a tray of liquor. When he poured himself a JD, neat, I eyed it warily—fucker didn't drink this early in the day.

Hadn't since he'd become Prez.

"What's going on?"

"Told Storm about the situation in Coshocton in this morning's council meeting."

The change of subject didn't bother me. I knew how it felt to need to work up to something. That Rex, this hardcore fuck, needed to build himself up put me on edge. "Didn't go well?"

"No. Didn't."

"Can't blame him. Wouldn't want to be away from my kid, either."

Rex hissed out a breath. "I don't want that. If the dumbfuck had kept it in his pants, Keira would still be with him, and they'd be going down together."

I scrubbed a hand over my jaw. "Whether you want it or not, you're asking him to leave his family behind."

"The family he screwed over."

My shrug said it all—I agreed with him, but it didn't take away from the truth, did it?

"We need someone we can trust down there."

"Steel—"

"Prefer him up here. Needs to be Storm. Fucker's killing himself here." Rex's mouth turned mutinous. "It'll be hard at first, but I ain't letting this drop. He can throw as many tantrums as he wants. Coshocton, fucking responsibility, leadership, it'll straighten him out more than any twelve steps." He took a deep gulp of JD, then rasped, "Second he's gone, I'm putting you forward as Enforcer and Nyx as VP. You down with that?"

"You know I am, brother."

Rex dipped his chin. "Shit's coming our way." He peered out the window like there were rolling golden hills out there, Elysian Fields and all that shit. Course, I only knew what they were because, while Tiff was in the bath last night and I was shaving, she'd told me about her trip to Paris and to the *Champs Elysees.*

Her life and mine couldn't have been more different up until now, but the truth was, more than just the baby in her belly meant our futures were entwined.

I loved that woman.

Enough to fucking shed blood for—mine and any cunt who got in her path.

"Shit's always coming our way," I countered, strolling over to his side, and leaning against the same window he was staring out of.

"The *Famiglia* are everywhere. They cast long nets. We've got caught up in the haul. I refuse to lose any of my men to them." His hand tightened around the tumbler in his grip, and I wasn't surprised when the fucker burst. He just stared at it, at the puddle of JD, the shards of glass at his feet, and the one burrowed into his palm.

"You won't lose any men, cuz," I told him. "Nyx and I will make sure of it."

He caught me a look. "Not sure you can make a promise like that, man."

I smirked at him, reached over, and pulled out the glass shard. "Wanna bet?"

THIRTY-THREE

TIFFANY

"SHE'S HIS SISTER?"

Lily's bewilderment wasn't exactly difficult for me to comprehend. I was still bewildered myself.

After all, Sin had introduced me to her before things had derailed, then later on, he'd explained some things.

In fact, a lot of things.

A helluva lot of things.

Stuff I was still scratching my head over.

"Half-sister, I guess is more accurate."

"Who's the shared parent?" she asked, as she sat back at her father's desk, crossing her legs at the ankle as she slouched.

The sight looked good on her, and I wasn't sure why.

I eyed her from across the desk before I inquired softly, "What are you doing here?"

She blinked. "Taking back ownership."

"Ownership? Of what?"

"Of me." She pursed her lips. "This was where he'd punish me."

My eyes flared at that, and I half-sat up, like the chair itself was infected by the taint. "You're joking."

"I wish I was."

"Lily, you don't have to put yourself through this—"

"Yes, I do. I want to. Link has already tried to talk me out of it, but I want to do this. It makes me feel better, knowing that he'll never be able to sit at this desk ever again. Not only because he'll get arrested the second he lands on U.S. soil, but because all of this is in my name." Her smile was gleeful—and who could blame her? "That makes me very happy."

"I can see that," I rasped, but I squirmed in my seat, uneasy with being in here now.

Lily, spying that, rolled her eyes. "You want to sit in another room?"

Warily, I shook my head. The ornate office was Donavan's style—overbearing, expensive, filled with questionable art.

I'd never been in here before, and to be frank, I didn't want to come in here again now.

Her bravery in staying in a house where her abuse had occurred astonished me. I'd always known she had the strength of ten women, but fuck, I was coming face to face with it now.

"What are you doing in here anyway?"

"The books."

"The books?" I frowned. "Who's books?"

"Link's. You know he manages the garage?"

"For the MC? Yeah."

"I think he has dyslexia. He was telling me that Rex was on his ass to do the accounts, and that he couldn't get his head around them, so I said I'd do them.

"It's relaxing. Plus, it's like a double 'fuck you' to the office."

Her grin beamed back at me in a way that had me laughing at her. Despite the situation, despite the trauma and the horror, that she could find the fortitude to overcome it all?

"I'm so proud you're my sister," I rasped, meaning every word.

Her eyes glittered at that. "Thanks, Tee-Tee."

We grinned at her use of the old nickname she'd called me before we'd known what 'titties' were, and I leaned over the massive desk, reaching hard until, when she did the same, our hands met and clasped.

Then, I wriggled and winced. "What is it?" she questioned, frowning at my fidgeting.

"My boobs are really tender," I told her with a huff, pulling free from her grasp and rubbing the side where I'd dug it into the edge of the desk to reach for her. "When Sin first got back home, he sucked on my nipples until I exploded and passed out."

Her mouth dropped open. "You came from having your nipples sucked?"

"Yeah. It was intense," I admitted.

"Sounds like it. I did...something to Link too."

I arched a brow. "What?"

"We still haven't...you know, but that doesn't mean we don't fool around," she hedged, her tone close to prim.

"I'll bet," I said drolly. "Go on, spill the details."

"I fucked him with a butt plug," she whispered, but her face was bright pink, even as she looked turned on by both the memory as well as proud of herself at having accomplished that much.

It was impressive too, considering she'd told the girls and me that Donavan had raped her anally.

It was hard, because I wanted to ask how she felt about what she'd done with Link, what head space it had put her in, but I could see on her face she'd enjoyed it. And I didn't want to make things serious by ruining the memory for her.

"He liked it?"

She bit her lip. "He loved it. I did too. It was so hot."

"Link doesn't look like the kind of guy—"

"He's kinky." Lily shrugged at the admission when I snorted. "He is. The stuff he suggests when he's dirty talking with me." She wafted a hand in front of her face. "I'm half terrified and half turned on all the time. And he loves going down on me. Like the man is obsessed."

"Woop woop!" I declared with a laugh, my eyes sparkling with glee. "Gotta love a man who knows how to treat a lady right."

Lily grinned. "Yeah, he sure knows how to do that."

"Lily?"

"Yeah?" she asked, her tone wary, but I understood her reticence as my tone of voice had shifted some.

"I know you're doing the books, but I'd kill for a burger and fries."

Her mouth rounded, and I knew I'd surprised her because she'd expected some serious talk, but all I was thinking about was my gut. Then, her lips formed a grin. "Is this a craving?"

"Shit," I whispered, "I think it might be."

She snickered. "Tiffany, I hate to break it to you, sweetheart, but you're a vegetarian."

My heart thumped in my chest at the thought. "I mean, I know, but I... I forgot."

Lily's nostrils flared delicately. "I think you can smell beef in the air. I think we're having steak for dinner."

My mouth watered. "I really need beef." I thought about yesterday. "Storm was eating a sausage biscuit thing at the clubhouse when all this was going down with Mary Catherine. I wanted to French him for it."

She snickered, her eyes dancing with glee as she remarked, "Maybe you can do what Phoebe and Joey did in *Friends*. When she was pregnant?"

"Oh God, do you think Sin would be vegetarian for me?"

"I think he's head over heels for you. Don't see why he can't sacrifice some meat while you sacrifice your body to that baby."

"Sacrifice is a hard word," I groused with a pout.

"Babies do the worst things to a woman's body."

"I know that. I'm the one who wanted to minor in biology."

"Well? Is it true or not?"

"It's true, but—"

"Nope. No buts. If you can do that, sacrifice bone density and a pelvic floor, then he can stop having a few fucking burgers."

My lips curved at her fire.

"What are you smirking at?"

"Not smirking!" I raised my hands. "Just—"

"Just what?" Before I could answer, she squinted at me. "Have you tried any of the diner's burgers?"

"No. Not even their veggie burger."

"Oh man, Link took me there the other night. We should go there. They had this one with PB and jelly." She made her mouth go slack. "I think my mouth had an orgasm."

"It sounds gross."

"It isn't. I promise. And I tell you what, until you cut a deal with Sin, I'll have like a salad or something while you have a burger."

I felt bad.

I did.

But the sudden need for beef? Fuck.

She was right—it was in the air. Enough that I felt like a dog sniffing the room to scout out where the damn beef was.

"Oh man, if you could see your face!" Lily burst out giggling as she stared at me. "I swear, I haven't seen you this intense since you took your SATs."

I flipped her the bird as I reached down and rubbed my stomach. "I'm starving."

"Did you eat this morning?"

"I had a smoothie." I frowned. "I wanted Sin's breakfast."

"What was it?"

"Bacon. Eggs." My mouth watered. "Oh God, the kid's a boy who refuses to let his mom be a vegetarian."

Lily snickered. "Man, this is too funny."

"No, it isn't!"

"It is, because watching Sin turn veggie so his kid can eat meat is going to be even funnier!"

I scowled at her. "You're no help."

"Oh, I am," she retorted, getting to her feet with aplomb. "Because I'm going to save your ass and take you for meat."

"I shouldn't. I mean, I'm barely pregnant. It can't be a craving, can it?"

"The kid knows what it wants. It's like its daddy," she said ruefully.

And damn, there was no arguing with that.

These men of ours...they certainly knew what they wanted and when.

"Anyway, you can tell me more about Sin and all these secrets he spilled last night on the way over there." She shot me a mischievous grin, which had me shaking my head at her.

"I probably shouldn't tell you."

"Screw that. You have to. You can't leave me hanging."

"I will, but only because you're going to have a salad so I can have a burger."

"You drive a hard bargain."

"I know I do."

As we sauntered out of the house, toward the driveway where Luke's line of sports cars was stored, as well as her dad's, she headed for the section of German cars. Only, she walked past her regular ride and straight into a teenaged boy's wet dream of a car.

Knowing she usually drove a Porsche, I arched a brow at her. "Feeling brave?

She shrugged. "It's just a car."

No, it wasn't.

It represented the difference between her freedom and the way she'd been forced to deal with her family and what they'd put her through.

It represented her choice.

I knew it had always grated on her that she hadn't been able to drive any of the cars in the garage that was like a stable of mechanical horsepower. I liked, though, that she was willing to break down those barriers with me.

She headed for a BMW that was low to the ground, a bright gleaming white, and whose doors opened up like wings after she grabbed the keys, which swung from a hook on the wall behind it.

There were dozens of vehicles here. Anything from boats to bikes, the kind Sin and Link wouldn't be seen dead on, ATVs, SUVs, and jet skis.

As I slipped into the passenger side, Lily joined me in the driver's seat.

The interior gleamed a bright blue the second the doors closed, thanks to a strange pipe of lighting that ran around the whole vehicle.

I didn't say anything, just put on my belt, and waited for her to do the same.

It took her a while, but I understood that. She started the engine a few times then stopped it. But with a huge inhalation, she pushed the ignition button and began to roll out of the car space and into the garage.

She traveled as slowly as a tortoise, but again, though before I might have teased her, I didn't. I just stayed sitting there, letting her know I had her back, that I was there for her.

As she crawled out of the driveway, I peered around, wondering where her tail was, but before I could ask, she released a shaky breath the second we were past the gates. When we veered onto the road, she blurted, "I felt like Luke was going to come out of the pool house at any minute and—"

When she gulped, I reached over and patted her knee.

Then, because she didn't say anything else, I explained, "Sin told me that he's Rex's cousin last night."

The brakes screeched to a halt as she stopped in the middle of the private road that led onto the highway. She whipped around to stare at me, mouth agape, and I almost laughed when she bit off, "And you didn't tell me this immediately why?"

I grinned at her. "We had other things to talk about?"

She huffed. "Oh my God, Sin's related to Rex? This explains a lot."

"Like why he let Sin go to Ohio? Why he didn't just chop off his head?" I arched a brow at her as I sliced my finger across my throat. When she grimaced, I had confirmation that Sin had been incredibly lucky.

It also occurred to me that Lily didn't know why Sin had left Giulia in the lurch...unless Link had told her, which I figured fell under the whole 'club business' guise that Sin used with me when he didn't want to talk about something.

"Crap, I have a lot to tell you," I complained.

"You wouldn't if you'd told me along the way," she grumbled.

"You kept Link from me!" I retorted without any heat, but I sputtered for sure. "And there's a whole lot of stuff we haven't been open with each other about." I thought about the secrets Lily kept, and I muttered, "I think we need to agree on something."

Lily placed her hands on the steering wheel, kept her focus on the road, and whispered, "That we don't keep secrets?"

"Yeah. That we tell each other everything. As much as we can without hurting Link or Sin at any rate."

"Or the MC. It's their lives, Tiff." At that, she cut me a look. "They're our family too, whether we want them to be or not."

"Do you mind?"

She shook her head. "No. I know what they do, I know a lot of it seems bad, but I know what true evil looks like. Link could never be a part of something like that."

"I don't mind either. I feel like..." My brow puckered. "Sin was a Marine. Then I look at Maverick, and how they took the girls in, and what they're doing for...well, everything. I just feel like their heart is in the right place, even if they go about it in really illegal ways."

"Illegal is relative."

"It really isn't," I countered dryly, making her laugh. "But, okay, I don't want this to upset you, but you know the night Luke died? Sin and I, well, we think...no, I know he drugged me."

"What?" she spat.

"Yeah." I released a shaky breath, feeling weird about telling her this because I didn't want to add to the burden on her shoulders. None of this was her fault, but Lily felt stuff more than others. She'd take my pain, her shame at Luke, and would twist it into a big thing for her—she didn't need that. Didn't deserve it either. "Truth is, I thought I was just drunk, but Sin said I wasn't acting like I was drunk, I was acting like I was drugged, and the next day, that was like no hangover I'd ever had before.

"I remember a few things—leaving your house, then Luke groping me and it hurting really bad, then waking up in Sin's bed the next morning."

Her hand snapped out, and she grabbed a tight hold of my fingers. "Oh, Tiff, I'm so sorry. You should have told me!"

"There wasn't all that much to say. Not in the aftermath of him dying. Then Sin left, and everything just went tits up. I-I..." I blew out a breath. "I guess I buried it, and to be honest, in comparison to what he could have done? I know I'm lucky. So, that's not my point. Sin was guarding Giulia that night, and he—"

"Left her to come and save you?" Her gasp was sharp. "Oh my God."

"Yeah. That. Luke got him away from the bar by drugging me. I have his texts on my phone and everything—"

When I reached for my cell, she scowled at me. "You're not wondering if I don't believe you, are you?"

My nose crinkled. "No, but I just wanted you to know I wasn't bullshitting."

"I never thought I could hate Luke more, but he just keeps on piling onto how many reasons I have to loathe him."

I squeezed her fingers. "So that's why Rex forgave him too. Because Sin told him about what happened to me, and I figure that Rex was more predisposed to listen because of who Sin is to him."

"His cousin, yeah."

"I mean, after what happened in school, it wasn't like I could say anything to the cops, was it?"

She winced, and as she'd been there for that particular meltdown, I knew we were on the same page. "They'd have vilified you, and Father being Father, i.e. a cunt, would have, I don't know, spun it so that Luke was the victim. Giulia would have been worse off—Luke would have been the saint, and all womanhood would be to blame for trying to trap innocent men in their webs."

Biting my lip, I nodded. "So, it's all been kind of complicated."

"What isn't in this world?"

"True." My lips twitched as I proceeded to explain the rest of the complications that had made a sudden appearance in my life. About Mary Catherine and Grizzly, and about how Sin had come to be a member of the MC.

When I finished, she didn't say a word, just started the engine once more and began to drive into town.

"Wow."

It took her a good five minutes, but I got it.

That was how I'd felt last night.

When she had to brake at a stop sign, we shared a look, and I nodded.

"Yeah. Wow."

The drive into West Orange only took a few minutes, and when we arrived at the diner, finding it busy, my heart sank.

Lily, having cast a glance at me and my long face, snorted. "The service is fast here." She grinned. "That baby is changing you."

I frowned, because she was right. It was actually unnerving. First meat, then a complete change of appetite? I was used to going hungry. Used to dieting and doing without just to stay slim.

To be allowed to do the opposite wasn't exactly liberating, more like confusing. How much more was my body going to change? I'd been waiting on Sin to book the appointment with my doctor, but had I delayed not only so that he'd be there for every step of the way, but so he'd hold my hand?

I didn't... Crap, I wasn't a very maternal person. I didn't look at a baby and get goo-goo eyes. In however many weeks, I'd be really round, and popping out a kid who was me and Sin combined, and that was the only part that didn't freak me out.

I wanted that.

But, shit, diapers? Baby vomit?

Hard pass.

Only, there was no hard pass, was there? Wasn't like I had a choice on those parts.

"Hey, are you okay?" she asked as we took a seat.

I gnawed on my lip as I pulled the menu over to me. The place was decked out like a real, vintage diner. All red vinyl with those rounded countertops like you saw in the movies or in reruns of *Happy Days*, which I only watched when I was feeling really down. I couldn't imagine how much the MC had spent to make the place look so old. The Formica wasn't scratched or scraped, the silver flourishes were all squeaky clean, and the counter was loaded down with vintage-looking sauce bottles and the like, making it seem even more old-school.

As I peered down at the list of burgers, my mouth watering as I read, I just shrugged at her question.

Of course, Lily being Lily, that wasn't enough. "Dude." She kicked my foot under the table. "What's up?"

I heaved a sigh. "It's weird, is all."

"What is?"

"Not being in control of my own body."

She didn't laugh like I thought she might. I figured Lily thought I was indestructible because I was stubborn, loud-mouthed when required, and ballsy—not frightened to make myself heard.

Sometimes, however, even the strong were weak, and it seemed I'd found my weakness.

A child.

Her hand covered mine. "It's going to be okay. Remember? Commune baby. Link and Sin as daddies, and me and you as mommas."

"That's going to be insane."

She winked. "What about our life isn't?"

"True," I admitted wryly.

The waitress bustled over, looking harried and faintly sweaty. I understood why—it was kind of hot in here.

"Everything okay, ladies? You ready to order?"

I smiled at her, thinking how glad I was that Lily had said I didn't need to work here, so I decided to be super nice. "Cherry Coke, please, and the bacon burger with avocado and large fries." I wrinkled my nose. "Can the bacon be extra crispy, please?" When Lily snickered, I shot her a wry look.

"If I'm going to hell for eating meat, I'm going to double the load with bacon."

Her grin widened, but she turned to the waitress and said, "I'll have the falafel buddha bowl, please. Lemon tea to drink."

The waitress wrote our order down, hustled away, and as she did, my brows rose at the sight of her shoes.

"She must be crazy," I whispered to Lily, who peered over her shoulder and whistled.

"Jesus, they have to be four inches high!"

I pulled a face. "I hate breaking heels in."

"Who'd wear those around here?"

"Do you think she's a stripper?"

"Not everyone who wears hooker heels is a hooker. Or in this instance, a stripper," Lily chided.

"Who the fuck works a busy service with high heels strapped to their feet unless they have to get used to wearing super high heels?" I argued, and as we bickered over shit, like we usually did, a sense of comfort flooded me.

This was normal.

This was life.

And it felt good.

Baby or not, Lily and I would always bicker with one another. We'd still get pedis, even if the kid was stuck to my boob, and we'd still ride around town blasting music—okay, maybe it would be quieter, but babies liked cars, didn't they? Hadn't I seen on a show that sometimes the only way to get a kid to sleep was from the vibration of the car?

Life would change dramatically, and it would never be the same again, but Lily wouldn't change. Our friendship wouldn't. Sin wouldn't either. Not really. He'd still be the same calm dude who was really hard to rile. Who didn't mind making me a cup of decaf first thing or kissing me with morning breath.

I had to just chill out and remember that.

The burger came, and it was heaven. Mouth orgasm bliss—Lily was right about that. I actually moaned a few times as the juices sank into my mouth, tissues that had been parched of their glory for way too long. All the while, Lily would laugh at me as I groaned and drooled over the delicious concoction while she ate her falafels which, while not standard diner fare, she actually said were pretty damn good.

Appreciating her sacrifice, I rasped, "God, thanks, Lily."

She winked at me. "It's what sisters do for each other, huh?"

I grinned, then felt a little guilty when she paid, but she arched a brow at me, clucking her tongue. "Don't start," she warned, making me huff. "You're working for the MC. That's all I asked of you, and you're doing it."

"While Mom spends a fortune on QVC."

"You haven't seen her in a few days, have you?" Lily inquired.

"Not since the meal. I tried to call her yesterday, but she didn't answer. Not only that, it's not like I haven't been busy. Plus, I'm still annoyed at her. That dig about Daddy rolling in his grave? Uncalled for."

"It was, but she's being weird."

"Weirder than usual?"

"Yeah. She's never leaving her room. Not even for food. You should go see her," Lily prompted gently, her eyes on the straw in her glass as she twirled the ice around. When it clinked, she murmured, "I think she's mad at your dad but misses him, you know?"

Because I understood entirely, gruffly, I muttered, "I know."

"I'm always here. To talk."

"I know, babe. Thank you. I just... Christ, at the minute, I don't have all that much to say." And I didn't. Sure, it hurt, and at random points of the day, it would feel crucifying. I'd be in the shower, and all of a sudden, I'd think of him and it would just hurt.

Like a knife in the hand pain.

Like a kick to the gut agony.

Lily's mouth softened as she looked at me, seeming to sense how I was feeling. "I get that. You've got a lot to process."

"Ain't that the truth," I muttered. "It hurts. It will always hurt. But at the moment, I'm just mad. I need that to disperse, then I think I'll grieve. It's funny," I mused soggily. "I know the five stages of grieving like the back of my hand, but it's different now that I'm going through them myself. While it's selfish, I can't deal with her grief as well because she's acting like a toddler, when we both need to pull on our big girl panties and deal with the shit Daddy left us in together."

She reached over and patted my hand. "I'm here when you're ready."

"Same goes, Lily." I caught her eye, made sure she knew what I was talking about, and when she nodded, I sighed.

"Come on, let's get back. I need to finish those books for Link. You wouldn't believe how much he gets for his custom jobs," she shared on a whisper.

I heard her pride though, and my lips twitched as I said, "I didn't know that's what he did. I thought he was a mechanic."

"He is, but it's his custom work that brings in the big bucks." She whistled. "Like, if he went off on his own, cut ties with the MC? No joke, he'd be a millionaire."

My eyes widened at that. "Christ."

"Yeah, my reaction too," she replied with a laugh as we headed on out.

There was a parking lot adjacent to the strip mall where the MC's businesses were based. I knew the Sinners owned this joint, simply because it had pissed my father and Donavan off when they'd received the licenses for the place. The Sinners had more pull in City Hall than our fathers had, which had blown their minds, and knowing the Sinners slightly from the few parties I'd attended, it had always amused me.

As we crossed the street, I wasn't even sure where the guy came from. One second, the sidewalk was empty, and the next, he was there. Walking toward us. I thought nothing of it until he was at our backs, hustling into us. Lily grabbed her bag, held it to her, thinking he was mugging us, but the guy was faster.

Only, he didn't want her purse.

I felt the barrel in my lower back, knew he'd done the same with Lily, because she tensed up and froze on the sidewalk.

"You're going to walk to your car, open it up, and not make a fucking move I don't order, do you understand me?"

Heart in my throat, I could hear the blood rushing in my ears as my gaze darted around for Lily's tail, but it wasn't there.

It.

Wasn't.

Fucking.

There.

Where were the rough and ready bikers who were supposed to be keeping us safe? Had they learned nothing from what had happened to Giulia?

Before the thought could paralyze me, the barrel dug into me, the cold metal right at the bottom of my back where my kidney was.

I was so proud of how fucking strong I was, so ready to fight, but at that moment, it all disappeared. I felt like a balloon with air whistling out of it, sagging as all I could think of was the child sleeping there, growing, waiting to be born, and I trembled as I whispered, "We won't do anything."

Lily tensed some more, and I knew I'd surprised her. Normally, I'd have screamed. I knew I would. I'd have grabbed her purse and hit him over the fucking head with it, smashing it into him and making him back the hell away.

But I wasn't just Tiffany anymore.

I was Tiffany who had a life in her belly.

I was a mother in the making.

I was different, and it went so much fucking deeper than the need for beef.

"Good," he grunted, making me wish I'd seen his face before he'd rushed up on us, but I hadn't been paying attention.

Why would I?

He was there one second, just walking toward us like a regular passerby, then he'd swooped in like a fucking magpie on the hunt for something shiny.

He shoved the gun into my back, making my hands fly up. It was stupid, but I covered my stomach like that could stop a bullet and walked forward the second he began to move.

We headed for the shiny sports car, and Lily whispered, "Can I get the key from my purse?"

"Yeah, but don't make any sudden moves."

He was so close to us that I could feel his breath on the back of my neck, and I wanted to close my eyes, wanted to scream as I wondered how stupid we'd been to just come into town without anyone on us.

Before Link, before Donavan had warrants issued for his arrest, she'd always been tailed by guards. Where were the Prospects who were following her? Or were they here and they didn't realize something shady was going down? Surely, we looked like we were being hijacked, so why were they leaving us alone?

Alone with a gun-wielding asshole who wanted something from us, and I was pretty sure neither of us had it to give.

This had to be Sinner related, didn't it?

Surely?

Or…

Daddy.

The mafia had ruined us. Had ruined him. Were they trying to take me too? As what? Some kind of payment?

Feeling nauseated by the endless wheel of thoughts, I was almost relieved to stop thinking when Lily opened the car.

"Go to the passenger side first."

His order had us shooting each other a look, but as I glanced around us, I saw there was no one.

Fucking no one who could help us.

Where the fuck was everyone?

The diner had been getting busy, but surely someone would come out soon?

Panic hit me, because I knew you weren't supposed to allow a kidnapper to take you to an alternate location, but I couldn't let him shoot us. Just...couldn't.

Fuck, why couldn't—

The barrel was shoved harder into my back.

"Open the door and get into the backseat," he rasped, digging the gun even harder into me, forcing me to obey.

My legs almost caved in as I did as he asked, and it stunned me how weak I was at that moment.

This was the time for Momma Bear to come out, to rip into him, to tear into him, but I couldn't.

I just...

I felt frozen inside.

Later, when we were safe, if we were safe again, I'd hate myself. I'd regret it. But now? I just needed to do as he said.

I needed to obey.

"Get in," he ordered Lily, who scrambled across the console, the move awkward in the tight confines of the car.

When I saw he was focused on her, I slipped my phone out of my pocket and quickly messaged Sin blindly, my thumb moving on instinct.

Me: SOS. LIly's cqr is bin hij9cced.

Seconds later, Sin replied, but I didn't get the chance to read it. I took advantage of the man dipping down and getting into the seat to drop our live location. As he settled in the seat, I slipped my phone between my legs so the guy couldn't see what I'd done. My timing was lucky. He twisted so that he could aim the guns at each of us, and now in place, he ground out, "Drive. I'll direct."

THIRTY-FOUR

STORM

WITH KEIRA'S angry words and Cyan's sobs in my ears, I rode too fast as I rolled into the town where I'd been born and raised.

The distance between us was nothing to what would be in our future, because, fuck, she wouldn't be coming with me, and I didn't have a choice about leaving.

I was being shipped down to Coshocton, to the currently Prez-less chapter who was in need of someone to take charge of their rudderless ship.

For years, I'd wanted more. Rex was the best Prez, though, and as VP, that was as high as I knew I'd ever get here. Unless he got hurt. And to be honest, I loved him too much to wish that, even if I knew I was at the end of the road here.

I meant that in more ways than one.

West Orange wasn't good for me.

It never had been.

Not until Keira.

My throat turned into fucking knots as I wondered what the hell was the matter with me.

The one good fucking thing in my life, and I fucked it up.

I fucked everything up.

West Orange was one huge mistake, and the only light at the end of the goddamn tunnel was Cyan.

She was the hope I had that I wasn't a total mistake.

She was my everything, but to get away from the man I was here, I needed to go to Ohio. Needed to move away.

At church this morning, Rex told us all how it had gone down in Coshocton, how Peggy and Butch were now pig food and how they'd betrayed us, but I'd never expected him to tell me to get my ass over there and run the chapter.

The second I thought it over, though, I knew it was a chance for a fresh start.

Knew it was a path rife with possibilities.

I'd thought they'd come with.

It had never not occurred to me that they wouldn't, but Keira had refused, and now?

I was fucking lost.

I had to go down there. I had to. I needed the change of pace. It wasn't enough to watch over the strip joint, to deal with the chop shop shit with Steel. I needed more responsibility, more room to grow. But leaving Keira and Cyan behind? Fuck, I wasn't sure if I could even do it.

I revved the bike harder, pushing it past the speed limit as I blasted down the highway on my way toward town.

When my cell buzzed, I almost ignored it, but along the wind, I heard Rex's ringtone, and I knew not to ignore his call.

The idea that, in Coshocton, a bunch of brothers would feel the same way about me, that they'd feel that same fear, was an unexpected thrill.

Power didn't get me going, but I figured the idea of being more, of doing more than just being Rex's lackey, was the only way I'd ever get out of this rut.

Too much pussy.

Too much drink.

Fuck.

Temptations were rampant everywhere, but I was wasting myself here. Wasting away because I was living with regrets for shit I'd done when I was even more stupid than I was now.

Keira was forever.

She had that vibe about her, and being the dumbfuck I was back then, I'd been unable to deal with that.

Now?

I'd give my liver to have her back.

With my phone still buzzing, I pulled over, not because of Rex's call, but because the tears in my eyes were getting in the way of my driving. I didn't need to crash my fucking bike. Moving away was better for Cyan than her daddy dying in a road accident, and even though I was crying like a pussy, it was, I thought, only a smart man who recognized what he'd done, the mistakes he made, and who could mourn for it and his stupidity.

As I rode to the side, cars whipped past me, a few blaring their horns at how I'd slipped through the lanes.

I ignored them, reached for my cell, and when I saw the messages, I didn't call Rex back, just dealt with them straight.

Seeing the live location I'd been sent a screenshot of, I typed out my reply.

Me: *I'm two minutes away. I'm on the highway, just need to pull around.*

Rex: *GO! We're sending back up. ETA, ten minutes. Her guards didn't realize she'd gone out.*

Me: *Fuck. Nyx needs to slam some skulls. On it.*

Thinking about how the brothers on Lily were going to get their asses handed to them didn't beat down my anger as I shoved my phone back into my jeans then revved my bike into life.

All self-piteous thoughts vanished, Keira and Cyan did too as my focus shifted at the same time as the tires screeched when I slammed back onto the road.

The vehicle was heading for NY, not the town, so I quickly headed for the turn off and made my way onto the freeway.

Speeding faster than ever, the wind burning every visible spot of skin as I raced toward the car that contained my brothers' women, I hunkered down, ignoring more horns as I looked for a car I thought Link's woman would drive.

No one had any idea of the vehicle, but when I saw a souped-up BMW in the distance that was lower to the ground than a nun's skirt, I knew I'd found my target.

As I slipped through traffic, I roared toward the car, trying to discern what the fuck was going on, and as I pulled up just behind them, I peered in and saw the glint of metal from the passenger seat, and I took note of Tiffany's terrified features as she peered at me with longing and hope in her eyes, like she knew salvation was on its way.

Fuck, I hadn't been that for a long time, but I vowed, then and there, not to let her or Lily or my brothers down.

I revved my engine, making it impossible for Lily not to hear the deep bass vibrating along the road. She had to know that a bike was in the vicinity, and she had to know what that meant.

I looked around and saw we were on a drag of freeway where there were a shit ton of trees on either side of the road.

Pushing my bike hard, I raced past her car, swiping from the side so she had no choice but to veer toward the shoulder or she'd crash into me.

But as I did that, disaster struck.

The boom of a gun trickled to me, even over the sound of the wind rushing in my ears. Glass shattered and screams sounded. The brakes screeched as Lily reacted to the gunshot. She and Tiffany screamed as more gunshots rained down inside the car as the bastard kept on trying to hit me, but succeeded only in terrifying the shit out of the women and fucking deafening them.

I swerved out of instinct, and as I did, rolling over to the side of the road, I saw a nightmare unfold.

The car drifted a few feet before the tire clipped the side of the asphalt. It teetered on that wheel, and my heart almost fucking seized as I thought it was going to ski, falling onto its side, and drift farther forward, but it didn't. It just ran forward, but the reason it stopped?

A tree.

The passenger side took most of the impact, thank fuck, but Lily soared forward, the web of the shattered windshield almost catching her as the airbags deployed.

Who wasn't caught in time?

The passenger.

I watched as the fucker soared through the glass, breaking it and any proof of the gunshots, except for the bullet casings, and I didn't have time to collect them.

Kicking my engine into gear, and knowing I had to act fast as cars started to pull in to watch the show, which meant the cops would be on their way soon, I drove into the copse of trees and headed for the body.

He was a fucked up mess, but that was nothing compared to what he'd be when we were done with him.

I bent low, grabbed him by the hand, and dragged him over to the other side of the road, away from Lily's car.

It killed me not to go to them, but I had to think about everyone here—the women and the MC.

Grabbing one of my two cell phones when I dumped the guy onto the ground in a heap of limbs, I quickly messaged Rex.

Me: *Need a cage. Stat. Bullets in car, need to collect them. Have the gunman.*

Sending him my location, I veered onto the dialer and called 911.

Shielding my voice, making it high-pitched, I said, "I saw a bike knock a sportscar off the Essex Freeway. Just off the storage place. The car's wrecked."

I cut the call before they could ask too many questions or tell me to stay on the line. Then I pulled off the back of the burner, grabbed the SIM, and pocketed it.

Rex: *ETA, two mins. Understood.*

I waited for the sirens that were going to come soon, but when a cage appeared, Hawk driving it, I nodded at him, even as I climbed off my hog and began to drag the fucker over to his ride.

When the passenger door opened, I heaved the breathing corpse onto the passenger floorboard, and ground out, "Straight to the clubhouse."

Hawk nodded, and while I appreciated him as a man of few words, I finally heard them.

Sirens.

With that, I slammed the door shut, raced over to my bike, gunned it, and I rode through the trees to the other side of the road, just off the freeway.

Taking the backstreets, I didn't stop until I was back in West Orange, pulling into the garage.

As I rode in, I wasn't surprised that Link wasn't there, but I dumped my bike and to Jaxson, a Prospect for the club, I stated, "Need new plates on this, new paint job too. Emergency."

His eyes flared wide, but he nodded. "Sure thing, VP."

I peered around the garage and saw no vehicle I could ride in except for a small Mini Cooper.

I shook my head at the sight, and under my breath, grumbled, "The guys see me in this, I'll never hear the end of it."

Jaxson snorted out a laugh, but I glowered at him, which shut him the hell up.

"Get me the keys."

I needed to get the fuck out of here, fast.

Christ, it looked like I didn't have a choice in whether I was going to Coshocton or not.

Fuck.

THIRTY-FIVE

LODESTAR

I COULD SEE it killed Rex to stay in his office. The second Sin had surged in without a knock, shoving his phone in Rex's face, it had made the Prez morph into a general directing his troops. Of course, most of those orders took place over his cell. The guys' phones lit up with only fuck knew what, and Rex snarled, "Go!" making me wonder what the fuck was even going on.

At his command, I watched Sin, Link, Steel, and Nyx take off like their feet were on fire, and when his face turned white as more pinging texts came in, I muttered, "Do you want me to go?"

He shook his head, just once, and I froze in place.

I'd called on Maverick to hit up a church meeting because what I'd uncovered lately was starting to add up. At last.

The guys had grumbled because everyone on the council wasn't around, but having impressed upon Maverick just how big of a deal what I'd discovered was, they'd come together.

Begrudgingly.

Five minutes into my explanation of what the fuck was going on, the guys had run off. I'd think that I stank, but I didn't.

I used three different deodorants to make sure I didn't.

See, I was smart like that.

When an antiperspirant didn't work, the deodorant might, and then I used that cream stuff as well just to make sure.

Didn't stop me from lowering my head to the side and cautiously sniffing my pits.

I mean, I knew it had nothing to do with my stench, but now that it was in my head, I needed to make sure, right?

When Rex looked up at last, there was fire in his eyes, and even though I'd dealt with nastier fuckers than him, most of those had been back when I wore a uniform and I didn't have to worry about being shot if I pissed off a superior officer. Stuck in a jail cell, sure! Maybe lose out on a promotion, maybe. But shot? Stabbed? Nope.

"Get on with it," he ground out. "I have shit I need to be doing."

Though he was rude, I didn't point it out, not when Maverick quickly shoved his head to the side in a sharp negative—the bastard knew me far too well.

Huffing, I muttered, "Knowing that Ghost and the rest of the girls were purchased by the Lancasters gave me a clear starting point. Throw in the fact that Tiffany's father was being funded by them, I've been able to identify several large corporations that are fronts of the Fieri family."

"You have actual names?" Rex demanded, sitting forward.

"Yeah. I do. More than just Fuoco as well. Lots of smaller companies, tiny in the grand scheme of things, but all of them allowed me to trace their overseas activity."

Never let it be said the man was slow… "You know when the shipments of women come in?"

I nodded. "Using information that Ghost gave me about when she was taken, I managed to track shipping records and found the actual tanker she was brought over on. That tanker sails across the Atlantic twice a month."

"You think each one brings in shipments of girls?"

"Shipments of something," I replied, "that's for sure. And each and every time, the shipments are secured by one particular dock worker, also signed by one dock manager—"

"So we have someone to trace?"

I nodded. "We do."

Rex rubbed his chin, then cast a glance at Maverick. "What do we do?"

"Depends."

I was surprised at how Rex shoved the news onto Mav, but then again, maybe not. He'd always been good at thinking outside of the box. Always been good at thinking about plans that no one really wanted to have to think up.

"On what?" Rex countered.

"What you want the reaction to be."

"We're in it up to our necks with the Five Points. We're already at war with the *Famiglia* as a result."

Maverick shrugged. "Then what's the hassle? We could bring down their empire."

"If I have a vote, that's what I'd like."

Rex shot me a look. "You don't have a vote."

I shot him a smug smile. "I do if you want to know where Donavan Lancaster is at this precise moment."

Maverick tensed. "You never said you were even looking for him."

I snorted. "If you think it took me a week to trace the money, then you're an idiot and you don't deserve my skills, because I'm way better than that."

Maverick rolled his eyes. "Sorry, Lodestar."

I grinned at him. "So you should be," I told him as I rubbed my nose with my middle finger.

Rex grunted. "Get the fuck on with it."

"No. I want a vote when it comes down to your movements with the *Famiglia*. I want in. Been hunting these bastards for a long time. I'm not about to let go of this," I warned.

"You're not a brother."

"Because I don't have a dick? I assure you, my dick is bigger than a lot of the guys who are Prospecting for you right now. Plus, I'm a damn sight more useful. Honorary member, fancy it up however the fuck you want it, but you won't get shit out of me about Donavan Lancaster unless I get some sway—"

Rex growled, "I don't appreciate being manipulated."

"Neither do I. Three years I've been working on this fucking trafficking business. Three fucking years. It brought Kat into my life, and it brought a shit ton of—"

Maverick stilled at that. "What? That's how you found Katina?"

"Yeah."

"Wait, that doesn't compute."

"What are you? Data?" I retorted. "Of course, it does."

"Start from the beginning," Rex ordered slowly, cutting Mav a look.

"Kat's mom," I started, then I pulled a face. "Ghost's mom too, she was like Ghost. Shipped over and sold."

Maverick's mouth dropped at that. "You're shitting me."

"No. She was one of the lucky ones."

"She was?"

"Her buyer married her."

"Fuck. If that's your idea of luck—"

"After what happened to Ghost you have to even question that?" I spat at Rex. Then, grinding my teeth, I growled, "I've been on the hunt for these bastards for a long time. If you think you can deny me the satisfaction of seeing their empire crumble, then I'll head to another fucking MC who'll help me."

"She'll do it, Rex," Maverick said.

"Yeah, I can see she's a fucking lunatic if she thinks she can threaten me, so why the fuck wouldn't she think she can fuck off to another MC?" Rex's mouth twisted into a snarl as he repeated, "I don't fucking like being manipulated." He jabbed the air, but he could jab all he wanted.

No way in fuck was this going down without me being involved.

"I can unravel their business from the ground up, but that isn't as much fun as seeing them bleed out too."

Rex blew out a breath, slowly. His gaze drifted over mine, and the look in them morphed from irritation into an anger that would raze an ordinary man to the ground.

Lucky for me, I wasn't ordinary, and I wasn't a man.

"You got your vote, because, to be frank, it sounds like a fucking blast watching them bleed out too."

I dipped my chin in agreement. "I have the last place he was staying, and I have a trace on the card he's using."

"Where is he?"

"After he left Vietnam, Cambodia."

Rex cut Maverick a look, but Mav merely shrugged. "Nyx is needed here. Storm will be heading down to Coshocton."

Rex sighed. "After what just went down, Sin and Link will need to be here." He pinched the bridge of his nose.

"What did just go down?" I asked softly, aware that all the men had received a text at the same time and that they'd all acted as one.

"Someone took Lily and Tiffany."

"Shit," I breathed.

"Yeah, shit."

"Leaves only Steel," Mav rasped. "He can go. He has a passport too."

"How do we bring the fucker back?"

I cracked my knuckles which drew their attention over to me. I winked at them. "Leave that to me, boys."

THIRTY-SIX

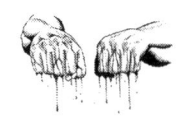

TIFFANY

I WOKE up to beeps and pain. That was all I heard, all I recognized.

Then a hand tightened around mine, and a mouth brushed over my knuckles. When the stubble rasped over my fingers, I whispered, "Sin?" When he tensed up, I mumbled, "S'that? Where...I?" My tongue didn't seem to want to work, and I figured that was because of how dry my mouth was.

"You're in the hospital, baby." His voice was raspy. "Everything's going to be okay."

"Is?"

"Yeah. It is."

I pried my eyes open at his words, grimacing as pain ricocheted through me as I did so.

"Hurt."

He winced, but he surged onto his feet, then twisted around to grab the jug. It rattled, and he pressed an ice chip to my lips.

The cold liquid sank into dry tissue, and I almost moaned at the relief. He fed me some more, graduating from the ice chips to a small cup that he pressed to my lips.

When I could swallow, I downed as much as I could until my mouth felt some semblance of normal again.

Only when I was done did he sit down, and though I shielded my eyes by letting the lids hood, I followed the move, and when I did, I saw the pain in his face.

For a second, I wondered if he'd been hurt too, then I remembered, and I knew.

I just knew.

Tears clogged my eyes, easing the pain of opening them, and I tipped my head back against the pillows as grief swirled inside me, amassing power like a hurricane.

When the whimper escaped me, when it morphed into sobs, he grunted before he carefully climbed onto the bed beside me.

Burrowing my face into his cut, I whispered, "Gone?" I knew. I didn't need him to answer for his eyes to have already told me the truth, but when he nodded, I released a keening cry.

Before things had derailed, I'd been worried about how things would change. How nothing would stay as it was now. Fuck. Had I wished this on myself? Was this my fault? Karma—

"I'm so sorry, angel," he rasped, and that last word was the straw that broke the camel's back.

My entire body ached. Every part of me, from the top of my head to my toes, but what hurt the most?

The emptiness inside me.

I'd never felt the baby. Hadn't felt it move. Hadn't even seen a difference in my breasts—aside from the hypersensitivity in my nipples—or in my belly, but I'd known it was there.

The food, the cravings, the nausea...

I sobbed hard into his cut, and even though it should have been alien, the leather hit my nostrils, filling me with a comfort I couldn't deny.

He was here.

He hadn't left me.

The baby...

It wasn't our glue.

I'd never been scared that it was, but feeling him here, feeling his distress, I knew what we had was real. I felt him shake. Felt the moisture from his eyes on the side of my face and knew, even though Sin had told me he'd never wanted kids, he mourned our baby too.

He grieved with me.

I wasn't alone in this.

I huddled into him as much as he huddled into me, and even though I knew what was wrong with me, knew why it had happened, I rasped, "You're going to deal with him, aren't you?"

"Yes."

One word.

I knew not to press.

Knew not to say anything in the hospital ward, but relief swirled inside me.

It didn't outweigh the grief. Didn't take it away. If anything, it just made a deeper, rawer ache grow—a rage so pure, I'd never felt the like before.

"Make him hurt."

"I will."

That was a vow.

A promise.

And I knew he wouldn't break it.

"Is Lily okay?"

"Bad concussion. Broken arm, dislocated shoulder." He blew out a breath. "Badly scraped up and severe whiplash, but she's alive."

"What about me?"

"Broken wrist, whiplash, concussion."

"Did they..." I trailed off and turned my face into his cut again, and into the leather, mumbled, "Was there surgery?"

"No. Well, you had a D&C, sweetheart. There was no damage other than..." He cleared his throat. "I'm sorry, angel."

"You keep saying that—"

"Our fault. *My* fault. We should have had more guards on Lily. More experienced ones. We don't know who the threat is yet, not precisely. Still, two Prospects weren't enough—fuck, I'm so sorry, angel."

"Maybe I should have fought more—" I rasped, ignoring his explanation, avoiding his apology, focusing instead on how docile I'd been when I was never docile.

Fight or flight? I'd done neither. I'd just frozen.

Weak. Goddamn weak.

"Lily said the guy had guns. No way you can fight a bullet."

My mouth trembled again. "She's awake?"

"Yeah, woke up a few hours before you."

"He had two. He appeared out of nowhere. I just thought he was someone on the street. Then he had guns in our backs, and I froze up." I gulped. "I've never done that before in my life."

"You're a fighter, but you knew you had something to protect." He pressed a kiss to my temple. "You did right."

"I should have hurt him."

"And maybe have been shot?" He shook his head, but his face burrowed deeper into my hair. "Worst case scenario wasn't you losing the baby, Tiff. Worst case was me losing you."

"You mean that?"

"I mean it." He released a breath. "I never wanted kids, but I wanted this one because the baby was yours. I want you, therefore I want anything that's yours. Does that make sense?"

I blinked back tears. "No, but I'm glad you feel that way."

He snorted out a soft, sad laugh. "I've learned along the way not to want that much, Tiff. I should have figured life would bite me in the ass again."

"You can't think that way—I won't let you."

"We don't even know who the fucker is," he whispered in my ear. "I can't even tell you why he did this to us—"

"You don't have to," I rasped, surprised he was talking about this when it was club business.

"Yeah. I do. I owe you the truth, and the truth comes with so much shit..."

I grabbed his hand, knotted our fingers together, and whispered, "I'm not going anywhere."

"You don't need to hear this shit now. Fuck, not ever."

"Maybe I do. I know you keep stuff to yourself, Sin. Maybe that's why, sometimes, I never know if this is real or not. I feel like it is, but when I'm at the clubhouse, all this stupid stuff comes into my head, and it's dumb, so dumb, because I trust you, but maybe you holding back on some stuff makes me think you're holding back on other things as well."

"That's not fair."

"Never said it was," I admitted rawly. "But you know me. You know everything there is to know, and what you don't know, you can ask. I kept things from you while you were away, and I regret that. I won't do it again, and I don't want you to hold things back from me. Not the things that matter. The things that make you *you*."

"I lived a different life than you," he whispered. "A completely different life, one you'll never be able to understand, and I'm ashamed of it. It's so fucking abnormal in comparison—"

"What's normal? Lily was rich, Lily was raped by her father. I was rich, my father was some kind of front for the mafia. He just killed himself. What about that is normal?"

"I have to go soon," he rasped, "but I can talk until then."

I knew what he meant, and I said, "You can go then with my blessing." I squeezed his fingers. "Just tell me one thing."

And he did.

It settled on him uneasily, his body was stiff at my side, and I knew opening up was hard for him, but I needed it.

At that moment, I needed him. The real him. I needed not to feel like there was a wall up between us, something that I'd never be able to cross because he'd never let me in all the way.

I didn't want to find out tidbits from his brothers, shit that he should have told me himself.

I wanted to hear it straight from him.

"Told you Mom abused me. I ran to the Sinners, but my dad was as much of a deadbeat as she was. I used to fight a lot in school, got a rep for it. Got in with some rough crowds that were basically setting kids against each other." He released a shaky breath. "Used to win because I knew if I didn't, I'd have no food. It gave me—" Another breath gusted from him, and he admitted softly, "I have anger issues. One day, I lost. Got beat up real bad. Mom refused to take me to the charity hospital, and the second I was on my feet, I hitchhiked to West Orange."

Talk about the Cliff Notes version, but I'd take it. I'd accept anything he had to share and take it for the huge step forward it was. Sure, this topic wasn't something I wanted to be dealing with now, but hell, it took my mind off the pain I was in, because Christ, everything hurt.

But two things stuck with me.

Anger issues?

Sin?

I'd never seen him lose his temper ever.

"Is that why you're always calm?" He was too. He rarely, if ever, got mad. That was why it was hard for me to accept that he had anger issues.

"Yeah. I had to teach myself to be that way."

When he wasn't any more forthcoming than usual, I sighed, and questioned, "Who took you in?"

"Rene. No one knew why. Bear didn't tell anyone, neither did Grizzly. They just took me in, and that was that."

"Who's Rene?"

"Rex's mom."

I pressed my hand to his stomach, felt the tension in him that was practically making him vibrate. "You stayed there for a long time?"

"Until I enlisted."

"You didn't go straight into the club?"

"No. I Prospected from the start. Got patched in as a brother when I was nineteen, but it wasn't..." He grunted. "Working with Grizzly was hard. He never told no one I was his kid, but as a Prospect and as a brother, he used to treat me like shit. He was Road Captain, so I had no choice but to take it.

"Only way out of the MC is death or jail or—"

"Enlisting?"

"Yeah. They accept that." He cleared his throat. "Laws are meant to be broken, you know that."

"But they can be patriotic when they choose?"

He turned into me, and I felt his smile against my temple. "Never said we had to make sense."

"Figures, especially considering how many ex-military you have in the club."

He shrugged. "Most of the time, they Prospect after they get home. Servicemen…it's hard. Getting out, then going back into civilian life. MCs, though it might seem crazy, have structure."

"Not crazy. There's a rank and file system. It makes sense."

He hummed. "Knew I loved how fucking smart you are."

Despite myself, and even though it was a little soggy, I teased. "He loves me for my brain."

"And other things," he rumbled, warming my heart enough for me to curl onto my side.

"Thank you for telling me that."

"Pretty short story," he rasped. "There isn't that much to tell."

"I want to know everything and nothing…but only what you want to share. I guess, what I mean is I want you to want to share it with me. Been thinking about Daddy. How much he kept from us. I don't want that for me."

"That makes sense. Angel, you need to sleep."

I squeezed his hand. "Has Mom been?"

"No."

"What the hell is with her right now?" I growled, hurting enough at her absence that my eyes pricked with more tears.

"Want me to bring her?"

"No. I don't want her to be forced to visit."

"I'll see what's going on with her. After."

I nodded, knowing what he meant. "Make them pay?"

"You didn't even have to ask, angel."

And I knew I didn't, but a girl had to make sure, didn't she?

THIRTY-SEVEN

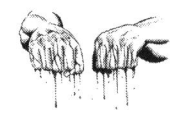

SIN

THE BUILDING STANK OF PISS, blood, and puke. Sadly, those were scents I was used to.

When I walked inside the bunkhouse that was on the farthest side of the compound, away from the clubhouse, away from the others, where Giulia's twin brothers were staying and where the girls were currently living, and reachable only by ATV or SUV, I dipped my chin to my brothers.

Link was here, Rex and Nyx too. Steel wasn't though, but I knew why. He'd already been shoved on a plane to Phnom Penh, and Storm? He was already on his way to Coshocton, as the 'biker' had been blamed for the crash, and not this piece of shit on the floor.

We called this place the Fridge.

It wasn't often we used it. Wasn't often we had the need to use it, but I got the feeling we'd be using it often in the coming weeks. Once Donavan was back on U.S. soil, this was where he'd be brought.

It was a bare cell with concrete walls and concrete floor with more stains on it than an abattoir.

Walking over to Link, I grabbed the baseball bat from his hand without asking, well aware that he'd gotten his licks in on Lily's behalf, then strolled over to the fucker on the ground. Because Link's wrath? Even Nyx's? Nothing compared to mine when I was in this mood.

Kicking him in the gut had him grunting as he curled into a ball.

"You'll regret this," he slurred, staring up at me through bruised and beat up eyes. His face was covered in cuts from his flight through the windshield, and even though he was a mess, it wasn't enough for me.

I felt the anger inside me baring its teeth. Christ. I worked hard to keep it under wraps, to keep it controlled. No one who knew me now would even recognize just how angry I could get. Some days, I felt like the fucking Hulk with how it could trigger me, but I worked hard to keep it contained.

Today was not a day for containment.

"I'll regret shit," I snapped, as I drew my leg back and kicked him hard enough for him to soar off the floor and collide into the wall.

"He's Luigi Fieri, Benito's third son," Nyx told me, his tone conversational.

"Fucker's been talking, has he?" I retorted, tapping the bat against my leg as I strode over to him.

"Yeah, thinks his papa will want him back."

Tension filled me, and I cut Rex a warning look. "No fucking way."

Rex shrugged. "Better for business if he goes home."

"Would you let the fucker go home if he killed your baby?"

Rex's jaw tightened. "She miscarried?"

"Yeah. She fucking did." I'd had my phone off during my vigil at Tiff's side, mostly because I'd wanted the guilt to eat at me.

I'd wanted it to tear at my insides, because here and now was where I wanted to pour out my grief.

The weird thing was, finding out I was going to be a dad had made me surprisingly happy.

Learning that wasn't going to happen?

The pain was unreal.

I thought it was something inside me being happy at the fact Tiffany was going to be tied to me forever, whether she liked it or not. But I wanted the baby.

Fucked up that I realized that now when we'd lost him or her, but then, what about my life wasn't fucked up?

The thought had me raising the bat overhead and bringing it down against the bastard's legs.

When an audible snap ricocheted around the small room, satisfaction flooded me in time with the cunt on the floor howling with pain.

"We could leverage him," Link suggested.

"For what?" I spat. "What the fuck do we want from the Fieris?" I squatted down and grabbed the bastard's head, shaking him until he had no choice but to focus on me.

His face was coated in sweat, his eyes sheened with the delirium of agony, but it was nothing compared to the pain inside me. The pain that had sharp teeth that were tearing at my insides for what Tiffany was going through.

I shouted, "Why the fuck did you come after the women?"

He didn't make a peep, but he pissed himself.

Great.

"Wanted to deliver Lily to his brother—"

Link's words had my head snapping around to face him. "What?"

"Lily's contracted to marry Gianni Fieri. They were supposed to be married already, but he got sent up."

"And you're okay with this?" I bit off, gaping at my brother like he'd grown two heads.

Link's mouth curved into a snarl, and as he surged forward, Nyx grabbed his shoulder and hauled him back. "The fuck do you think?"

I gaped at him some more, then demanded, "You let Lily carry on thinking the bastard was going to come after her?"

"I knew I'd deal with the fucker when he came for her—"

"Too fucking late. He sent his prick brother after her, and because of that, I've lost my fucking kid," I roared at him, leaping to my feet. No one stopped me when I slammed my fist into Link's face, not even Nyx, and I figured they knew that was because I'd beat the shit out of anyone who came close.

I had a rep.

I knew that.

It wasn't often talked about because I liked it that way, but you didn't grow up scrapping for food without getting good at fighting.

And good was an understatement.

Twice in my life, I'd beaten someone to goddamn death with no other weapons except for the ones attached to my arms. I'd boxed for the fucking Marines for a reason, had even killed someone in the ring before by accident.

This was the shit I didn't want Tiffany to know.

I didn't need her to know that side of me, because I kept it under wraps purposely.

That anger?

That rage?

My Mr. Hyde.

It was why I was called Sin, the reason for which I hadn't been able to share the story behind my moniker with Tiff.

Wrath.

That was me.

I'd killed my father.

With my bare hands.

And I'd do it again.

Just like I'd kill the cunt on the floor.

"Padraig."

My real name came from Rex's lips, and it was the only thing that would have stopped me from beating the shit out of Link.

Head swerving to glower at him, I snarled, "Don't fucking call me that."

Rex just grunted. "Then don't beat Link to death. We have bigger fish to fry than him being a dumbfuck." He cut Link a look, who was mopping up his broken nose without any grumbling. "We were always going to be dealing with Fieri, but I was hesitant to make a first move. There are only sixty of us in this chapter, that's not enough to fight the *Famiglia*. With our allies at war with them, we can throw ourselves into the battles without the risk of losing everything we've fought hard to earn."

Link grunted, "I owe the club."

"We all do," Rex rasped, his gaze trained on the broken body on the floor. He studied him for a second, then muttered, "What do we know about this prick?"

Nyx, leaning back against the wall, stacking his boot against it, stated, "Mav says he's the third son. The second died of leukemia when he was a kid. The first boy is following in the father's footsteps, but this one keeps fucking up. Gets sent to rehab a lot—"

"Another fucking junkie." Rex grunted. "Great."

With a sniff, he turned on his heel and began to walk toward the door. "Take your anger out on him, Sin, but after, that's it. I want you contained. I wasn't bullshitting about having bigger fish to fry, and I don't want you wasting that temper of yours on men who have your back."

Before he could leave, I demanded, "What fish need frying?"

He turned to look over his shoulder at me, and his smirk was pure arrogance. "We have a family to destroy."

Satisfaction had me tipping my chin up before I dipped it immediately, telling him silently I agreed with him, that I'd obey.

When he saw I understood, he stated, "The Prospects on the detail...let Nyx deal with them as his final task as an Enforcer." His mouth tightened as he shot Nyx a look, and I sensed Rex's displeasure with his best friend.

"I'll make them regret being dumb fucks," Nyx vowed, and though I heard the gravel in his voice, it wasn't enough.

"Do that. And Sin? Remember what I said. Burn off your anger on this shithead, not on brothers. Even if they're dumb, they're family." Before I could agree or disagree, he left, and though I knew he was right, I moved away from my brothers, who all backed up toward the door.

I wasn't surprised when they left me with the guy who paid for the stupidity of the Prospects who'd let my woman head out into danger, who suffered for the loss of my child's life in ways he could never have imagined.

And me?

I couldn't have imagined it either, because the rage that whispered through me?

It was a thousand times more powerful than that of discovering my father in my wife's bed.

A thousand times more powerful than learning Luke Lancaster had drugged my woman.

He bore the brunt of my rage more than any man ever had.

Or would ever wish to.

And he died a sack of sorry shit as he became the third man I tore to shreds with a rage that festered inside me like a gangrenous wound.

THIRTY-EIGHT

TIFFANY

"IS IT TRUE?"

The whisper had me jerking awake with a groan, because that was exactly how my head was right now.

It was dark out, and the room was hit with low lights that made it easy to see, yet it was impossible to peer into the shadows.

The voice, though, I'd know that anywhere.

"Mom?"

"Is it true?"

"Is what true?" I snapped, then instantly winced as the pain in my head made me clench my eyes closed, but I was annoyed at the cloak-and-dagger arrival. Annoyed at her not coming to see me today. Annoyed at her period for her behavior since Daddy had died.

"I heard those bikers discussing the Fieris in the garden tonight." A noise escaped her, and it sounded oddly like a sob, but what was there to cry about?

"You're here for that? I lost my baby, Mom. Don't you care about that?"

"I care about your life," she rasped, and she finally moved out of the corner. When she did, I saw why it was hard to see her.

She was dressed in black.

Her hat, her coat, her shoes. Even when the coat shifted aside, she wore black pants and a shirt.

Fuck, she looked like a cat burglar.

"What's going on?" I whispered, too in pain to be dealing with this, with her and her childish goddamn ways right now.

"We have to get you out of here."

"What? Why?" I shook my head, but as I did, the concussion made itself known to me yet again.

I'd been woken up every hour on the hour, so that meant Mom had come in sometime between the first and last nurse making sure there were no complications from my situation.

This was beyond weird, though, so maybe her watching and sneaking in wasn't outside of the realm of possibility.

"I can't leave. I'm sick," I rasped, and I fucking felt it. My body was still aching, and I felt raw deep inside, but my head? Pounding. It hurt like nothing else. In fact, it hurt more now than it did when I'd woken up with Sin at my side.

He hadn't come back to the hospital, but he'd called, and it had been so good to hear his voice, even better to hear him whisper, "He'll never hurt you again."

"You'll be in worse danger if you don't come with me."

I frowned at my mother, who was on some kind of parallel universe. "What's going on with you, Mom? I don't get you."

"The second I found out just how involved your father was with the Lancasters and Fieris, I knew this would happen," she murmured, her hands coming to the side of the bed. Her weight depressed the mattress, tilting my body and making every joint ache.

Trying not to lose my patience, I muttered, "Knew what would happen?"

"He said he'd broken ties with them. Said he'd never go to them again, but I should have known he would when the business went through a downturn." She swallowed. "He never could deal with losing everything. His parents did during the nineties. He never got over it."

My eyes widened at that. "He never told me."

"He never spoke of it. Only when he was drunk."

"Drunk?" I repeated in disbelief. I'd never seen him drunk, not once in my life.

"It happened rarely. Usually on our anniversary." She gulped. "We don't have time for this, Tiffany. We need to go."

"I'm not going anywhere. My life is here."

"You can do better than that biker," she argued, her hand curling about my arm like she was going to drag me off the bed or something.

"He's not just a biker. I love him," I snarled, jerking my arm from hers, instantly whimpering as my head pounded with the flurry of activity. "I'm not going anywhere until you tell me what the fuck is going on."

"We don't have time."

I could hear the frantic note in her voice, and because it confused me, I sucked down a breath and, begging for patience, demanded, "Mom, you need to start at the beginning. If you explain, maybe I'll come with you."

"You have to come with me," she fretted, her nails turning to claws as she dug them into my forearm.

"Explain what's going on," I repeated sternly, trying to think what Daddy did when she was like this. He got all stern with her, talked to her like a teacher would to a naughty student.

"Y-You'll hate me," she whimpered.

"I'm not happy with you right now," I retorted. "What with not going to Daddy's funeral and behaving so disgracefully at Lily's—"

"That's nothing compared to what I've done in the past."

My eyes narrowed. "Like what?"

"I-I don't come from a good place," she whispered, and she sounded so broken that it made me wonder if she was on drugs or something. I'd never heard her so irate, so all over the place before, not even after she'd found Daddy.

The thought had me wincing with guilt. Sure, she was being weird, but she'd been the one to find Daddy. To find him with his head exploded from a bullet. So, I sucked in a breath. "It's okay," I soothed. "I'll understand."

"You can't. I don't." She paused. "My father was a loan shark. He used to work for some bad people. One day, he was robbed. All the money was taken. His backers came for him, and they took me as payment for him not being killed." Even as my mouth dropped open, she rasped, "I was sixteen, terrified, and when I met Benito, I was relieved. He was beautiful. Older than me, sure, but he was gorgeous. And he treated me so well. I was stupid. I never thought—"

"You never thought what?"

"I was his mistress. He kept me at his side for years until I got pregnant." She swallowed. "With you. That was when he changed. He never came around, he never slept with me again. He broke my heart more than when my father gave me to him as payment."

Speechless, I could do nothing other than stare at her, mouth wide open, because...this wasn't true. She was a Southern fucking belle!

She hadn't finished though, and she whispered, "He was at school with Donavan and Richard. Richard's family had lost everything just a few years earlier, and Benito, being the clever bastard he is, always knew which strings to pull. He agreed to back Richard's business, if he married me and took on my child."

I gulped. "Daddy...?"

"Your father in spirit. Your father of the heart. But not your biological father," she whispered, and I heard her tears. "God, how we both wished you were. It broke us both. We loved you so much, but—"

"But what?"

She released a shaky breath. "I was upset when Benito told me what he'd planned, but when I met Richard, it was love at first sight."

More like Stockholm syndrome.

The thought hurt, so I shoved it away for another time.

Another place.

Fuck, *another life.*

"We both fell for each other. It was like something from a movie." Her voice had turned dreamy, and because I didn't want to break her train of thought, I stayed silent, just absorbed every damning word she had to say. "We grew closer all the time, even though," she whispered shyly, "the age gap between us was significant. I was terrified you'd push us apart, but you never did. He was fascinated with me being pregnant, and I only found out why a few years after you were born."

"Why?"

"He had mumps as a boy. It left him sterile. So he was grateful to have you, but he was scared."

"Why?" I inquired, anxiety lashing at me.

"Benito isn't someone who forgets what's his." She shuddered. "Funny how love can turn to hate."

"You hate...him now?" My biological father.

My real father.

What the fuck?

How was Daddy not mine?

"I never loved him. I was sixteen and terrified. He treated me kindly, but I was too young, and my age never stopped him. He was my jailor, but he was beautiful, and I was stupid," she scoffed. "Benito would never have left you alone if we hadn't done what we did."

Warily, I pressed, "What did you do?"

"When I was due to give birth, we traveled to Mexico. Richard said it was for business, but he arranged for the clinic where you were born to say you were stillborn." She laughed. "It seems insane now, but we were so desperate.

"We knew what he'd do, we knew he'd take you from us when you were old enough, and Richard loved you so much, and I loved him so much—I've never known a man to love a child before he even met her." A muffled sob escaped her. "It worked too. We stayed in Mexico long enough for it to seem natural that I grew pregnant again, and you helped by being so small as a baby. When Benito visited us when we came home, I knew why.

"He wanted to check we weren't lying to him. But you were tiny. If he'd been a woman, he'd have known, but men are all the same. Newborns aren't of interest to them. He was more interested in my breasts.

"God, I hate that man." A shudder whispered through her like she couldn't contain her revulsion for the man who'd impregnated her. A man she'd once thought she loved. "It was why we sent you to St. Lawrence Academy.

"Donavan was always in Benito's pocket, and Richard said that hiding you under his nose would keep you safe because it would be hiding you in plain sight. Benito would never think we'd be so brazen—"

I processed that, *badly*, registered how she was saying my friendship with Lily was founded on a lie, how my entire existence, from my heritage to my age, was one massive falsehood, but I also recorded how her hands had loosened about my arm, and could only think to ask, "Why do you think I'm in danger?"

"Why else would those bikers be talking about the Fieris?" she snapped. "He must have learned the truth in the aftermath of Richard's death." She sucked in a breath. "If we don't get you out of here, if we don't get you away, Benito will find out. He always finds out," she rasped, and I could hear the terror in her voice and knew it wasn't feigned. Knew it was real and true, and that she believed every word she was uttering.

In turn, that terrified me.

Was she right?

Did I need to be scared?

Sin had never mentioned anything about the Fieris to me, and the only person who had was Rex.

"Pass me my phone," I demanded.

"No time!" she hissed. "We have to get out of here. Now! I lost Richard to him when Benito decided it was time to call in his debts, but I won't lose you too!"

The door opened just as her voice turned high and loud, and when I saw the biker in the doorway, my heart almost burst out of my chest when I thought it was Sin. Only, it wasn't. It was Link, whose nose was bloodied and quite clearly broken. As desire for Sin whispered through me, Link stared at us both in confusion before he turned on the light, which instantly made my eyes feel like a thousand needles were stabbing them.

"What are you doing here?" Mom spat at him.

"I'm guarding your daughter tonight, Laura," was his calm response.

"Badly if I got in—" she snapped, and God help me, but she wasn't wrong.

Ignoring her, he cut me a look, and maybe he saw how stressed out I was, how fucking confused, because he reassured me, "I saw her come in and allowed it, Tiffany. You're safe. Is everything okay?"

Mom backed away from the bed and huddled in the corner of the room like a frightened child. I gaped at her, then at him, but the pain was overwhelming. I shielded my eyes with my hand, then whispered, "Could you close the door, Link?"

Warily, he eyed us both but did as we asked. "What is it?"

"The man...today, what did he want? Do you know yet?"

He nodded. "Club business."

The password for secrecy.

I grunted under my breath. "I need to know!"

"Not my place to tell you."

I ground my teeth together, then rolling onto my side, ignoring the pain spearing my head in two, I grabbed my phone from the nightstand, my fingers scraping over the shattered screen as I hit the Siri button, and demanded, "Call Sin."

The second the call connected, he rasped, "Angel?" He sounded gruff, sleepy, a little different than how he usually sounded, but it was such a relief to hear from him that I sank back into the pillows, needing him to ground me. To balance the equilibrium my mother had just turned on its head.

"Sin?" I whispered, voice raw with emotion. "We have a situation."

And if that wasn't an understatement, I didn't know what was.

THIRTY-NINE

EPILOGUE
TIFFANY

"ANGEL?"

My brow puckered as pain slammed through my head. Fuck, that was *bad*. Worse than when I'd been drugged, worse than any hangover I'd had in the past. Moving from the hospital to back home had been a nightmare, even if I was glad to get away from all the beeps and the machines.

Wincing, I reached up, rubbed my temple, then whispered, "Sin?"

"Lily called. She wants to come see you," he relayed.

"Tell her to come visit." I rubbed my hand over my face. "Please?"

He dipped down and pressed a kiss to my forehead. "She says to come visit, Lily."

I peered out from between my fingers, watching as he cut the call soon after. "Where's Mom?"

That had him rolling his eyes, even as he reached over to the nightstand for a glass of water. As he passed it to me, he gathered some pills from there too. "Barricaded in her room at Lily's."

After I took a sip, then swallowed down the meds, I sighed. "I'm surprised you managed to make her stay."

"We Sinners can be persuasive."

My eyes widened at that, which, of course, made the extra light make me feel like each individual ray had turned into a knife that was spearing me in the eyeballs. As the pain ricocheted inside me, I managed to get out, "Does that mean you locked her in?"

He snorted. "Do you really want to know?"

Christ.

I cleared my throat. "She's safe, though, right?"

"Yes, of course. You both are." He grunted. "I let you down, angel, but it won't happen again."

"You didn't know."

"No, but we could have predicted it. I'm Enforcer now, and I'll make fucking sure no one touches you again." He blew out a breath. "He didn't come for you."

I tensed at that. "He didn't?"

"No. He came for Lily."

That didn't make me feel a whole helluva lot better.

"Did you think she was under threat?"

"Link said he knew that Donavan Lancaster had arranged for Lily to marry Gianni Fieri, but he thought she was safe because he's still in jail."

"Shortsighted," I rasped.

"The whole MC was. Sometimes, we forget—"

"Forget, what?"

"That not everyone is afraid of us." He rubbed his jaw. "I'm sorry, angel."

"You keep saying that, but it's not your fault. It's Donavan Lancaster's for thinking he can marry Lily off like she's a commodity. It's not your fault my father got involved with the mafia, and that—" I bit my lip, unable to think about my biological father or deal with the clusterfuck there. "Who was he? Specifically?"

"You sure you want to know?"

I didn't. But, also, I did. "Yeah."

"Your half-brother."

My stomach roiled at that, but I nodded as I swallowed it back.

All this time, I'd thought I was a cut above the rest, but crime was in my blood on both sides.

Mom's father was a loan shark, and my biological father? Only God knew what he'd done in his time.

I pressed a hand to my mouth as I closed my eyes. It had been two days since I'd learned the truth from Mom, and I still couldn't handle it.

"I miss my daddy," I whispered, feeling like a five-year-old, but it was true.

We'd always been close. Always.

"Whether or not you know the truth, he was always your father, angel," Sin murmured, somehow digging to the heart of the matter without even trying. "Miss him, and grieve him, but don't worry about things that don't matter. And Fieri? Doesn't matter."

My throat felt tight. "You can't say that."

"Can't I?"

"What if he finds out—"

"He won't. The kid was here for Lily. Not you." He reached down and cupped my chin. "Sweetheart, your mom overreacted. If she hadn't eavesdropped on a conversation she should never have been listening in on, you wouldn't know. There's no point in worrying about this shit."

"You can't—"

"I can, and I know how I'm going to stop this in its tracks."

I narrowed my eyes at him, even as, carefully, I started sitting up. The meds weren't doing much yet, but lying down felt wrong for this conversation. It made me groan a few times, but I felt jubilant when I was upright.

"What are you talking about?" I inquired gruffly, pain making my voice deeper.

"I'm talking about this." A box appeared out of nowhere. He placed it on my lap. "You can read into this as many ways as you want. Me doing this to protect you. Me doing this out of guilt. Me doing this because I'm ashamed. Me—"

I scowled at him. "If this is your idea of a proposal," I butted in, "then you're shit at it."

His lips curved into a wide grin, but he surprised me by jabbing his finger at me. "That. That is why I want to marry you."

"What is?"

"Tiffany. The way she is. Who *you* are. What you are. That's why I want to make you mine every way I can." He pulled open the box, revealing a pink diamond that made me gasp. The clarity was incredible, and the size?

Jesus.

Sin wasn't lying when he said he could support me.

Not that it mattered. I didn't need supporting. I just needed him.

"Yes," I told him simply.

His lips twisted. "You didn't give me the chance to ask you."

"You already asked. I want to be yours. Every way I can be."

Nostrils flaring at that, he rumbled, "Don't talk dirty when you're out of action."

I snickered, then winced when my head pounded with it. "I always talk dirty."

"Nah, you actually don't." He winked at me. "We have time to give you lessons in it."

Sticking out my tongue at him, I grumbled, "Meanie."

"Hardly." His grin revealed how happy he was, but what confirmed it? When he slid the ring down my finger, raised my hand to his mouth, and kissed it. "I do feel guilty. I am ashamed. I will always protect you. But I can do that without this ring. I want you tied to me this way so that the entire fucking world knows you're mine. No question. No doubt. Do you hear me?"

His words sent a thrill through me, and trust me, I was in no state to be thrilled.

My body hurt. My head hurt. Deep inside, I hurt.

My belly was empty, where once life had bloomed. My heart was raw from losing not only the baby, who'd barely had the chance to be alive, but from my dad, and from learning the truth of my lineage.

Everything was upended, but not this.

Never what Sin and I had.

The ring represented what it had for thousands of years—eternity. A couple destined to be together for eternity.

"Sin?"

He hummed under his breath. "Angel?"

"I hear you." Then, I reached for his hand, cupped it, and huskily asked, "I want to wear your brand."

His eyes lit up. "You do?"

Slowly, I nodded. "I do."

"I didn't want to ask—"

"Why?"

"I don't know. You're not a regular woman, Tiff."

"I know I'm not. I'm yours."

He grinned at me. "Yeah, you are."

"So you should have known that if you wanted the world to know I'm yours, I'd want the same."

His eyes sparkled. "That can be arranged."

"Good. Now, will you help me shower, please? I don't want Lily to see me like this. The last time she did, she started sobbing and she broke my heart. I don't want that. I want her to see my ring and to be happy."

"Of course, angel." He pressed a kiss to my ring. "And then I'll make an appointment with my regular tattooist."

Even though my world was in chaos, I still had it in me to smile at him.

My happiness was entwined with his, and he'd just proven that by slipping a ring on my finger when, in his world, rings meant nothing.

For us, however, we'd always be different.

When he reached over, he proved how perfect we were for one another, as he bowed his head, pressed a kiss to my stomach, and whispered, "Goodbye, little angel."

My eyes flooded with tears because he didn't say, 'there'll be more kids in the future.' He didn't discredit this child, this loss. He said farewell, and he tied my heart up in him with those three words, earning a love that was undying, and a loyalty that could never be equaled.

I was his.

He was mine.

And Benito Fieri? Could get fucked if he thought he could tear us asunder.

FORTY

EPILOGUE
SIN

AS INDIANA FINISHED up Tiffany's brand, which sat on her left hand, I eyed her bruises, which weren't even close to fading, and the cuts from the glass that had rained inside the car, causing little tears to mar the perfection of her face.

The collision with a fucking tree on the island on the freeway was something that had killed our baby, but it hadn't killed us.

Here she was, my ring on her right finger for the moment, while on her left, on her true ring finger, sloping from the bottom where her digits joined to her hand and all the way along to the first knuckle, ink blossomed. It was a lacework filigree design in a multitude of rainbow colors, and amid the lace were my names.

Both Padraig and Sin.

One man she'd meet, the other, I'd do my fucking best to keep from her, even though it was time she knew the truth of what both parts of me could do.

It had rammed itself home when she told me she felt like I was keeping a part of me away from her. Mostly because she was spot on.

I did keep that side of me from her, because Padraig?

Insane.

As raving fucking mad as Nyx, but Sin kept that bastard under control. Just. Until he needed to come out.

Just as Padraig needed to be let loose on the Fieri fucker who'd hurt her.

But it felt apt that she'd have both names slotted in the lace, both of them tied to her for eternity, because she owned both of us.

Both twisted parts of this fucked up soul.

As I fingered the gauze-wrapped brand on my wrist, one that wrapped around it like a bracelet, her name entwined with a plaited inked cord, I watched as Indiana hunched her shoulders, evidently in the zone. She drifted back and forth on Tiff's hand before she started moving out wider, swiping a mandala over the back of her knuckles, the pair of them talking all the while.

In the distance, I heard a bike's engine, and when I moved toward the window away from the desk where Indiana's creepazoid receptionist sat, I peered out and saw Nyx and Giulia clambering off the back of his hog.

Well aware why they were here—time for Nyx to add to his bag of souls and for Giulia to commemorate the soul she'd taken too—I shuffled back toward the doorway, watching as the arduous process came to an end.

"You can't put that ring back on until it's completely healed," Indiana advised Tiff. "And it's going to be a pain in the ass for a few days, because the skin will tighten up around your finger and itch like a motherfucker."

Tiff just shrugged, but her smile was serene. Settled. It still surprised me when I saw her look like that. I was used to her being far blunter, a lot more outspoken.

Right now?

I knew she was in a daze.

Her father wasn't her father.

Our baby was dead.

She was the daughter of a mafia don.

Lily and she had almost been kidnapped.

I'd killed a man in her and our baby's honor...

The list went on.

I watched as she thumbed the diamond on her right hand, twisting it nervously as Indiana patched up her other one with gauze.

When she was finished, I moved to David, the receptionist, and paid the bill. As Tiff walked out, Indy at her back, Nyx and Giulia walked in. But rather than greeting either of them, she arched a brow. "You didn't make an appointment."

The accusation had Nyx snorting. "You can't make time for your brother?"

Indiana sniffed. "Nope."

David cleared his throat. "Actually, Nyx asked me to book time for him and his partner, but he asked me not to mention it to you."

His nerves were clear, and I understood why the second Indy whipped her head around to glare at him. "Dammit! Who pays your wage, David?"

He hunched his shoulders. "I mean, you do, but Nyx insisted."

"For a reason. You won't pick up my calls," he rumbled.

"I told you. I'm mad at you. And you know why. If you can't talk to Caleb, then I can't talk to you." She raised her head and tipped her nose in the air before storming off into the back room where she did her ink.

"What the hell did you do? And who the fuck's Caleb?" Giulia groused, but I tuned out their argument, and instead, grabbed Tiff's non-bandaged hand, bowed my head at Nyx, then made my way out into the big, wide world.

When we were outside, I sucked in a deep breath as I curved an arm around Tiff's waist.

It was stupid to feel like she was fragile. Made of porcelain. But to me, at that moment, she was.

When I walked over to the cage I was driving for her sake, I opened the door and helped her in, then as I moved to the driver's side, I found the Prospects who were tailing us, and dipped my chin at them before I got behind the wheel.

Jaxson and North didn't appear to have suffered under Nyx's wrath for having let Lily and Tiff out of her family estate without a tail—they sported no visible bruises, at least—but they were my woman's shadow now. Having heard what I'd done to the Fieri piece of shit? They blanched whenever I made it a point to catch their eye.

I'd been ashamed all my life of the parts of me that made me Padraig—the wrath, the control issues, the violence I was capable of—but I'd embrace them if it meant making sure Tiff was never hurt again.

"When are you going to let me ride bitch again?" she complained as I set off.

"When you have your checkup," I replied calmly.

She hummed, but as I focused on the road, I couldn't stop myself from noticing how she kept on making her fingers dance. On both hands.

I eyed the one wrapped in gauze. "It hurts?"

"No." She fell quiet, and I knew to wait. Knew she was building up the courage to say something. When she sucked in a breath, I braced myself. "You know a brand and a ring won't stop him if he wants me."

We both knew who *he* was.

"He doesn't know about you," I reassured her, like I'd keep on doing when doubt hit her, when fear made her voice tremble, and I cut her a quick look before returning my attention to the road. "And even if he did, we're about to rain hell on him, angel. He's going to have more shit to worry about than you."

Her shaky breath told me she was relieved, but still cautious. Who the fuck could blame her? "You only proposed because of him," she murmured a few seconds later.

"Maybe. It's certainly why I asked when I did, but if you think I don't want you tied to me in as many ways as I can, you're the crazy one."

Her lips twitched into a smug smile at my version of a compliment, before she turned her head to the side, revealing a profile that would make my namesake for her—an angel—weep.

I sucked in a breath, knowing confession time was here. Was it shitty of me to have waited for her to be branded before I told her the truth? Before I let her know who Padraig really was?

"Tiff?"

"Yeah?"

"I need to tell you something."

When she twisted to the side, giving me her full attention, I cleared my throat, not altogether certain I wanted all her focus. "Go for it."

"I lied to you."

That had tension rippling through her. "About what?"

"My father."

I quickly glanced at her, saw her frown was more confused than worried. "What about him?" she asked slowly.

"How he died." I sucked in a breath. "He died because of me." The second the words fell from my lips, all five of them as much of a lie as what I'd told her before, I had no choice but to pull over. No way was I going to trap her in the truck with me if she wanted out...

"Because of you?"

Arms on the wheel, I hunched my shoulders as I stared over the main street of Verona where Indiana's Ink was based. It was a small town, but it was getting a name for itself because of Indy. That was how good her work was.

"Sin? Talk to me."

Her soft voice kind of irritated me. I knew why too. It was her therapist voice, but though I definitely needed a shrink, it wasn't like I could go to one. I'd never be able to tell her the full truth about what I did as an Enforcer for the club, not without her running screaming for the hills. But this? I could tell her. It wasn't club business. It was family shit and about honor and disrespect, to the point where, though my father had been the

Road Captain under Bear—Rex's dad and the old Prez, Grizzly's goddamn brother—had sided with me.

He'd just asked me to kill someone cleaner next time.

"I found him in bed with my wife," I said. "I'd just got back from deployment. I'd been stuck on a fucking FOB for months on end, and I get back, and there they are. Boning away. I knew why too. He hated me. Always did, and I knew then, like I know now, if he lived, he'd do everything in his power to take what I have. We got into a fight, and he wouldn't stop. Wouldn't back the fuck down, even though he wasn't in great shape and I was at peak condition." My jaw clenched. "I warned him, but he didn't listen. Just kept on hitting me back, and then he said some shit, and I lost it." On those words, I released a breath that was loaded down with my shame.

"Why?"

"Why did I hurt him? Why did I lose it?"

"No, why did he want to take everything from you?"

Her whisper had me tensing. "I don't know. I genuinely don't. I never did shit to him. If anything, he was okay with ignoring me for most of my life, then out of nowhere, he just focused all his hate on me."

"When you turned eighteen?"

I huffed. "Yeah. I guess."

She laughed gently. "Sin, you don't look in a mirror often, do you? Aside from shaving."

I grunted. I mean, I knew I was okay in the looks department but—

"You're a woman's wet dream. Everything about you. And it's mine. No matter what you've done, no matter what you do." She tilted her chin up. "You protected me. You have from the start. Whatever you do, you'll do it for my protection, even if I don't like it." She reached over, and when her thumb brushed over my messed-up knuckles, the skin flayed from beating Fieri, she whispered, "These wounds didn't happen by chance. These came as vengeance for our baby. For the pain I went through." She leaned farther forward, cupping my chin, making me look her in the eye. "I know you say you have a temper, and I consider it a blessing that I haven't borne the brunt of it, considering what I've kept from you—"

"You never will," I vowed, and I meant it. Never would she come face-to-face with the fucker that was Padraig. "Ever. I'll kill myself first—"

Her head swiped to the side. "Never say that to me. I can deal with anger. I can handle it. You won't hurt me, not physically. I know you won't. But you can hurt me by leaving me—without a goodbye." Her voice turned choked at that, and I knew why and cursed myself for being a fucking fool for talking shit like that when her dad had done what he had.

"I'm sorry," I whispered.

"Don't be. You didn't mean it that way, and it's only because of Daddy—" She sucked in a breath. "You've got a past. I get that." Her eyes caught mine. "But together, we're going to make a better future, aren't we?"

I wanted, so badly, to tell her we would, but I couldn't lie to her. Not again. "I'll do things for the club—"

"I know you will." She pursed her lips. "I don't need to know, and you won't tell me."

"You're okay with that?"

"I'm okay with knowing you'll protect me unto death." Her smile was rueful. "I'm happy you're not a banker. I'm happy you don't belong to a country club and—" She winked. "You get the picture. Maybe you're not every woman's idea of Prince Charming, but I never needed a prince." Her grin morphed out of nowhere. "I needed a biker."

My world sat on the other side of the cab from me. My reason, my heart.

I'd never thought to fall in love, never thought to bring a child into this world, and I never thought I'd want to tie someone to me in all the ways the law allowed, but here she was.

Living proof of it.

She came with more baggage than even I did. Her mother was refusing to leave her room at Lily's, her father was in a grave because his business was torn apart by *Famiglia* sharks, and her blood relative was a Don the MC and its allies were at war with.

But for all that, she was perfect.

More than that, she was mine, and the tattoo on her finger and the ring on her other hand declared it to the world.

I reached for her hand, pressed my fingers to her knuckles, and whispered, "Mine."

"Yours," she instantly confirmed.

Benito Fieri could come for her.

But if he did?

Padraig had been let loose, and he would be waiting on him, and what was left of him in the aftermath was something that'd make Nyx feel queasy.

FORTY-ONE

EPILOGUE
REX

"PREZ?"

"Where the fuck have you been?"

"Sorry, man, been stuck in solitary for three weeks."

I grunted, pissed even though it wasn't Quin's fault for being stuck in solitary—well, aside from whatever shit he'd done to get punished, that is. "Wondered why you were off grid. Wasn't sure if you'd been moved."

"No. I'd have made sure the message got back to you if I had."

"Speaking of making sure...your sister got that birthday gift I promised," I hedged, changing the subject.

It was never easy speaking to Sinners who were locked up, but the second a man was patched in as a brother, we all learned the basics for when the shit hit the fan.

Gifts were payments.

We all knew that, when we were inside, sometimes we could do work for the club, even if we were behind bars. It was code for us paying their family the imprisoned brother's cut for a job or a run.

"Really?" Quin asked, his voice deepening with his interest. "How big was it?"

"Very. I had to put it on ice."

"Ice? Huh."

"Yeah. Your sister will be around with some pictures of it in the next few days, I think she said."

"Yeah," Quin drawled slowly. "I think she's due for a visit. Can't wait to hear all the gossip."

"Have fun."

"Yeah, I will."

"Speak later once you've had a chance to see the gift?" I asked.

"Thanks, man. I'll be in touch."

"More than welcome. My pleasure." I cut the call, shot my council a look, and nodded. "Fieri'll be dead by the end of the week."

THE NEXT BOOK IN THE SERIES IS NOW AVAILABLE TO READ ON KU!
www.books2read.com/SteelSerenaAkeroyd

UNIVERSE READING ORDER

FILTHY
NYX
LINK
FILTHY RICH
SIN
STEEL
FILTHY DARK
CRUZ
MAVERICK
FILTHY SEX
HAWK
FILTHY HOT
STORM
THE DON
THE LADY
FILTHY SECRET
REX
RACHEL
FILTHY KING
THE REVELATION
THE ORACLE
FILTHY FECK

FREE BOOK!

Don't forget to grab your free e-Book!
Secrets & Lies is now free!

Meg's love life was missing a spark until she discovered her need to be dominated. When her fiancé shared the same kink, she thought all her birthdays had come at once, and then she came to learn their relationship was one big fat lie.

Gabe has loved Meg for years, watching her from afar, and always wishing he'd been the one to date her first and not his brother. When he has the chance to have Meg in his bed—even better, tied to it—it's an opportunity he can't refuse.

With disastrous consequences.

Can Gabe make Meg realize she's the one woman he's always wanted? But once secrets and lies have wormed their way into a relationship, is it impossible to establish the firm base of trust needed between lovers, and more importantly, between sub and Sir...?

This story features orgasm control in a BDSM setting.
Secrets & Lies is now free!

CONNECT WITH SERENA

For the latest updates, be sure to check out my website!
But if you'd like to hang out with me and get to know me better, then I'd love to see you in my Diva reader's group where you can find out all the gossip on new releases as and when they happen. You can join here: www.facebook.com/groups/SerenaAkeroydsDivas. Or you can always PM or email me. I love to hear from you guys: serenaakeroyd@gmail.com.

ABOUT THE AUTHOR

I'm a romance novelaholic and I won't touch a book unless I know there's a happy ending. This addiction is what made me craft stories that suit my voracious need for raunchy romance. I love twists and unexpected turns, and my novels all contain sexy guys, dark humor, and hot AF love scenes.

I write MF, menage, and reverse harem (also known as why choose romance,) in both contemporary and paranormal. Some of my stories are darker than others, but I can promise you one thing, you will always get the happy ending your heart needs!